the elm stone saga
SCARRED

D0971002

shayla
MORTENSEN

Scarred

Shayla Morgansen

Scarred

ISBN: 978-1-742845-18-0 (pbk.)

Published by Book Pal
www.bookpal.com.au

Contents

prologue

The landing was perfectly timed and executed. Jackson and his eight men each stepped out of the wormholes they had used to travel here, to this quiet street in Italy, and Jackson sealed off their exit points with magic. Normally he wouldn't have bothered but tonight's raid was Lisandro's brainchild and this cautiousness was a direct request of his. And what Lisandro requested was what came to be, inevitably, so here Jackson was, carrying out Lisandro's carefully laid-out plans.

The men he'd been assigned were brutes; scum and low-lives the upstanding villain Lisandro preferred not to associate himself with, but who were too strong and efficient to simply *not* have on board. Jackson was glad to have them. This team was *his*, and they were so starkly different from the team he'd been part of when he was a councillor for the White Elm. This team respected him and what he had to offer. This team got stuff done, without spending weeks or months in talks, deliberating the ethical, socio-political and whatever other ramifications of action. This team was a force to be reckoned with, and best of all, this team listened to Jackson.

The White Elm had never done much of that. If they had, he might not now be a fugitive and outcast from their ranks, and he might not now be on his way to attack the home of one of the council's newest members.

'Suit up,' Jackson hissed at them, jerking his head at the furthest of his men to gesture him closer. Cloaking spells were most effective over a small area, so the closer the nine stayed together the more powerful the spell would be. As the most powerful sorcerer present – and they knew it, he thought smugly – Jackson was the one to cast the cloak over them. An invisible blanket of magic settled over the group. For them, wearing the cloak spell was almost unnoticed. They couldn't feel it; it didn't affect their vision, their hearing or their extended magical senses; it didn't slow their motions or impede them in any way. However, for anyone outside of the cloak, such as a nosy neighbour peeking out their window into the street, where moments ago there stood a bunch of strange men, there was now nothing to be seen except empty air. For any sorcerer nearby, accustomed to being able to sense the presence of approaching living things, where moments ago there was the distinct sense of life, of energy, of emotion, of intention and thought, there was now only void. The cloak redirected the senses *around* those hidden beneath it, and that was exactly the cover Jackson and his team required.

The target was not a large or stately home, but it was the address the informant had provided, and inside the small, tidy cottage near the top of the street Jackson could feel several powerful magical presences. The one he was most interested in, he couldn't feel, but that did not mean she wasn't there. He grinned at the thought. He didn't like for anyone to be better at things than he was, but there was no denying that Emmanuelle Saint Clair of the White Elm was the *best* at wards and cloaking spells.

The nine drew knives as they approached the home as a group. Knives for sorcerers were more than tools for cutting the physical; pointed and precise, often they could be more useful than wands for directing magic. Jackson paused ahead of the group and extended a hand slowly. Invisible, almost undetectable, a delicate web of protective energy lay over this house. To pass through it would trigger a mental alert in the mind of the spell's creator. The people inside were strong and of unknown competence – the less warning they received of Jackson's arrival, the better.

Beneath Jackson's hand, a silvery strand of energy, as thin and indistinct as a spider's web, quivered into visibility: a very basic ward. Blade glowing with his own power and intent, Jackson drew his knife across the strand. It resisted destruction, as all things do, but soon gave. The knife went through, severing it cleanly. The taut line of magic snapped and pinged apart with a spark of pale light, but the remainder of the net remained intact. The group waited in tense silence – would the inhabitants notice? How in-tune was the young councillor to her spells? – but there was no energetic shift inside the house to denote an increase in activity or anxiety.

'Keep outside this radius,' Jackson instructed his team in a low voice. He pointed his knife at the perimeter of the spell's reach – at his will, dozens of the same silvery strands lit up faintly, stretching up into a dome over the cottage's roof. 'No rushing. No mistakes. Anyone who screws this up is staying behind to answer to the council when their *real* warriors show up.'

Because though Jackson liked to sneer at the mere mention of his former brotherhood, the fact remained that their collective and individual might was both impressive and formidable. The White Elm allowed onto their council only the best and brightest thirteen of the world's sorcerers: Seers who knew too much of the future, Displacers who could teleport through space on a whim, Healers who could mend most any wound, Crafters who could twist and manipulate the very essence of magic, Telepaths who could hear the thoughts of those around them, scriers (too busy being stubborn and self-righteous to allocate themselves a capital letter) who could see what was happening anywhere in the world... It was probable that right now, the White Elm's duo of scriers, Qasim and Renatus, were becoming aware of this very event, and it was only a matter of time before they arrived.

Jackson would prefer not to cross paths with either of them, if possible. He'd woven wards into his cloaking spell that would postpone the moment when these events were brought to the scriers' attention, but Fate, unfortunately, worked for scriers, not for Crafters like Jackson. Sooner rather than later that ward would break and the countdown to confrontation with the White Elm would begin.

Jackson wanted to be gone, with the prizes he was sent for, by that time.

The team moved slowly but efficiently around the cottage, stepping carefully over rows of vegetables in the garden and low fences separating properties. Each strand was cut with care, but as more came away, the quicker the process became. The remaining strands glowed much more brightly, forced to carry more power than when other parts of the net had been in place to share the load of protecting the house, and became much easier to spot and sever.

Jackson's men gathered at the front of the house around the final strand. Its light was so bright it made Jackson squint. Nico, a stocky Austrian wanted by the mortal law in several European nations for violent assaults in bars and nightclubs, carved his silver-bright blade back and forth across the strand of magic while the others held their breath in apprehension and excitement.

'Only one to go and they haven't even noticed?' Saul breathed, eyes manic. Jackson looked at him sidelong and said nothing. Bad eggs occurred in all types, both magical and mortal. Saul had come into Lisandro's employ – and subsequently shifted into Jackson's taskforce almost immediately – when his human trafficking enterprise had been uncovered and dismantled by Interpol, and the White Elm had rejected his pleas for sanctuary. The government of the magical world took a similar stance on human rights as did the governments of mortal society, and had attempted to apprehend Saul, with the intention of either providing him, gift-wrapped and powerless, to the police, or of imprisoning him themselves in their prison in Valero. With nowhere left to turn, Saul had sought out Lisandro, a former authority within the White Elm and a political revolutionary, and taken refuge among the ranks of Magnus Moira, Lisandro's new but quickly growing movement against the White Elm council's leadership.

Jackson really didn't care what Saul or the others had done before they came to work under him, but Lisandro had made his opinions on Saul's history very clear to Jackson. 'If it happens that you lose one, or need to leave one behind,' he'd said, 'don't stress too much if it's him.'

A spell is a near-living thing, almost sentient – it *wants* to endure. As Nico drew his knife carefully across the strand of magic defending the cottage, the spell shuddered and grew brighter, strengthening its now-weak point of attack.

'Why is it taking so long?' someone hissed, bouncing on the balls of his feet in excitement. Jackson irritably caught him across the chest with one of his gloved hands, stilling his annoying motion.

'If they haven't noticed yet, rushing will only tip them off,' he whispered back. He looked back at the trembling strand of magic, felt the rise in energy all around him as the spell prepared to break and his men prepared to take the house. 'Look alive, boys.'

A bright spark signalled the end of the ward; the spell gave under the pressure of Nico's knife and power, and the nine grinned. There was nothing more to be said. They rushed at the cottage. Nico traded his knife for the wand in his coat pocket, and blasted the door open.

They had a weapon to steal and a war to ignite.

chapter one

As I had expected, the door opened for me, and I walked into the study. Renatus, my headmaster and the Dark Keeper of the White Elm council, was at his desk, a pile of letters, forms and documents either side of him.

'You're here,' he noted. Tonight was the last of the nightly detentions he'd issued me three weeks ago when I'd accidentally upset one of his colleagues, Qasim, my scrying teacher. Far from being the dull punishments I was sure Qasim hoped them to be, my evenings with Renatus had been enlightening and interesting. 'I wasn't sure.'

'I had to. We have stuff to talk about, I think.'

Understatement of the year. We'd talked a lot yesterday, but now there was new stuff. There was always so much *stuff*. There was the freaky half-imagined vision of a blood-soaked girl in the orchard at the back of Renatus's property. There was my stupid friend Sterling's demand that I flush my dignity to investigate whether her pathetic infatuation with the headmaster was reciprocated. There was the list I'd pulled off the door on my way in, which I held in my hand but I'd still not bothered to look at. Plus there was always something else, something unexpected, whenever I talked with Renatus.

'I think you're right.' He held my gaze as he lifted a typed letter from the top of a very tall pile of the same. He was pretty much the most attractive human being I'd ever met, but the more I got to know him, the less I noticed. The less important it seemed, compared with all the other "mosts" I found him to be. The most powerful. The most abrupt. The most complicated. The most broken. 'About a few things.' He broke eye contact to look down at the letter as he signed it. 'You can tell Sterling Adams that it isn't going to happen.'

I sighed and nodded, relieved that I'd been spared having to ask that, but only felt marginally better. I was on edge, shifty, uncomfortable, and I found myself pacing. My relatively youthful headmaster eyed the list in my hand but did not bring it up.

'Renatus,' I said, trying to sound much more casual than I looked or felt and much less crazy than I was probably about to appear, 'are ghosts real?'

It sounded stupid in my head and even stupider out loud, especially considering I was quite sure I either knew the answer or at least knew what *my* truth, my belief on the topic, was. But somehow, in Renatus's office, stupid questions had a way of feeling much less stupid. Maybe it was the way my headmaster never treated my questions like they were stupid but instead gave me insightful and thought-provoking responses. It was this ability of his, I thought, that had made my time spent in detention worthwhile and intriguing. At first he'd loaned me books to read every night; later we'd gotten to talking while I helped with some of the more mundane aspects of his job, like sealing envelopes.

And our conversations had yielded some remarkable insights. Despite being two very different people – he a super-powerful, painfully wealthy, twenty-something professional warrior for an elite council of sorcerers, me an eccentric, naive seventeen-year-old girl with little direction in life and no impressive accomplishments or talents to my name – we'd learnt that we in fact shared an unlikely tragic history.

We'd discussed this in depth last night, and Renatus had said I didn't need to come to this last session, that I'd given enough time yesterday, but things had transpired since that had driven me here.

Now he was staring at me, surprised by my question. I might have felt smug at any other time, since he struck me as someone difficult to surprise, but tonight I was too jumpy following my strange experience out on the estate.

'No, they're not. What made you ask that?' he said finally, strikingly violet eyes flickering critically over the space around me. My aura. Despite his age, Renatus was a very high-level member of the White Elm council – the best of the best of sorcerers, and our people's government. Observing a person's mood and emotions from their energy field was no effort at all to someone like him. For a newbie student like me, it was all part of The Dream, the hope that one day I'd possess those kinds of automatic skills and be half as awesome as he and his colleagues were.

'Something weird happened,' I said, exercising what passed for self-control in my books and not just blurting it out. Last night's aborted conversation came to mind and stilled my tongue. This was my teacher, not my friend or parent. 'Something...' Black, white and red. In the orchard. Quite clear. 'Indistinct. I don't know. I probably imagined it.'

While I spoke, Renatus slipped the now-folded letter into an envelope and sealed it with the White Elm's stamp. But questions and confusions bubbled away beneath my skin. I was sure Renatus could hear them. He possessed a not-always-welcome ability to overhear my wonderings and my thought trains, and often he would respond to my thoughts as though I'd spoken them aloud. Now he looked up at me sharply, and I knew I'd been unable to keep my thoughts to myself. As usual.

'Aristea,' he said seriously. 'What did you see?'

'A girl,' I burst out, glad I could share with someone. None of my friends would have understood. 'Or at least I think I did. I was waiting for a sign, like you said, and there was this girl, for just a tiny wee second, standing in the orchard, and she had white skin, long black hair and she was covered in blood-'

'Stop.' Renatus held up a hand to punctuate his forceful word. My description had quickly drained his already-pale face of blood, making him practically as white as the imagined girl. His silky black

4

hair, worn long, and his smooth, symmetrical features – the picture of human beauty – could be likened to my vision, too, and I realised with a start both why he was getting upset and why I was drawing connections between his face and the girl's.

'Oh.' Last night's lengthy discussion had come after our conversation had accidentally stumbled across Renatus's deepest heartbreak, and it had been revealed to me that his beloved sister had died here seven years previously. And that he'd never gotten over it. And that I reminded him of her. And that she'd looked just like him. But she was very dead and very gone. 'You just told me ghosts aren't real, though.'

'They're not,' he said, frowning, clearly not liking this conversation. We'd come a long way in three weeks, from speaking very delicately and politely about inconsequential things to now, talking quite openly about our beliefs, histories, fears and losses. 'You must have tapped into a trace leftover from when Ana was alive.' An energetic footprint that lingers on the Fabric of the universe after events of significance, that can be tapped into by a scrier, like myself. 'I'd rather not discuss it tonight, if you wouldn't mind.'

'I don't mind,' I agreed immediately, not wanting to upset him like I did yesterday when I forced the issue. I sat down quickly in my usual seat opposite him at his desk and tried to paste a look of acceptance onto my face, and to emulate these feelings at the same time. Curiosity could wait. I laid the list I came in with across my lap and looked at the envelope in front of Renatus, expectant. 'What can I do?'

I felt like I was learning to read him much better, the more time I spent with him. Renatus was the quiet, mysterious type. I'd never seen him smiling, and his expression didn't tend to change much, but his eyes – if you were looking – often betrayed his emotional reactions. He pushed the envelope to me without a word, without any expression, but in his eyes I read his gratefulness for my discretion.

I fell easily into the routine of sealing envelopes, stamping the back, copying name and address onto the front, and ruling a line through the names on the list. I'd been helping with these kinds of ordinary tasks for weeks, and normally we'd talk, too. Tonight Renatus stayed silent. Yesterday we'd reached a strange new place in our student-headmaster relationship and agreed to be open with one another, to be allowed to ask the other anything in exchange for the same in return, and for the right to simply decline to answer if we chose. I was glad of this; he was intriguing, certainly, on a personal level, but he was also a treasure trove of information on the magical world that I wanted unlimited access to. I really admired and respected him, and despite not knowing him all that well yet and despite that most people seemed to find him abrupt and unsettling, I felt comfortable around him. Like I used to feel around my brother, before his death many years before.

Renatus's handwriting was neat and spidery, much neater and nicer than mine, but I came across a name I wasn't sure of. A letter in the middle was smudged. I squinted and tilted the page to no avail. I turned the paper so Renatus could see.

'Is this an *i* or an *l*?' I asked, pointing. I looked up at him when we didn't lean forward to check.

He never answered. His eyes had slipped out of focus and a frown of concern formed. My interest in the envelope task gave way to my interest in his behaviour. He was scrying. He had the skill and talent necessary to be able to remotely view past and present events without even trying. A scrier myself (though embarrassingly less knowledgeable and skilled) I hoped to one day be able to do this, but for now I had only my less-extraordinary means of accessing the same visions. I remembered the night he'd postponed my first detention. He'd touched my hand to get my attention and I'd somehow witnessed a troublesome situation occurring elsewhere, like watching a DVD inside my head. Was something terrible happening again? Without pausing to think about it, I reached across the desk and touched the back of his wrist.

A small, homely cottage in Italy with neat little gardens... Nine men, led by a tall sorcerer with rich, dark skin, use glowing knives to carefully carve at the air around the property... The resistance against one knife gives, and a spark in the air indicates the destruction of the spell... 'Only one to go and they haven't even noticed?'... They gather behind a stocky man, watching eagerly as his knife, silver-bright with his own power, cuts through the last strand of magic guarding the house...'Why is it taking so long?'... 'If they haven't noticed yet, rushing will only tip them off.'... A spark as the magic snaps... Nine bright grins... No longer needing to sneak, they rush forward... Someone exchanges his knife for a wand and casts a spell to blast the door inward...

The images stopped abruptly when Renatus flinched away from my touch, apparently having just realised what I was doing. We'd realised three weeks ago that I was able to channel visions from him through touch – it had not been established whether this was a good thing or a bad thing.

'What's happening?' I asked worriedly, not caring if he was angry with me for spying. He ignored my question.

'You probably don't want to see this,' he told me, giving me a meaningful look. 'It's Jackson, sent by Lisandro.' He placed his hand back on the desktop as his focus slipped again. I hesitated – his words and actions seemed contradictory – but, taking his action as an invitation, I touched my fingertips to his knuckles, and the stream of images began again.

Inside the cottage now, a joint kitchenette, dining and lounge room with a freestanding bench and a small dining table defining the areas... The nine men crowding at the door, weapons grasped tightly in heavy hands... Jackson at the front... Aubrey and Teresa standing by the table... Aubrey's wand is out, prepared... 'She's not here.'... Jackson scoffs, disbelieving, and a blaze of flame shoots between his wand point and the councillors... The flame glances off an opalescent wall, deflecting into the kitchen... A small cupboard door is blasted from its hinges... A flicker of fear from unseen parties...'See that ward? Did you think I wouldn't recognise her work? It's Emmanuelle's – where is she?'... Another faint pulse of nervousness, this time from several people... 'She's not here. She's gone.'... 'I don't think so. I know you're in here somewhere, darling. I've been looking forward to seeing you again.'...

This time, the vision faded before I broke the connection, and I became aware of the office once again. My emotions were a mess, as usual. What was going on? What was Jackson going to do? Was this Lisandro's doing? I'd never met the White Elm's former brother-turned-nemesis, but I knew enough to be at least distantly afraid of him. He'd betrayed his council and killed his own friend. I didn't know what else he was capable of. What was going to happen to Aubrey and Teresa, two of Renatus's more junior colleagues? Emmanuelle, my favourite councillor and possibly Renatus's only friend – she had been mentioned, but was she alright? I pulled my hand back as Renatus stood, muttering Emmanuelle's name softly.

'Is she there?' I asked, watching him. He pushed his chair back and opened the smoky-glassed cabinet behind the desk.

'You tell me,' he responded, pocketing several small items. I recognised the box that held the pendant he'd loaned me to stop my Haunting. 'It's where I sent her.'

I wondered how I was meant to know whether or not Emmanuelle was in that cottage. I hadn't seen or heard her. In my mind I sifted through the various images, sounds and feelings I'd channelled before I understood. Renatus didn't feel *anything* when he scried. I, on the other hand, was an Empath: I felt things much more intensely than other people, and I could sense feelings and motivations through scried visions. He hadn't felt that spark of fear when the door had fallen – that fear of being struck, of being discovered – nor when Jackson had asked after Emmanuelle.

My instincts told me that Emmanuelle was there, hidden somewhere, somehow, and that I'd felt the feelings of others, too.

'I think she is,' I said finally, doubtful. 'I think she's hidden with someone else.'

'Jadon should be there, too,' Renatus said, closing the cabinet and turning back to me. 'They are under attack. Jackson is extremely dangerous. He could hurt or kill them.' His gaze flickered from my face to the door and back again.

'What does he want?' I asked, willing myself not to panic. I wasn't even there, or even connected to the situation, but scrying it and feeling what the people there felt made it seem close to me. I got to my feet, catching the sheet of paper that fell from my lap.

'Emmanuelle has the White Elm's ring,' Renatus said, waving a hand at his door. I moved over as it began to open. 'She's calling for me to help.'

Telepathically, of course, not with phones. I wasn't even sure the White Elm used phones.

I'd forgotten my ghostly encounter in the orchard but now I had other things swirling about my mind as I went to the door. Sterling would ask why I was back so early, she'd ask what Renatus had said, I'd have to tell her "tough luck"... I was lost in my disordered thoughts of Sterling, Emmanuelle and Jackson, so I passed Renatus and reached the door before I realised that I was still holding the list of potential apprentices. That would have been the second time I'd walked out of the office with it in an emergency evacuation. I went to hand it back but saw that it had changed.

Everybody's name had a neat line drawn through it – except mine. I looked up at Renatus as he approached me. I was more confused now than I had been all night. Did this mean...? What?

'Are you coming?' Renatus asked, his tone telling me that there was no trick. I stared for a moment, uncertain. He grasped my wrist, and the images took over once again.

Teresa pulls Aubrey backwards a step... Aubrey's spell hits a man in the neck... The man falls, shouting, hurting... Aubrey's next spell is aimed at Jackson but is deflected... It strikes Aubrey in the stomach... Aubrey is on his knees, gasping, pain written across his face and his hands clenched... 'Just give me the ring, pretty thing...' Two more spells hit Aubrey and he is lying on the floor... Teresa steps over his motionless form... 'Stop. He's not a threat.'... 'I know'...

Renatus released me. I gasped, overwhelmed. Aubrey had been both surprised and terrified by the realisation that his spell had backfired. For one intense second that fear had been all I'd known.

'He's hurt,' I said, frightened. Was he alive?

11

'Are you coming?' Renatus asked again, tensely. I knew there was no question at all, really.

'Yes, I am,' I said, nodding quickly. Renatus's hand closed around my upper arm and he walked forwards, into the wall opposite the office door, pulling me along. I instinctively paused before any of my body could hit the wallpaper, but he had not stopped, and I found that when my elbow struck the wall, I felt nothing. In fact, my elbow had hit nothing, and when the rest of me followed, forcibly, I discovered why.

I melted through the wall as though it did not exist, except to my eyes, and the world around me became dark and cool. I blinked and continued to walk forwards into my new surroundings. The hallway had been completely replaced by the dim, spacious underground kitchen. There were no windows, and the floor, walls and ceilings were all made from cold stone. The oven was large and old-fashioned, and pots and pans hung above every bench top. A few of the house's staff were still here, washing up the cutlery and crockery used at dinner. They all glanced over with mild interest as Renatus dragged me across the room and up a small flight of stone steps, but nobody looked too surprised to see him randomly appearing out of a wall with a teenager in tow. Some sort of portal? To save the time that would have been wasted on stairs in this huge, four-storey estate home.

He pushed open the heavy wooden door at the top of the steps and strode out of the kitchen. This new room was better lit, I saw, as we moved quickly around the staircase and into the entry hall. Our footsteps echoed in the large empty space, faster and more urgent now than before. I had to extend my stride to keep up with his. We had almost reached the door when I heard a third set of footsteps echoing from the foot of the stairs, and both Renatus and I glanced back just as the person spoke.

'Renatus!' It was Qasim. Renatus stopped immediately before the doors, which were still closed, but didn't release his tight grip on my arm.

'Italy,' Renatus called across the space, waiting for the older scrier to catch up. 'Most of the council will meet us there. Somebody needs to stay.'

'Susannah has agreed to stay behind,' Qasim said, speaking to Renatus but watching me. The older sorcerer from Saudi Arabia both frightened and interested me. He was tall, more powerfully built than Renatus, around fifty years of age, with a neat beard and a tattoo on his left wrist. He had an expression and an air that you simply did not mess with. He did not like me: he'd made this very clear. I wasn't sure yet, but I didn't think I liked him much, either. Our interactions were usually intense, and often negative. He'd tried to have me expelled a month ago – I'd been lucky to learn that my enrolment at the White Elm's Academy was subject to Renatus's whim, essentially, and I'd gotten off with a warning and a stack of detentions. 'Where do you think you are going, Aristea?'

I didn't know exactly, only the country, and I wasn't sure how to answer, because his tone implied that I was about to be in a great deal of trouble. Thankfully, Renatus spoke for me.

'She's coming with us,' he told Qasim. The Scrier blinked, apparently wondering whether he'd heard correctly.

'She's what?'

'She's coming.' Renatus, in my experience, despite his comparative youth, never seemed afraid of putting his foot down with the White Elm's Scrier.

'What are you talking about?' Qasim demanded, emanating frustration, looking between us. 'She isn't going anywhere. You can't take a student out of the grounds.'

'I think you'll find I can,' Renatus answered, his tone calm and cool. I wondered whether he could feel my arm trembling in his grasp – Qasim's mood was darkening, becoming ugly and angry, and it scared me.

'I think you'll find it difficult pulling the "headmaster" card this time. Nowhere did Angela Byrne sign to give you permission as headmaster to take her sister out of the country, for *any reason*.'

A brief image of my sister appeared at the front of my mind. What would she say if she were here?

'The Academy's headmaster has no such right over our students; in that, you are correct,' Renatus agreed. I glanced between them as Renatus went on. 'I am exercising my rights as master, granted by the old laws, which even our council cannot overrule.'

'As *master*?' Qasim repeated, slowly. His dark eyes moved between my face and Renatus's.

'That's right,' Renatus confirmed. 'Aristea is my apprentice.'

The words rang in my head. *Aristea is my apprentice.* He chose me, out of a whole host of better students. I was still clutching the list that confirmed it. Qasim was silent for a long time, his emotions bubbling like boiling water as he turned this information over in his head until it made sense. When it did, he turned to me suddenly, his hand snatching for mine. His fingers closed over my left wrist before I could move away, and though I instinctively tried to wrench it back, he was much too strong.

'Hey,' I said, but he ignored me. I expected him to take the list from me again. He did not even notice I held it. He twisted my hand uncomfortably so that the smooth underside of my wrist was facing upwards. He smirked at Renatus, relaxing slightly.

'Unmarked,' he commented. 'She's not yours yet.'

'The old laws accept a verbal contract as sufficient until the ceremony at the first full moon,' Renatus disagreed, plucking the list from my hand and pocketing it. He looked to me as Qasim relaxed his grip. 'Aristea, I wish to take you as my apprentice, for life. Do you consent to this?'

'Let her go,' Qasim snarled, grabbing my wrist again and yanking me free of Renatus's grip; the Dark Keeper did as he was told. 'You won't control her answers. Aristea,' the Scrier said, taking my shoulders and turning me to face him, 'you don't understand what you are doing. If you agree, you are

15

accepting a *lifelong* commitment. You are giving him access to your every thought; you are agreeing to a connection that will exist until one of you die. If you agree, you are agreeing to share your gifts, your power – do you understand that? You are agreeing to *belong* to him, to do as he asks, share his work, and one day to take his place on the White Elm. You don't know him. You don't know what he does. *You don't understand what you are doing.'*

It took me a moment to process all of this. What he'd just described was basically what I'd read in Renatus's books. Qasim was trying to make it sound like a curse, but what difference did it make? Renatus would see into my mind whether I let him or not, and it would not surprise me if he had the power to borrow magic from those around him regardless of whether they were connected to him. By coming to this school, I had known that one day I might be asked to work with the White Elm. It was not a curse; it was a dream come true. My sister would not be angry with me for agreeing. She would be so, so proud that I had been chosen over everyone else.

My whole family would have been proud of me to agree to serve the White Elm.

I was proud of me right now.

I lightly shrugged Qasim's hands from my shoulders and looked back at Renatus. My master, I thought vaguely, convinced that I was making the right choice.

'I understand what it means,' I said, hoping I was telling the truth. 'I accept.'

I felt Renatus's relief; apparently, he had not been sure whether I would say that.

'You're not prepared,' Qasim said, a note of desperation in his voice.

'She has read each of the texts required of any apprentice,' Renatus said, an arm appearing around my shoulders and steering me towards the door, which was opening of its own accord. 'She read them in her detentions. Can we go? Aubrey and Teresa are down. Jadon and Emmanuelle need us.'

Qasim hesitated as the door opened. He was not happy with the situation, but seemed to have run out of excuses. His sense of duty overpowered his anger and he nodded once, tensely.

'We'll talk about this later,' he warned Renatus, shoving past him to exit first. He was almost visibly seething with fury. Renatus pushed me through the door and we followed Qasim across the lawn, keeping a fast pace.

No one said anything until we reached the gates, which, like all the doors here, opened at a gesture from Renatus. The White Elm's Academy used for its campus Renatus's old family home and the whole place seemed sensitive to his whims. I followed the two scriers out. I normally would have noticed the cold air or the clear, starry sky, but now I felt somewhat numb. My thoughts were whirling around in my brain, but kept coming back to a few key sentences – Renatus picked *me*. I am his apprentice. Several of the White Elm's councillors are in danger and Renatus and Qasim are going to help, and I will... what? Stand and watch?

17

What did Renatus expect for me to be able to do?

'Have you been to Teresa's before?' Renatus asked of Qasim when we passed through the gates. *The* Scrier, the only one of our class who got to use a capital letter, shook his head, coming to a stop several metres away. This was where Angela had parked when she'd dropped me off. Had that really been only five and a half weeks ago?

'Elijah is there now; we can go to him,' Qasim answered. He turned his dark glare on me, and I tried my best not to quail. 'This may be a hostile situation. If you become endangered, you will hide and build your wards around yourself. You will stay by Renatus's side at all times; you will not wander off alone. If you become separated, find Lord Gawain and *stay* with him. *Nobody else.* Do you understand that?'

I nodded automatically, not really understanding at all why I couldn't go to anyone else on the council. Renatus did not try to argue or contradict Qasim's orders.

Renatus grabbed my arm again and I felt his power running through his being as he cast a spell I couldn't see or understand. He pulled me with him as he took a step forward. For a moment I felt a strange resistance, as if I were in water, and then my foot landed on a solid paved road, my body followed and when my second foot followed the first, I was standing in an entirely new time zone.

I had Displaced. I was in Italy. It was warmer here, though not quite warm. The winding street I

18

stood in rose before me with the hill it was built on, and cute cottages lined it, spaced apart to give generous garden and lawn areas to each.

It was as I had seen.

There was a commotion behind us. Qasim appeared beside me and took off down the hill. Reminding me quietly to stay by his side, Renatus followed at a jog, and I tried to keep pace. In the dimly lit street I could see several people spill out of the house from Renatus's vision. I could hear voices; they were drowned out by a sharp *psshhh* sound, like a rocket flying past. I ducked and slowed, but nothing happened and the scriers didn't even miss a step. When I straightened I saw the small band of men dart between two houses and begin to disappear. I pointed, horrified as I noticed human forms slung over the shoulders of the bigger men.

'Stop!' Qasim shouted, and both he and Renatus did so, pulling wands from inside their coats and aiming them in the direction of the escaping attackers. Before they could do anything, the last man disappeared with a small female body. They were gone.

Renatus swore loudly, and looked back for me. I caught up, wondering what the neighbours thought of all this noise. Nobody appeared in any of the other doorways and no windows suddenly brightened.

Further along the street, some more people appeared and began to enter the house behind those who had hurried out before. As we neared, the last of them turned and looked at us, hesitating only a moment before raising a hand in acknowledgement.

The light from inside the house spilled through the open door onto his face, and I saw that it was Tian, another of the councillors and one of my teachers.

So the newcomers were White Elm. At least we were walking towards the good guys. I felt so disorientated by the suddenness of everything, our arrival here, the action...

We were nearly at the cottage of interest when I felt a flicker of emotion where those strangers had disappeared and stopped, grabbing for Renatus's arm. Distantly, through him, I overheard some of what he was scrying: *'He just took them, I don't know why he would'*... *'Why didn't he take you, too?'*... *'Teresa's illusion saved us. She didn't have time to guard herself and Aubrey'*... *'She was wearing one of the rings – what if it was the real one?'*... *'She's the only one who would have known. I didn't even bother to ask'*... *'How did they know where to find us?'*

He stopped immediately at my touch, and even Qasim pulled up. I wasn't sure at first whether I'd been right to stop them, because I couldn't see anything in the shadows between the two houses, but I *had* felt something, not ten metres away.

'What?' Renatus asked, voice low. I slowly shook my head, unsure. There was nothing there – my eyes were very certain of that – but *someone* was exactly there, feeling apprehensive. The more I looked the more concern I felt. Not mine; someone else's. Air didn't have feelings so where were these reactions coming from? The unease built as I scanned and squinted and as my eyes slipped into the focus Glen had taught me...

The shadows remained dark but a small, blurry figure with thin blonde hair became apparent. His dark eyes were staring straight into mine. Where had he come from? He'd just *shimmered* into existence between those shadows.

'Renatus!' I stage-whispered, too scared to speak any louder as I pointed. He followed my gaze, and, without warning, he levelled his wand at the mostly-hidden figure and shot a sphere of fire the size of a tennis ball at his torso. It made a cracking sound like a gun and I leapt backwards in shock. The fireball travelled as fast as a bullet, too. On impact, the man became completely visible and his whole body caught alight, burning like he was bathed in petrol. He screamed, his agony and horror rolling from him like smoke, choking me as it hit me. I pressed my hands to my ears, terrified, hoping that by blocking the sound I could block the awful feelings.

He burned, and he burned, and it seemed he'd been burning forever, but it was only a few seconds before Tian came to his senses and ran over. He raised his sword, letting it fall through the air in a cutting motion, severing Renatus's connection with the spell and extinguishing the flames.

'Renatus, that's a person,' he snapped, shoving past us to tend to the man, who was by now lying curled on the lawn, moaning. 'You could have killed him.'

You could have killed him. That's a person. You could have killed him. I slowly lowered my hands from my ears but in their place I could feel the pounding of my pulse through the fine blood vessels.

What had I agreed to back at the house?

'Whoops,' Renatus responded, his tone sarcastic, as Emmanuelle, the council's official Healer, arrived. Obviously drawn by the sudden fire and the scream, she hurried to Tian's side to take over, and we followed her to watch. The White Elm's swordsman immediately moved aside as she ran careful hands across burnt skin, millimetres from contact.

'Second degree burns,' she muttered, mostly to herself. For such a brief fire, the spell's flames had done a lot of damage. I couldn't draw my eyes away from the mess that was supposed to be a man. Much of the clothing had been burnt away. The skin was red and raw, peeling away in some places and shiny with blood in others. There didn't seem to be a single patch of unharmed skin. What had Renatus done?

'Nothing you can't fix, of course,' he said coolly, addressing Emmanuelle. She shot him an annoyed look before her eyelids slid shut and she ceased to move.

Others arrived and tense conversation began around me but I wasn't listening. My attention was locked on Emmanuelle and the man from the shadows. His raw, blistery skin had repulsed me at first, but now it didn't seem so bad. A skinless patch on the neck and including the ear still oozed blood; I looked elsewhere, watching Emmanuelle's hands, which trembled just slightly but otherwise remained poised above the patient's heart. The skin on his chest looked quite healthy, I thought, except for the blood on it, but the wounds were not apparent. Involuntarily, I looked back to the ear. To my surprise, there was no skin missing from the ear or the neck. Shiny, fresh new skin had replaced the wound. I looked back and forth across the man's body, and before my very eyes, blood clotted and wounds closed up.

Less than thirty seconds and the man was essentially healed, his wounds patched up, his damaged skin regrowing. Emmanuelle opened her eyes and looked up.

'He's fine,' she said, French accent affecting her English. 'The shock of 'is trauma and my healing should keep 'im docile for a few hours at least. 'is system doesn't know what to think, and some of 'is nerves are still rebuilding, so it will be a while before 'e regains full awareness of 'is body.' She gave Renatus another look. 'Not that I care in this case, but you ought to take more caution. Another few seconds and 'e would 'ave been dead.'

Renatus didn't respond. I imagined he didn't care either. He tossed a balled-up golden chain to Emmanuelle and she secured it around the patient's shoulders.

His carelessness blew my mind. I'd assumed all along that he was someone not to be crossed, but I'd not expected...

'We don't even know if he was one of them,' Qasim chastised.

'Renatus just doesn't give a flying fuck about anybody but himself,' Jadon said, very coldly, 'which is why he turned Teresa and Aubrey over to Jackson.' Renatus only frowned as everyone else turned to him. Jadon carried on, asking, 'Is there any point in telling you that Jackson just broke in while we were working on *your* project and attacked Teresa and Aubrey? That he *took* them, and one of the rings? Or do you already know?'

'Of course I already know,' Renatus answered tightly. He gestured back at his fellow scrier. 'Qasim and I both saw the whole thing.'

'Don't drag Qasim's name into it like it's your lifeline,' Jadon sneered. I rubbed my arms self-consciously. Like the rest of the councillors, Jadon was one of my teachers, and I'd never seen him angry before. I'd never seen him upset. He was always cheerful at school, always prepared to show the class another magical party trick. Tonight it was like I was looking at a whole different person.

Lord Gawain, the white-haired Welsh sorcerer charged with leading the White Elm, raised his hands, palms outward, trying to calm Jadon.

'Jadon, please consider your words,' he requested. 'Now is not the time for mislaid blame.'

'I don't think it's mislaid. Thirteen people knew what Teresa was doing here tonight. Only one of them would benefit from this council falling beneath Lisandro's feet.' Jadon narrowed his eyes at Renatus. 'It was *your* idea to bring the ring here tonight; *your* idea for Emmanuelle to come, knowing that Jackson was tracking her. Nobody but the thirteen of us knew what was going on tonight, and you're the one who set it all in motion. You betrayed us.'

Everyone started talking again, and I listened in silence. Glen turned up, demanding to know what had happened. Voices kept lacing over and through one another; negativity wove over and through itself, over and over. The White Elm were superheroes, incredible sorcerers of incredible capabilities, but apparently they could argue just as loudly and strongly as any gaggle of hormonal preteens.

'Jadon, stop it,' Emmanuelle snapped, as I struggled to make sense of the conversation. 'You cannot take out your frustrations like this.' She turned to face Renatus. Nobody seemed to have noticed me yet, standing in the shadows. 'Renatus, tell us. Whose side are you on?'

Everyone stared at him, waiting with apprehension, while he looked around the room.

'The same side as the rest of you, I hope,' he answered. Truthfully. Sorcerers as sensitive as me, and therefore of course the council, could detect the energetic flicker that accompanies a lie, and Renatus wasn't lying.

'Thank you. That should be good enough for everyone,' Emmanuelle said firmly, eyeing each of her fellow councillors. Her gaze almost drifted over me, but clung, and for a long moment she stared. 'Aristea? What are you doing here?'

Everyone turned to me, shocked. I stepped forward a little, still unsure what to say. Again, Renatus spoke for me.

'I have chosen an apprentice,' he said simply. 'She works with me now.'

A tense moment of silence was followed immediately by another breakout of arguments and disagreements – '*What*?', 'I don't believe this' and

'You're not old enough' were the loudest – until Qasim interrupted.

'He's heard it already from me,' he said, his tone making it very clear that he agreed with them all and was not happy. 'We have bigger problems tonight than Aristea. This can wait; Teresa and Aubrey can't.'

Qasim had an authority the others could not argue with. Lord Gawain nodded briskly, quickly assuming control, but the shock of my presence and Renatus's words still showed in his eyes.

'First of all, we need to secure the area,' he said, glancing quickly over his councillors as though counting them. 'Qasim, Tian and Renatus – and Aristea – this entire property and the street needs to be investigated. We need to know if anyone else has stayed behind. As they search, this house will need new wards, Emmanuelle; and I will need that ring to learn whether Jackson has taken the true one. Jadon, take Samuel back to Morrissey House until we're done and fill the others in. Glen, Anouk; we will need to question our friend here,' he nodded briefly at the unconscious prisoner, 'as well as the one we found inside, so we need to talk to Valero.'

Qasim and Tian immediately walked off in opposite directions. Renatus knelt beside the detainee and slipped the pendant he'd once loaned to me around the man's neck. I knew it was designed to lock one's magic inside their body. In my case it had been to prevent any accidental subconscious magic while I learnt to control it; in the prisoner's case things were a little more dire.

'Look, my girlfriend is missing,' an unfamiliar man said suddenly, his tone barely controlled. Anouk laid a gentle hand on his arm, soothing him with soft words, but he shrugged her away. 'I am not going anywhere until I know how you're getting Teresa back. Do you even know why she was taken? Do you even know if she's alive?'

Teresa's partner. Had he just been forced to watch in useless silence as his girlfriend was abducted by hostile strangers? He looked young, only in his early twenties, I supposed about the same age as Teresa herself. And he looked scared. I couldn't blame him. I felt the same.

'She's alive, Samuel,' Lord Gawain promised. 'Our circle of thirteen is unbroken. Teresa and Aubrey are alive, and that is not without reason.' He accepted Emmanuelle's ring from her. 'If Jackson had wanted to, he could have killed them both, but he did not. I suspect Lisandro has other plans.' He smiled briefly at Samuel, holding up the ring. 'If this isn't real, Teresa's illusions are even more impressive than I had ever expected. We're going to get her back, Samuel. She is our sister, and Aubrey is our brother. We will do everything in our power to bring her back to you.'

'But-'

'Samuel,' Jadon interrupted, 'I promise we're going to find her. Alright?'

The conviction in his voice was many times more convincing than Lord Gawain's spiel, I thought, and Samuel must have thought so, because he reluctantly followed Jadon into the cottage, presumably to pack some things for a short stay.

Glen and Anouk pulled the prisoner upright. The man's head lolled to one side and I looked away from his eyes, which had rolled back.

'Will the prison take anyone so short-notice?' Glen asked, while Elijah helped get the captive upright.

'They will from me,' Anouk answered. Renatus took my arm again and led me away, onto Teresa's front lawn. I went where he dragged me. After his display of power I wasn't about to disobey.

'Stay with me,' he ordered. 'Put more wards up.'

Obediently I built layer upon layer of shields around my mind and body. No one would be able to get at me without a fair deal of work. I hoped nobody would try.

I was quite sure I was in the very last situation I should have ever put myself into.

chapter two

Searching turned out to be a tedious task. Renatus slowly circled the house, his wand pointed wherever he was looking as though it were a flashlight. He seemed willing to check every square centimetre of the cottage wall, possibly for sigils or other symbols binding magic to this place, and had me check the gardens, although I wasn't sure exactly what I was looking for. I just did what I was told.

Elijah went with Anouk, Glen and the bad guys, but he was the only one to return. Lord Gawain met him on the edge of the street while Renatus and I worked our way around to where the attackers had disappeared from.

'Qasim says if there were any traces of them to follow, they've faded now,' I overheard Lord Gawain saying. 'Elijah, if there's anything at all you can do...'

I glanced up from the carrots to watch as Elijah moved a few steps away from Lord Gawain. I expected him to Displace mid-step, as I'd always seen him do and as I'd seen my friend Hiroko do hours before. But he slowed, sensing something, and stopped. Then he disappeared entirely, his image flickering a few times in place a second later. For a long moment, he was gone, and then he reappeared, looking worn out.

'It's like the wormhole they used has been cemented shut,' he admitted, slightly breathless as though he'd been straining. 'I can feel it; it's like a door, just standing right here.' He waved a hand to indicate the space he occupied. 'It's blocked from the other end. I can't see where it goes or follow it.' He squinted at the air around him thoughtfully, as though looking at something the rest of us couldn't see. 'I'll keep trying.'

'Has anyone checked the shrouds over the neighbours?' Lord Gawain asked the group as Elijah resumed his flickering in and out of space. 'We don't need anyone popping out to get the cat in and seeing us here.'

'Master, there's nothing here,' Renatus called to his leader. I reluctantly glanced back at him. I'd avoided looking at him since he fire-bombed that stranger in the shadows, expecting to feel a lump in my throat or a flutter in my stomach – some physical representation of the fear his action had inspired in me. But when my gaze met his, I didn't feel any such thing. I didn't feel any need to drop my eyes. I didn't feel afraid at all. It was almost like I couldn't *be bothered* being afraid of him. Like it was an actual effort to be afraid.

What was wrong with me?

Qasim and Tian returned from each of the neighbouring properties. Lord Gawain approached to listen while Tian shook his head.

'There is nothing uphill,' he reported.

'Downhill is the same. Jackson is not as organised as we are giving him credit for. Did he leave anything at the house?' Qasim asked, turning to Renatus. My new master was still tracing his wand through the air, following a line, it seemed, his eyes changing focus as though trying to spot something quite transparent.

'They didn't. There's magic around, but it's mostly Teresa's. The wards are in tatters all over the place.' He dropped his wand to his side, apparently giving up. 'There's no spy magic, anywhere. No sigils to alert anyone to new presences. I couldn't find any wards against us, but if I missed any, Emmanuelle will find them.'

'Can you see them?' Qasim asked, changing tact. Renatus shook his head.

'I'm looking but I can't find either of them,' Renatus answered, businesslike. I assumed they were talking about Aubrey and Teresa and their mutual gift of seeing things that were far away. 'They're being blocked from us.'

'I see only black when I scry for them,' Qasim admitted. 'I expect it's because they have not regained consciousness. Perhaps it will change when they do.'

Still talking, the two fell into step, walking towards the house, leaving me, Lord Gawain and Tian to trail behind. Considering their mutual dislike for the other's character, I thought, the two worked quite well together and obviously respected each other's gifts.

'Aristea,' Qasim snapped, jolting me out of my thoughts. 'What did I tell you?' I looked up at him and saw that they had all stopped to look at me. Renatus returned to my side as Qasim continued, his voice scathing, 'Stay close. And get out of Teresa's garden. You can pick flowers when you get back to school.'

I glared back at him, stung. I wasn't a councillor, or a warrior, or a particularly accomplished spell caster, but I wasn't a baby, either, and I hadn't been rude to him at all today. I wasn't even sure I'd spoken to him.

If he wanted to convince me I shouldn't be Renatus's apprentice, he was definitely going about it the wrong way. At this point I would take potentially homicidal over needlessly mean.

'We should be heading back now, anyway,' Renatus said. 'There's nothing to find here. Was the ring real?'

Lord Gawain nodded once, and held out a dull silver ring. All of this was over that old thing? I stepped closer to see.

'I've seen that before,' I said before I could stop myself. Then I clapped my hands over my mouth, realising my mistake. I'd seen the plain band with the black stone carved with the White Elm's tree of life emblem on Emmanuelle's hand a month ago while illegally (and accidentally, it should be mentioned) Haunting. That was what I'd gotten my detentions for. Had Renatus not agreed to cover the whole thing up I would have been expelled, and possibly charged for my gross misdeed; if anyone other than Qasim ever *knew* he'd covered something like this up, he'd doubtless be in trouble, too. Nobody else was ever supposed to know. Renatus's expression did not change but I felt his sudden tension. I saw Qasim raise his eyebrow, waiting for me to slip up and give him the proof he needed to show that he was right all along. Renatus had just burnt some guy's skin off but I was still determined that Qasim would not get the better of me, and so I felt myself innately siding with the headmaster. I lowered my hands and cleared my throat. 'Um, that tree. It was on the stone I picked up when you tested me.'

Qasim blinked at me. 'The emblem of the White Elm. Obviously.'

Obviously. *Obviously* your patronising nastiness is going to do nothing to deter me from my decision to become Renatus's apprentice. Renatus attacked bad buys without warning but he was never as needlessly unpleasant as Qasim managed to be, at least not to me.

'Meet back at the house as soon as you're done,' Lord Gawain said tiredly. 'There's nothing to be found here and much to discuss.'

Renatus asked Lord Gawain to take me back to the school while he, Emmanuelle and Qasim finished rebuilding the wards at Teresa's house. Lord Gawain offered me his hand, which I took, and a few steps later we were in the dark moors surrounding the estate.

'You can never be sure when you Displace whether you'll get it right,' he said, smiling at me awkwardly as we trekked to the top of the nearest hill. We'd never spoken before; I realised that he was making the effort to be friendly, so I forced a return smile.

'I can't do it at all, so I'm not complaining,' I answered.

'All skills will come to you quicker after the ceremony,' Lord Gawain said, glancing up at the sky. The moon was waxing towards its full form, just a few days away. 'We'll have to do it Monday, when the moon is fullest. Magic is strongest then – your bond is most likely to be approved.'

We spotted the house, only a minute's or less walk away. I knew he was talking about the initiation ceremony, which officially bound a master and apprentice to their word and to one another. I didn't know much more about it, but it seemed prudent to find out, considering I was apparently going to undertake the ceremony.

'What do you mean, "approved"?' I asked, following the council leader down the hill, picking my way through the knobbly grass and various holes and ditches.

'Well, consenting to the apprenticeship is the first step – I trust you have?' Lord Gawain checked, looking back at me worriedly. I nodded despite my new doubts and listened carefully to Lord Gawain as he continued. 'Good, good. The ceremony itself formalises the relationship, and we call on magic to officiate and carry out its will. If you are fated to be Renatus's apprentice, you will be. Otherwise, Fate will intervene. Fate will always have its way.'

Fate sounded like a bossy thing. I wasn't sure yet whether I liked it.

'However,' he warned, looking up at the house, 'you'll still need the approval of the council. Because Renatus is White Elm, the council has the right to assess you and decide whether they want you joining them one day. If they decide they don't, the ceremony will not go ahead and you won't be able to be his apprentice.'

So, there was more disagreement yet to come, I thought. I could definitely think of a few councillors who would oppose Renatus's decision. *Our* decision – I'd decided, too.

As shocking as it was, especially to me, I still wanted to be his student.

We had to use a key to get back inside the gates of Morrissey House, and then we walked up the winding, sloped path to the big front doors. I looked up once more at the stone mansion's imposing visage. It was Renatus's family home, the base of the infamous Morrissey family for generations. He was the last one left, and so everything had fallen to him. The house. The money. The reputation. It wasn't all positive, and after tonight's exercise of power I was starting to respect why that was. But Renatus was White Elm, and their application process was a stringent one, their expectations of their members high. When the council had decided to form a school to upskill the youth of their society in finer magical arts and to help them seek out potential apprentices, Renatus was the only one of the thirteen whose residence had provided an appropriate campus. And so what was being called the "Academy" was here.

Most of the windows on the second floor were lit behind the curtains, indicating that most of my thirtyish classmates were still awake. I cast my eyes down to my wristwatch as we stepped over the threshold. Of course they were. It was late, but not late enough that teenagers with no parents around would have yet sent themselves to bed. I lowered my gaze; my dorm room had no windows, so I wouldn't be able to tell whether my friends had a light on. Were they wondering where I was? Lord Gawain led me through the silent house and to the ballroom. The council had already begun to gather. Lady Miranda, Susannah and Jadon turned as we entered.

'Gawain, I came as soon as I could get away,' Lady Miranda said, striding over. As usual, she looked exhausted. Her day job was as a surgeon in London; when she wasn't saving lives there, she was here, helping Lord Gawain govern the magical world as his co-leader. 'I can't feel anything from Teresa or Aubrey except that they are alive. Hopefully Teresa's illusion lasts long enough that they can wake up and make their escape. Jadon says the attacker was Jackson.'

'It seems so,' Lord Gawain confirmed, looking around. 'Where is Samuel?'

'He's staying in Teresa's usual room,' Jadon said. His anger had abated, and he seemed young and a little lost now. He stood slightly apart from the older, female councillors.

'We heard about Renatus's latest stunt,' Susannah commented coolly, nodding once at me.

'I'm not a stunt,' I argued, a spark of defiance giving me a moment of strength. It quickly faded, and I was soon staring at my feet.

'We know you're not, Aristea,' Lady Miranda insisted quickly, laying a hand on my shoulder. Her touch was warm and soothing. 'We're just... surprised. That's all. Nobody is angry or upset with you.'

Just Renatus. I could gather the unspoken end to her sentence.

'We just have to talk it all over,' Lady Miranda added, smiling kindly at me as I looked up. 'As Renatus is one of us, his decisions affect the entire council.' She turned to Lord Gawain, her smile becoming strained. 'Did he mention anything to you?'

'I had no idea,' Lord Gawain admitted.

'You know him better than we do,' the priestess pressed. 'Has he been acting strangely?'

'No stranger than usual,' Lord Gawain said noncommittally with a small shrug, glancing back at the door as Glen and Anouk entered.

'The Valeroans are happy to hold them as long as we want,' Glen confirmed. 'Any news?'

'I can't reach either of them,' Jadon said, misery tinging his voice. 'There's some sort of block.'

Glen crossed the ballroom, shaking his head, and came to a stop beside Susannah, keeping some distance from Lady Miranda. Anouk left a space between herself and Susannah. I realised that the councillors seemed to be forming some kind of large circle, leaving big spaces for those who had not arrived. When Elijah and Tian returned a few minutes later, they took the spaces either side of Anouk, and the circle became more defined.

Almost exactly twenty minutes after Lord Gawain had called for the council's return to the estate, Qasim shoved open the ballroom doors, obviously still annoyed. He was closely followed by Emmanuelle and Renatus. My hand clenched at my side when I saw Renatus, suddenly reminded of tonight's events. He'd lit a man on fire, hadn't he, without knowing whether the guy was good or bad? I'd been correct to think he could be dangerous. What was I thinking, agreeing to work for him, to have him train me?

Emmanuelle crossed the middle of the circle to stand beside Tian, keeping a gap for two people between herself and Jadon. Renatus and Qasim occupied the space between Lady Miranda and Glen.

I stood awkwardly behind Lord Gawain. The circle was large but just too tight for me to stand beside anyone. I heard my name called very softly, and glanced to my left. Emmanuelle had her hand extended to me, a slight smile gracing her features. I hurried to her, taking the empty space beside her. Aubrey's place, I realised.

'Blessed be,' Lord Gawain began, his voice rebounding in the large space. Very Wiccan, I thought. The other ten councillors present echoed his sentiment.

I didn't know whether it was proper for me to repeat it, so I stayed silent.

'Jackson has taken Aubrey and Teresa, along with Teresa's illusion of the Elm Stone, presumably on Lisandro's order,' Lord Gawain stated. 'At this time they remain alive. We must hope that it serves Lisandro's purpose to keep it that way. He has blocked all of our efforts to reach him or our councillors. Therefore we are left with only one option – to wait.' Jadon looked away. 'Whatever his reasons for taking them, his problem is not with Aubrey or Teresa. It is with me, and so he will come to me when he is ready.'

'Do you mean to say we won't look?' Jadon asked, glaring out of the tall windows.

'We will search,' Lord Gawain said, 'but I doubt it will do us any good. Lisandro does not want to be found.' He paused, but Jadon would not look back at him. 'We will talk about that next. We have another matter of business, which needs to be attended to immediately.' He raised a hand to indicate me.

'You never cease to surprise us, Renatus,' Susannah commented. With barely a glance in her direction, Renatus left his place in the circle to stand in its centre.

'Renatus has chosen to take Aristea as his apprentice,' Lord Gawain explained, as if anybody present hadn't already heard and made their opinion known. 'I am of the understanding that Aristea has already accepted the offer, and that she is aware of what this means. Is that correct?'

Everybody was staring at me, waiting for my response.

'Yes, it is,' I said, somewhat terrified, because I wasn't sure it was entirely true. My instincts, my heart told me, *yes, it's true, go with it*, but my head kept butting in, saying, *you don't know what you're doing, you aren't ready*. Luckily for my heart, I wasn't known for making rational choices.

'This decision affects us all,' Lady Miranda said again. 'If Renatus trains Aristea, she will eventually join our council, and will one day have the right to the chair of Dark Keeper. We all have the right to vote who joins the White Elm, so we also have a right to vote here. If you have something to say, now is the time to say it.'

Emmanuelle nudged me gently, pushing me into the circle with Renatus. We were on show, I thought. I went to his side, glancing up at him nervously. I still couldn't bring myself to be afraid *of him*, not after weeks of sitting alone in an office with him stamping envelopes and coming to absolutely no harm, but I was definitely afraid. Tonight I'd seen a side of him and his colleagues I'd not witnessed before. I had entirely no clue what the outcome of this circle would be for me.

'Obviously, I'm voting yes,' Renatus said, 'for what it's worth.'

'All votes are equal,' Lord Gawain was quick to reply. 'We each have a vote. Because Aubrey and Teresa are not present, we will assume their votes to be neutral until we can retrieve them. If they are not returned by Monday night, we will be forced to act without their vote.'

I looked over my shoulder at the faces of my teachers. Renatus's colleagues. Until tonight I'd not realised how unfriendly the ten of them could look.

Lady Miranda spoke first.

'I will lend my support to your decision,' she said, her voice slightly strained, as though to even say it was difficult for her. 'I can't believe I'm saying it, but despite everything, I won't be one to question Fate. This is happening for a reason. I can imagine you on our council, Aristea, and I would welcome that future. But you should know it won't be easy. Believe me, I know.' She extended her left arm, turning it so that a black tattoo of some rounded, alien symbol could be seen on the underside of her wrist. It looked nothing the same, but I was re-minded of Qasim's tattoo on the same section of skin. I had no idea what they meant.

'I know, too, and I won't support this,' Qasim said bluntly. The warmth I'd felt from Lady Miranda's words dissipated at Qasim's tone. Everyone listened. 'This is all wrong. Renatus is too young to have an apprentice, and Aristea was not adequately prepared. They don't know each other well enough to make this choice. Would you marry someone you'd known five weeks, Aristea?'

I didn't answer – obviously, I would not, being seventeen years of age and being a little sceptical of the idea of love at first sight. Qasim continued.

'This is entirely unprofessional. Renatus has not followed council guidelines. The council should have been informed of his intentions months in advance. Aristea's guardian needs to provide her consent before any formalisation can commence. Has Angela Byrne been consulted, Renatus, or did you forget that detail?'

'I didn't forget,' Renatus answered frostily. 'I just haven't had a chance yet. Things have been slightly chaotic lately.'

He wouldn't have a problem, I knew. Angela never said no. If it was what I wanted, I would get it.

'There is also the tiny problem of your apprentice's sex,' Qasim added, brutally cold. 'All the Fate in the world can't change the fact that she is a girl, and White Elm guidelines command you to select a male.'

I froze, quickly flicking through my memories of that White Elm book. Had it really said that? I suspected he might be right.

'The guidelines are not the old laws,' Elijah spoke up. He looked as though he wished he didn't have to take the side he was taking. 'They are traditions only. The old laws do not stipulate the sex of either party – magic decides whether the pairing is right.'

'That said, Renatus is breaking many of our traditions tonight,' Qasim said. 'It is disrespectful. He has chosen an apprentice to one day take his chair as Dark Keeper, forgetting that no woman has ever held that chair.'

'What, is it a man's job?' I demanded, unable to hold back the sarcasm. 'The book I read didn't say anything about females being prohibited from holding that position.'

'They aren't,' Lady Miranda said, a dark glare silencing Qasim. 'It just hasn't been done before. We've heard from you, Qasim. Glen?'

'I'm sorry, Aristea, but I can't believe that you fully understand what you've agreed to,' Glen said, his eyes genuinely apologetic. 'You're a child. I have a daughter, younger than you, and looking at you tonight I see only my Madlen. You don't know how vulnerable you are, and I don't want to see you manipulated. I feel like at least one person here should be looking out for you, and not just the might of the council or themselves.' He glanced between Qasim and Renatus, and back to me. 'I'm sorry. I do not support your choice.'

I nodded, but Susannah was already talking.

'Neither do I,' she said. She wasn't looking at me. She was looking only at Renatus, her eyes challenging. 'Do you think we don't know what you're doing? Don't you have enough power without taking hers?'

'I'm not *taking* anything,' Renatus answered frostily. 'A master's power is granted by the will of magic.'

'What makes you think you need that power?' Susannah asked. 'How can you prove to us that you'll use that power responsibly? Why should we grant you that power when there's every chance you'll drop us at a moment's notice? And why should we give you responsibility of one of the

Academy's students? If you leave the council we'd lose a student.'

'That would be most unfortunate,' Renatus agreed. I admired his resilience, because Susannah's accusations were very open. 'Perhaps you should be grateful that it isn't going to happen. Surely you've Seen that already.'

The American sorceress pursed her lips.

'It's not for me to tell you what I've Seen,' she said finally. 'It would be unethical. The future changes as quickly as we change our minds, and what matters, Renatus, is that many of those potential futures see you damaging this girl, or yourself, or both, and I won't support that. She's not as strong as you are – she can't be expected to match you.'

'I support you both,' Elijah, beside her, said with a small sigh. 'People do not have to be equal to be perfectly matched. The stronger does not necessarily rule, possess or ruin the weaker. Sometimes the weak, damaged or uncertain can teach the strong, the whole and the educated some very important lessons. Often, the old learn from the young. I suspect these two have much to learn from one another.'

'But neither is old,' Anouk countered, continuing the debate around the circle. 'They are both young. Renatus, you are not old enough for an apprentice. There is too much for you yet to learn. And if you must train someone for your chair, let him be male – there is a very good reason why a sorcerer's apprentice must be the same gender.'

'I know, but that won't be a problem,' Renatus insisted. I didn't ask, but I had an idea as to what that reason might be. 'It would never happen.'

'My answer is still no,' Anouk said, half-shrugging. 'It doesn't seem right.'

'My answer is the same,' Tian said. 'You aren't ready for an apprentice. I See many futures for you, Renatus, but none are clear. Your direction is not yet decided – if you don't know the way, you should not be leading anyone.'

Those sorcerers against me had some very good points, and so far they were winning the debate – five against three. Only Emmanuelle, Jadon and Lord Gawain remained to cast their vote, and, I realised with a jolt, we would need the support of all three to gain the majority.

'You 'ave my support, my loyalty and my trust,' Emmanuelle said firmly. She looked around the circle, her gaze pausing on the faces of those who did not share her view. 'Renatus 'as proven 'imself over and over and never yet let us down. He is now doing exactly what we're all supposed to be doing – passing on knowledge, ensuring that when the time comes, our roles can be filled – and some still *insist* on criticism.' She looked at me; her very bright blue eyes seemed to be burning with intensity. 'Aristea and the other students are 'ere in the 'opes that they will 'ave this opportunity. She 'as been offered it and she 'as taken it. It is what she wants; otherwise she would not be 'ere tonight. This is what is meant to be.'

I tried to smile at her. I wished I could think and speak with as much confidence as she did. *She's right,* I told myself. This is what's meant to be. Yes, Renatus could be scary, but I'd known that from the first time I'd spoken to him, and he hadn't scared me *then* any more than he scared me now. Being scary was his job as the White Elm's warrior, and whatever he was capable of doing to other people was really only further evidence that the best place to be in times of crisis was right beside him.

Renatus nodded ever so slightly to Emmanuelle in acknowledgement and we turned to Jadon.

The youngest councillor took several long moments of silence before he spoke. I had to remind myself to breathe, not to hold my breath.

'I don't know what to say,' Jadon admitted finally, surprising me. Earlier he'd been so passionate and certain. Now when he met Renatus's eyes, I saw that he was more upset than anything else. 'I won't pretend I don't blame you for what's happened to Teresa and Aubrey. Whether you passed the information on or not, you're the one who put them in the situation in the first place. I blame you and I don't want to see you get your way right now.' He turned to me, and I tuned into feelings of worry and powerlessness. 'However, I don't believe in punishing anybody for someone else's mistakes. I didn't have the opportunity to study under a master. It's not done enough anymore and a lot of magical knowledge has been lost already as a result. I think Aristea's stronger and smarter than a lot of us are giving her credit for, and I think she deserves the benefit of the doubt. We don't turn into our teachers – we learn from them and from their mistakes. Aristea,' he said, pausing for a second, 'I support *you* and *your* choice. Good luck.'

I almost couldn't believe what I was hearing. Jadon had voted *yes*, which made five – didn't it? I counted our supporters: Renatus himself, Lady Miranda, Elijah, Emmanuelle and now Jadon. All we needed was Lord Gawain to take our side, too, and then... maybe I could go to bed. I realised now that I was feeling exhausted. The excitement was catching up with me.

When I looked at Lord Gawain with a flicker of smile, I felt the weight of doubt in my stomach. He was not smiling.

'It's unorthodox, to say the least,' he said finally, ignoring me completely and looking only at Renatus. The younger councillor said nothing, and his face didn't change, but his energy did. It surprised me: in my experience Renatus always maintained the upper hand in any interaction, even at the expense of general politeness. Being addressed by the Lord of the White Elm, he was suddenly submissive and attentive. His authoritative aura of power slipped out of focus and he took on the air of a teenager preparing for a lecture he knew he probably deserved. 'You're ignoring traditions of *my* council, the council *I* worked so hard to put you on. Those traditions might not be laws but they are rules I live by and which I thought you at least respected enough to roughly adhere to. You didn't even tell me what you were planning. I am disappointed. After all I have done for you – all I have given, all the questions I haven't asked – I expected better.'

I was too scared to look at Renatus. Lord Gawain had done a complete 180 from the way he'd spoken to me earlier. He'd sounded so supportive, but now, talking to Renatus, it was clear that this was not the whole case. His face showed that he was being completely honest. He was hurt and disappointed. Vaguely, I wondered what Lord Gawain had done for Renatus to think he was owed.

'I understand,' Renatus said, his tone low and almost remorseful. He didn't apologise – I wondered what it would take to make him say it, what he considered worthy of "sorry", since he refused to ever say or hear it – but it was clear in his tone. Lord Gawain didn't seem to expect the words. Presumably he knew Renatus well enough to know the words weren't coming.

'I hope so,' Lord Gawain said finally. 'You aren't a child any longer but you still report to me. I need to know what you're planning. Or at least,' he corrected suddenly, 'I don't want to be surprised again. Your role begs privacy for your work. I can understand that. I am sure that there is plenty that you get up to that I want to know nothing about.' He hesitated. 'I would like to be *warned* of any impending surprises.'

'I should have warned you of my intentions, Master,' Renatus agreed. There it was again, I realised. Master, instead of Lord. I wondered what that was about. 'I was concerned you would try to dissuade me; and then tonight I was forced to act earlier than I had anticipated. Please forgive.'

He still hadn't actually apologised but his request for forgiveness visibly reached Lord Gawain's softer side. His frown relaxed, softening his face, and the disappointment faded from his eyes.

'Of course,' he said, the strength and power he had emanated before gone, hidden. He regarded the young councillor for a very long moment, in which I realised that he had not actually given his vote. I tried to read his emotions, but he kept them close, trying hard to block them back. I vaguely sensed disappointment, still, and affection, and something that could have been pride.

Lord Gawain eventually turned his gaze to me, and broke the long silence: 'Welcome to the White Elm, Aristea.'

'Thank you,' I said automatically, though it was a few seconds before I really understood what he'd said and what it meant. The vote had been won. I was allowed to be Renatus's apprentice. I was going to be on the White Elm one day.

'Thank you,' Renatus repeated.

'The initiation will be held Monday night,' Lord Gawain reminded the circle. 'I want everyone to be present, regardless of your stance on the situation. Renatus, you'll need to gain the consent of Aristea's guardians before then.' He waited for a nod of acknowledgement. 'Aristea, you'll understand when I ask that you not mention a word of tonight's events to the other students. Not even your new role. We won't announce that until it's official. You may go.'

No one else moved but it was clear I was being dismissed. Renatus caught my arm and pressed a piece of paper into my hand. The list; the list that had changed so much already. I turned and left, knowing the council had a lot to discuss and do.

Like find two missing people. Like track down their enemies, who after months of silence had suddenly chosen tonight to reappear. Like decide what to do with the captives they'd gained from tonight's events. Like pass judgement on Renatus's actions regarding the stranger in the shadows.

What a night. I tried to recount the events in my head but they were such a blur. I could hardly believe those hazy recent memories were mine. *I* was the one who had been chosen as Renatus's apprentice – the first of thirty-whatever students to be chosen by any of the councillors. I had scried an attack on the White Elm. I'd been to Italy tonight, watched two arrests, and watched my master almost kill a man...

My master – that would take some getting used to. Dogs have masters. Slaves have masters. I, too, now had a master.

I had barely ascended two steps; I ran up the rest of the flight to the next floor. I wanted to get to my room, where I had friends who didn't want to argue about loyalties and traditions and masters and apprentices.

I reached my dormitory before I knew it and I stepped through into normality. I shared the room with three girls my own age, from all over the world, like the other students here. Hiroko was sitting cross-legged between our beds, surrounded by tangles of green wool and holding a pair of knitting needles. A scarf was taking shape. On the other side of the room, Xanthe was lying on her back in bed reading, and Sterling was sitting beside her feet, flicking through an old magazine she'd brought with her for her flight from America.

'Hey,' Sterling said brightly, while I clipped my key back around my neck. I was exhausted, but I made the effort to smile. I wanted to be normal right now; I wanted to put the craziness of my night at the back of my mind and just listen to Sterling talk about nothing, watch Hiroko knit, ignore Xanthe, and then go to sleep. She glanced at her watch. 'You're back late.'

'Yeah,' I agreed tiredly, checking my own. Nearly eleven, and I was usually back at eight. 'I lost track of time.'

'You don't have to lie to us,' Xanthe assured me. She smiled cheekily. 'Whose room did you come from?'

'What?' I asked, uncomprehending, completely missing the point.

'You come back late, flustered,' Xanthe said. 'Your hair is a mess. Your skirt's backwards and,' she leaned forward to squint at my leg while I hastily corrected my wayward skirt, which had indeed twisted, 'your tights have a ladder in them. You should be more careful with your clothes – were you just in a rush to get them off?' She grinned playfully while I continued to stare at her with my blank expression. My skirt must have twisted while I'd been racing down Teresa's street after Renatus and Qasim, or while I'd been picking my way through the moors outside the estate. And I'd probably

51

caught my stockings in Teresa's garden. I hadn't noticed my deteriorating appearance in the excitement of the night.

'Who were you with?' Sterling asked, standing and looking apprehensive.

'Come on, we're your friends,' Xanthe pressed. 'You can tell us. Who is he? More importantly, was he any good?'

I suddenly clicked. Oh. I felt my face heat up just thinking about the implication. I had never been there and these were not the friends I would want to talk to about it when I did.

'It's not like that…'

'Ooh, she's blushing,' Xanthe teased, and the realisation flushed more blood through my cheeks. The fact that I was blushing so deeply was probably more embarrassing than the conversation topic.

'Look,' I tried again, 'I'm not... I don't *do* that. I've just been in the headmaster's office. Really,' I added quickly, when Xanthe opened her mouth to ask something else.

'Did you talk to Renatus?' Sterling asked hopefully, happily dropping the old conversation, but this one wasn't much better. How uncomfortable normality was tonight. I avoided her eyes, regretful now that I had to pass on the rejection.

'No,' I said initially, forgetting I was talking to other witches. My lie was immediately clear to everyone. 'Alright, aye, I did.'

'What did he say?' Sterling's apprehension was overbearing. I felt her terror, mostly, and within it I sensed a fine strand of hope, of desperation... How could I tell her that the man she idolised wasn't interested in her, and how would I explain on Monday night that I was now his assistant and trainee?

'He said it's not going to happen,' I said, going to my drawers and seeking my pyjamas. I needed to get away from this. I avoided looking at Sterling but it made no difference. I could still feel everything she felt, wave after wave of disbelief, hurt, disappointment, and finally, a deep feeling of betrayal. 'He read my mind,' I added, deciding that I should be as truthful as possible. 'He knew what I was thinking. I didn't have to ask anything. He said, "you can tell Sterling it isn't going to happen". I'm sorry, Sterling.'

She stared at me for a long moment, hurt evident in her eyes.

'You bitch,' she said finally, her voice very soft and wavering. Xanthe's mouth fell open.

'Oh, Aristea, you didn't,' she accused.

'Didn't what?' I asked, so confused. Now what? Sterling's expression hardened and her self-control broke.

'You *bitch*!' she screamed, frightening me. 'I trusted you! I told you everything I was feeling and you just went ahead and did it anyway?'

'Did *what*?' I demanded.

'You *screwed* him!' she shouted. She looked ready to cry. 'You slept with him. You're meant to be my friend.'

'What? No!' My stomach clenched with horror and twisted with disgust. I couldn't believe she'd come to such an insane conclusion. 'Yuck, no. Sterling, I didn't! That's not-'

'Aristea, that's so low,' Xanthe said, shaking her head and getting to her feet. 'I can't believe you.'

'I can't believe *you*,' I said, starting to feel less horrified and more annoyed. I faced Sterling, trying to appeal to her common sense. 'This is just stupid. Think about it. I've never looked at him twice.' She looked slightly doubtful so I continued. 'I wouldn't do anything like this – what you're saying I've done – to you. I still have to live here, remember? I would never mess around with someone you care about and expect you to be okay with it.'

'So...' Sterling looked hesitant. 'You didn't sleep with Renatus?'

'No,' I confirmed, relieved. For good measure, I threw in, 'I never, ever will. The idea of it is...' Repulsive. 'I just wouldn't.'

It didn't matter that the headmaster looked like he belonged on TV. It didn't matter that other girls my age were falling over themselves for his attention. That kind of attention was *not* the kind I wanted from him.

'So where have you been?' Xanthe interjected. I turned to her, intensely aware of how much I did not like her. I'd had a few of these moments, more and more frequently as of late. My youngest roommate suffered regular bouts of being a spiteful and unkind person, and I was losing patience with her affliction. 'If you weren't having sex, what were you doing?'

I wished I was a better liar. I wasn't forthcoming with a simple excuse – "I was reading", "we were talking" – and Sterling watched me struggle to explain the events of the night without giving away any details.

'I can't tell you,' I began apologetically, 'but it's absolutely not what you think, I promise.'

'Whatever, Aristea,' Xanthe snarled, putting an arm around Sterling's shoulders. I stared at her, unable to understand what had brought this on. Sterling said nothing. I could see in her eyes that she didn't know what to think.

I couldn't deal with this anymore. I let myself into the bathroom and slammed the door behind me. What was their problem? Who even jumped to such stupid conclusions based on such insubstantial evidence? Adolescence was crap.

Looking at the White Elm's band of superhuman brothers and sisters, adulthood wasn't much to look forward to, either.

I kicked a towel rack and spun quickly around when I heard the door opening. Bitches. But it was just Hiroko. I felt my anger fade. The first person to have spoken to me when I arrived here, my most trusted friend, my *first* friend in a very long time; Hiroko, surely, had some sense...

'Hiroko, I didn't-'

'I know.' She shut the door behind her and leaned against it. 'Do...' English was not her first language, and sometimes the phrasing she wanted eluded her. 'We can talk?'

I nodded, feeling like I wanted to cry. She knew. She was capable of rational thought and had concluded that Xanthe and Sterling were being insane.

'I'm not allowed to tell anyone, though,' I said, but even as I said it I knew there was a way around it. I was still holding Renatus's list. Had he known I would need it? I gave it to Hiroko.

She accepted the list and I watched her dark eyes scan it carefully. With less suddenness than Qasim had exhibited, Hiroko took my left hand and turned it so that she could see the underside of my wrist. She frowned when she saw that it looked the same as ever.

'Official as of Monday,' I told her, not knowing what she was looking for but inferring that it was the same thing Qasim had been checking for.

'Ah.' She nodded and looked up at me. 'And you are not to speak of it, in case it fails. I see. I knew it must be something like this.'

'Thank you,' I whispered, immeasurably grateful for her, 'for just believing me.'

'Renatus has chosen well,' Hiroko said, squeezing my hand affectionately. 'Did *he* tell you to say nothing?'

'No, Lord Gawain did.'

Hiroko smiled.

'You belong to Renatus now. Orders only count if they come from him.'

chapter three

The circle went on for hours. Blame bounced backwards and forwards as everyone dealt with their personal fears, issues and conclusions. It came to nothing, and Emmanuelle was bored and irritable long before the circle's end. Tian was terrified of Renatus, and his show of power in dispatching the now-prisoner had only deepened this – he wanted something done, but Lord Gawain heard the evidence in brief and near-immediately ruled the apprehension above board. Which it so wasn't. But Emmanuelle wasn't going to argue. She'd had her own problems with Renatus in the past, and she was privately horrified by the damage his spell had inflicted on the man, but given the choice between siding with Renatus or against him, she was going to choose "with" every time. He was brash but his heart was in the right place, and he'd proven himself both trustworthy and *good* in Emmanuelle's eyes. Two months ago she wouldn't have expected such a thing to transpire, but now she counted him as a friend. She wasn't sure what his opinion of her was in return – she didn't think he had any actual friends; it was possible he didn't remember what friendship looked like. He was something of an outcast, but he fought for the right side, albeit with sometimes distasteful methods.

The other side had Lisandro, a liar, a betrayer and a murderer, and following him was Jackson, a sadist and a brute.

I promised Peter I would find you.

The arguing continued all around her. The core issue was Renatus, and the rest of the council's feelings towards him. As usual. Susannah's deep mistrust of Renatus had begun years before, during her friendship with Lisandro, and his impending empowerment as Aristea's master was setting her on edge. Jadon had just watched his two best friends taken out right in front of him and had been forbidden to step in. He was furious with the situation, but mostly with Renatus for his part in creating it and with Lord Gawain for not trusting him to stop it. Emmanuelle, for her part, completely agreed with that particular gripe of Jadon's. She and Jadon were young but both were extremely capable. She was certain that together, they would have been able to take on Jackson and his men, or at least hold them off and get the other three out of there.

All she and Jadon would have needed was to keep Jackson and his men occupied until Renatus had the chance to show up, and she was quite sure she and Jadon had the firepower and defensive skills between them to have fulfilled that task. Renatus would have finished them off.

'And what would have happened to Samuel?' Lord Gawain demanded, losing patience with them both when they refused to back down. 'Don't you think I had reasons for commanding you to stand down? If you two had stepped in, I *promise* that Samuel would have been killed in the cross-fire. It was in every possible future.' A great Seer, Lord Gawain saw things before they happened. Because the future is not entirely set, he saw all possible paths created by different choices. Emmanuelle couldn't imagine what it would be like to make decisions with the weight of that gift sitting upon one's shoulders. The council's High Priest continued, 'We protect civilians. We don't throw them into harm's way. And there were few futures in which you escaped with the rings.'

That quietened Jadon, but Emmanuelle knew he was still stewing on the inside.

Lord Gawain went on to allocate temporary tasks, spreading resources as effectively as he knew how: Seers and scriers searching, Displacer tracking, Telepaths listening. And Emmanuelle doing nothing, as per usual.

'Renatus, Qasim, Susannah and Tian are coming off general crime search and as of right now are searching exclusively for Lisandro,' he pointed at Renatus, 'Jackson,' he turned his authoritative finger to Qasim, 'Aubrey,' he assigned Aubrey to Susannah, 'and Teresa,' he finished with Tian. 'They are your highest priorities right now. Elijah, your every effort to trace Jackson's path will be appreciated. Glen, Anouk, Jadon; please continue your efforts to reach Teresa and Aubrey, however futile they might be. Emmanuelle, you're still the Elm Stone's protector –

it still answers to you. You should stay within the walls of the estate. Jackson may be targeting you.'

Emmanuelle broke circle and went to Lord Gawain to collect her charge. The legendary Elm Stone. The White Elm's ancient source of emergency power. The plain old ring was nothing much to look at, but once it was on her thumb she could feel it thrumming with untapped power; power which was, should she direct it, all hers, until the ring chose someone else. She'd guarded it for less than a month yet it felt like a part of her.

'Jackson can target me all he likes,' she told the Lord. 'Just let him try me.'

A part of her wanted him to try. A little part of her mind, the part that still wondered what might have been if Peter had come back, wanted to know what Jackson meant when he said, 'I promised Peter I'd find you'. He was there when Peter died, she just knew it. He'd watched Lisandro murder Emmanuelle closest friend. And he'd let it happen, if not taken part.

If only Jackson had been the last man standing, the one lagging behind the group, the one Renatus had burnt half to death.

It was an awful and inappropriate thought, and she could tell from Jadon's intense gaze that it was not particularly private, but she didn't care.

'We must all be wary of our words and our thoughts,' Lord Gawain said to the group. 'Only *we* knew that the Elm Stone was to be at Teresa's tonight, yet somehow Jackson knew, too. Teresa's surname and address have been withheld from the public, yet somehow Jackson found the exact house. He knew the time, the place and who would be there. He knew the *Stone* would be there.'

Jadon shot a nasty look at Renatus. This time he said nothing.

'Lucky he's only got a fake,' Glen commented, but Lady Miranda looked to him seriously.

'Teresa's illusion was undoubtedly very good if it fooled him but no spell lasts forever,' she said. 'Before long it'll fade and Jackson will know he's been duped.'

'She estimated a maximum of one hour outside her auric field,' Renatus spoke up. 'It's possible they already know.'

'We have to hope that a situation arises in which Aubrey and Teresa are able to make an escape,' Lord Gawain said. Emmanuelle could hear the chatter inside the collective hive mind of the council and knew that everyone was thinking that if the young councillors weren't able to resist capture, what hope did the pair stand of waking from unconsciousness and escaping those same kidnappers? It seemed unlikely. 'If not... we must ensure nothing like this happens again while we seek them out. Someone may have misspoken. It must *not* happen again.'

The circle finally dispersed and the other councillors went off to begin their tasks or get some rest.

'Emmanuelle.' Renatus stopped her as she went to follow Anouk out. He looked almost anxious, except of course at the same time he didn't. He was cool and mostly expressionless, and very hard to read. Yet something about the way he leaned into her view rather than assuming she was just paying attention, and the way he held eye contact like he was looking for indications that he might be overstepping the boundaries of their new friendship, convinced the Healer that he was nervous about speaking to her. 'I have a favour to ask.'

He'd never been nervous around her before. Then again, he'd never asked her for a favour before, and maybe he didn't know how to gage whether or not he was allowed to. Anouk glanced back, nosy and suspicious, and Emmanuelle ensured her voice was loud enough to carry.

'Anything,' she promised, because that's how a friendship works.

When Emmanuelle arrived in Cairn Gardens, Coleraine, the following morning, she saw that it had been raining overnight. The road was wet and the sky was grey, but it was still early. It could still turn out to be a beautiful day, though Emmanuelle doubted it would.

Number nine was unoccupied, but Emmanuelle was happy to wait. Any time wasted waiting was time spent away from Morrissey House, where Lord Gawain wanted to keep her as a virtual prisoner. Even now, she was sure, he was stressing, convinced she would be swiped away from under his nose. Every few minutes she felt his nervous consciousness brush past hers, "checking in". Suffocating her. He had his reasons, and she knew they were good ones, but she was a person, not a pet. She was part of the White Elm but she did not *belong* to it, not like a coat belongs to a man, or a bouquet belongs to a bride, or a chair belongs to a dining set. Lord Gawain was the master of the council, not of Emmanuelle specifically. He did not own her, or any of the other councillors.

The relationship between a master and his apprentice was different, as both Renatus and Aristea would soon find out. An apprentice belonged to his or her master, like a coat, bouquet or chair.

Renatus had asked Emmanuelle to approach Aristea's guardians and formally request approval for the apprenticeship. He had a few leads to follow and didn't know how long it would take. It would take him god-only-knew-where and require him to speak with Emmanuelle-didn't-want-to-know-who.

While it really should have been him to ask, Emmanuelle could appreciate his situation and also felt that *she* had a better chance of convincing the family than he did. Renatus, for all his good intentions, did not make the best first impression with everybody. She herself had feared and disliked him for five years before realising how childish she was being.

Emmanuelle had slept until morning and visited the dorm of her four girls before breakfast. Xanthe and Sterling had not been present; perhaps they'd gone to breakfast early. Hiroko was to be found sitting on her bed knitting a long green scarf, and Aristea had not yet woken. Understandably, Emmanuelle had been reluctant to wake her. The poor girl was exhausted. She'd had an unexpectedly long and exciting Thursday night.

'Aristea, I'm visiting your sister today,' Emmanuelle had explained clearly after shaking the student gently awake. 'Will she be 'ome?'

'Uh, she goes for a jog first in the morning,' Aristea had answered groggily, blinking, 'but she has Fridays off so she'll probably be home.'

'Is there anything you want me to take? A letter?'

'No, I haven't written anything.' Aristea had struggled to sit up in bed, and looked around the dorm. 'Can you ask her to send me some more of *my* clothes? *My* stuff? She'll understand.'

So fifteen minutes later, Emmanuelle was here, standing in front of Aristea's empty home. It was a small place, modest but tidy. The small garden spaces were neat and well-kept, the path swept, the lawn mowed. Emmanuelle had expected Aristea to have come from a less organised environment.

A lone figure appeared at the bottom of the cul-de-sac and began to make her way up the street. Brushing her senses over the woman unobtrusively, Emmanuelle guessed that this must be Angela Byrne. A witch, strong in magic but probably not aware of how to use it, otherwise she would likely be cloaked in wards. She was dressed in tight sweat clothes, her hair up high, earphones fitting snugly into her ears, evidently returning from a walk or jog. She didn't sense Emmanuelle through her wards, and did not even see her until she'd reached her mailbox. She checked it absent-mindedly, then looked up, noticing the stranger standing on the other side the road watching.

'Good morning,' Emmanuelle called, smiling and walking over.

'Hi,' Angela answered, smiling back but obviously confused. She was probably used to being able to sense other people around her – mortals rarely make an effort to be invisible. In a street this small, she most likely knew all of the neighbours, and Emmanuelle, with her accent, her deep blue medieval dress and unfamiliar face, was clearly not a local out to grab the newspaper.

'I'm Emmanuelle.' She reached Angela and offered a hand, which was shaken politely. 'I'm with the White Elm.'

'Oh, of course,' Angela said, her confusion clearing. 'Hi. Um, I wasn't expecting visitors.' She vaguely indicated her outfit and slightly dishevelled state, mildly embarrassed.

'I apologise for arriving unannounced so early,' Emmanuelle said. 'My visit today was not planned and so there wasn't time to provide more notice.'

'Oh, no, it's fine,' Angela quickly assured her, brushing stray locks of brown-blonde hair from her eyes. Her complexion, though flushed from exercise, was clearly a lot fairer than her sister's, and her eyes and hair were different colours, but otherwise Angela Byrne looked very much the same as Aristea Byrne. Her aura showed a more refined personality, possibly the result of the years she had on her little sister. Angela looked to be about the same age as Emmanuelle, mid-twenties, but she hadn't bothered to do any research on Angela before coming so she didn't know for sure.

'I'm wondering whether you 'ave a few minutes this morning to discuss your sister,' said Emmanuelle.

'Is she alright?' Angela asked, concern clouding her face. 'I wrote to her last week and she wrote back saying she was alright – she said everything was okay – she said she wants to stay.'

'She's fine,' Emmanuelle promised. 'She's doing very well. That's what I've come to talk to you about.'

Angela nodded, clearly mystified but too polite to say that. She extracted a set of keys from her pocket.

'Would you like to come in? It's warmer in, and I'll put some tea on,' Angela suggested, going to the door already. Emmanuelle followed, smiling.

'Yes, please,' she said, entering behind the other witch. At Angela's offer, she took a seat at the six-seater table while the resident of the home set about making tea. She'd been sitting at a different table, adjoining a different kitchen, only the night before, and that had not ended well. She rubbed the ring that had started this mess, wondering whether it had been the best idea to bring it here. The alternative had been to leave it with someone else on the council – one of whom, it seemed, was feeding information to Lisandro. Not an option. To redirect her thoughts, she said to Angela, 'Your sister is a wonderful student. She's one of the best in my class.'

'What do you teach?' Angela asked, raising her voice over the rising noise of the kettle.

'I instruct the students on casting wards, though Aristea doesn't need much instruction. It seems to come naturally. She's already quite adept. By the time she joins me on the council she could be better than I am.'

Angela laughed.

'She just *did it* one day,' she admitted. 'She'd never done it before, and then, all of a sudden, she's casting shields all over the place. Of course, she could be good at anything, provided she's interested and thinks she'll be successful. She's like that.'

Emmanuelle thought about her student, one of the best in her subject. Angela Byrne's description seemed to fit the opinion Emmanuelle had formed of the girl. Bright, gifted, but aimless. Hard-working... when it suited her. A swift learner... of things that either caught her interest or which she considered herself good at. Emmanuelle continued with the small talk, both women having made a silent decision to leave the meaty part of the conversation until they were sitting together drinking their tea.

'One of my tasks at the Academy is to supervise one dorm group of students,' Emmanuelle explained, loud enough for Angela to hear over the bubbling water. 'Aristea is in my group. She and the other three girls 'ave been my personal responsibility.'

'So you're getting to know her, then?' Angela asked, in part polite, in part amused.

'She's a very sweet girl – very perceptive,' Emmanuelle commented. 'She's Empathic, or so Qasim and Renatus believe. She's made a lot of friends.'

'Good,' Angela said, relieved. She checked with Emmanuelle how she liked her tea and poured the drinks. 'She hasn't had proper friends since... well, I suppose since we moved here, when our parents and brother died.' She shrugged, bringing the cups over. 'She didn't go to school and she worked in a very obscure little shop so there wasn't really anywhere for her to meet people.' She set down the drinks, smiling in response to Emmanuelle's "thank you". She had an eager-to-please air that reminded the Healer of the younger Byrne. For a moment they sipped their tea in silence. 'So. There was something you wanted to talk to me about?'

'Yes,' Emmanuelle agreed, all business. 'Aristea 'as been offered a place as an apprentice to one of my colleagues, and she 'as agreed.'

'Oh.' Angela sat back in her seat, honestly taken aback. Her aura swirled with colour as she emotionally reacted to the news. It was not something she'd expected to hear.

'The White Elm council 'as voted and approved the partnership, which will guarantee Aristea a position on the White Elm later in life,' Emmanuelle carried on. 'The training will be ongoing, continuing from 'er initiation as an apprentice until 'er initiation onto the council. The bond forged between Aristea and 'er master will be lifelong and unbreakable except by death. By joining 'er magic with a stronger sorcerer, Aristea's potential for magic will increase, and 'er abilities will flourish. 'owever, as 'er guardian, your permission and blessing is required before we can go ahead with the ceremony.'

Angela stared at Emmanuelle for a long moment, digesting the information.

'Who is it?' she asked finally. 'Who wants to train her, or whatever?'

''is name is Renatus,' Emmanuelle said, watching for Angela's response. She wasn't sure whether Angela had heard of him before; if she had, she probably hadn't heard anything good. Nobody had.

'Didn't Qasim want her as an apprentice?' Angela asked, clearly confused. 'Aristea wants to scry, more than anything. She really admires Qasim – isn't he the best?'

Emmanuelle had not gotten the impression that Aristea held Qasim in such high esteem. Aristea had ended up in detention before anyone else because of her disagreements with the White Elm's Scrier on the day of Peter's funeral, although that was Renatus's story and Emmanuelle knew better than to take his words on face value. She didn't necessarily think he was lying – he couldn't punish Aristea for nothing, after all, and expect her not to say something – but she expected that what she had been told was only a part truth. She was just as sure that there was a good reason for it, so she'd not pursued it. She valued her new friendship with Renatus too much to question his judgement.

'Renatus is a scrier, too,' said Emmanuelle. ''e can teach Aristea everything Qasim would, and because Aristea is still a student at the Academy she will have the benefit of learning extra skills from all of us. 'e's very powerful – more so than you or I, or even Qasim. Whether or not 'e is better than Qasim at scrying, I would not know. What I do know is that Aristea and Renatus seem to get along very well, and that in itself says something because he is... unusual. Much like your sister, I suppose.'

'Aristea's a scrier, too, isn't she?' Angela checked.

'She is. In fact, she is the only scrier at the Academy. She is a very gifted and unusual girl. She and Renatus 'ave...' Emmanuelle thought for the right English word, and settled on, '"clicked".' She shrugged helplessly, because it still escaped even her how it had happened that anyone in the whole world had "clicked" with Renatus, let alone a mild-manned seventeen-year-old witch.

'Clicked?' Angela repeated, a suspicious lilt to her voice that Emmanuelle couldn't place.

'They are both determined,' Emmanuelle said. She paused. 'Is your sister... *stubborn*... in your experience?'

Angela laughed quickly, an answer in itself. How fitting, Emmanuelle thought wryly. Renatus, it seemed, was in for a rude look in the mirror in the coming years.

'I'm sure 'e would not have selected 'er if 'e was not certain she could manage the work,' Emmanuelle commented instead.

Angela thought on this for a long moment.

'Isn't he really young? I thought he only joined the council a few years ago?' she asked finally.

'He did, about two years ago,' Emmanuelle confirmed, 'but he's been connected to the council a very long time, since before I was initiated. He's very capable. He is very close with Lord Gawain.'

That was probably Renatus's saving grace.

'Why didn't he come himself?'

'We 'ave a lead on Lisandro, and Lord Gawain 'as put Renatus in charge of locating 'im,' Emmanuelle answered, because she wasn't allowed to go into details regarding the kidnapping of Teresa and Aubrey. ''e is very busy, and I was given a much less active responsibility, so I came instead. It is better this way – Renatus 'as the terrible habit of saying the wrong thing at exactly the wrong time, and for a good person I'm afraid 'e makes a poor first impression.'

Angela laughed again, only one breath of laughter, but it broke the tension.

'He does sound like he might have something in common with my sister,' she said. She sipped her tea. 'I can't believe Aristea is going to join the White Elm one day. We joked about it before she left. I wasn't sure how likely it was.' She set the cup down but kept her hands wrapped around it for warmth. 'Is it what she wants, do you know?'

'She said it was,' Emmanuelle said, thinking of the circle the night before. 'She said she understands what it means.'

Angela nodded, looking away. Fine locks of her hair had made an escape from her ponytail. Her skin was clearer now, the flush of exercise gone. She had the air of someone very normal, very rational. No passer-by would expect that she was a witch by blood, or that her potential for power likely equalled

Emmanuelle's. Had her name come up for consideration for the White Elm when Emmanuelle's did? Might their places have been traded if Fate had twisted just that little bit?

'You said something about a ceremony?' Angela said finally.

'It's to be 'eld on Monday night to coincide with the full moon,' Emmanuelle explained. 'We call on Magic itself to officiate the partnership, and if it is fated to be, it will be. I know it sounds insane,' she added, smiling when Angela only nodded slowly. Angela gave a half-smile of acknowledgement. It *did* sound insane but it put her at ease to have this fact confirmed. 'I 'aven't before seen a master and apprentice joined by Magic but Lord Gawain called on the same powers to initiate me onto the White Elm, and I 'ave now been present for four further initiations, besides my own. It's beautiful.'

'What's involved?'

'Once we 'ave called on Magic as the ultimate overseer, each party is to identify themselves and select one witness, who is to oversee the ceremony and will 'ave the responsibility of ensuring that both parties uphold the partnership.' Emmanuelle sipped her tea; it was cooling, but she liked it hot. She rested her hand on the side of the cup, channelling energy into the liquid inside. When she took her next sip it almost burnt her lips – almost, but not quite. Perfect. 'Only White Elm can be present at the ceremony itself, so I expect Renatus will call Lord Gawain as 'is witness, and I anticipate that Aristea will choose me. The witness for the apprentice passes on the permission and blessing of the guardian – you – so in a way I will be representing you and anything you want said.'

Angela swirled her tea.

'Do I have to write a speech for you?'

'No,' Emmanuelle said. 'If there's something you want for me to say, you can tell me and I will remember. We only require from you verbal consent for Renatus to train Aristea. Anything else is optional.'

'Do you trust Renatus?' Angela asked suddenly, a desperate tone to her voice. Emmanuelle blinked, wondering how many times in recent weeks she'd discussed or heard this question discussed. 'Would you trust your baby sister's life in his hands? You said this is a lifelong commitment. Masters and their apprentices can hear one another's thoughts – I read about one pair who learnt to *see* through one another's eyes. They became like one another; their personalities blur. They could rifle through the other's memories, thoughts, feelings... What business does this man have sifting through Aristea's memories? Would you let a man you didn't know become that close with your sister or daughter?' She looked down, colouring slightly as she thought of something else. 'And what if he's after a partnership of a different kind? I'm not insinuating that's the case,' she hastily assured. 'I don't know him – I can only take your words and form a picture from that. How do I know she won't be taken advantage of?'

'It would never happen,' Emmanuelle echoed Renatus's words from the night before. 'Renatus 'as not only to answer to Lord Gawain, the rest of the White Elm, to me and to you if 'e oversteps 'is role, but also to Magic itself. To enter into such a relationship is forbidden – the equivalent to incest in magical terms – and any power 'e gained upon 'is initiation and from 'is connection to Aristea will be stripped away. 'e would lose 'is seat on the council and lose favour with Lord Gawain. He would never risk it.' She said this sentence with emphasis and firmness. Whether she trusted him or not, Renatus was purposeful and driven. He'd never allow a distraction like a pretty young girl to put his plans, whatever they were, in jeopardy. 'I know you can't be as certain as I am because you 'ave never met 'im, but *I* know 'im, and you know Aristea. You must know she's smarter than that. She would never allow 'erself to be taken for a fool. He's not interested. She's not interested.'

Angela nodded, reluctant. Emmanuelle leaned forward.

'Yes, I trust 'im,' she said, because she hadn't answered the last question. 'I would trust 'im with my life because I must. My life is in the 'ands of every person on that council, every day.' *Aubrey and Teresa's lives are, too, and someone gave them up*, she thought, but didn't say. 'Renatus 'as never let me down, even when 'e should 'ave. If I 'ad a sister, or even a daughter, yes, I would trust 'im with their lives, too.'

To buy time, Angela pulled her ponytail free and massaged her scalp. She stared at the table top.

'Aristea is not my daughter,' Angela said finally, 'and if our mother was alive I think she'd say no. She would say Aristea's too young to make this kind of commitment. She's only seventeen, and a young seventeen at that, isn't she? Our mum would have said no. And I would have agreed with her.' She looked conflicted. 'But that's not my decision to make. I'm not our mother. I want whatever Aristea wants – a place on the White Elm? To work with or for someone I've never met for the rest of her life? I don't know exactly, but it's her path and as long as it's safe and she's not alone, I think I'm happy for her to make her own choices. I *think*.' She smiled at Emmanuelle, a more open expression than any preceding it. 'This is an opportunity I never thought she'd get. Our mother would have refused, out of fear for her; I will not be an obstacle to her future.' She brushed her hair back from her face. 'Do I need to sign anything?'

'Your words are fine,' Emmanuelle said, 'if you are sure.'

'I am,' Angela agreed, a determination in her voice that reminded Emmanuelle strongly of the younger Byrne sister. 'I give permission for Renatus to train Aristea as his apprentice. Is that right?'

'That's perfect.'

'And...' Angela hesitated. 'And, tell Aristea... Make your own fate.'

Emmanuelle nodded, committing the words to memory. She wondered what effect the words would have on the ceremony, which relied so heavily on the notion that Fate itself had brought Renatus and

Aristea together with the intent that they would become a great team.

Vaguely, she felt the faint energetic tickle in her mind as Lord Gawain ran his watchful, disapproving mind's eye over her. Less vague was her responding feeling of annoyance. *Go away*, she almost thought, but dared not, knowing he would hear and she would be in more trouble. But really, what could he do? Pull her up in front of the circle and chastise her like a little girl, like he had Renatus? Well, maybe Renatus would put up with that sort of treatment, but she wasn't going to. Emmanuelle was a grown-up with a bonus Renatus didn't have – she didn't owe the High Priest anything. Lord Gawain had *not* picked her out of an extinct family and raised her into adulthood before organising a place on the council for her. Emmanuelle's ascension onto the council had been less controversial. The previous priestess, Lady Jennifer, had passed away unexpect-edly the same month that the then-Wandcrafter, Boris, had passed peacefully after a long illness. Peter had been brought on to replace Boris; Emmanuelle, a Healer, had been chosen to replace Miranda, who had of course ascended to Lady.

'I'll tell 'er,' Emmanuelle said, forcing her atten-tion back to Angela. 'I spoke to 'er this morning. She said to ask you to please send her some more of *her* clothes. She said you'd understand.'

'She's awake already?' Angela asked, surprised, looking about for a clock.

'Not by choice.'

'I know the clothes she's talking about. Would you be able to take them to her?'

'Absolutely.' Emmanuelle drank some more tea. Angela excused herself and hurried into one of the bedrooms for a few minutes. She returned presently with a plastic bag filled with clothing and shoes. Emmanuelle noticed purple tartans, black lace, dark denim and what had to be a cropped leather jacket – very different from what Aristea had been wearing at the Academy before now.

'She dresses a little... unconventionally... left to her own imagination,' Angela admitted, handing over the bag. 'I did try to send her with an appropriate wardrobe. I apologise for the mess she's going to look from now on.'

Angela sat down again to finish her tea. She seemed much more at ease now that she'd gotten used to the French councillor. Emmanuelle took another mouthful of her own tea, concentrating for a moment on Angela's aura. It was a second or two before the swirls of colour were apparent to her eyes. Calm, mature blues and greens intermingled with compassionate pinks and creative peach. A second of further observation, and Emmanuelle's attention was drawn to several strange features – dark spots, around which the colours flowed, as though the dark patches were holes the energy was avoiding.

Emmanuelle wondered what it meant to have those holes in the aura. She'd seen it before, in only three people. Aristea was one, Renatus another, and Lisandro the third. Before meeting Aristea she might have suspected that it was a sign of evil, but now she knew that Renatus was not that, and the Byrne sisters were even further from. Perhaps it was the mark of someone with a significant contribution to make to the future, good or bad? Emmanuelle suppressed a shiver. Lady Miranda might know, she thought, or perhaps Glen.

Something beeped in Angela's kitchen. She finished her tea in one last mouthful and took the two empty mugs to the kitchen, looking about for the source of the noise. She found a silver phone on a counter and opened the cover to check the screen. She read something on it quickly, presumably a text message, and sighed.

'My cousin wants to come and stay for the weekend to keep me company,' she explained. She snapped the phone shut without replying. 'I made the mistake of telling my aunt that I was lonely without Aris here making a mess. Now I have to entertain.' She fiddled with a charm dangling from her mobile phone, and an idea seemed to come to her. 'Hey, do you have a cell? Or does anyone else on the White Elm? Is there a number I could call or text to check in with Aristea? Writing is such a slow means of contact.'

'I 'ave one,' Emmanuelle said, 'but I don't often 'ave it with me. I can't take it to Morrissey House – it would short out, with all the energy around the estate. I leave it at my apartment, mostly, and check it daily.'

'That's still quicker than the post.'

Emmanuelle recited her rarely-used phone number to Angela, who typed it straight into her mobile. When Renatus had helped her to clean her apartment after Jackson's break-in a few weeks ago, he'd found her new-model touch phone under a magazine and asked what she had it for. She'd been surprised that he even knew what it was – Renatus had never used a phone in his life – but she supposed he would have seen mortals using them when he scried. She'd explained that not all the witches she knew could communicate telepathically, and besides, when she met new people and they asked for her number, they would look at her strangely if she were to say she didn't have one.

'Thanks,' Angela said, closing her phone again. 'I'd give you mine but I suppose there's no point.'

'We have other means,' Emmanuelle agreed, standing. She felt the faint tingle of Lord Gawain's attention once again. 'I should be going. Lord Gawain expects me back at Morrissey House. Thank you for the tea.'

'Oh, that's fine,' Angela said, waving aside the thanks. 'Thank *you* for coming today. And please thank Renatus for me for choosing Aristea. It'll take me a while to get used to the idea, but it really means something to our family that someone would give Aris this opportunity – well, it means something to me.'

Emmanuelle smiled.

'I'll pass it on,' she promised. Angela led her to the front door.

'Did you all sort out those parents? The ones from the internet?' Angela asked, hand paused on the doorknob. Emmanuelle sighed and stopped beside her. A week or so ago a disgruntled parent was approached by Lisandro and had decided to withdraw her son. It would have been fine – well, not fine, but manageable – had the mother gone no further, but instead she'd spammed almost the entire community of Academy parents with Lisandro's message of necessary revolution, sending the families into a panic.

'A few students 'ave been withdrawn over it, but we think we've identified the families most likely to react and spoken to them before they could be contacted by this group,' she said. 'It's a hoax, orchestrated by Lisandro. I didn't realise they'd contacted you, too.'

'I don't know how they found me,' Angela admitted. 'I thought it sounded like trash but it still scared me, knowing how easily I could be tracked down and how passionate the other side was getting people. I nearly came straight to Morrissey House to get Aristea but…' She shrugged. 'It was hard not to. I don't like making decisions for her. That's not a sister's job. I wrote a letter instead.'

'If you had done any differently, I wouldn't be 'ere now telling you that Aristea was going be Renatus's apprentice,' Emmanuelle countered with an encouraging smile, 'so it seems to me that you did the right thing by 'er by waiting.'

'Aye, I'm glad now,' Angela agreed. She opened the door.

'So am I.'

'I suppose I'll see you next time,' she said as Emmanuelle stepped outside. The councillor turned back with another smile.

'Next time,' she agreed. With a wave, she left the house and walked down the street. Someone was pulling out of their driveway at number two so she couldn't Displace yet. Dressed like a witch from Arthurian legends and carrying a plastic bag full of clothing, walking down a quiet Irish street at breakfast time, she looked strange enough already without disappearing into thin air. She wondered briefly what the people in this street thought of the pedestrian visitors to number nine. What did her own neighbours in Paris think of her when they saw her leaving or entering her apartment?

Emmanuelle felt Anouk in her mind only an instant before she heard her colleague's voice.

I think you should come quickly.

Frowning, Emmanuelle reached lightly for each of the other councillors, worried, in the same way that Lord Gawain had been checking in on her. Lord Gawain, safe at home... Lady Miranda, safe at the hospital... Renatus, as safe as he ever was... Qasim, safe at the Academy... Glen, safe at the Academy... Susannah, safe at home... Elijah, safe... Anouk, safely at the Academy... Tian, safe... Aubrey, unreachable, nothing but blackness and the awareness of life...Teresa, the same... Jadon, safe... There was no emergency with any of them.

It's the students, Anouk said, tersely. *Your students.*

Emmanuelle's thoughts touched on each of the girls in her dormitory, ending on Aristea. Now what?

Which one? What's happening?

All four of them, Anouk answered, *screaming at one another in the dining hall. Will you hurry, before my two get involved?*

The driver from number two left the cul-de-sac, glancing at her in the rear-vision mirror. Emmanuelle expanded her net of awareness, checking that nobody around was paying her any heed. Angela Byrne seemed to be the only one in the entire street who even knew she was there. Certain of her discretion, Emmanuelle opened a wormhole and stepped through to a completely new physical space. To her left now was a high stone wall, and thirty paces away was the front gate of Morrissey House. Aristea, Hiroko, Sterling and Xanthe were friends. What was going on? Why would they be screaming at each other?

Emmanuelle had the gates open in an instant and was through; she locked them behind herself quickly and ran. If it wasn't one thing, it was another. Secret magical artefacts, mysterious lists, tragedies, break-ins, suspicion, kidnappings, ceremonies, lesson after lesson, task after task... It was lucky that Emmanuelle had no other life to be getting on with.

chapter four

I was sleeping very deeply when I was gently awoken by Emmanuelle. She told me she was going to visit my sister (Emmanuelle, visiting Angela? Strange – I was sure they'd never met. Were they friends?) and I think I said something about Angela jogging in the mornings. I gained enough awareness to ask Emmanuelle to bring me back some of my clothes. I'd been wearing crisp, pressed attire akin to my sister's sense of style since arriving here and had recently decided it wasn't working for me.

'Alright. Sorry for waking you.'

Emmanuelle left. I fell back on my pillow, rubbing sleep from my eyes. I felt like I hadn't slept at all, except for the grogginess and the fact that my eyes were somewhat glued shut. I must have slept, though, because yesterday felt one hundred years ago. For a long moment I struggled to remember the details. A circle – White Elm – Emmanuelle calling me over – an unfamiliar street, a cute cottage – Renatus, his list, Qasim's frustration, going to Italy, Teresa and Aubrey missing, a man on fire, Emmanuelle healing, back with Lord Gawain, the circle, the words spoken by each of the White Elm...

They had voted and I had passed. I was Renatus's apprentice, or would be soon.

I stumbled out of bed eventually. Hiroko, feeling sorry for me, unlocked the bathroom door for me. I remembered to thank her before going to my usual shower stall and locking myself in.

A hot shower does a lot to bring me to consciousness. After a blast of hot water to the skin (and several minutes of standing very still, enjoying the warmth) I felt ready for another day.

When I was dressed I went to the mirror to do something with my hair.

'They went to breakfast early,' Hiroko said, entering the bathroom and sliding a bobby pin into her hair to keep her ever-growing fringe out of her eyes. I assumed she was talking about Sterling and Xanthe and wondered why I was meant to care.

'I'm so tired,' I complained, although after my shower I was feeling considerably more refreshed.

'Classes might not even be on today,' Hiroko commented. She checked her reflection in the full mirror opposite the basins. Her asymmetric bob of shiny, straight black hair always looked so trendy and glossy with what seemed like no effort whatsoever. Meanwhile my longish, supposedly-straight-yet-more-often-than-not-wavy, dark brown hair always resisted my efforts to glam it up... not that I really bothered all that frequently. I was a low-maintenance kind of girl. 'Two of our teachers are gone, you said. I expect the White Elm has some work to do today.'

She was right. Lord Gawain would probably announce a classless or shortened day over breakfast and I would be able to come back up here and go back to sleep if I wanted. I followed her from our dorm to the dining hall, realising that I was lying to myself if I thought I'd get a chance to go back to bed. At breakfast I would sit with the twins and Addison, who would want to discuss the news and share their conspiracy theories, and then Hiroko and I would spend the day with them. I wouldn't be able to share what I knew, but other than that, things would be as normal. Nothing had to change just because I was Renatus's apprentice now. Sterling and Xanthe would get over their little misunderstanding with me once I'd undergone the ceremony to become an official apprentice. Sterling would probably even be happy then – I would be an even better source of information on Renatus when I started working with him.

It seemed that most people had already gone to breakfast because we didn't see anyone until we stepped into the dining hall. Most people were seated; the emotional level in the room was some-what normal (as normal as emotions come, anyway) so I gathered that Lord Gawain had not yet dropped the bombshell that Aubrey and Teresa had been kidnapped by Jackson. I glanced over at the White Elm's table and saw that Lord Gawain was not present, and neither was Lady Miranda or Renatus. The only councillors here this morning were Qasim, Glen and Anouk. The table looked sort of lonely with ten empty seats. I wondered whether the others would appear later or if someone else would be speaking on Lord Gawain's behalf.

I felt eyes on my face and turned my attention back towards the student table we were approaching. A couple of the boys had been watching me, but when I looked at them they dropped their gazes, grinning. I wasn't really that disconcerted – boys are a strange species, after all – until I met the triplet glares of Khalida, Bella and Suki. Every school has its little clique of catty queens, and these three were the Academy's. Until now, I'd had no run-ins with them. My stomach clenched a little as I followed Hiroko to our usual place at the table. What was their problem? Bella shook her head disgustedly while Suki stood abruptly and walked the length of the table to the opposite end, where her brother Isao sat with his friends.

Kendra and Sophia Prescott were sitting opposite Sterling and Xanthe, deep in conversation that looked too intense for breakfast time. Approaching from behind Sterling, I smiled at Sophia when she looked up. She blinked once, as though surprised to see me, and then offered a hesitant, fleeting smile. Her eyes flickered to her sister as though for confirmation. My heart sank – what was this?

'It's just sick,' I heard Xanthe say. 'Even if he came onto *her*, like she made it sound, she should still have had the self-respect to say no.'

'Are you sure that's what happened?' Kendra asked, doubt in her voice, as I stopped suddenly behind Sterling. Only Sophia had noticed me, and she was silent, staring now at her orange juice.

'Aristea said she went to the office and he read her thoughts and knew what she wanted from him before she even had to ask,' Sterling said, bitterly. 'She just came out and said it.'

The cold fear in my stomach began to feel heavy. That was *not* what I'd said. Hiroko waited beside me, concern emanating from her like cold air falls from an open freezer.

'No respect or thought whatsoever for the feelings of her friend,' Xanthe said angrily. 'I mean, if she can bring herself to do it to Sterling, what's to stop her from doing the same to you, with Addison?'

Kendra blanched, taken aback. Sophia looked up at me suddenly, and I knew with dread that she was wondering whether I *would* do such a thing as to steal her twin's new boyfriend. The other three followed Sophia's gaze to my face.

'Oh, you're awake,' Sterling said, standing to face me. Her tone was cold and bitter as she continued, 'I suppose you needed a sleep in after your big night with Renatus.'

'Sterling, I told you,' I said, struggling to keep my voice stable and clear. My stomach was twisted with fear of confrontation and I could hear the blood pumping in my ears, dulling other sounds. 'It didn't happen.'

'Right,' Xanthe agreed with sarcasm. She rose from her chair. 'But you can't tell us what *actually* happened.'

'Yes, that's-'

'No!' Sterling interrupted, her voice rising and becoming wobbly. 'It's because you're a *liar* and a *bitch* and you were having sex when you were supposed to be helping *me*. You're meant to be my friend!' She stamped her foot to vent some anger. A few nearby conversations ceased at the magic word. 'You knew I loved him and you didn't even care – you just took what was offered.'

'That's not what happened,' I insisted.

'It is!'

'It's not. You don't understand.'

'You're such a liar!' Sterling shouted, causing all remaining conversations in the dining hall to die out. The three White Elm councillors were standing at their seats, looking very grave, but they did not step in.

'I'm *not* a liar; I *am* your friend-'

'Not anymore,' Sterling said loudly, shaking her head and breathing slowly and deeply as though to hold back tears. 'Not anymore. You don't give a *shit* about me. All you care about is yourself.'

'Sterling, this isn't true,' Hiroko said, her voice soothing and placating. Her smile seemed to calm Sterling slightly. 'I think we have all misunderstood.'

'Shut up, Hiroko,' Xanthe snapped, impatient. 'Nobody cares what you think.'

'Hey!' I said defensively, feeling Hiroko's stab of hurt as though it were my own. 'Leave her out of it.'

'You've probably been screwing around with the headmaster for weeks, and Hiroko could have known all along and not bothered to tell us,' Xanthe said, looking down on Hiroko with disgust. 'I don't know, maybe you even encouraged the relationship.'

Tears began to well in Sterling's bright brown eyes.

'There is no relationship!' I shouted, frustrated. 'Nothing happened! There was nothing for Hiroko to know and there's nothing to tell. I told you that yesterday.'

'Why should I believe that?' Sterling demanded, verging on a breakdown.

'Because it's true.' I shook my head; this could *not* be my life. I dropped my voice back to normal conversational level. The whole room didn't need to hear this. 'Sterling, if I had wanted Renatus for myself, wouldn't I have said something from day one? Would I have teased you all these weeks if I felt the same way?'

'Maybe,' Sterling said. 'If you were too embarrassed to say so.'

'I'm embarrassed *now*,' I admitted, gesturing to our less-than-subtle audience, 'because this whole thing is *stupid*. We're arguing like wee little kids and it's stupid. I wouldn't and I didn't... you know... do *that*, to you.' It was too gross to verbalise out here in front of everyone else, all these semi-strangers and *boys*. 'I'm not lying, okay?'

Uncertain, Sterling sniffed.

'Aristea, you're such a manipulative little slut,' Xanthe snarled, stepping forward slightly to be in front of Sterling, just that little bit too close to me – a challenge. Her words cut me, but I didn't back down. I felt a sudden welling of anger beside me.

'You are just an instigator, Xanthe!' Hiroko shouted. I think everyone jumped slightly then. Nobody had ever heard Hiroko shout before, or quite believed her capable of it. 'You knows it is false but you try to make this fight between Sterling and Aristea-'

'Shut it, Hiroko!'

'Don't you dare talk to her like that!' I shouted into Xanthe's face, furious.

'-and it has nothing to do with you!' Hiroko was still shouting over us. Her usually careful English was slippery in her rage. 'You will make a problem where there is not. Aristea is done nothing wrong. *You* are the one who is manipulative-'

'Hiroko, shut the hell up!' Xanthe screamed, lunging forward with her hands outstretched as though to shove my friend back. Without thinking, I raised my hand quickly between them, and Xanthe hit something shimmery and solid. She rebounded from my ward into the back of her chair, which made a clattering noise as it skidded across the floor and hit the table. She clutched at the chair, trying to regain her balance. Sterling stepped back a bit, her nerves already too rattled by the argument to deal with this. Kendra and Sophia were watching on in absolute silence, wearing identical wide-eyed expressions.

'You attacked me,' Xanthe whispered, then said again, louder. 'You attacked me.'

'I don't think anyone is going to listen to that one,' I said coldly, dropping my hand and letting my little ward dissolve. 'I'm pretty sure everyone just saw what really happened, so you might have a bit of trouble spreading your version of the story.'

The whole hall was deathly silent. Xanthe straightened, her narrow eyes like daggers.

'That will depend on the telling,' she said finally, her voice constrained. 'I think you should probably find somewhere else to sit for breakfast.'

'Not that we care what you think, but we were just about to,' I said, taking Hiroko's hand. I looked past Xanthe to where Kendra and Sophia sat on the other side of the table. 'Are you coming?'

Startled, the twins sat back in their seats, apparently surprised that they were expected to have any part of this. They looked at one another, as though expecting the other to be the one to make the decision. The weight of the tension in my gut seemed to double when I felt their hesitation and saw the uncertainty in their crystal green eyes. Sterling and Xanthe, I could live without. I was mad with them, which made walking away easy. Kendra and Sophia I adored, and the realisation that I had lost their trust hurt almost physically. I turned away quickly, Hiroko in my wake, so when they looked back to me with nods or smiles, I didn't see.

Hiroko and I had barely taken six steps towards the doorway when Emmanuelle appeared in it, a plastic shopping bag in hand.

'What's going on?' she demanded, striding into the dining hall. She glanced up at the three White Elm councillors standing at their table; following her gaze, I saw Anouk nod in my direction.

'Nothing,' Hiroko told Emmanuelle. 'It is finished.'

'What's finished?' Emmanuelle asked, looking between the four of us suspiciously. Somehow, I could tell, she already knew something of what had just gone down. Lying to her was useless.

'Just a misunderstanding,' I said, trying to sound normal. My body was slowly returning to its usual functioning – the adrenaline receded and the tension released as the threat of conflict moved further and further into the past. The rushing sound in my ears was gone, but my stomach still felt full of lead.

'Something like that,' Xanthe agreed when Emmanuelle turned to her. Sterling started to cry. Emmanuelle moved past me to go to Sterling, and I felt Hiroko tug gently on my hand. Without so much as a glance back, we left the hall. Silence and apprehension followed us, and I knew that the only reason excited conversation hadn't already broken out was because Sterling was still in the room, falling to pieces.

Hiroko and I went straight to the library and found a cosy pair of armchairs at the back. She was still seething with anger; mine had gone cold and very still. After the heated argument I felt numb and shaky. I collapsed into my chair and wished I could melt into the upholstery. Hiroko initially sat, too, but within seconds had to get back to her feet and took to pacing, restless. I let her. I just sat there and picked at lint on the arm of my chair, reflecting with glaring clarity on the confrontation, and reflecting more dully on how completely I'd managed to screw up my life here in only a single day.

'I hate Xanthe,' Hiroko said eventually after several minutes of silence, startling me with the suddenness and the brutal honesty. She threw herself into her chair again, much less gracefully than I'd ever seen from her. 'I never hated a person before, but she is very mean.'

'She is,' I agreed, thinking. Things would be rather harder to patch up with Sterling and Xanthe now. I still couldn't believe they'd come to the conclusion they had, and I was even more dumbfounded by the fact that they'd gone ahead and told other people as though it were established truth. I recalled the sniggers of the boys and the disgusted looks of Renatus's admirers and felt slightly ill. How many people had Xanthe and Sterling spread their rumour to before they'd sat down with Kendra and Sophia?

No – this was not Sterling's fault, I realised with some difficulty. Hiroko was right. Xanthe had instigated this whole thing right from the start. It had been she who had put the insane idea of me sleeping with Renatus into Sterling's impressionable head last night, and she'd pushed the issue the whole way. Now, because of her, I'd lost at least three good friendships. Bitch.

'I think I might hate her, too,' I said, pulling my legs up onto the seat so I could curl up. We sat in companionable silence for a few further minutes, mulling things over. Hiroko's anger slowly evaporated.

'Thank you for standing up for me,' she said softly after a while. 'You defended me when Xanthe spoke cruelly. You protected me with your ward.' She smiled. 'Your wards are very good and you are a very good friend.'

I sat up, touched by her words. What most people would leave unsaid she verbalised with honesty and conviction, and I owed her the same in return.

'You are the better friend,' I said, brushing one of my plaits back into place when it swung into my face. 'You stood with me when you didn't have to. You didn't have to step in.' I paused, embarrassed. 'You probably would have been better off if you'd walked away.'

'Why?' Hiroko asked, slightly challengingly. 'So people will think I am a bad friend?'

'No,' I said, surprised by her argumentativeness. This was not the Hiroko I was used to. 'To spare you taking the brunt of Xanthe's problems with me. You didn't need to put yourself out there for me like that.'

'Yes, I did. If Xanthe said these lies about me, you would tell the truth.'

'Well, yeah,' I agreed, 'but no one would believe them about you. You're so nice. Normally.'

We shared a quick smile, our shared sense of humour surfacing, but mine was short-lived. Kidding aside, Hiroko was definitely the nicest person under the Academy's roof.

'Perhaps no one would believe it,' she said, fiddling with her shoelace. 'Perhaps people think I am nice. But Xanthe has been unfriendly to me since the start and you are the only person who has told her not to. No one else notices when she ignores me or takes my seat. No one else has spoken up for me. Except for you.' She angled her gaze up at me. 'Because you are my friend.'

One day, I realised, I might look back on this awful day and call it the best day of my life – the day I'd worked out that I had a best friend, the very best friend in the whole world. I'd never had a best friend before. I'd spent my life as the *other* friend at school, the *other* sibling at home. Casual staff at the little shop I got work at; only called in when someone else couldn't make their shift. Nobody's first choice. Second-best. Third-born.

Now I was not only Renatus's first choice for apprentice, I was Hiroko Sasaki's first choice for the role of friend.

Distantly, I heard the click as the library door was closed. Hiroko and I craned our necks to see, but it was a few moments before Garrett Fischer came into view, his pale, freckled face turning red the second he met Hiroko's eyes.

If ever there was an adorable sight, it was watching Garrett crush desperately on Hiroko, which seemed to be his main function since I'd first met him a few weeks ago. He was our age, roughly, and a Displacer, like Hiroko. Painfully shy.

'Hi,' he said, at least two octaves too quietly, stopping in front of us and shifting his weight awkwardly from one foot to another. 'Uh... breakfast is over. Qasim made an announcement – I thought you'd want to know, since you didn't hear it... Lisandro has, um, attacked again, and Aubrey and Teresa were taken prisoner. It's all, like, really bad.'

Hiroko and I already knew this, of course, so our responses were limited to polite nods, which only served to deepen Garrett's blush.

'Are classes still on?' I asked, giving him a chance to provide us with new information. He shrugged slightly.

'Some,' he said, trying and failing to meet my gaze. 'Qasim's level one class is on this morning, and Glen, Anouk and Emmanuelle's classes are still on, but none others.'

I felt relief, because my two classes – healing and illusions – were cancelled. Hiroko looked to me in horror.

'I must go to learn wards after morning tea,' she said, tugging nervously on the ends of her dark sleek hair. 'Xanthe is in my class. I don't think I can be so brave without you there.'

'I thought you were really brave this morning,' Garrett spoke up, the most solid sentence I'd ever heard from him, eliciting a smile from Hiroko. I expected his blush would have reddened if it could, but his entire volume of blood seemed to have already gone to his face. He opened his mouth to continue, but no sound came out. Taking a deep, embarrassed breath, he tried again, apparently having already said too much to back out now. 'I, uh, I thought it was really awesome how you stood up to Xanthe. Both of you,' he added quickly, taking the reprieve that was the inclusion of me into the compliment. He chanced a swift glance at Hiroko but finished his announcement by looking at his shoes.

'She was really great, wasn't she?' I agreed, smiling warmly at Hiroko. 'You'll be fine in wards. You're brave and strong. Emmanuelle won't let Xanthe do a thing to you.'

'Xanthe tried to tell Emmanuelle that you two had, like, started them,' Garrett said without looking at us. 'I don't think she believed it, and the other councillors will tell her the truth of what they saw, but maybe you should talk to her.' He shifted his weight again to his other foot. 'Um, I have to go to scrying. I'll, uh, see you both later.'

He quickly turned away, but Hiroko called him back.

'Garrett,' she said, and he spun around before she'd finished saying the word. 'Thank you for finding us. You are very sweet.'

The blush that had been slowly receding returned in full, and with a mumbled reply he quickly left. We waited until he'd exited the library before giggling.

Realising that I was starving and that Hiroko hadn't eaten breakfast either, the two of us eventually returned to the dining hall in the hopes that the buffet table would not yet have been completely cleared. The room itself was abandoned by all students and councillors, and only two of Renatus's staff remained, packing dishes onto trolleys. To my disappointment, the buffet table had already been dismantled.

'Morning tea is not so far away,' Hiroko reassured me. Her voice alerted the nearest of the staff to our presence, and she turned to look at us. I recognised her face, which brightened with a hesitant smile. She bustled over, abandoning her trolley.

'Aristea?' she asked, her eyes on me. I nodded, glancing once at Hiroko. My friend was looking at the table beside us, where two heaped plates of bacon, hash browns, breakfast sausages, mushrooms and tomato waited, apparently untouched.

'Yes,' I confirmed. The woman, dressed in green, smiled wider. She was in her fifties, I guessed, with greying hair that once was quite fair. She was full-figured and her face was softly lined with age. Everything about her seemed soft.

'I am Fionnuala,' she said, extending a hand. When I shook it, she warmly placed her other hand over mine. 'Head of staff. Welcome to the family.'

'Uh, thanks,' I said, uncertain. She released my hand and indicated the plates beside us.

'I heard you and your friend missed out on breakfast so I had these made up for you before the buffet was cleared,' she explained, an apologetic note in her voice as she added, 'but I didn't consider whether either of you might be vegetarian. I'm very sorry if-'

'No, we're not,' I said quickly, before she could apologise. 'Thank you so much for saving it for us.'

'Yes, thank you,' Hiroko echoed. Fionnuala smiled at us both.

'You're very welcome,' she said kindly. 'Don't hesitate to ask if you ever need anything.'

She returned to her heavily burdened trolley and, adding another pile of plates to it, wheeled it from the room. Hiroko and I sat down for our breakfasts. For a day that had started off so badly, it seemed to have recovered itself reasonably well.

But of course, it was barely ten o'clock. It had only just begun.

Emmanuelle found us in the minutes before the first session was due to end. Hiroko and I had decided to just sit here right through to morning tea, by which point the excitement of the morning should have worn off for most people. Emmanuelle sat down beside Hiroko to address us both.

'I want to know what 'appened zis morning,' she said, her tone firm and very French. 'This is quite serious. Qasim and Anouk told me what was said between you two and Sterling and Xanthe, and I'm quite disturbed by what I heard. I gave the other two a chance to explain themselves but their story does not match that of Qasim. Don't think you can lie to me and get away with it.'

I wasn't going to try.

'Sterling is infatuated with Renatus,' Hiroko began, setting the scene for the rest of the tale. Emmanuelle rolled her eyes, but motioned for her to continue. 'She is upset... *was*... upset with Aristea last night when she returned so late – Xanthe suggested that Aristea must be carrying on a relationship with the headmaster without we knowing.'

Emmanuelle rested a hand across her forehead, evidently stressed.

'I just assured your sister that such a thing would never 'appen, so tell me it's not true,' she said, her tone both tired and pleading.

'Why are you asking me that?' I asked, trying not to sound like a demanding child. Emmanuelle, honestly? She was there last night, she knew where I was. She understood me, or so I'd thought. 'Do you believe them?'

'No. But I need to hear it from you.'

'Of course it's not true,' I said, unable to avoid sounding snappy. 'It's gross.'

'Lord Gawain is coming up this afternoon,' she said. 'Anouk is demanding an investigation. As if we don't 'ave enough to worry about. You must be present, Aristea. Don't look at me like that. It's a serious charge.'

'It's a rubbish charge,' I muttered. I managed to find a knot in the timber of the tabletop and I ran my fingers along the contours of that to distract me, but the angry, frustrated words still spilled from me. 'Someone gets to tell the whole school that I'm... I'm a... that I'm a *slut*,' I stammered on that word, discovering that despite how little I cared about Xanthe, the name still hurt, 'and she can attack Hiroko, but *I'm* the one under investigation?'

'I am afraid so,' Emmanuelle said grimly, standing. A clock chimed somewhere. 'Welcome to Renatus's inner circle.'

I didn't know then what this was supposed to mean, but later I'd look back on this moment and cringe at the less-than-veiled truth to her words.

'What did my sister say?' I asked suddenly. 'Is she okay with everything? Hiroko already knows,' I added when Emmanuelle glanced subtly at my friend. 'She's my best friend. She... Renatus didn't tell me not to tell anyone.'

Hiroko smiled, pleased, looking down into her lap. Emmanuelle was unfazed by my rule-bending.

'Finding the loopholes already, hmm?' she confirmed. 'Why am I not surprised? Angela gave 'er permission for you to begin your apprenticeship. These are yours.' She gave me the plastic bag she'd carried in earlier. 'I 'ave a class but immediately after you are to meet me for the examination.'

I agreed, and she left. A small group of boys walked into the dining hall a minute or so later. One of them grinned when he saw me, and turned to whisper something to his friends. I pretended not to notice, but it didn't stop the attention from feeling bad.

Qasim, Glen and Anouk were once again the only White Elm at the meal, at least until Emmanuelle returned, now accompanied by Lord Gawain. All five of them glanced over at me periodically, obviously discussing me and possibly trying to be discreet about it, but not doing a particularly good job of it.

Sitting in the library with Hiroko, alone, talking, listening to Garrett try to compliment her, I'd felt good. That was quickly draining away as more people entered the hall. Some stared, some ignored me completely. Khalida and her friends glared at me as though I had no right to be in the same room as them; an older guy walking with Isao and Dylan, boys from my scrying class, wondered aloud, 'How much do you think she charges?' as they walked past. Isao laughed. Dylan didn't laugh, but I could sense that he still found the comment amusing.

The worst thing of all was when Addison and the twins turned up. Kendra and Sophia were laughing as they stepped through the doors, and I looked over. My stomach flipped nervously when I met their eyes and they both looked down. Had they been laughing about me? Addison, his arm slung casually over Kendra's shoulders, met my gaze for an instant before leaning down to murmur a question in his girlfriend's ear. Uncertain, she shrugged, looking past him to her sister, who mirrored her gesture. They sat down in our usual spot, where they were joined several minutes later by Sterling and Xanthe.

I turned back to my still-clean plate, hurting. Renatus's apprenticeship was already costing me.

I went with Hiroko to her class, arriving right on time. Sterling and Xanthe, I imagined, would just be leaving the dining hall now. Xanthe would need to return to the room to grab her book, so I didn't plan on hanging around there waiting for her. I waited with Hiroko while Emmanuelle set up the space inside her classroom, and when Hiroko went in and sat down at a desk, I stood at the door. Emmanuelle walked over to me while someone entered beside me.

'I'll see you here in two hours,' she said. I nodded and agreed, turning to leave and almost walking straight into Xanthe. My once-friend-turned-apparent-nemesis stared at me for a long moment, her narrow eyes cold and hateful. Then Addison squeezed between us and I used the break in our eye-contact as the moment of my escape. I walked to the stairs and down, through the entrance hall and out the front doors. I kept walking until I reached the edge of the lawn, where the orchard began. It was cold and dreary and grey outside, and I was convinced that the orchard itself was haunted, but none of that was enough to put me off. I sat down with my back against an apple tree and stared back at the house. I had been so excited to come here. I'd thought I was so lucky. But was it lucky to be the apprentice of a White Elm whose own council didn't like him? Was it lucky to have only one friend in the whole world, even if that friend happened to be a very good one?

I was definitely lucky to have Hiroko, I decided, but other than that I wasn't lucky at all. I was alone.

chapter five

Two hours is actually a very long time, especially if you are sitting in the cold, alone, for that length of time. You do a lot of thinking, but that doesn't pass as much time as chatting and laughing with friends.

I slowly made my return to the house, encountering Hiroko as she left her classroom. Her classmates walked straight past me without acknowledging that I was even there. Not that I was particularly friendly with any of them, save Addison James, who I saw inside still talking with Emmanuelle, but it was still off-putting to be so deliberately ignored. No one wanted to appear to be staring, so instead they chose not to look at me at all. Once they had cleared off, and when Xanthe's shiny brown bob disappeared into the stairwell, I asked, 'Did she try anything?'

Hiroko shook her head.

'I worried she might, but Addison came over and sat with me,' she said, looking infinitely grateful for this fact. 'He did not speak to me but Xanthe could not say anything rude to me while he was there.'

I smiled, relieved. In my two hours of solitude, I had wondered whether I had ruined Hiroko's life today – whether anyone would want to be her friend

rehearsed answers in my mind – things like "master", "honest", "totally platonic male mentor-type person" – but none of those fell out of my mouth.

'Black.'

My answer seemed to surprise everyone but Lord Gawain. I broke eye contact with him to look at Renatus. "Black" was unexpected, even for me. His hair was black; his usual attire was generally black. His role on the White Elm was as the Dark Keeper, meaning that he had access to study black magic. But beyond those facts, I couldn't work out where the association came from. I mean, I didn't think he was black-hearted, or evil, or anything. I hope it didn't offend him or make me look any stranger than these people already probably thought I was.

Even furthermore unexpected, Lord Gawain was *not* finished questioning me.

'Aristea?'

'What?' I snapped my head back to look at him. I realised how rude I sounded. 'Sorry. Yes?'

He gave me a level look. 'Aristea.'

Oh. More word associations. *Aristea* goes with-

'Stars,' I said quickly, without thought. Again, I had no idea where all this came from. There were lots of more appropriate answers: Byrne, scrying, Angela. But stars? I understood the basics of stars – big balls of burning gases, very old, varying ages and temperatures, often orbited by planets, stuff like that – and had a workable knowledge of star signs from working in a new age store, but in the larger fields of either astrology or astronomy, I would find myself severely lacking in things to talk about. My name meant nothing to do with stars... although, as a child, I'd gone through a phase of signing my name with a star in place of the dot for the "i". That was probably the most relevant link between my name and the word I'd chosen to associate with it, and though my logical mind cringed at my display of incoherence and weirdness, I kept my mouth shut and declined my better judgement's offer of a correction.

Lord Gawain released my hands.

'Thank you, Aristea,' he said. 'That's everything I need. You may go.'

'What? That's not much of an investigation,' Anouk argued, standing. 'We owe it to the families of the children we are protecting to ensure they are completely safe.'

'I'm convinced that there is no reason here to suspect Aristea is any less safe than the other children,' Lord Gawain answered. He nodded towards the door, gesturing for me to take my leave. I glanced at Renatus as I turned away. He didn't say anything but appeared relieved by the outcome of the investigation. I headed out as the door swung open. Anouk stepped into my path.

'We need to check her memory,' she insisted. I stopped and looked about at the others. Renatus pushed away from his desk when he saw my anxious expression. This was what I'd been trying to avoid. I knew there was nothing strictly intimate to be found in my entire memory bank of experiences with Renatus – some inappropriate conversations, perhaps, but more of the "that's a state secret, don't tell anyone" or "you and I share the same horrific past, what a coincidence" type, rather than the "take your clothes off" type – but I also knew that if someone *did* go looking through my memories, they'd find I was accidentally witness to an embarrassing scene between two councillors, and that the reason it was accidental (and not public knowledge) was that I'd illegally scried myself into this very office. If Anouk saw that, not only would two people present be potentially humiliated (three, if you include me), but I would very probably find myself either expelled or on trial of sorts. At the very least, my likelihood of being ultimately approved as a White Elm apprentice would be significantly decreased.

'There's nothing to find,' Renatus said smoothly, and to me he said, 'Just go.'

'If there's nothing to find it'll be quick,' Anouk replied coolly, looking into my eyes like she was looking for something deeper than irises, deeper than pupils. I averted my gaze instinctively and glared at the floor, for whatever that was worth.

'No,' I said, firmly. Several of the councillors looked at me in surprise, although Qasim and Renatus seemed to have expected this following their confrontation three weeks beforehand. 'No one is looking around in my head. There's nothing to find and what *is* there is not anyone's business.'

'Aristea-'

'You can't read a mind without permission,' Qasim interrupted Anouk. 'Aristea won't give it so we can't look.'

I looked up to him, grateful, even though he wasn't really on my side.

'You'll know for sure on Monday night, Anouk,' Renatus added. 'If I've done what you're determined to suspect, Magic will turn me down as Aristea's master. I would be stripped of much of my power. Why would I risk the repercussions?'

No one answered. Anouk took a breath and exhaled slowly.

'We'll see on Monday,' she agreed finally, though with apparent reluctance. 'I'll go ahead and let them know we're coming.' She moved towards the door. Emmanuelle and I moved over so she could pass. I didn't know "they" were.

'I've been unable to make any progress with Teresa or Aubrey,' Glen said, standing, speaking mostly to Lord Gawain. 'Wherever they are, they're separated from us by some kind of energetic wall.'

'What about you two?' Lord Gawain asked of Qasim and Renatus. Both shook their heads.

'Jackson has hidden himself well,' Qasim admitted.

'No lead on Lisandro, either. If anyone knows anything, they're not talking.'

'So, we keep looking,' Lord Gawain said with another sigh. 'In the meantime we will need to speak with Jackson's men in Valero. When I left, the one Aubrey put down was just coming around. It's too bad he wasn't quicker with those spells; he did quite a number on the one he did manage to hit.'

'I want to come,' Emmanuelle said quickly.

'Very well,' Lord Gawain agreed. 'The one you healed has made good progress except for one shoulder, which seems very inflamed.'

It surprised me that the White Elm had not yet questioned their prisoners but had instead locked them up somewhere and waited around patiently for them to wake naturally.

Glen left. Emmanuelle directed me through the door after him before I could say anything. She released me and remained in the room, so I supposed I was finally free to go. I wandered down the hallway towards the stairs, fiddling with the aging leather strap of my watch. Lord Gawain was a strange man, I thought. He was at the same time impressive, with his eccentricity and unusual approaches, and worryingly unimpressive for the same reasons. He didn't seem to be a man cut out for action. He was slow to act in emergencies – Qasim was the one who'd taken charge last night when it looked like paranoia was going to overtake the White Elm outside Teresa's house – and he took his time rising to challenges. He was a great man, obviously, with an immense capacity for compassion and an abstract, open mind, but he was not a warrior. It was lucky, I supposed, that he had Renatus onside, and other strong and wilful councillors like Qasim and Emmanuelle.

Something thudded on the floor, and I looked down to find my wrist naked and my watch bouncing from the carpet through a slightly opened door. Disappointed that it had broken (the strap had been wearing very thin for some time) on today of all days, I followed it into the darkened room beyond. I couldn't find a light switch, so I crouched down, running my hands across the carpet in the direction in which I had heard it skitter to a stop. I bumped my head on what I assumed was some sort of side table or coffee table. Some instinct kicked in as though I was being attacked, and a thick, opalescent ward formed quickly around me. I'd always been good at wards – one of my few talents.

'Ouch,' I muttered, annoyed, rubbing the top of my head with one hand just as the fingers of my other hand closed around my warm watch. Stupid watch, stupid everything... This really was the worst day. I crawled back to the doorway, where light spilled in from the hall, and examined the broken strap. It was as I'd guessed. The leather had worn through on one side, breaking it cleanly right through the notch I most often used. I found the other half of the strap lying in the doorway and looked at it sadly. My late brother, Aidan, had given me this watch for my thirteenth birthday. Several days after, actually, as he did every year. He was dead now but he'd always been known in our family for his tardiness, especially with birthday presents. I tried to smile at this thought; seeing my broken watch lying in two pieces in my palm killed that expression. I had plenty of possessions from my parents but few from my brother, and I stared at it now, missing it already.

I heard voices in the hall and looked out as Lord Gawain and Emmanuelle walked past. They didn't notice me – perhaps they were accustomed to my presence and to being able to sense students and councillors all over the house? Then I realised that my ward was still up. Had I shielded myself energetically, too, without realising? Was I invisible?

'I'll be there in a few minutes,' Qasim said, though he was still out of sight. 'I have something that needs to be done first.'

'Alright, don't be long,' Lord Gawain agreed. In a lower voice, he asked of Emmanuelle, 'Is it usual for a trauma victim to sleep this long after an... attack... like Renatus's?'

'I'm not a doctor,' she answered bluntly, 'but I'm not surprised. I took a lot of 'is energy to work the 'ealing process...'

Their voices faded down the stairwell, and Renatus and Qasim walked past me. With a suddenness that made me jump, Qasim turned on Renatus, grasping the collar of the younger man's shirt and throwing him against the wall to their right. I shuffled back, shocked, but I needn't have bothered. Neither man was remotely interested in his surroundings.

'I could throttle you,' Qasim hissed, tightening his grip on Renatus's collar. 'How could you be so irresponsible?'

'What are you talking about?' Renatus demanded, shoving the older scrier away and freeing himself from Qasim's grasp.

'You've done stupid things before, but this by far exceeds anything I ever considered you capable of,' Qasim said. 'What were you thinking? Manipulating children to suit your purpose?'

'Aristea was not tricked into anything,' Renatus replied. 'She made her choice, knowing it would be a difficult path.'

I nodded to myself; his words echoed exactly what I'd been trying to tell myself. It would be hard, probably, and already had begun to be, but it would be worthwhile.

'She barely knows you. She doesn't understand the work you do.'

'I suspect she'll very quickly work it out.'

'This is all wrong, Renatus,' Qasim said angrily. I could feel his frustration, and Renatus's cold indifference. 'You're not old enough for an apprentice, and definitely not disciplined enough. She was not properly prepared. The council was not prepared for this, either.'

'Qasim, if you'd wanted her for yourself, you might have said something,' Renatus commented.

'Everyone knew. I thought you might have guessed.'

'I did, but you didn't act.'

From my hiding place, I blinked in surprise. I had just assumed that the Scrier hated me. The idea that he wanted *me* as *his* apprentice had never crossed my mind.

'I wanted to wait until she was ready, as should you have,' Qasim answered, annoyed. I peeked around the edge of the door to see Renatus shrug in response.

'Time is not always in our favour. The council needs me to be the best I can be, and to do that, I needed to become a master, immediately.'

'The choice shouldn't have been about *you*, self-ish brat,' Qasim snarled. 'Listen to you – a spoiled child yourself. The decision should have been made in Aristea's best interests.'

'It was,' Renatus defended. 'Only under the instruction of a scrier like you or me can that girl become what she is fated to be. I just acted quicker.'

'You acted impulsively and rashly – hardly in a way appropriate of a responsible adult guardian, which is what a master should be to his apprentice.' Qasim took a deep breath, but seemed unable to check his emotions. 'You do not fit the bill, Renatus. How can you expect to fulfil this role? You don't understand what it means to be responsible for another life, a child's life and her learning. You aren't old enough to be a father and a teacher to her. How many years are there between you, Renatus? Six? Seven?'

I listened with interest, because I didn't actually know how old Renatus was. I'd assumed he was twenty-three or twenty-four, about the age of my sister or maybe slightly older, as my brother had been.

'Five.'

Five plus seventeen is twenty-two.

Angela was twenty-three, and would turn twenty-four in July.

'Five,' Qasim repeated, frustrated. 'How can you possibly be a positive adult role model to a girl who was born when you were five years old? You'll never have the master-apprentice relationship, the parent-child relationship that it represents. The closest you

117

can be is her brother. This is why there are rules! Masters and their apprentices should be of the same sex; a master must reach a certain *age* before he can select an apprentice. This is not only unusual. It's wrong. It defies tradition.'

'I'm sure you didn't expect any action of mine to be conventional.'

'You're almost her age! You're supposed to be her guardian!'

'She *has* role models already,' Renatus asserted. 'I can protect her better than any of them.'

'Aristea's current guardian is almost the same age as you,' Qasim disagreed. 'There is no other stable adult figure in that house. Her sister has given up her hopes and dreams to raise Aristea; you only want to use her to achieve *your* success. What Aristea needs is a strong adult role model – a *parent* – to nurture her abilities and direct her along the best paths. That person is not you.'

I stared at the ticking hands of my broken watch as the ensuing silence lasted and lasted. My stomach felt full of lead, as if I were the one involved in the confrontation. Was Qasim right?

'Well,' Renatus said finally, 'I'm so glad we have these talks, Qasim.'

The two stared at each other for a long moment, before Qasim turned away and descended the stairs. Renatus stayed where he was, glaring after him.

'You shouldn't have had to hear that, Aristea,' he said, turning his intense gaze on me. I flinched, caught, and stood quickly.

'I didn't mean to eavesdrop,' I said, avoiding the word "sorry". He and I had established a no-apologising policy whereby neither was allowed to use the "S" word that made us both so uncomfortable to hear. I stepped out of the room and extended my hand, showing him the broken watch strap as explanation. 'I was looking for something I dropped.'

'It isn't your fault.' He took the pieces of my watch from me. When his skin touched mine I imagined a brief second of blackness – was he scrying that? As always, he explained as if I'd asked. 'This is what I see when I search for Lisandro, but it is only a matter of time before I find him. Nothing stays hidden forever.'

'I thought Qasim hated me,' I said, changing the subject.

'I told you he didn't.'

'Why would he treat me so badly if he wanted me as his own apprentice?' I asked, confused. It made no sense.

'A test, I gather,' Renatus answered. His hand was closed with my watch inside. He uncurled his fingers and offered it back to me. My watch fell into my palm, mended. 'I hope you haven't changed your mind.'

I lifted my gaze to his. He had very unusual, and very intense, violet eyes, which could capture anyone's attention, and he was the kind of attractive that never has to check his reflection to see if his hair is sitting right because it really doesn't matter. In my experience Renatus had been nothing short of perfectly confident in himself, and that wasn't surprising, but his words now bore a loaded weightiness that felt new. He was asking, in his round-about way, whether I was wishing that Qasim had gotten in first. Did I wish that?

Hadn't Renatus lit a man on fire without warning? Wasn't Renatus offside with nearly the entire council? Wasn't associating myself with him a very bad career move? Hadn't it already cost me dearly?

Yes on all accounts, but no, I decided with surprise. My brain was absolutely right – association with Renatus was a risky idea – yet I couldn't bring myself to wish for Qasim in his place. I had probably hoped for it at first, weeks ago, but getting to know Qasim I had realised that I didn't really like him any more than he liked me. Renatus had not only overlooked my accidental criminal activity, but had trusted me with secrets I had no business knowing. He trusted and respected me; he seemed to like me. He deserved the same in return.

'I haven't.'

'Good.' Ever smooth; like it hadn't worried him in the slightest that I might have said something different. 'I need to go; it will be my task to interrogate Jackson's men.'

'Why did Lord Gawain wait so long before questioning them?' I asked, curious. I strapped my watch back on.

'Partly for ethical reasons,' Renatus said. 'Both were apprehended by magic and were taken into custody while unconscious and possibly undergoing self-healing. Just as you wouldn't wake a sleepwalker, you shouldn't wake someone who has fallen into a comatose state following magical trauma. It could damage memories, brain connections... Lord Gawain was also hoping that Jackson or Lisandro would come back for them. He must have forgotten for a moment who we are dealing with. Lisandro is loyal only to himself.'

'What will happen to them?'

'We have a standing arrangement with an all-magical colony in Russia,' he said. 'Anouk is from there. They have the most secure prison in our world. They detain our criminals; we protect their colony from the modern world.'

'But Lisandro must know of it?'

'He does, but he can't get to it.' He glanced at the stairwell, and back to me. 'Aristea, I'm truly sorry for what you've been through over the past twenty-four hours, between the council's votes against your character, misunderstandings with your friends, spreading of rumours and now an investigation into those lies. I suspect that for me to deny the rumour to the students would only fuel the fire, so I hope that you will manage to ride out the storm, so to speak. I'm very sorry that things aren't working out the way either of us planned.'

I played with the end of my newly mended watch strap. Good as new. He was sorry, but none of it was his fault. Not *really*. He had been planning to choose me, and then last night his hand had been forced and he'd had to ask me earlier than he'd expected. Rash, perhaps, impulsive, probably, but if his philosophy was to be believed, a mere act of Fate. I was meant to be in Italy last night. And Renatus could not be blamed for Sterling's obsession, especially when he'd done nothing to encourage it, nor could he be held accountable for the fact that Xanthe was an utter *bitch*. It was not his fault that rumours spread like wildfire amongst teenagers, or that people in my classes were stupid enough to believe them, or that Anouk was flighty and gullible.

'You're not meant to apologise until you do something wrong,' I reminded him, and then turned to the stairs. I sensed his gratitude. Unseen, I smiled at my watch, able to relate. I took three steps down before something occurred to me, and I stopped and looked back. He had started in the opposite direction, back towards his office, and I remembered the magical portal in the wall that would take him directly to the kitchens downstairs. 'Renatus? About what I said, when Lord Gawain asked those weird questions. I don't know where that came from. I don't really think you're dark or anything.'

'Everyone is dark,' he responded. 'Everyone has something to hide or something to feel ashamed about. We're all just different shades of dark, trying to be lighter.'

'Why do you think those words came to me?' I blurted out, unable to contain the burning curiosity. '"Black" and "Stars"? Does that mean anything to you?'

He looked thoughtful. 'Not yet. But it might make sense in time. It's certainly not *nothing*, or meaningless. Lord Gawain knows what he's doing – those words came to you then for a reason. Nothing is random-'

'For people like us,' I finished, remembering his words. He nodded a goodbye and stepped into the wall. He disappeared through it like he was walking through a film or a liquid, but when I ran over and touched the same place, it was solid and unforgiving.

There are no random pages for people like us.

That's what Renatus had said to me, just the other day, when I'd opened a book to a "random" page. When I'd looked later I'd found the page boring and unhelpful... but today, not even a full day later, the information about apprentices succeeding their masters onto the White Elm seemed slightly more relevant. A lot more relevant, in truth. The words Lord Gawain had encouraged from the void of my scattered mind were less than useless to me right now, but perhaps, given time and experience, they would make sense. Maybe?

I found Hiroko and we hung out for ages, alone, ignoring everybody else. Eventually the need for a bathroom drew us back to our room. We paused at the door and glanced at each other. We could both sense the two presences inside. Why they'd decided to abandon their rumour-spreading and return to their room, I couldn't imagine, but I wished they hadn't. I slid my key into the lock and turned it. No explosions; no screams or accusations. Yet. Taking a very deep breath as though I was diving into a deep, dark sea, I stepped inside.

Xanthe was sitting at her desk, writing in her journal, and Sterling was strewn across Xanthe's bed, on her stomach, facing her friend. They had apparently been talking, but glanced over when we walked

123

in. I waited just inside the room as Hiroko moved to my side. If they had something to say, now would be the time.

For a moment, we all just stared at each other. Then Sterling let her hand slide across the bed, falling back onto her elbows and looking back to Xanthe.

'So then I just grabbed my brother's keys and, like, ran,' she said, evidently continuing whatever story she had been telling Xanthe. 'I didn't have a licence yet but Dad was teaching me to drive so I knew what I was doing. I was just *so sick* of her and all her crap, you know? She's my stepmom, not real family. She can't treat me like that.'

I glanced back at Hiroko, who shrugged very slightly, handing me back my key. Apparently we were getting the silent treatment, which despite being very awkward suited me quite fine, because I wasn't prepared for yet another confrontation. Things might sort themselves out in time, I thought as I followed Hiroko into the bathroom. We shut ourselves in, soundproofing our conversation and blocking out most of Xanthe's last comment, something about her sister's friend's stepfather.

'I hate Xanthe,' Hiroko said again. 'Now they will pretend we do not exist?'

'It's better than arguing,' I reminded her, going to the furthest toilet stall. In the mirror, I saw her fold her arms moodily.

'Perhaps we should ask Emmanuelle to move us to another room?'

Another room? I flushed my toilet as I considered this. As nice as it would be to get away from our current roommates, was there any other pair of girls who hated me less right now? Kendra and Sophia's roommate Marcy had returned home, leaving at least one spare bed in that dorm, but right now, I certainly didn't want to swap the enemies I had for another two. And I really didn't want to be separated from Hiroko, which would happen if there were no other dorms with two spaces.

'We didn't do anything wrong,' I told her finally. 'We shouldn't have to go anywhere.'

She said nothing else. When we returned to the room, Xanthe and Sterling were still talking, acting as though we didn't exist, and when I addressed Hiroko, our hostile roommates pretended not to be able to hear us.

It was an awful, awkward situation, I thought as I slipped out of the room after Hiroko, but it would have to do, at least until things settled down a bit.

chapter six

Anouk saw the illusion of rocky, uninhabitable land – the visual defence of her hometown – in the near distance, a bit under a kilometre away. Sometimes she wished her Displacement skills were a little better, but really, she knew they were most sufficient. Russia was a long way away from Northern Ireland – to have gotten this skip spot-on, she would have to be Elijah.

Space moved beside her and Glen appeared nearby. He didn't say anything and neither did she. When you share thoughts with someone continuously for a decade, you find that there is little to actually talk about.

Unwilling to walk so far, they Displaced the nine hundred or so metres to the edge of the town's magical perimeter and walked through the shimmery wall of magic protecting it. Anouk felt the energy flickering all about her, alerting those who ran the town to the arrival of a permitted visitor. On the other side of the illusions and wards, the high walls of the place she'd grown up in became suddenly apparent, and she felt herself relaxing. There is no place like home.

Valero was an all-magical community, wanting no contact whatsoever with the technological, ever-expanding world of mortals. There were many like it around the world, but Valero and Avalon were the most powerful, with the closest and most tenuous affiliation with the White Elm. Protected by convincing illusions, impenetrable wards and imposing stone walls topped with archers, nobody got in or out without Valero's governors and guards allowing, making it the perfect place to keep those dangerous sorcerers the White Elm couldn't trust in mortal custody.

Anouk noticed the archer standing atop the arch of the massive iron gate and waved once in greeting. She didn't recognise his face in the glare of the sun, but after a moment he lowered his bow and waved back enthusiastically. He disappeared from view, and a moment later, the heavy gate began lifting, allowing her entry.

She loved her medieval community, with its security and close-knit atmosphere. Once through the gate, Anouk glanced about, enjoying the familiar sights of old little houses lining hard dirt streets and wishing she could take a left and wander down to her elderly aunt's house for a surprise visit, or continue past to visit her second cousin... Visitors to Valero, including Glen, had said in the past that the town reminded them of a prison camp, so enclosed and controlled and so poor, but Anouk couldn't see what those people saw. To her, this was home – safe, stable, certain. She could easily while away her day here. But there was work to be done. Reluctantly, she turned right instead and began the trek up the sloping street, leading Glen to the prison at the centre of the town.

She saw the prison long before she reached it. Unlike the other buildings in Valero, it was several storeys above ground, with two subterranean levels reserved for the worst prisoners. Like the town itself, the prison was walled off with stone. Loops of barbed wire lined the top, and guards patrolled the perimeter.

Most of the people Anouk passed on her way smiled or nodded in acknowledgement, clearly recognising her from her childhood and young adulthood spent here, but it was not until she reached the prison gates that she was recognised by someone she actually knew.

'Anouk!' Viktor exclaimed when she smiled. She waved once and approached her childhood sweetheart, now a guard for the prison, while the second guard eyed her with uncertainty.

'Viktor,' she said, and spoke in Russian, 'I can see you are being kept busy.'

In her head, however, she said, *It is good to see you.*

'I am,' Viktor agreed, adding, *It has been too long. Why do you never visit?*

'I was here last night, but someone else was on this gate,' Anouk said, answering his telepathic question. 'I am being kept busy, also. The outside world is in chaos.'

'As always,' Viktor commented. *Do you see now why I asked you not to leave?* 'Hello, Glen.'

Her very oldest friend, Viktor had discouraged Anouk's decision to nominate herself for the White Elm a decade ago. He'd insisted that the world the council presided over was a vast and depressing world full of arrogance, ignorance and danger. He was right. The outside world was not always a nice place. It was populated with dangerous people, holding the self-assured belief that the rules did not apply to *them*.

Rules, as far as Anouk and the other Valeroans felt, were for everyone. No excuses.

'We would be lost without her,' Glen told Viktor with a smile, undoubtedly having overheard the last comment echo through Anouk's thoughts. To an outsider, listening in on this conversation, it would be entirely incoherent and scrambled. People in Valero, however, were accustomed to this kind of disjointed communication. Valero was known for producing Telepaths – only very rarely was a child born into a different Class, and even when one was, a secondary talent for telepathy was inevitable.

'Glen, I believe it is time that you, too, leave the White Elm, marry our Anouk and join our nation instead,' Viktor said, shaking Glen's hand. Glen laughed easily, and Anouk rolled her eyes. Glen was her partner-in-crime, her closest connection on the council and almost certainly a soulmate, but there was absolutely nothing romantic between them. Viktor, like many Valeroans, was simply looking to collect another Telepath for their city and for an excuse for Anouk to leave the council. Because, of course, married women didn't do this kind of work.

Tell that to Susannah or Lady Miranda, she thought, but kept it to herself.

'Ask again in another year,' Glen suggested. To Anouk, wryly, he added, *We might be looking for an excuse to get out of this line of work by then.*

Anouk nodded and Viktor smiled, hearing Glen's voice in her head. The second guard leaned forward to interject.

'The warden extends his welcome to Anouk and Glen of the White Elm,' he said in Russian, passing on a message from those he'd informed of Anouk's presence. 'He permits you entry and will meet you inside.'

'I'll take them up,' Viktor said, beckoning to Anouk while the second guard unlocked the gates for them. The prison grounds were grassless and hardened, like the rest of the town, but surrounded by the stone and wire, it seemed so much more austere. The prison itself was a windowless stone tower, rectangular and rough. Completely cloaked in spells, not all of them nice, those unfortunate enough to be locked inside had no chance of escape.

You're upset, Viktor observed as he led her and Glen along the worn path to the prison doors. The two guards there nodded and let them through. *Something has happened.*

It is the past, Anouk insisted, determined not to think about the reason she was here. The two men she'd incarcerated last night were at least in part responsible for attacking and stealing Aubrey and Teresa. Where were those two now? Anouk had had so little to do with any of the newest councillors but still she feared for them deeply. Both were so gentle and harmless. What did Lisandro and Jackson have in store for them?

Viktor allowed the councillors to enter ahead of him, and the doors closed behind them. The sunlight was cut off completely, and Anouk paused, waiting for her eyes to adjust to the torchlight. Viktor touched her back with one hand, encouraging her forward along the hall until they reached one of the torches. He took it and led on, showing her up the cold, dark, stone stairs.

It was an eerie place. The halls on each floor were lined either side with dank, dark cells. The residents were silent behind their wooden doors.

They grew silent very quickly, she knew, but she recalled several who had started their stays screaming, back in the days when Lisandro was in charge of interrogation. It had seemed okay then, she remembered, to let Lisandro mentally torture criminals if it paid off in good information. Now they were going to ask Renatus to do the same job. Was it still okay, given what they now knew about Lisandro? Would Renatus have the captives screaming and begging, too?

It was not hard to imagine.

The warden was another familiar face.

'Anouk,' Ivan greeted her warmly when she, Glen and Viktor reached the second floor. 'Twice in as many days! We welcome you, and your friend. Welcome back, Glen.'

'Thank you,' Anouk and Glen said together, and Anouk added, *We are both pleased to be here, or would be if we had better reasons for our visit.*

Ah, yes, Ivan agreed grimly, leading them along the dark, deathly hall. A thin wailing sound began and grew louder as they neared its source. *They have both awoken. The larger one woke half an hour ago – he has been noisy. That is what you hear. The other, the small burnt one, woke first. He hasn't made a sound.*

'How long?' Glen asked. He was not familiar with Ivan, and the ethics of telepathy dictated that a Telepath not communicate non-verbally without permission.

'He woke four hours ago,' Ivan said. 'I thought with his wounds he might have some screaming in him, but nothing. Sometimes that is the case. This one, though...' He tutted disapprovingly through the bars of a heavy wooden door. Anouk peered past him into the cell. Inside was unlit. An old bed stood against the furthest wall, and what passed for a toilet around here was tucked just beyond that, in the corner. The prison boasted running water, so a showerhead sprouted from the wall to Anouk's right and a small drain marked the floor beneath it. Tilted as far as it could go, the showerhead could probably spray water onto the bedclothes. But that was not the prison warden's concern. In the centre of the room, curled into a foetal position with his back to the door, was a big middle-aged man. He slowly rocked himself, moaning and wailing in an incoherent pattern of high and low volumes.

Maybe it's a song, Glen suggested. Anouk spared him an amused glance as she became aware of Lord Gawain and Emmanuelle arriving at the outskirts of the town.

'What happened to this one, anyway?' Ivan asked with interest. The prisoners brought to him by the White Elm always interested him much more than those who committed crime within his own community. 'He doesn't seem... right.'

'They never are,' Anouk answered, her eyes on the wall as she ran her fingertips across the stone. Dozens of spells, weaved tightly together, protected this wall from being broken or damaged in any way. Every protective spell, every ward, every barrier charm, every piece of magic designed to hide things or obstruct the senses that had ever been written was knotted and sewn all through this structure. Even through this one wall, the man inside was completely energetically invisible. Valero's prison put Morrissey House to shame. There was absolutely no getting in or out of this place unknown. Not that it mattered these days. The prison had developed a much more efficient way of keeping its building safe from magical harm and its inmates under control. 'That's why we bring them here.'

Qasim and Renatus had arrived nearby, too.

'The gatekeeper has just allowed your Lord Gawain into Valero,' Ivan said, his head tilted to the side as he listened to his other, silent conversation. Conversations like this were being had all over the city, all the time. A massive hive mind, like a giant White Elm, all capable of knowing the same thing within minutes. If anyone ever did breach the walls, the entire city could be aware and ready to repel them in a matter of minutes. There never had been or ever would be an army so easily mobilised as the community of Valero. 'He and the one with him are being escorted this way as we speak. Others are approaching the gates. Do you know them?'

He could not sense them – the magic around this town reduced its people's abilities to sense beings and events beyond its walls – but Anouk's connection to the White Elm gave her powers beyond those of other sorcerers.

'They are also with White Elm. They will pass through the perimeter with ease,' she said.

The brands are ready, Viktor told her. *They are coming now.*

There wasn't long to wait. Two armoured guards with their faces obscured by visors arrived, bearing long iron posts, and at the end of each was a flat, circular brand. They stood back, prepared to wait until after the questioning was completed. Lord Gawain and Emmanuelle came soon after with another guard. Ivan made a show of welcoming Emmanuelle, a first-time visitor.

Don't even go there, Ivan, Anouk advised him, although he pretended not to know what she meant.

'Has he been making that noise the whole time I was gone?' Lord Gawain asked concernedly, checking on the wailing prisoner through the bars. He looked back down the hall towards the stairs just as Qasim arrived, and moments later, Renatus.

Anouk avoided looking at Renatus – even thinking about him made her angry. Sometimes, Lord Gawain's ongoing adoration of that stupid boy completely astounded her. How could anyone love a person who so very clearly could not be trusted? He kept secrets from the council, betrayed their ancient traditions, manipulated young girls to suit his purpose and set councillors against each other. He was trouble. *Why* did Lord Gawain have such a special place in his heart for Renatus; *how* did he look past all those warning signs and still see what he wanted to see?

Was it really only the storm? Was the reason behind Lord Gawain's love so simple – only that he'd rescued the vulnerable boy and felt responsible for him? Lord Gawain had saved other lives before, but Renatus was the only one he'd taken under his wing like a nephew. He'd even moved his whole family, work and life from his home in Wales to live in Northern Ireland, closer to the orphaned Renatus. Anouk remembered Lord Gawain and Lisandro bringing the adolescent Renatus to a White Elm circle days after the storm had wiped out the rest of the Morrisseys. *Missed one,* she'd thought at the time, knowing even then that Lord Gawain was mistaken to think that a *Morrissey* could be anything but a problem.

'What took you two so long?' she asked.

'We had to sort something out,' Qasim responded shortly, his energy tinged with a frizzy edge – a sure sign he had just been involved in some sort of confrontation. A glance over Renatus's aura showed the same sign, but he nodded in agreement with Qasim's explanation.

'I hope it's sorted,' Lord Gawain said, obviously noting what Anouk had seen.

'It is, Master,' Renatus agreed. He looked past Anouk into the first cell. 'This one first?'

'That's right,' Lord Gawain said, stepping back and trying not to look anxious. Apparently he wasn't completely sure about this, either. 'Open it.'

'Excellent,' Anouk murmured, pressing her hand over the lock and working on the tightly woven magic holding it shut. After a moment it unravelled, and she pulled the heavy wooden door open. The hinges creaked – this was no hotel. Renatus took half a step inside and froze.

'No. This one knows nothing.' He walked out and had a guard direct him to the other prisoner.

And he knows that how? Glen asked of Anouk, and together they stepped inside the cell and rounded the huddled figure.

The prisoner's noise had lessened but now he burst out with a tuneless, warbling cry. Except for his size, there was absolutely nothing remarkable about this man – brown hair shaved short, plain features, no scars. Anouk knew she would have trouble remembering this face, and considered that Lisandro had probably chosen this sorcerer for this task simply for that fact.

They didn't need to say anything else; Anouk understood, from the second she entered the room and became aware of the prisoner energetically, what Renatus had meant. There was a man on the floor, yes, and he was alive and breathing, but there was no mind to read. His mind was gone. His every memory, skill and belief had been wiped clean.

Ivan had said there was something wrong with this one. No wonder. Assuming, of course, that he'd been like this *before* Renatus announced he knew nothing.

How could that have happened? Glen asked, mystified. Apparently he'd never seen anything like it. Anouk had, a few times here in the prison, but it was still surprising. *Can that really be a result of Aubrey's spell? I didn't think he knew that kind of magic.*

He thought he was going to die. We are all capable of greater things in what we believe to be our final moments.

Glen followed Anouk from the cell and asked, *Is Aubrey strong enough for that, even in desperation?*

'Brand him,' Anouk instructed the waiting guards in Russian. She chose to ignore Glen's question, afraid of the possibilities brewing away in her own head. 'Brand him.'

Glen patiently explained to Lord Gawain the implications of what Anouk and Renatus had found and why they wouldn't be bothering with questioning him. Anouk followed the quickly receding glow of Renatus, his guard and their torch flame as they strode down the hall. No way would she let it go if *both* prisoners *just happened* to *both* have lost their minds.

The wailing had almost faded into the distance when it was cut off by a piercing scream of shock and agony. Anouk did not flinch. They all had to be branded – the process permanently locked the prisoner's power inside their body, forever inhibiting them from performing magic. Normally prisoners would be extensively questioned and the council and Valero governors would convene to ensure justice was carried out properly, but their first captive was a special case. He would not ever attempt to escape; he would never try to attack his captors with magic. If he ever rediscovered his magic, however, he could accidentally hurt himself or cause damage to his cell, so the branding was necessary.

'Is the other one fit for questioning?' Lord Gawain asked of Emmanuelle as they walked. The torch ahead stopped and the guard began unravelling the magical lock.

'I've told you, 'e's fine,' Emmanuelle said, pushing past the other councillors and sounding annoyed. The guard moved aside and she gestured through the barred window. Renatus's burns victim was lying on the thin grey mattress, breathing slowly and deeply. 'You don't believe me?'

'The skin on his shoulder seems infected,' Lord Gawain said, slightly hesitantly.

'Well, you can tell 'im how lucky 'e is to *have* skin at all,' Emmanuelle answered, her accent becoming more pronounced as she became more irritated.

'Perhaps it's better we don't remind him that Renatus torched him,' Qasim commented, leaning against the doorframe and glancing inside. This one was more memorable. Covered head to foot in shiny new skin, with patches of thick blonde hair that had survived the fire, the short, thin sorcerer Aristea and

Renatus had found disguised within shadows had fine, dainty features and a pierced ear. Renatus's golden chain had been removed to clothe him in a grey jumpsuit and had been rewrapped around his arms and torso.

Renatus let himself into the room and Emmanuelle followed closely. They had become friendly very quickly, Anouk observed privately. The pair had rarely spoken more than to acknowledge each other before the Academy had started, and now they seemed as tight as... well, their new relationship was like Anouk's with Glen.

The dainty man on the mattress turned his attention from his ceiling to his captors. His gaze clung to Emmanuelle.

'You can call me Saul,' the man said without prompt. His English was clear; his accent placed him as being European, perhaps somewhere to the north. Belarus? Lithuania? 'You must be the lovely Emmanuelle my friend Jackson speaks of.'

'You mean your friend who left you behind to be caught by the White Elm?' Emmanuelle asked scathingly. Saul, who was still lying down and bound with the golden chain, made a shrugging movement.

'I didn't say he was a good friend.'

'Where is he?' Renatus asked. Saul dragged his gaze onto the Dark Keeper.

'Wouldn't know.'

Emmanuelle leaned over the bed and ran her hand through the air above the occupant, feeling for infections and other signs of bodily illness. She leaned closer to check his furthermost ear and Saul made a sudden movement to sit up, cheekily trying to kiss her. Anouk felt a snap of annoyance within herself and automatically moved closer to put Saul in his place; Renatus, too, twitched as though he were about to step in. But Emmanuelle was quick enough. She caught him by the chin.

'Don't try us,' the French sorceress advised.

'Saul Matheson, born 1969,' Qasim said from the doorway. The other councillors looked back at him as he recited a case file he must have once read. Scriers had the ability to develop a photographic memory, and given enough time to review his own thoughts, Qasim would be able to reproduce and remember the entire document as he saw it. Less experienced scriers like Renatus, and totally beginner ones like his new apprentice, had a long way to go before they found themselves possessing this skill. 'Arrests in 1992, 97, 98, 2001 and two in 2002, for various assaults, battery, kidnapping, fraud, blackmail... Nothing much stuck. Most recently, wanted by Interpol for high-level involvement in human trafficking.' He glanced between Lord Gawain and Renatus. 'Approached us last year for protection. Denied.'

'Why do you think I went looking for Lisandro?' Saul asked with a humourless smirk.

'Things might have turned out better for you if you hadn't,' Anouk suggested, looking around at Saul's new surroundings. Crimes against humanity were the mortal world's jurisdiction, and generally speaking, the White Elm would have simply branded him and turned him over to a police agency like Interpol. His involvement in political kidnapping, however, made him the White Elm's to prosecute, and that made it unlikely he would ever again leave this building.

'So... we're looking at scum,' Emmanuelle commented, and Qasim nodded.

'Essentially, yes.'

'I know what you want from me,' Saul said to Emmanuelle. 'You want to know about your boy and your girl, sure – and I know nothing about that, so forget it – but more than that, you want to know whether I was *there*. And I was. I was there at the end.' He grinned, coldly, a smile that didn't reach the eyes. 'Funny, to meet you, knowing he died for loving you too much. Do you think about it every single day?'

Peter. Anouk knew this had to be about Peter, a former councillor and Emmanuelle's closest friend, who had been found dead several weeks ago, murdered by Lisandro for refusing to hand over the Elm Stone... the ring of power that now lived, plain and still, on Emmanuelle's thumb. When Qasim and Renatus had finally scried the murder, they'd both said it had been committed before an audience of Lisandro's followers. Saul, apparently, was one of them.

With a suddenness that surprised Anouk, Emmanuelle shoved Saul back onto the mattress. The captive gasped as his chains dug into his shallow wounds.

'You know nothing about me,' Emmanuelle whispered harshly, holding him down.

'I know you can't hurt me,' Saul mocked, too soon. Emmanuelle grasped the chain and twisted hard, ripping softer sections of skin even through his jumpsuit. Saul grimaced.

'You'd be surprised what I can fix,' she said. Anouk glanced at Lord Gawain concernedly, but Emmanuelle took control of her own emotions and left the cell. She paused in the doorway and told Renatus, 'Don't call me back 'ere unless you've made a mess too big to clean up on your own.'

Anouk let the Healer past; Ivan was quick to accost her and suggest she check on another inmate of theirs, presenting with such-and-such symptoms... Anouk tuned out as they walked away. Now her fears would be realised. Now, Renatus would question their witness. Would he rip open Saul's mind and leave him a blubbering mess? Would he have Saul whimpering and begging for death? Lisandro's techniques were effective and cruel. Renatus, doubtless, knew them, too.

'Ooh,' Saul mocked quietly in his healer's wake. He smiled coldly at Renatus. 'Does she think you'll make a mess of me?'

'She must think you won't be cooperative.'

'She's right. I have nothing to say.'

'I think you'll find that you do.' Renatus shoved his sleeves back and clicked his fingers once – theatrics, nothing more, Anouk thought, but suddenly a massive snake was wrapped around Saul's midsection. The man stared at it for an instant,

'*I* have no idea what he's like?' Renatus repeated. '*I* don't know what he's capable of? Saul, do you know who I am?'

Saul nodded quickly as Renatus moved closer and the snake illusion began winding around his neck again. Anouk looked away and stepped back out the door; she'd had a sudden, unwelcome flash of memory – Lisandro, asking that same question to Peter, his friend, supporter and eventual victim.

'He speaks of you often.' Saul's voice was jagged now as his breaths came faster and faster, and the snake began constricting. Anouk resisted the urge to look back at her colleagues. *Lisandro speaks "often" of Renatus?*

Do you really want to know? Glen asked, sounding tired even as a voice in her head.

'And you think *I* don't understand him?' Renatus leaned over Saul, gently stroking the python's smooth scales. 'I'm the most qualified person alive to tell you what Lisandro is really like.'

Alarm bells went off in Anouk's head. She was going to ask Saul to elaborate on what Lisandro had to say about the new Dark Keeper, but he did it anyway.

'He calls you a *problem*,' Saul spat, clearly terrified. The snake was fully wrapped around his neck now, and tightening its coils. 'He says... He says everything would be different if you were out of the way. But when we suggest, "just kill him", he only laughs and tells us no.' He gasped and struggled, and his next words came in a rush. 'I thought, maybe, it must be you – our informant within the

White Elm, the Friend he speaks of. He doesn't give us a name... Just the information.'

Anouk's insides felt suddenly cold. There it was, hard proof, that someone within her beloved council was leaking information to their enemy. Her head told her it was Renatus. He was the logical conclusion. However, her heart told her to trust in Lord Gawain, and Lord Gawain both loved and trusted Renatus, so she would wait.

'Saul, if you had been actually listening to Lisandro, you would know that he trusts me even less than he likes me,' Renatus said, his tone short. Saul could not answer; he was utterly convinced that he was being choked. 'Imagine how happy he's going to be with you when he learns that you gave up his secrets to me – his *greatest secret*, you say, although I doubt that – all because of a little snake?'

He clicked his fingers and the snake dissolved like smoke. Saul drew a deep and grateful breath. Anouk overheard Renatus's thoughts and knew he was finished; she gestured for the guards with the brand. They slipped into the cell as she stepped out, and Renatus followed her to the doorway.

'Lisandro is playing this one close to his chest,' Renatus murmured to the other councillors as the guards unwrapped the golden chain from Saul's shoulders. 'He's not sharing information further down the chain than he needs to.'

'It would be Lisandro's way to keep the power of information to himself,' Qasim agreed softly.

'So Saul is just following orders? He mightn't be as at-fault as we thought,' Lord Gawain suggested cautiously. Renatus shook his head.

'He knew exactly what he was doing,' he argued quietly. 'He just didn't know why. It didn't worry him. He-'

He froze and turned abruptly back into the cell. Anouk leaned to see past him. Saul was sitting up now, with the help of the guards who were pulling his jumpsuit aside to expose the back of his shoulder. Saul's dead, dark eyes were staring sightlessly at Renatus.

'Stop,' the Dark Keeper ordered the guards. 'He's doing something. What's he doing?'

Anouk wasn't inside the room so she couldn't detect any magic, but the guards had their hands on the captive and would be able to feel if any magic were moving through his body.

'He's not doing anything,' one guard said, staring hard at Renatus.

'Ah, I should have known,' Saul said now, still staring with unfocused, dark eyes. 'Of course it was you. And now that you've played your part and I've played mine, it's time, is it?' He smiled his cold smile. 'You'll see Lisandro again, I'm sure. Tell him about the little girl, the one who sees through illusions.'

Anouk saw the tightening of Renatus's usually expressionless face and felt Qasim, beside her, tense worriedly. Both scriers, whether admittedly or otherwise, felt protective of Aristea. Anouk knew that was who Saul was speaking of, but found it hard to care in light of what he was *really* saying.

'Saul, what are you talking about?' Lord Gawain asked, a tiny waver in his voice betraying his concern and his fear.

The prisoner did not turn his gaze from the Dark Keeper, but his eyes did seem to focus and his smile grew colder.

'Renatus, Lisandro has chosen well for this task,' Saul said. 'We all have our parts to play, so play yours now and kill me.'

Anouk's stomach dropped and she told herself to run forward to stop it, but instead she found herself backing up. As though punched by an invisible fist, Saul was suddenly thrust back into the stone behind him. The guards flung themselves away, brand out like a pike, as the prisoner seized once and gasped loudly, then lay still.

Everything went crazy. Viktor turned and ran up the hall, shouting in Russian for backup. Glen raced back to the first cell, to protect him if need be. Renatus turned helplessly to the other councillors, for the first time in Anouk's experience looking shocked and, in so doing, looking *young*. Qasim slid into the cell with his wand out at Renatus's throat and the two guards unsheathed their other weapons and pointed them at the same obvious perpetrator. Lord Gawain turned away, pressing himself against the wall, apparently hoping it would all just go away. In the confusion Anouk tried to enter the cell but hit something invisible. Rubbing her shoulder, she tried again to get inside and found the obstruction gone. A temporary ward, she realised, one of the many protective measures taken by this institution to keep prisoners in and accomplices or assassins *out*. It hadn't helped in this case when the attacker was already inside.

Anouk had the foresight to call for Ivan and Emmanuelle, not that she could do much now for Saul, and went into the cell. She avoided looking at Saul – the *body* of Saul, anyway. He was dead, eyes open and crossed, tongue hanging out of his mouth. Awful.

And the killer...?

'It wasn't me,' Renatus insisted, keeping still against the wall, head high to keep a good distance from Qasim's wand tip. 'I did nothing. Qasim... No, Qasim, check him, check Saul, there won't be a trace of me on him.'

'For *her* sake, you'd better be telling me the truth,' Qasim snarled. He jerked his head, indicating for Anouk to take over watch of Renatus. She lifted her leg and pulled free the knife she kept in her boot. Growing up in paranoid Valero, Anouk never went anywhere without a blade. Normally it was useless, and Glen teased her about it sometimes, but today she was glad. She held it in her practiced grip at Renatus's neck where she could act quickly if he acted against her first. Which he easily could – he'd killed Saul so unexpectedly; she needed to be alert and ready for anything from him. Qasim and one of the branders checked over the body. Emmanuelle and Ivan burst in, both white.

'Let me,' Ivan offered, noting what Qasim was trying to do. He withdrew a thin wand and began tracing sigils in the air, seeking the source of the magic. Ivan was one of the rare Valeroans who was born a Crafter, able to manipulate magic at its most essential level. He finished drawing and flicked his wand to close the spell: the last spell's energetic signature lit up a ghostly blue.

Saul's chest was splashed with the translucent blue glow, and, suspended in the air, a string of blue light – the spell's trajectory – connected him with the wall beside Renatus, which was bathed entirely in mottled, swirling shades of blue.

Had he pulled energy from the very fibres of this structure?

'There's no trace of you, as you said,' Qasim told Renatus, gruffly, but Anouk did not lower her knife. That meant nothing to her. Spells could be covered up. 'There's no trace of anyone.'

'How can there be no trace?' Emmanuelle demanded, kneeling beside the deceased prisoner and checking him over. She cast a dark, impatient look over her shoulder. 'This man is dead. It is as if 'e 'as been electrocuted. 'is internal temperature is...' She shook her head and went back to her examination, apparently lost for words. 'I 'aven't seen this before. What 'appened?'

'He started talking to Renatus about roles and seized up and died,' Qasim summarised. Anouk narrowed her eyes and looked to him, annoyed with the information he left out, but Glen, down the hall, overheard it in her head and added, to her, *That's all we really know.*

He would say that. He would give the unbiased perspective.

I think we can infer the rest, she replied. Her short blade did not waver from beside Renatus's neck, and he did not move. She thought he was the type to fearlessly push her threat aside, but either she had him all wrong or he was too shaken by the events to act his usual self. She herself could hardly believe it. Renatus was the council's loose cannon and she'd always assumed he'd eventually implode and do something like this, but *in front of everyone* seemed out of character for someone so intelligent and cunning.

'The power that killed him came from where your interrogator stood,' one of the branders spoke up, gesturing to the wash of blue light that glimmered on the wall and in the air between the Dark Keeper and the dead prisoner.

'I didn't do it,' Renatus said again. 'I *know* it wasn't me.' As if it could be him by *accident*.

'I don't think it was you,' Ivan said slowly. He looked extremely unsettled. He motioned for his guards to stand down and moved to closer inspect the wall beside Renatus. The blue glow was slowly dissipating but the concentration of light on the wall was definitely attention-grabbing. 'This is very worrying. Lord Gawain,' he called, and the old Seer came in, looking cautiously relieved. 'We have a terrible problem. This trace,' he indicated the light, 'has been wiped clean of an energy signature. We cannot determine its creator.'

'But we have determined its point of origin,' Anouk pointed out. 'We all saw – there was no one else here.'

'This is a huge manipulation of magic. The magic *within the walls of my prison* has been manipulated here. My *own prison* has been bent for someone else's protection. If this was not your man's work, and I desperately hope it was, then there was someone else in here with him, unseen, and he is about to become the first sorcerer to break in and out of my prison in history.'

At that, Anouk finally did lower her knife.

chapter seven

The following weekend felt like the worst one of my life up to that point, although I'd undoubtedly experienced worse and just forgotten about them.

I learned late on Friday that my school life was actually the less horrible of my two parallel existences of student and future apprentice. Qasim grabbed my arm as I reached for a book from a high shelf in the library.

'I want you to read this,' he said in a low voice, showing me a small book. It was old but not ancient, with a tatty dust cover and some pages peeping out of one end, indicating that they were coming away from their binding.

'Is it homework?'

'Not for class,' he answered. 'Consider it *personal reading*. It's quite informative, especially regarding your master's position.'

I raised my eyes from the book's cover, which read *"The Facts Behind the Darkness"*, to meet his. I knew quite little about Renatus's role, except what he'd told me and the small section I'd read from that White Elm history book I borrowed from Anouk. Which I should really return, come to think of it.

'It's something of a controversial publication,' Qasim told me. 'It's no longer printed, and very difficult to find existing copies. Most of them were destroyed.'

'By who?'

'The White Elm Council.'

I blinked, surprised. The council had deemed this book unworthy of print or existence. Was it dangerous? Misleading?

'Why are you letting me read it, then?' I asked, slowly, because I really didn't get it. Qasim was a very high-up member of the council – the next Lord, Renatus had said.

'The information was destroyed because of the light it shone on the council,' he explained. 'The writer was actually a former member of the council, and broke oaths to distribute these secrets. However, you already know what we do and how we work, and I think it's important that you have access to information that is well-researched and from an unusual perspective.'

'Well, thanks,' I said, reaching for the book, still not really understanding why this warranted grabbing me in the library but not really wondering about these things so much anymore. He withheld it from me.

'You have until Monday, you remember.'

He was referring to my initiation. He was re-minding me that I could still back out if I wanted to. Hiroko was standing nearby, looking on, and I felt her gaze on the side of my face.

'I won't be backing out,' I said finally. 'I made my decision. I'm not changing my mind.'

'Of course not,' I heard Emmanuelle's voice say, firmly and encouragingly. Qasim released my arm and stuffed the book into the nearest shelf with a meaningful look at me. I read it loud and clear. We both turned to Emmanuelle and Renatus as they approached from the tall, thin door. 'Qasim.' Her tone suggested a warning. 'Hiroko, could you come with me? I have a ward-strengthening technique I think would help you.'

Having artfully redirected everybody else in the vicinity, Emmanuelle left, followed by my friend and the Scrier. Renatus moved to me and took my arm, less forcefully than Qasim had, and walked me through the shelves. I didn't question him; this was no weirder than Qasim's abrupt interruption to my reading time. We passed a pair of students taking notes from a thick old book and they looked up at us just as Renatus pulled me into a shelf. I instinctively balked; when he kept pulling, I closed my eyes and braced for the inevitable impact... which of course didn't happen. We walked straight through the wall of wood and books and into Renatus's office.

He let me go and I spun around. The wall we'd materialised through looked solid enough, and when I touched it, there was no give whatsoever. I pushed harder. Nothing.

'The portals are sensitive to my bloodline,' Renatus told me. 'They don't exist to other people unless I willingly pull them through.'

'That's so incredible,' I said. I hadn't had much chance to think on it in light of everything else happening, but walking through walls was really a pretty special talent and a pretty cool thing to tick off the bucket list.

'What did Qasim tell you?'

I turned back to Renatus and was surprised by the young man I saw standing in the centre of the office. Yeah, I'd known he was *young*, like, for a world leader, but until right then it hadn't occurred to me that twenty-two is actually not old at all. Maybe it was because I'd thought he was older and now that I'd deduced his true age my mind was reconstructing him to fit this new knowledge. Or maybe, and more probably, it was to do with the slightly shaken expression in his eyes and the fear he was only barely managing to keep from me.

'What happened?' I asked, my stomach immediately full of lead. I could tell just by looking at him that something terrible had occurred and if he looked that worried, I should probably be very frightened indeed.

'One of Jackson's men, the one you picked out of the shadows, was killed, while we were questioning him.' He watched me closely for signs of... I didn't know what, exactly. 'What did Qasim say about it?'

I'd already forgotten the book.

'He didn't. He just said I can still change my mind about Monday night. I said I won't be.' Strangely, this didn't seem to calm Renatus very much, which led me back to the other topic. 'I don't understand. How could someone be killed while you were there?'

'He was murdered. Executed. Lisandro's spy must have done it, but no one saw anything.'

'Wait, how?' I asked, raising my hands in confusion. The weight in my stomach was lightening. This was bad, admittedly, but didn't really affect me in the way it had obviously affected my headmaster. Had he seen the awful death? Was that why he was so jittery? 'I thought you said that place was secure. You said it was the most secure place in our world, so safe that even Lisandro can't get in.'

'I did. It is.' Renatus turned away and stalked to the window, exhaling sharply in frustration. I followed, a little bit relieved that he was moving out of his vulnerable mood. Frustration was not a new emotion for Renatus in so far as I'd observed, and I certainly preferred it. Frustration I could deal with. 'I don't know what happened. We were watching, there was no one else there, but then he was killed, and he was definitely *killed*. He didn't just *die*. Emmanuelle says his insides were fried.'

I considered the firmness in my Wards teacher's voice when she approached me in the library with Renatus. She saw and dealt with some pretty horrific things in her day to day working life, yet it didn't seem to weigh on her like this was weighing on Renatus today.

'Was it awful?' I asked in a small voice, not sure I wanted to know but feeling like it was the right thing to ask, in case Renatus wanted to talk about it.

He shook his head once, giving me all the answer I needed to that question.

'He was electrocuted, virtually,' he said. 'That energy came from *somewhere*, channelled deliberately by *someone*. The Valeroans say that their wards picked up on our energy signature as White Elm when we came into vicinity of the city, and there have been no other arrivals since Anouk and Glen delivered Saul and the other one last night. So... unless it was a local, which seems doubtful considering their allegiances and the harsh punishments Valero would serve... it had to be one of us. One of the council.'

That conclusion seemed totally out-of-court and shocked me.

'Who? You said you didn't see what happened.'

'I saw him killed. *Someone* killed him.'

'But you didn't see anyone,' I reasoned, not seeing the chain of deduction as clearly as he seemed to, 'so you can't be one hundred percent sure.'

'There was this big welling of power; everything around you reverberates when there's a big spell in the making,' Renatus said vaguely, staring out his window. Already he seemed more like his usual, mature, weird self. 'I don't know what happened. I don't understand how it *could* have happened.'

I was still so insufficiently informed that I said nothing, unable to make any decent contributions to his thoughts. I waited patiently for him to return from those thoughts; it only took half a minute or so.

'Aristea, I didn't do it.'

'I know,' I answered, surprised he would even imply I might believe that. For once his remark was totally out of sync with my thoughts. 'Why would you? He was already in jail. And besides, you could have done it yesterday if you wanted to.' He nearly had. I squashed the thought before it could form and redirected the topic. 'It's a shame that all Emmanuelle's amazing effort fixing him went to waste, though.'

'It is an amazing gift.' He paused again. 'Do you remember promising you wouldn't believe anything you heard about me?'

'Aye. Yes.' The book. Did he know? Should I mention it?

'Good. Because no matter what anyone else says, I really didn't do it.'

Had he been accused? He must have been. Where else would this be coming from? I folded my arms. This was the guy who'd mended my watch just a few hours ago. This was the councillor who'd crossed off seven names from his list of potential apprentices and decided to pick *me* as his student. This was the man Emmanuelle had stood up for before the whole council last night. I didn't have any evidence to the contrary at this point and so I absolutely refused to accept that *this man* could have done what he was describing. Renatus was going to be my master. He couldn't be my master *and* a murderer. Not possible. More than anything yet, this internal denial cemented my certainty.

'I really know,' I said. 'Who said you did?'

'I'm on suspension,' he told me, and my mouth dropped open. 'I was closest to the source of the spell that killed the prisoner so I'm under investigation.'

'Someone accused you?!' I asked, shocked. I didn't know the White Elm *did* suspensions. It certainly hadn't occurred to me that Renatus could be *suspended* in the days leading up to my initiation onto the council. Selfishly I wondered how this would affect me. Immediately I felt bad for thinking this and tried to stamp the thought out before Renatus could overhear it, but the effort was in vain.

'It shouldn't impact on you much at all,' he said. 'Except for the usual, the concerned looks and the leading questions.' He paused; I cracked a half-smile at him. 'Your initiation is to go ahead as planned – it's part of my suspension conditions, actually.'

I took a breath, still regretting that I'd had that thought. 'How does it affect *you*?'

'I'm on house arrest until further notice,' Renatus admitted. 'My access to usual White Elm resources is frozen. My White Elm duties and workload are being adjusted – my tasks regarding the running of the Academy are unchanged at this point; it's just my research and investigative tasks that are on hold. I'm also not getting paid, but, you know.' He shrugged and looked around the study. I got the drift. Missing out on whatever sum of money the council's accounts paid him to do this job was not going to hurt him. He'd probably do it for free if they wanted him to. Getting paid was a formality. 'I had to hand my wand to Lord Gawain.'

Again, I thought that this presented as more of a formality than anything else, because Renatus was the kind of sorcerer who could perform perfectly worrisome magic without the use of a wand. Lord Gawain taking it from him was just a show of the council exercising power over the case. It wasn't any kind of prevention or punishment.

'How long is all this for?'

'Indefinite,' Renatus answered. I raised my eyebrows.

'Did you tell them that's ridiculous?' I demanded.

'No. I took it. I wasn't in a position to argue.'

I shook my head, incredulous.

'Your initiation on Monday will be the deciding factor in the length of my suspension,' the headmaster told me. 'If I murdered Saul, Fate will know and the ceremony will fail. Fate doesn't tend to give murderers charge of minors. If I'm telling the truth, everything should be fine.' He paused again, hesitant. 'You can still change your mind, up until Monday night.'

Change my mind? 'I don't need to change my mind. Unless you're telling me to.'

'No. I don't want you to change your mind,' he said. He looked at me for a while. The youngness had gone from his demeanour. Back to business. 'Monday night's ceremony will go smoothly, I'm certain.' He paused as though finished, then added, 'Lady Miranda recommended not eating anything at all on Monday, suggesting that the bonding is quite physically taxing. But I'm sure it's just a precaution.'

'I'm sure,' I agreed, slightly sarcastically, slightly weakly, trying not to imagine throwing up in front of the whole White Elm council. I looked around the office for something to distract me from those thoughts. 'Well... I don't know what you were researching before you got suspended-'

'You don't want to,' Renatus filled in, and I didn't push that issue, even though as soon as he said this, I suddenly *did* want to know what sort of things he researched.

'-but I suppose now that you're banned from doing anything productive, you'll have a whole lot of extra time to do other things,' I finished. I gestured at a pink, sparkly notebook that rested at the very extreme edge of Renatus's desk, so glaringly out of place and unwanted in this very classical and masculine space. Three self-centred teen queens – namely Khalida, Bella and Suki – had dropped that in for Renatus to peruse just the other night. Apparently it contained a compilation of their suggestions for social events to be held for the students. I was quite sure Renatus had next to no interest in their suggestions whatsoever. 'You could catch up on some reading.'

'I could,' he answered dubiously, casting an un-inspired look over at the book. 'I have excuses in mind but I suspect I'll run out of them eventually. Three days is a long time.'

'It's really not,' I assured him, trying to be gentler. I'd meant it teasingly but I knew also that having some of his responsibilities taken from him, not to mention being accused of and investigated for a criminal act, was at least a little bit upsetting for my headmaster, even if he didn't really show it. It had to be. 'It'll be Monday before you know it.'

'I'm sure,' Renatus replied in the same tone I'd used before. He made the door open for me so I could leave, but I had just one more thing to say.

'This is all going to go away,' I said with certainty. 'For you, and for me. The girls will stop being catty, the council will lay off you for choosing me and this suspension of yours will be dropped after Monday. Maybe sooner. You didn't do anything wrong and that'll come out.'

Renatus didn't answer, but I could tell from his posture and energy that he was pleased with my surety. I knew what he knew: it's nice to be trusted and liked.

Waking up in a room of people who hated me was *not* nice, conversely, but I was going to have to get used to that, because Xanthe and Sterling made no attempt to look at me or speak to me all morning after we woke up on Saturday, even as we all made our beds and got ready for breakfast. It was like an invisible line had been drawn down the middle of the room, separating their half from mine and Hiroko's. I was so, so glad now that Hiroko's bed had been situated on my side of the room. Fate must have known that this was in store for me when it decided to let her key fit the wardrobe beside mine.

When the other two left, I sat on Hiroko's bed and told her about what Renatus had told me the day before. She looked quite taken aback with the idea of Renatus on suspension and under investigation by the council, but I failed to feel the same concern. They weren't going to find anything. It was a waste of time and resources. I'd seen them arriving last night for yet another circle, and I didn't know how long it had stretched out for, but the energy of the house felt the same as yesterday, so nothing big and world-changing had impacted on the White Elm.

'Are you still going to accept the apprenticeship?' Hiroko asked. Not judgementally, more curiously.

'Of course I am,' I said. 'It's such garbage. It will blow over soon, you'll see.'

I didn't know where I got my certainty from, because my knowledge of the White Elm's procedures and the severity of their processes was vague. I just had this feeling in my gut that Renatus's suspension was a tiny bump in the road. I suppose my distance from that situation allowed me to belittle it, while I also had the excuse of being distracted by my own problems.

'Oh my goodness, look,' Bella stage-whispered as she entered the dining room that morning, loud enough that I knew I was meant to hear. I stared hard at my cornflakes, concentrating on shovelling spoonfuls into my mouth as gracefully as I could manage. I tried not to listen but I heard it all anyway. Apparently I wasn't forgiven for Sterling's misunderstanding, and other people were jumping on that bandwagon.

'Ugh, look at that – do you suppose she thinks she looks good?' Khalida asked of her friends, and they all giggled. I resisted the urge to quickly inspect my outfit. I looked *fine*, and I didn't want their approval, anyway. 'That jacket is so second-hand shop. Look, it's falling apart.'

The safety pin on the shoulder was a brooch; it was not holding the jacket together.

'Those stockings are awful – purple stockings? Eww,' Bella added.

'Oh, those shoes... yuck...' Suki mentioned, infuriating me. She had been wearing similar shoes not one week ago. I doubted I'd be seeing her in those again anytime soon. She wouldn't want to look as though she was dressing like me.

It occurred to me that I could just wear outfits like theirs every day, and eventually the trio would run out of unique and trendy outfits and would be forced to wear frumpy and boring clothes in order to avoid dressing "like me". That would totally serve them right.

'It must take a lot of effort to put together an outfit as ridiculous as that,' Khalida concluded as they took their seats down the far end of the table. I let my spoon fall slowly into my cereal, breathing out slowly and trying my best not to feel hurt. I felt their satisfaction and pleasure at my silence – what exactly did they think they were gaining by treating me like this? What had I actually *done* to deserve their malice?

The internal urge to fight back (to stand up, throw my cereal into Khalida's hair and scream that *she* was the stupid one who, because of her own shameless flirting, had missed out on the opportunity of a lifetime that *I* had been lucky enough to snap up) was powerful, but Hiroko beat me to it.

'Aristea,' she said loudly, definitely loudly enough to be heard, while I instinctively ducked my head to stay out of sight, 'I am thinking. Sometimes when girls has unrealistic expectations of unavailable men, they project their insecurities onto other girls to convince themselves it is other people's fault that he is not interested.' Everyone at our table froze with their spoons halfway to their mouths. 'So if someone must comment that she do not like your clothes, perhaps it is because she's worn through her entire wardrobe since she arrived and the headmaster has never looked at her any differently *because he doesn't date teenagers.*'

I heard several snorts of surprised laughter along the table but no one dared to say anything as Hiroko turned her unrepentant gaze directly onto Khalida and her friends. She glared back, but Bella, whose wardrobe was notably extensive, blushed and looked down. There really wasn't anything to be said in response, and no one else spoke up. I went back to my breakfast, calmer. Even though I had only one friend in the whole world, she was the very best one that anyone could hope for.

I spent my whole weekend with Hiroko. I'd hung out with her closely for six weeks now but was only just starting to see the attitude beneath her super-sensible and super-lovely outer shell. She glared openly at Isao and his friend as they walked past us in a hall, murmuring to one another. Their smirks disappeared immediately and they quickened their pace. When we watched the sunset from the front steps and two older girls inched past us, pretending not to see us, Hiroko smiled up and greeted them, asking if they were only pretending to ignore us because of Xanthe Giannopoulos's stupid story. Both blushed deeply at Hiroko's awkward and blunt questioning and mumbled something about not liking to listen to rumours. They hurried inside, and Hiroko and I smirked at each other.

Renatus mostly kept to himself all weekend, or sat in his office in deep discussion with Lord Gawain or Lady Miranda; when he did venture out, and joined the other councillors at the smaller table for a meal, I noticed that the hall was distinctly quieter. Students glanced between us curiously, and I overheard a pair of girls with a volume control problem further along the table wondering what had actually gone on to spawn Xanthe and Sterling's story. I took some comfort in that, realising that some people had brains and were able to look past a dumb rumour and think for themselves what other explanations might have existed. Some people were just intrigued, and I wasn't allowed to sate their curiosity with the truth because the truth was a state secret until Monday night.

The whispers and looks were persistent because they weren't allowed to be addressed, but with Hiroko they were bearable. After a walk in the drizzly rain on Sunday afternoon someone called out to me in the reception hall. I turned, and saw two boys struggling with one another, both grinning.

'Hey, Aristea!' one, Jin, I think, called, trying to restrain his friend. 'Con's been a little tense lately – do you think you could help him out?'

I recognised them suddenly as Addison's friends and realised what they were implying, and I felt my face heat up. For a moment I stood, frozen on the spot, because until now, no one had actually addressed me in their teasing.

'Ignore them,' Hiroko advised, deliberately loud enough that they could hear. 'I heard that those two boys were both turned down by Khalida in the first week.'

Stunned, both boys' jaws dropped, and when we stayed exactly where we were, they were forced to metaphorically back down and walk away. It wasn't nice to be so at odds with my peers, but it would be over soon, I reminded myself, and with Hiroko I just might survive this weekend.

Renatus was right. Three days could be a long time.

We were now met by Renatus's housekeeper, Fionnuala, who appeared from behind the staircase with big fresh towels.

'Look at you both, all soaked through,' she chided, wrapping our shoulders with towels. She did not say how she knew we were coming in, or even how she knew we were outside in the rain in the first place. She rested the back of her hand briefly on Hiroko's cheek. 'Just as I thought, completely freezing! Go and have long, warm showers, both of you, and for dinner make sure you have something good and hot. I've made pumpkin soup – I hope you like that.'

'Yes, thanks, I do,' I agreed immediately, while Hiroko nodded appreciatively. Fionnuala smiled at us indulgently, and disappeared through the door behind the staircase. Hiroko and I looked at one another and began our walk back to our room.

'She is very nice to us,' Hiroko mentioned as we started up the stairs. She used a corner of the towel to pat dry her dripping black hair. 'This is because she considers you now to be part of her family?'

'I suppose,' I said, although I hadn't realised that the bond between a master and apprentice was a familial one. It was a nice thought, though, I decided. It would be nice to be able to include another person in my very small family circle, and I was sure that Renatus liked the idea of having any family at all.

When we got back there we found our room was not currently occupied by Xanthe and Sterling, although it wouldn't have made much difference if they *had* been there, because they had decided that Hiroko and I had turned completely invisible and inaudible. They hadn't even looked at us all weekend, or responded in any way to our conversations or general presence.

Over dinner, Fionnuala beamed at Hiroko and I as we ladled pumpkin soup into our bowls. I loaded my plate with dipping bread, fried rice and chicken drumsticks, remembering that I wasn't going to be eating anything for the entirety of the next day.

The council had kept their distance from me all weekend except for that once exchange with Qasim,

Emmanuelle and Renatus on Friday night. There had been so few of them around since last week's mishaps, presumably on damage-control. Whenever I did see them, they seemed extremely tense, especially with one another. I alone amongst the students could recognise their sudden suspicion of one another, even if I couldn't really understand it. I thought of the way Renatus had tried to insist that Saul's death was caused by one of his colleagues, and the fact that Renatus himself had been accused. I remembered Thursday night, Jadon claiming that Renatus was responsible for Teresa and Aubrey's abduction. Why were they wasting time pointing fingers at one another? The real bad guy in this case was the one who died, and there was only so much sorrow I could muster up for someone who helped kidnap two people. I felt that the White Elm needed to pull itself together. It didn't occur to me that there were facts I was missing, just as the nasty girls who spitefully commented on my clothing were missing facts about my connection with Renatus.

After dinner we went to the library and wrote down our classes for the week.

'I hope Elijah will take my class again to the hills,' Hiroko said while we copied down our timetables. She tapped her pencil against the Monday column of the main timetable and I saw that she had her Displacement class in the afternoon. Mine was first thing in the morning, but I found it difficult to be excited about that. To my further dismay, I saw that my Tuesday was completely full of classes – that Spelling and Energies class with Jadon, Wards with

Emmanuelle and then Scrying. It sounded like I was going to need my rest after this ceremony, so I was going to have to make tonight's and Monday night's sleep count.

My plan to sleep well was foiled almost straightaway, because I really struggled to fall asleep that night. For hours after the other girls dropped off, I laid awake, staring at the ceiling and listening to their soft, slow breathing. Tomorrow could change everything – my whole life. I'd read that joining with another sorcerer as I was about to would make me different, give me greater powers, but did I really want to be any different from my friends and peers? Childish dreams of becoming a Scrier for the White Elm aside, did I want to be extraordinary? Wasn't it better, sometimes, to just blend in? Was that me? And aside from that, tomorrow was a big deal for Renatus. I'd not seen a lot of him over the last two days but when I had, he'd looked and felt pent-up and fidgety. House arrest did not suit him. So far the council had not dropped the suspension, as I'd thought they soon would. I wondered why. Did they have an actual decent reason for thinking Renatus was responsible for a part in a crime, aside from just proximity? Was I jumping into a situation I didn't belong in? Was this highly suspicious White Elm a council I wanted to be part of? I tried to tell myself that it was fine, unimportant, and that I should just sleep, but my mind remained active, unwilling to shut down.

Eventually I must have fallen asleep, because I woke the next morning feeling exhausted.

Hot water, as I'd tell anyone, is life-giving. The sharp droplets of my morning shower made my skin tingle, the heat woke up my nervous system, the steam opened my pores and seemed to clear my head; the whole cleansing process is like a physical removal of all the previous day and night's energetic grime in preparation for a new day.

I'd forgotten to bring clothes with me, so, wrapped in a towel, I returned to the dorm. Sterling and Xanthe carefully ignored me on their way out the door, and Hiroko smiled at me from her bed, where she was sitting cross-legged and knitting.

'I did not think I would like to be ignored like this, but now I think it is best,' she commented. 'I do not have to listen to Sterling discuss Renatus – have you noticed; now she does not say his name? You have saved us.'

I laughed shortly. Inadvertently, I'd forced Sterling to keep her promise and stop talking about Renatus, although I'd lost her friendship and her ability to even look at my face in the process. Fair trade? I didn't think so, privately.

'And Xanthe was not good,' Hiroko continued, 'so it is not a big problem she no longer speaks to us. She did not talk to me before.' She shrugged. 'It is good this way. It is obviously this way for a reason.'

I laid a few of my clothes across my bed and picked an outfit – black skinny jeans, black t-shirt, black leather jacket.

'So you think all this stuff was *meant* to happen?' I asked, returning to my closet drawers to find underwear and socks.

'Of course.'

'We're meant to be alone and unwanted? I'm *fated* to be known as horrid and promiscuous?'

'It is a challenge and seems bad now, but all that is, is meant to be.' Hiroko turned her attention to a missed stitch. 'Experience changes a person. You will grow from this into the person you must become. One day, I think, this will be clear to you, but now it is too close to see.'

Reflecting on her words, I went back into the bathroom to get dressed.

Breakfast was fast becoming an unpleasant but familiar ritual. Hiroko and I would turn up and you'd think a spotlight had been switched on, because people would suddenly glance over as if their attention had been forcibly drawn to us. Khalida, Bella and Suki would fix me with cold glares. They'd regained their confidence since Hiroko shut them down, and whenever I passed close enough to overhear them, they would begin discussing my outfit in loud and obnoxious voices. Today the discussion was focussed on my leather jacket, how leather is so old-school, how it did me no favours, how it's skanky, or tarty, or lame, or whatever, blah, blah, blah... Hiroko exhaled in frustration as she turned to give it to them, but I sighed and touched her wrist. I shook my head when she looked at me. Not worth the effort. I gestured to the line and followed behind Hiroko with my plate to get some breakfast, realising that I was finding the undercurrent of negativity less and less affecting each day.

'Aristea.'

Qasim was just leaving the dining hall, but paused as he was passing me. He beckoned me away from Hiroko slightly.

'Morning,' I said, feeling slightly wary. Was he happy with me today, or no?

'I'm not sure whether Renatus bothered to research it for you-'

'He's banned from researching,' I couldn't help but throw at him, 'because he's-'

'-but the ceremony tonight calls on some very old, very powerful magic, and the channelling of such energy can be quite overwhelming to the physical body,' Qasim carried on as though I hadn't spoken, keeping his voice low. 'During lesser initiations I've seen sorcerers stronger and more capable than you faint or collapse. If the ritual fails, and you are rejected as master and apprentice, the sudden departure of magic has been known to cause brief, but severe and violent, side-effects, such as seizures or heart attacks. I'm not saying it will happen,' he added, when my jaw fell open in horror, 'just to be prepared. Even very successful bonding ceremonies usually cause temporary weakness. Either way,' he said, taking my empty plate from me and placing it down on the buffet table, 'the day of the ceremony is a day of fasting.'

I'd forgotten.

'Alright,' I said with a small shrug, trying to metaphorically shrug off the insecurities that had suddenly arisen inside my head. 'That's fine. I guess I'll just be really hungry tomorrow.'

'I wasn't,' Qasim answered, already leaving. I watched him go. Hiroko returned to my side, her plate laden with scrambled eggs and bacon.

'What did he say?' she asked, and we began to walk back to the table.

'I'm not meant to eat anything today,' I said, ignoring the fresh giggles from Khalida and her cronies, 'in case I, like, throw it back up during the ceremony.'

'Why would you throw it?' Hiroko asked after a long pause, in which I heard Bella say loudly, 'Did you see that? Even Qasim thinks she should lay off the fatty foods.'

'No, I mean, vomit,' I explained to Hiroko, pretending I hadn't heard anything but her question. 'I don't think it sounds like a very nice ceremony. I don't want to be sick everywhere.'

'It will not happen to you,' Hiroko said, sitting down with me. I rearranged my now useless cutlery as she began to eat.

'Maybe this whole thing – Renatus, the apprenticeship, the White Elm... perhaps it's not right? Or just too much, too soon?' I wondered aloud, keeping my voice down. Hiroko frowned and shook her head, quickly swallowing her mouthful. I added, very quietly, the first worms of doubt niggling at me, 'You said yourself: Renatus is under investigation for some heavy stuff. Is that something I want to be involved in?'

'Stop,' she said, firmly. She pointed her fork at me. 'You cannot let those who are not supportive rule your decisions Khalida and other girls are jealous; Sterling is misinformed; Qasim is angry. The council is... I don't know. They all wish you to be doubtful. You *cannot*. You already made this choice, and it is right. They must not destroy your chance.'

'How do you know it's the right choice?' I asked. Hiroko didn't even hesitate.

'Because you made it already,' she said simply. 'The choice is made and now it is part of the Fabric. All of the past, it makes what is now. You should not try to undo what you already do. Done. *Have* done. That is not how to walk onward.'

Her answer kind of blew me away with its depth.

'Why are you so wise, Hiroko?' I asked, sparing her a quick smile. She shrugged, turning back to her breakfast.

'Because I must, or where would you be?'

I went to Displacement, and, unsurprisingly, it was lame. Despite having been actually Displaced, twice, since my last class with Elijah, I was still completely useless at it and didn't have the faintest clue how it was done. Thankfully, however, there was no one in the class who openly hated me, and no one used the outdoor opportunity to mock or humiliate me. When we were all finished failing at Displacement, Elijah cheerfully assured us that it wouldn't be long now until we saw some real improvement as a result of our hard work, and bid us a good day.

'And Aristea,' he added, and I glanced back. He waited until Willow had walked far enough away to not overhear. He looked so tired, I thought. 'Good luck.'

'Thanks,' I said, trying to smile back. A definite sense of nervousness had begun to build within me. It was only a friendly comment, but my imagination had taken hold and I was starting to see hidden meanings. Good luck – you'll probably need it. Be strong – it's not going to get better too soon. Don't eat – you might throw up while you're having a seizure because your body will be overwhelmed by the rejection of ancient magic, and, well, you could choke and die, couldn't you?

Later, Hiroko and I passed Garrett, who was standing in one of the library aisles reading an atlas, completely oblivious to the presence of anyone else. Hiroko glanced at him forlornly, but didn't try to get his attention as we walked towards the back of the library. I nudged her gently.

'So?' I asked softly. 'What's happening?'

'I have not seen him all weekend,' Hiroko reminded me. He'd studiously avoided us. Probably we had been gaining too much attention for his liking.

'But you like him.'

'I wish he would speak to me,' Hiroko answered, dodging the question artfully. 'I wish he could *look* at me.'

'He's just intimidated,' I said as we found our now usual seats. My stomach growled softly.

'Boys are so…' Hiroko struggled to think of the right word, and right then, Garrett wandered out of the aisle we'd spotted him in before. He was trying to walk and read at the same time, but when he tried to turn a page, he dropped the whole book. He hurried to catch it but missed, and looked around as he stooped to pick it up. He spotted us down the back of the library, and when I smiled and Hiroko gave a tiny wave, Garrett's milky skin flushed bright red. He nodded once in acknowledgement and quickly left the library. Hiroko sighed.

'Strange,' she decided finally. I couldn't help but nod in agreement.

In the afternoon session I had a history class with Anouk. Usually I sat with Kendra, I thought as I walked to my lesson, but today I supposed we'd both be sitting alone. Probably best; I could just sit there and worry and stew about tonight's impending ceremony in peace and near-starvation.

I was one of the first to arrive for the class. Anouk was sitting at her table at the front of the room, looking completely exhausted, much as Elijah had that morning for my first class. I waited just outside the door, thinking she hadn't noticed me yet. She yawned, and flicked her long hair behind her very bony shoulder. She was *so* thin. How does a person stay that skinny and remain healthy?

'Genetic gifts,' Anouk said, turning to look at me. The boy beside me looked startled, and I felt myself start to blush. I approached her desk and stood in front of it. 'You must learn to quell your curiosity and resist the urge to wonder. A question must be posed to another.'

'But I didn't say it,' I argued. 'I didn't actually want it answered.'

'The mind doesn't work that way. When you wonder something, anything, as a question, it is projected from your mind. Not far, and not strongly, unless your desire to know is strong, but still, it projects from you and if nearby, very advanced Telepaths can usually pick up such trains of thought.' She shuffled her notes and smiled tightly at me. 'You've been wondering what is happening with Renatus's suspension. I have heard it from you over the past two days.'

I hadn't said a word to anyone except to Hiroko, but I knew we weren't talking about physical eavesdropping here. I nodded once, willing to admit I'd been thinking about it on and off all weekend and for parts of today.

'I don't understand why he's being investigated,' I said. 'He's one of you.'

'White Elm isn't synonymous with perfect,' Anouk said vaguely. 'We must cover all possibilities. Loyalties can be misplaced. Information can escape us by our traitorous thoughts. Our minds are only as safe as we make them.' She paused. 'Whatever the outcome this evening, you're about to be trusted with secrets and work worth more than you can imagine. Please – don't let us down.'

I glanced at the door. More people had arrived, and they were all talking and laughing. No one was paying any attention to me, or Anouk. I looked back at my teacher and found her waiting, looking me straight in the eyes as though challengingly.

I remembered that she'd voted "no" when asked if she wanted Renatus to train me to be on the council one day. She hadn't been aggressive about it, but she'd still said no, and since then my only interaction with her had been quite negative, last week during the "investigation" into Xanthe's lies. *She thinks I can't hack it. She thinks I'll screw up, or I'll fall for my master and ruin everything. That's what a weak girl would do.*

I stood up straighter. Elijah's encouragement hours earlier had terrified me, made me doubt I was doing the right thing. Anouk's certainty that I was not right for this life did the exact opposite, cementing in my mind my resolution. If it was the last thing I ever did, I would prove her, and Qasim, Glen, Susannah and Tian wrong, and I would show Sterling, Xanthe, Kendra, Sophia, Khalida, Bella and Suki – and whoever else – that they were wrong about me.

'I'm not going to let anybody down,' I told Anouk, surprised by how firm my voice sounded. She seemed surprised, too. 'I know I'm doing the right thing.'

She raised her chin a little but kept her emotions tucked away.

'Good,' she said simply. 'Keep your thoughts – and your heart, body and soul – to yourself, and we will not have any further problems.'

My peers started milling in, and I turned away, feeling like I'd just won a round. Automatically, I went to my usual chair at the back, placing my hand on the top of it just as another hand closed on the top of the one beside it. I raised my gaze to meet Kendra's.

chapter eight

The awesome feeling of empowerment of only seconds before evaporated. She looked at me for a long moment, then pulled her chair back and sat down quickly, never breaking eye contact. She took a deep breath, and I knew she had something to say. I waited, but she didn't say it. Did I really want to hear it, anyway? She could ask me to find somewhere else to sit; she could say she hated me. I pulled my gaze away and walked back to the front of the room. I found an empty pair of desks and sat down, staring at my hands. This whole situation just *sucked*. One day, I vowed, I'd be strong enough to just ignore it all. I'd be at peace with my lack of relationship with both Kendra and Sophia, and my stomach wouldn't flip with nervousness whenever I encountered either of them.

'Boys and girls,' Anouk began, standing and searching her desk for a stick of chalk, 'what can you tell me about apprenticeships within the White Elm?'

I looked up suddenly; Lord Gawain was meant to be talking about this tomorrow. A few people raised their hands.

'White Elm councillors pick a student between the ages of sixteen and nineteen and train them to eventually take their spot on the council when that councillor dies,' someone offered.

'They don't have to die for their apprentice to get a spot,' somebody else countered. 'After the apprentice turns twenty, the first place on the council to become available goes to them, so they don't actually have to wait for their master to die to get on the council.'

'That's correct,' Anouk affirmed. 'A master and apprentice can both be on the council at the same time, although because of the *usual* age gap, this is very rare.'

The *usual* age gap, hey?

'What else can you tell me?'

'The councillor has to choose a kid that best suits their skills,' a girl said. 'Like, there's no point in you choosing someone who struggles with telepathy if that's your gift. They pick the student they can offer the most to.'

'Yes. Councillors most usually choose students with gifts matching their own. Seers train young Seers. Displacers train new Displacers.'

'Does that mean that people like me have no chance of getting onto the council?' a boy with chocolatey brown hair asked. 'The only Crafter on the council is gone.'

We all turned to look between him and Anouk, waiting.

'Daniel, you don't have to be an apprentice to get onto the council,' Anouk said, turning her blank left wrist over. 'I wasn't. Only two of our current councillors were specifically trained for initiation onto the White Elm. The rest of us were recognised for our talents and skills and invited to apply for the positions. Crafters are always sought-after.' She handed the chalk to a student to my left. 'Can you write these points up on the board? Thanks. Keep shouting out everything you know about apprenticeships.' She turned back to Daniel. 'And Aubrey isn't *gone*. He's going to be fine. Yes, Kendra?'

I dropped my gaze back to my hands as Kendra began to speak.

'I just remembered some other stuff about the apprenticeships,' she said, and Anouk nodded encouragingly. 'Um, there's a bunch of old laws to keep it pure, like age restrictions, and don't the councillor and apprentice have to be the same sex?'

A few people nodded, possibly having heard the same thing, and I found myself sitting up and turning in my seat.

'No,' I said immediately, meeting a few gazes, including Kendra's. 'That's not a law. It's just the way it's usually done.'

'It's usually done that way for a reason, though,' Anouk said, her tone light. She wasn't trying to pick a fight with me or humiliate me, or at least I didn't think so. She was trying to get a point across to me, while preparing my classmates for Lord Gawain's news tomorrow.

'Only because it's assumed that a male and female can't be trusted to be alone together without having sex,' I said flatly, and a couple of people giggled. Kendra didn't, and neither did Anouk.

'That's so rarely true. I think it's unfair to just assume that two people would be so weak.'

'You may be right,' Anouk conceded, and turned away to ask the class to continue contributing what they knew.

We went over the whole bonding process, from selection and verbal contract through to the White Elm's ability to vote for or against the apprentice and then the setting of a date for the ceremony. Most of it I already knew or had personally experienced, so I sat in silence. I paid more attention when we talked about the ceremony itself, and what it entailed – the invocation of ancient magic, the selection of overseers to represent each party, but Anouk only briefly mentioned the bonding itself. I sort of wanted to ask how it happened, what went on, but decided against it, thinking it might make me look nervous. I was not going to look nervous.

But I was nervous, *so* nervous. I sat on the front steps of the mansion until Hiroko returned from her Displacement lesson, and we sat for ages, just talking. We watched clouds obscure the sun as it started to set and slowly the light left the sky pale and colourless. We went to dinner, and it was the same old routine of being ignored and disliked and, in my case at least, very hungry. Watching Hiroko dig into her vegetables made my stomach growl. It had gone a full twenty-four hours now since my last meal. The fact that her dinner smelt delicious didn't help either.

I resisted, though, and stayed in my seat even after Hiroko finished eating. A member of Renatus's household staff took her plate away and several people left the hall as they also finished eating.

The White Elm, I noticed, were dressed in their white robes. Other students seemed to have noticed, too, and spared them odd glances, but clearly did not understand the significance. Renatus was nowhere to be seen, much as he had been all weekend, but Emmanuelle smiled at me when I looked at her. She stood and approached me.

'The ceremony is in 'alf an hour,' she said softly when she was standing beside me, leaning over my shoulder, 'in the ballroom. It shouldn't even take an hour. Unfortunately, Hiroko, you cannot be present.'

My friend nodded immediately, but I wished she could be there. I looked at my watch and read the time as seven-thirty. I supposed I had better go and get ready... however I was meant to do that.

We went back to our dorm, but all too soon it was five to eight. I said goodnight to Hiroko and left her sitting on her bed knitting, while Sterling and Xanthe tried very hard to look disinterested and inattentive. I knew they were dying to ask where I was going, and I made sure I didn't give away any details in my talk with Hiroko. It was coldly satisfying to keep them in the dark.

The house was quiet as I walked downstairs. Apparently everyone else was in bed or hanging out in their dorms. I was the only one not curled up on my quilt talking and laughing with my friends before bed. I was doing a terrible job of fitting in here.

The reception hall was abandoned and silent, and the ballroom door was closed. I wondered whether I was too early, but gently opened the door anyway.

The whole council was already gathered inside the candlelit room. I paused for a moment, letting my eyes adjust to the darker space. The councillors were standing in their circle again, with two spaces between Emmanuelle and Jadon in honour of their missing colleagues. Most had their heads bowed and eyes closed. Praying? Meditating? I moved my gaze around the circle of white-robed councillors until I spotted Renatus. He looked strange in white, I thought, still standing in the doorway, unnoticed. Like Qasim beside him, Renatus had his head bowed but eyes opened, staring at the floor. He was going to be my master, I thought, finally going inside. This was it. I closed the door, and several councillors looked up at me.

'Please join us, Aristea,' Lord Gawain said, nodding at the centre of the circle. I moved there quickly, but stopped suddenly when I tried to pass between Elijah and Anouk. Magic I had not sensed until then was flowing between the councillors like a river. I couldn't see it, but when I got close enough I could feel it. Were they powering up in preparation for the ceremony? 'Come into the centre. It's very safe.'

I took a breath and stepped through. It was so weird. I felt the pressure against my left arm, like a gentle wind. My skin tingled all over, and then I was through the odd energy field and the feeling was gone. Magic was so incredible and so beyond my understanding.

Renatus met my eyes when I reached the middle of the circle. Was he nervous? Could he tell that I was? He'd fought so hard to make me his apprentice, and I'd fought right alongside him, against both the doubtful councillors and my doubtful self. Now, at the very last moment, was the very wrong moment to be having doubts.

Did I have doubts? I'd seen Renatus attack someone without concern for their life. Was that someone I wanted to be bound to? I remembered that my sister had told Emmanuelle it was okay and felt certain again. I wished my head and heart would work together instead of separately.

'Remove your watch, please,' Lady Miranda instructed me. Surprised, I did as I was told, and handed it over to her when she asked me to. I went back to the middle of their circle, rubbing my wrist and feeling naked.

'Blessed be,' Lord Gawain said, very quietly, and the other councillors echoed him. He raised his hands to chest height, and I felt the council's apprehension. 'As Lord of the White Elm, I call upon the Ultimate Powers to witness and bless this circle, and I offer myself and my council as conduits for those powers.'

The candles flickered, and the *feel* of the ballroom changed. Something new was here. The spaces between councillors shimmered slightly, and the stream of magic between Lord Gawain and Lady Miranda slowly became visible as a gentle golden breeze. I watched as the golden breeze flowed to Renatus, and then to Qasim, and all around the council to Emmanuelle. She extended a hand towards Jadon, though he was too far away to touch, like she was helping the magic to reach him. He reached back and the gold flowed to him and through him to complete the circle with Lord Gawain.

The candles went out but I hardly noticed, because the golden breeze became suddenly much brighter, illuminating the circle completely. I tried to look like this wasn't all overwhelming and a little scary. Renatus didn't look scared. He looked alert. I tried to emulate that same air.

'We have gathered today to bond together a master and apprentice,' Lady Miranda said, turning to look at Renatus beside her. No mention of the suspension or the investigation. 'The prospective master is a councillor of the White Elm, and so the student he chooses will be destined to one day hold a chair on the White Elm council. Renatus of the White Elm has chosen Aristea to train and educate. Is this correct?'

'It is,' Renatus agreed.

'Aristea has agreed to study under Renatus of the White Elm, to serve him and to one day succeed him as Dark Keeper on the White Elm. Is this correct?'

There was a long pause, and I realised it was my turn to speak.

'Yes,' I said before I could think about it. 'It is.'

'Renatus, join Aristea,' Lord Gawain instructed. Renatus did as he was told, moving to stand to my left. 'Though our council is incomplete tonight, the vote has been cast, and this union is supported by the White Elm council. Aristea has been welcomed into the family of the White Elm as a younger sister, and as a prospective equal at some point in her future.'

Welcomed was not quite the word I would have picked, but it would do, I supposed. The golden breeze still flowed around and around, and perhaps it was my imagination, but it seemed to be getting faster. Lord Gawain continued speaking.

'Renatus's choice has been approved by the council, and now we leave it to magic to verify and endorse the partnership. If it is fated to be, then it will be. We, the White Elm council, will act as vessels and voices for the great powers of Fate and Magic as needed.'

The breeze was undoubtedly faster. I felt my hair lift gently as the wind picked up at Lord Gawain's words, and saw the loose and long hair of Emmanuelle and Susannah flow over their right shoulders, propelled by the energy being received in their left.

'Aristea is seventeen years of age, and so her guardian has given permission for her to take part in this ritual and partnership. Is this correct?'

'Yes,' I said at the same time that Emmanuelle did.

'Did the guardian have anything to add to this ceremony?' Lord Gawain asked.

'Yes,' Emmanuelle repeated, looking to me. 'Angela said "make your own fate".'

The effect of her words was more abrupt than anything else yet. The golden energy visibly faltered, flickering like a faulty lamp, and as it recovered, a spurt curled away from Emmanuelle's right side and to me. I jumped but it was faster. The energy flowed through my body just briefly, but it was the most electrifying, invigorating feeling I had ever experienced, like fifty hot showers all at once. I closed my eyes. My heart and mind blossomed like a flower, and visions came to me. I could see everything Fate had in store for me, happy and painful, and knew I was going to be okay. Some things could not be changed, but not all those things were bad, very few in fact. Good things awaited me on this path. Everything else was up to me.

The gold faded, and I battled to hold onto the images of those events and people I could not avoid no matter what choices I made. The face of the man I would love one day, the name of the apprentice I would train (*You! No way!*), the birthday of my firstborn nephew... But it was like grasping sand; I couldn't hold it, and every little picture and feeling trickled away. It wasn't for me to know now, and less than a second later I knew nothing of it, not even *what* I'd experienced. I just knew I was finally sure that this path was right, and I'd been given undeniable proof, although I couldn't for the life of me remember it.

So that's what it felt like to channel Fate.

'Aristea?' Lord Gawain said, his tone concerned and enquiring. I could see in his face that this was unexpected. 'Are you alright?'

'I'm perfect,' I said. I was smiling uncontrollably. Lord Gawain smiled back, more tentatively.

'Entering into such a partnership is a great responsibility,' Lady Miranda took over, 'and it is important that both parties uphold their obligations. Therefore, each party is to select a witness to oversee this ceremony and to ensure that duties are fulfilled. Aristea? Who will you choose to witness this ceremony and to hold Renatus to his responsibilities to you?'

I'd heard of this part but hadn't given it any thought. I had to choose someone who would essentially police my apprenticeship, and who had the power to remove me from my master if he overstepped or did not meet his role. It didn't really seem that important now – I knew it was all going to be fine. I looked around, but there was only one logical answer, one person in the circle I really knew or connected with at all.

'Emmanuelle.'

She smiled at me, encouraging as always. She looked so pretty, lit by the golden stream of magic flowing around the circle. It was bright again, and getting faster still.

'Renatus, who will you choose to witness this ceremony and hold Aristea to her responsibilities to you?' Lady Miranda asked.

Renatus didn't pause or wonder like I had.

'Lord Gawain,' he said straightaway. The old Seer tried not to smile, but I could see how pleased and proud he was. I glanced back at Lady Miranda as she began to speak, and unconsciously took a half-step backwards when I saw her withdraw two daggers from the pocket of her robe.

'Emmanuelle; Lord Gawain; you have been selected by the parties to represent their interests
throughout their apprenticeship,' she said, apparently not noticing my sudden movement. No one else
seemed alarmed as she held out the sharp, shiny
blades to display them to the circle. The councillors
in the circle stared at the blades, clearly focussing,
and Lady Miranda let the daggers go. Instead of
falling to the floor, as normal gravity might have had
it, both blades remained in the air, prone, pointy end
down. I stared. 'If you accept this role, you will have
the joint responsibility of supporting and policing
this partnership. Do you understand?'

'Yes,' they both said. The gold was definitely
glowing brighter.

'Will you allow Fate to work through you to
bring this apprenticeship to be?'

Instead of answering immediately, Emmanuelle
broke away from the circle, leaving a huge gap
between Tian and Jadon, and crossed to stand before
the floating knives. Lord Gawain extended a hand
and grasped the handle of the nearest dagger, and
she wrapped her ringed fingers around the other
one.

'Yes,' they repeated together, and took the
blades. They turned to face me and Renatus.
Everyone still in the circle, the eight that remained,
bowed their heads and closed their eyes. Lord
Gawain extended a hand to Renatus, taking the
younger councillor's right wrist when it was offered
in return.

'Renatus, tonight I speak for Fate when I make you a master,' he said, pride clear and obvious in his voice. Despite everything he'd said on Thursday night about disappointment and being let down, despite whatever Renatus had done to be accused of murder on Friday, he was as proud of Renatus as he would be of his own son. 'Will you pledge your mind, heart, soul, power and blood to your role and to Aristea?'

'Yes, I will,' Renatus said, looking only at me as Lord Gawain raised the dagger ritualistically.

'You understand that in the event of your death, Aristea will be placed under my care until I can find a suitable master to complete her training?'

'Yes, I do.'

'You understand that any breach of your role will result in Fate withdrawing your power from you, and that Emmanuelle at any point may act for Fate?'

'Yes, I do.'

'Then tonight, Fate and I make you a master,' Lord Gawain said, and brought the dagger down to trace a straight line across Renatus's palm. I stared at his hand as blood welled, and Lord Gawain closed his young friend's fingers over the dagger. Was I going to be sliced, too? No one had told me this, although I probably should have guessed that there was blood involved. It was *old magic*, after all, hardcore magic where a blood oath was really a blood oath.

Renatus uncurled his fingers and Lord Gawain lifted the dagger away, now bloodied. They looked now to me and to Emmanuelle, expectant. I glanced up at Emmanuelle beside me, a little scared. Was she going to hurt me? Renatus hadn't showed any sign of pain when his hand had been sliced open, but he was braver than me.

Emmanuelle smiled warmly at me, gently laying a hand on my shoulder. I felt warmth spreading throughout my body from where she touched. She took her hand away and held it out to me, waiting. She meant me no real harm, I knew, and a little cut would heal. After a moment I rested the back of my left hand in her palm. This was it.

'Aristea, tonight I speak for Fate when I make you Renatus's apprentice,' she said. 'Will you pledge your mind, 'eart, soul, power and blood to your study and to Renatus?'

I recalled Anouk, only today, telling me to keep all those things to myself. I didn't glance at her. I looked only at the French Healer, who I trusted very much more.

'Yes, I will,' I agreed. Emmanuelle raised the dagger, but not ominously.

'You understand that in the event that Renatus is unable to complete your apprenticeship, you will fall under Lord Gawain's care, and if you choose to continue apprenticing, an appropriate replacement will be chosen by Lord Gawain?'

'Yes,' I said, although I couldn't really picture that happening. If an apprenticeship was really the kind of familial, close relationship it had been portrayed as, why would I want to replace a master who had passed away? That would be like replacing my dad, wouldn't it? Disrespectful?

'You understand that any breach of your role will result in Fate withdrawing your power from you, and that Lord Gawain at any point may act for Fate?' Emmanuelle asked, and I nodded.

'Yes, I do.'

'Then tonight, Fate and I make you Renatus's apprentice,' she said, bringing the knife down. I fought the urge to pull my hand away or close my eyes. She kept her eyes on what she was doing except to glance up at me just once, very quickly. She rested the point of the dagger on the heel of my palm, and flicked it back towards her. My skin twinged as a small cut opened, but it was only a centimetre or so long and I barely felt it. She gently pinched the skin around the cut, encouraging blood flow. As red warmth welled from the nick, she rested the dagger's point against my hand, reddening the tip. When it was appropriately bloodied to her satisfaction, Emmanuelle took the dagger away and ran her thumb across the cut. I felt a tiny tingle, and the cut stopped bleeding, although it was still open.

'Now Fate may speak for itself,' Emmanuelle told me, turning away from me to face Renatus. Lord Gawain stepped around her to stand before me. He took my hand and placed it into Renatus's upside-down, the back of my hand resting in his palm, which was wet and warm with blood. I tried not to think of how alarmed my neat-freak sister would be if she saw this. Even *I* should be worried, really, about disease and infection. I had an open wound, mere centimetres away from someone else's blood...

But Emmanuelle was a Healer – she would have healed the cut properly if she thought I could get sick. I glanced at her, and she smiled encouragingly, so I looked back to Renatus. I couldn't read him; I wished I could.

'I invite Fate to make its mark,' Lord Gawain invoked, and Emmanuelle repeated his words as they both raised their daggers again above our hands. As I watched, both blades glowed bright gold, like the circle of energy still encasing this ritual. Both witnesses lowered the daggers to rest the tips on mine and Renatus's upturned wrists. They let go of the handles and stepped back, and the daggers remained upright, held there by some unseen force. The blade's glow continued to brighten, and it quivered as though overwhelmed by the amount of power building inside it and inside the circle. Lord Gawain's dagger was essentially coated in blood, while the one Emmanuelle had used to cut me was only bloodied at the tip.

Slowly, the blade started to move. It didn't cut or even graze me; instead it acted like a pen, tracing an obscure symbol in blood. I noticed that the other knife was drawing on Renatus's wrist, too. Strangely, it seemed to be drawing the same thing. It looked sort of like a letter but not any letter I'd ever seen before.

When the knife was finished, it shook a little more violently and simply fell off my wrist. It clattered to the floor, and was momentarily joined by its brother. The councillors, whose heads had been bowed until now, looked up at the sound, and stared at the blades as the glow abated.

I wasn't sure what was meant to happen now, and I could see in Renatus's face that he had no idea, either. The golden wind was whipping around the circle now, audible like a real wind. My hair flicked around my face, and I sort of wished I'd tied it up. Streams of gold curled away from the ring, encircling those of us standing in the centre. It was gentle at first, but power was building again, and the wind started to howl. Lord Gawain and Emmanuelle stepped backwards to resume their places in the circle, tasks completed, apparently.

When the circle was complete (or as complete as it could be without Renatus, Aubrey and Teresa), the golden wind flashed suddenly, blindingly. I closed my eyes briefly, and heard a harsh ripping sound, and before I could open my eyes again, the wind was upon me, almost blowing me off my feet. It had come away from the councillors. I shuffled my feet back to get a better stance. My hand was still in Renatus's, and I felt his grip tighten. I turned my hand so I could grasp his wrist. I tried to open my eyes. I was surrounded by blinding gold, whirling ever tighter and closer to me, and the only other things I could see were my hair as it whipped my face and Renatus as the gold took over him. I felt the same golden force flowing through my body, and forgot every-thing. The invigoration was back, that truly alive and all-powerful feeling as I glimpsed things I wasn't allowed to know, things I wouldn't remember after tonight. I was free. I was free from my life, from my problems, from whatever was happening to my silly little body. It was like flying, like dreaming, like eating chocolate, like running, like scrying, like lying on a hill watching clouds...

My wrist began to tingle. What wrist?

My head started hurting, like it did when it was under huge strain. Why? Being part of the gold was no strain. Channelling Fate was so beautiful, so wonderful.

My cut began to bleed again as my heart rate soared. Blood? Cut? What was going on?

I remembered that I was actually standing in a ballroom, being buffeted by a golden wind and holding onto Renatus to keep from falling over, and barely an instant later, I felt the gold abandon me, all in a rush, and it was like my head split open.

The pain was incredible, and I'm sure I would have screamed, but the gold went away and everything went dark.

chapter nine

Jadon had never felt so fulfilled and alive. Well, he had, once before, the first and only other time he'd ever felt the flow of Fate through his body – his initiation onto the White Elm. But that memory seemed so distant and dim compared to this incredible moment. The presence of Fate grew and grew, and when it was ready, turned its attentions fully to Renatus and Aristea. They held onto each other as the whirlwind of Fate closed in on them, and Jadon sighed, the ecstatic feeling slowly ebbing but not dying. He found it very difficult to feel any concern about the two people struggling to stay upright, disappearing from his sight in a cocoon of golden light. He merely breathed, feeling good and content for the first time since... well, he couldn't remember anything bad right now.

The golden cocoon flashed super bright and silently exploded like a bomb, dispersing outwards to the walls of the room and beyond, not bound by physical boundary. Jadon looked away momentarily, and when he looked back, it was dark, except for pale moonlight streaming through the windows. Aristea collapsed to the floor, all the life gone from her in an instant. Beside her, Renatus stumbled, dropping to his knees and pressing his hands against the floor. His head hung listlessly, his arms shook with the effort of holding himself off the floor and his shoulders heaved as he struggled to draw enough breath.

Emmanuelle broke circle – she often was the one to do it – and ran to Aristea. Breaking circle was like turning the TV off and switching the lights on after a really engaging movie, and Jadon responded accordingly, blinking a few times and trying to come back to Earth.

'How is she?' Qasim demanded, crossing past Renatus without looking at him. 'Is she alright?'

'She's fine,' Emmanuelle said, as the other councillors came closer. She brushed Aristea's hair away from the girl's face and turned to Renatus. 'And you?'

He didn't answer right away. Finally able to feel normal feelings again (not that that was really such a great thing), Jadon approached Renatus, feeling concerned. He looked a lot like he'd been run over several times by a train, minus the track marks. It was slightly disconcerting to see someone in this state when you always imagined them to be invincible.

'Renatus, did it work?' Jadon asked, not sure what else to ask. He didn't really care whether he was alright, but he was curious about the ritual. He didn't know what he was meant to have been looking for during the ceremony. It had seemed successful enough to him, except for the effects on Renatus and Aristea, but considering he'd had his head down and eyes closed for the majority of the ritual, he couldn't be sure.

'It worked,' Renatus agreed, clearly exhausted. He raised a hand to his head. 'My head... feels horrible.' He tried to sit back on his ankles, and Emmanuelle took his wrist. 'I'm fine,' he said, pulling away, but she yanked it back. He didn't have the strength to fight her off. Jadon saw that his right hand was slit open across the palm, and had bled plenty. A messy, bloody handprint marked the floor where he'd placed it moments before.

'So 'eal it then,' Emmanuelle challenged. 'You're making a mess.'

Renatus visibly hesitated, then acquiesced. 'You do it.'

Too tired to heal himself? The most basic of magical skills? Renatus was the strongest sorcerer on the White Elm; definitely the strongest sorcerer that the council was even aware of, in their society or outside of it. The ritual must have utterly wiped him out. Emmanuelle enclosed the Dark Keeper's hand in hers. There was a dim glow, and when she took her hand away, his hand was healed and hers was wet with blood. She looked at him oddly.

'You feel different.'

'There's another person in his head now, re-member,' Lord Gawain said.

'What does that mean?' Glen asked, sharing a look with Anouk, the other Telepath. Those two were like one person in two different bodies after sharing thoughts constantly for a decade. Jadon wasn't sure he ever wanted to be that close with anyone. 'The suspension-'

'Glen,' Lord Gawain interrupted tiredly.

'Is he cleared?' Anouk pressed. 'Is he safe?'

'Of course he's safe,' Emmanuelle snapped at her older colleague.

'Fate has said its part and now it's our part to make a decision with that knowledge,' Susannah said finally. 'It'll be our choice. But not tonight's choice.'

'That's enough talk of that,' Lord Gawain said, moving to help Renatus up. 'Let's get them out of here and somewhere they can lie down and rest.'

Jadon, the nearest person, obligingly hooked the Dark Keeper's arm around his neck and pulled him to his feet. Emmanuelle and Lord Gawain helped, then stood back when he was standing. Jadon was surprised by how heavily Renatus leaned on him.

'Where to?' he asked. Qasim lifted Aristea off the cold floor and turned to Lord Gawain, waiting for a direction.

'Kitchen,' Renatus mumbled. 'Fionnuala... She'll take care of us.'

With a glance at Qasim, Jadon turned and started for the door. Renatus was unsteady and slowed Jadon considerably. His feet dragged on the floor and his usual aura of unimaginable power was hugely diminished. Energetically he felt like a mortal. Flat. Tonight would be a very unfortunate night to meet Lisandro or Jackson.

Jadon felt a heaviness in his heart at the thought of Jackson. Thinking of Jackson made him think of the ring on Emmanuelle's hand, which made him think of Teresa's brilliant illusion, which made him think of Aubrey, lying prone on Teresa's floor, which made him remember that they were far away and in terrible danger. And despite how strong and empowered he felt after the ceremony, there was nothing at all he could do about it.

Elijah held open the ballroom door while Qasim carried Aristea through it. Jadon looked down at his feet, struggling to ignore the memory of Teresa being carried unconscious from her home. Tonight was the fifth night without her and Aubrey, the fifth night without sufficient sleep, the fifth night without *doing* anything. They could be anywhere, in any horrible state, and he was here, half-carrying Renatus like a drunken friend after a party.

Not that Jadon and Renatus were friends. That would be a stretch, seeing as Jadon still blamed Renatus for what had happened on Thursday night (not to mention the Valero issue…). None of this would have happened were it not for Renatus and his stupid plans. The memories of Thursday night haunted him like ghosts, from Aubrey's failed spells and Jackson's obviously much stronger magic, to Teresa stepping over Aubrey to protect him and ultimately losing consciousness.

And her thoughts… Jadon had been lucky to catch her gaze for just an instant, which was all he'd needed to start conversing with her mentally. Her thoughts had been jumbled, panicked, but he knew she'd heard his voice in her head, and he hoped it had done something to reassure her. He'd heard her, too. He'd heard her assertion that Renatus was at fault for her plight, and he'd believed her, because he always believed her. It made sense in every way. But did that make it correct?

If he was honest with himself, the reason he was so eager to blame Renatus was the fact that he blamed himself, too, on some level. He and Aubrey had chosen to be present while Teresa made her ring, with the intention of protecting her against any malicious ruse of Renatus and Emmanuelle's. Ultimately it had been Emmanuelle's wards that had given Aubrey the chance to knock out one of his opponents, and had held off the attackers long enough for the rest of the White Elm to be alerted. Teresa's magic had protected her friends, keeping them hidden and safe.

Everyone had contributed, except for Jadon. He had just *stood there*. Worst. Friend. Ever.

Brought onto the council only half a year ago, Jadon had immediately found that, while the other White Elm were friendly and kind, they were unwilling to properly accept him into the fold. They never shared thoughts or theories with him, or asked his opinion. Along with Teresa and Aubrey, he was the new guy, and no opportunities to prove his worthiness of trust and respect were offered. Frustrated by the same treatment, Aubrey and Teresa had banded alongside him and in less than a year had proven themselves the best and closest friends Jadon had ever been lucky enough to have.

And in one night he'd lost them both.

When you're helping someone to walk, the hardest part is walking them down a set of steps. The kitchen was sunken, and Jadon nearly dropped his colleague trying to help him down the steps.

'Careful!' Fionnuala, Renatus's housekeeper, fretted, hovering nearby. 'Is he alright?'

'I'm fine,' Renatus said again, though his voice sounded very much the opposite. Jadon led him to a chair near the bench Qasim had placed Aristea upon, and let him down. 'Thanks.'

Manners? Graciousness? Not something Jadon had expected to hear from Renatus.

'I'll make you some soup,' Fionnuala said, looking around helplessly as if she'd never been in this kitchen before. Renatus waved a hand no.

'I don't think I could eat it.'

'What about Miss Aristea?' Fionnuala asked, turning to check the unconscious teenager. 'Is she alright? What happened to her hand?'

Jadon glanced over at Aristea as Qasim turned her hand over to see the damage. Expecting a gash like Renatus's, Jadon was surprised to note that despite all the blood, Aristea's cut was only very small, perhaps only a centimetre across. Apparently Emmanuelle had decided to go easy on her favourite student, while Lord Gawain had gone all-out traditional and performed the cut just like it would have been done a thousand years ago.

'It's not her blood,' Renatus assured his adoring housekeeper, and she moaned when she saw his hands. Lord Gawain clapped Jadon's shoulder.

'You go,' he suggested. 'I'll stay with them.'

Jadon nodded and did as he was told, Qasim right behind him. He had long admired Lord

Gawain, but now that he was a member of the White Elm he found, just as Aubrey had, that being treated like a kid when you were meant to be an equal was extremely tiresome.

Especially when a possible, if not probable, murderer was being treated as a better and more capable man than you were.

Jadon had not been present in Valero when Saul was executed but knew, of course, what had happened. They'd spent hours afterwards in an urgent circle to discuss the implications. Anouk had demanded Renatus be strung up then and there; Emmanuelle had told her to do something inappropriate. Jadon would have been easily convinced of his colleague's guilt except for two things. One was Qasim's reluctant admission that he did not believe Renatus had any part. Qasim had absolutely no reason to take the Dark Keeper's side unless it was where he believed the truth lay, and Jadon found that a rather powerful decider. The other thing was the look on Renatus's face during the circle. It was the look of someone who had just had control swiped from him for the first time in a while. He was actually *afraid*, like a real person. Because someone had died in front of him and he couldn't stop it? Because the victim had named him as the killer in his last words and this would impact on the council's view of his apprenticeship? Who knew, but Renatus was *always* in control and he always knew what he was doing. With his impending bond with Aristea still a precarious topic among the White Elm, surely he wouldn't have done something so stupid right in front of them and not expected this outcome?

The evidence against Renatus had been deemed inconclusive so the White Elm had taken a huge leap of faith by suspending his duties and letting Fate decide whether the last Morrissey was worthy of Aristea's – and their – trust.

The golden light had spoken, and Jadon was quietly relieved, partly for his student's sake, because she was a nice girl, but also because a careless and overconfident Renatus was a better mental image than a murderous one.

The remainder of the council was waiting in the reception hall.

'Where's Lord Gawain?' Glen asked when only Jadon and Qasim exited the kitchen.

'Guess,' Qasim said, jerking his head in the direction he had come from. Glen looked away, clearly frustrated. Jadon could understand the feeling – it was the same thing he'd been feeling for the past four days. Once again, Lord Gawain was playing "Proud Daddy" instead of "Leader" and leaving what should have been the highest priority – finding Teresa and Aubrey – for yet another day.

'I think we've put enough time and energy into Renatus and Aristea for tonight,' Anouk said, her tone slightly cold. She turned to Lady Miranda. 'Can we *please* do something?'

Her home city had been infiltrated for the first time in living memory. She was in a complete panic. She didn't look it but Jadon could hear it in the way her thoughts flew wildly about. He imagined that

Valero, with all those panicked Telepaths connected to one another through a giant web of family ties, friendships and working relationships, would not be a pleasant place to be right now.

'Anouk, where do we start?' Lady Miranda asked, massaging her temples and looking over-whelmed. 'Qasim and even Renatus, despite his suspension, have been searching all weekend. As Lord Gawain keeps saying, Northern Ireland is small on the map but it's a big place to comb for a tiny, invisible beach house. The two greatest scriers in the world haven't been able to find a trace of Lisandro – what are we meant to do?'

'Something other than sitting around waiting for Renatus to feel better,' Anouk said, sounding angered. The ceremony had bolstered the energy of each of them, and they were all yearning to get out of the house and *do* something. 'We're strong, too. We're all gifted and strong. If Lord Gawain doesn't want to lead us, *you* do it.'

Lady Miranda looked extremely uncomfortable with the idea of making decisions without the Lord's stamp of approval, but after a very long, still pause, she nodded briskly. Jadon mentally checked on Lord Gawain, but the oldest councillor was paying them no telepathic heed whatsoever.

Whatever.

'Alright,' Lady Miranda said. She looked around at them all, and Jadon did the same. Even without their leader, their star or Jadon's two best friends, the council looked impressive. Qasim and Tian were powerfully-built men; Susannah's mouth was set in a determined line; Anouk and Glen were emanating displeasure and a need for action; Emmanuelle's arms were folded across her chest. Lady Miranda nodded again and said, 'Alright. Jadon, did you get anything from the families that would help us?'

After escorting Samuel back to his home on Friday morning, Jadon had met with Teresa's family for the first time. A large, poor Romanian family, many of the older family members didn't understand English, which sadly was the only language Jadon spoke. They had all been mortified to learn that their little Teresa, their pride and joy, their jewel, their high achiever, had disappeared without a trace.

'How did this happen?' Teresa's brother, the most conversant in English, had demanded of Jadon while his grandmother had sobbed loudly. 'How will you get her back?'

'Teresa was to take over guardianship of an artefact,' Jadon had explained, being careful with what he said. He couldn't give away many details. 'Somehow this fact was leaked and discovered by our enemies, and we became compromised. They attacked us,' he clarified, when the brother only stared, uncomprehending. 'She and our friend Aubrey were both taken.'

'How? Teresa is…' The brother looked around at his family, unable to think of a word. A cousin supplied it.

'Very strong,' the cousin told Jadon, nodding. 'Very clever. Very good magic.'

'She is,' Jadon agreed, wholeheartedly. 'She is outstanding. However our enemy is more experienced. Teresa and Aubrey were standing alone. When the enemy came in, she had only a moment, and she chose to use her magic to hide the rest of us. Our colleague, Emmanuelle, built shields.' Jadon used his hands to demonstrate a wall. 'Teresa was very brave. She saved me, and Emmanuelle and Samuel. We are looking very hard for her.'

'And you will bring her back to us?' the father asked, a desperate plea. Hope lit the expressions of every family member. 'You will find my daughter?'

Not knowing whether it was the truth, Jadon had found himself nodding firmly.

'I will,' he'd promised.

It had been a stupid thing to say, but he hadn't been able to stop himself. He might not ever find Teresa or Aubrey, and that thought scared him, but if he never found them it would be because his efforts had killed him, *not* because he'd given up.

Then he'd visited Shell. He couldn't decide which was worse.

Shell's tummy was big and obvious now, her first pregnancy, Aubrey's baby, and when she saw Jadon at her door she'd ushered him inside delightedly, eager to show someone the ultrasound photos. Shell lived a very normal, mortal life, so limited was her ability in magic that her housemates didn't give it a second thought when she told them she was a witch.

'The doctors say it's going to be a boy,' she'd said, positively glowing as she forced the black-and-white pictures into Jadon's hands. Aubrey's baby. Three months to go.

'Aubrey's missing,' was all he'd been able to say, and her response was an immediate and unconcerned, 'Okay.'

'He and Teresa are missing.'

Shell blinked, as though realising that he was not kidding. She averted her eyes to the picture Jadon still held.

'I think he'll be a redhead,' she said, retaining a normal tone, though everything she said sounded odd because of her mix of accents. Scottish. American. British. The occasional hint of Aubrey's French. 'Aubrey and I were both redheads as babies. That'll be so cute.'

'He was kidnapped last night,' Jadon added, and Shell just nodded, not looking at him.

'I hope he has his daddy's eyes,' she continued. 'Aubrey's eyes are prettier than mine.'

'But I'm going to bring him back to you,' Jadon promised again, unsure whether he could fulfil it. He waved the photo briefly. 'Can I take this? I'll give it to him when I find him.'

Jadon struggled now to return to the present moment, to the reception hall where the council waited for his response.

'Nothing that would help us find them,' he answered. Lady Miranda nodded again, turning to the next person.

'Anouk, Susannah, take the east coast. Work your way north. You're looking for anything unusual, and any trace at all of Aubrey or Teresa. Keep me posted. Jadon and Tian, I want you to do the same on the west coast. Glen, Qasim... I don't know, just pick somewhere and look. Elijah, I know it's an ask, but I'd like Displacement policed across the whole country. If anyone teleports into, out of or within this country, I want you to know about it. When you can, I want you to trace and follow the wormholes... Can you do that? I know it's a lot.'

'It's not a problem,' Elijah said. Jadon tried not to feel too overwhelmed by the awesomeness of some councillors' gifts.

'If you have classes tomorrow, make sure you get at least some rest tonight,' Lady Miranda added, turning to Emmanuelle last. 'Emmanuelle, come with me to London.'

With a quick nod, Emmanuelle hurried up the stairs to change into normal clothes. Lady Miranda often did this. Invariably, the hospital in which she worked would be overflowing with patients, and she would bring Emmanuelle in, citing her as a French medic. A little magical persuasion, and nobody asked any questions, but lives were saved and cuts were healed and patients could go home.

Jadon thought that what Lady Miranda really needed was an apprentice, but she maintained that she didn't have time to train one right now. She was going to have to find the time.

Anouk and Susannah left, followed by Qasim and Glen, and after consulting a map in the library and working out exactly where to begin, Jadon and Tian headed out after them. Elijah finished his conversation with Lady Miranda and hurried to catch up with them.

'Isn't it amazing that a ceremony that takes so much out of its main participants can leave the rest of us so revitalised?' he commented. 'I've never seen anything like it. Our initiations weren't anything like that.'

'Perhaps it didn't really work?' Tian suggested as they walked down the stone path to the gates.

Jadon reached out telepathically around the ring of minds that made up the White Elm, past Lord Gawain and Lady Miranda and to Renatus. Renatus did indeed feel different. His mind was connected to their collective one, and also, by a thin, growing link to another, sleeping one. Aristea.

'It worked,' he said, certain. 'I suppose it's different from an initiation, though, isn't it?'

'Yes, very different,' Elijah agreed. 'We were added to a collective consciousness that already existed. We didn't compromise our identities; we progressed. Those two are changed forever. Their minds had to be broken open to be joined together. I doubt it was a pleasant process, and it's not over yet.'

'What about the tattoos?' Tian asked, touching his own wrist. 'When will they appear?'

'They usually show up in the first twelve hours following the ritual.'

Two people appeared on the dirt road outside the gate. Jadon was still too far away to see any distinguishing features, but one was much taller than the other. He reached his senses towards them but felt nothing but a void. They were shielded.

'Who is that?' Tian asked, squinting. Jadon shrugged and shook his head. The taller person was a man and the shorter one a female, but neither of the White Elm women who had left before him were that short, so he couldn't think for the life of him who they might be. Why would anyone but a councillor arrive here so late at night? And why would they stand so still, ten metres or so from the gate, and make no move to approach the house?

'Parents?' Jadon guessed, thinking of the sleeping students. Elijah looked back at the house, as though expecting to see a student standing on the front steps waving to their mom and dad. There was no one there. Tian's unspoken questions – *why would parents shield themselves? Wouldn't they make themselves known?* – escaped him and Jadon privately agreed. They continued down the path, cautious and curious. He had an unsettled feeling in his stomach. The incredible feeling left over from the ceremony did not make them any stronger than they were an hour ago.

They were closer now, and Jadon was able to make out some features. The man was tall, and well-built. Strong. The woman, or girl, was little, but with an adult shape. Her hair was loose and dark.

With a feeling that might be comparable to electrocution, Jadon recognised her.

'*Teresa*!!' he shouted, bolting to the gates. He heard Tian behind him, calling him back, but he didn't listen. His every thought was focussed on Teresa, standing just beyond those gates. As he got closer he was able to make out her face, her curly hair framing her cute features, her eyes on him, her mouth unsmiling. Wasn't she pleased to see him?

Relief coursed through his blood to know she was alive. He shoved a hand through his ceremonial robes and into the pocket of his jeans, and his fingers closed on the little silver key at the end of his wallet chain. Maybe she'd lost her key, and that was why she hadn't come in yet. Maybe they both had, she and Aubrey. Jadon's eyes flickered to the man right beside her, hoping, but a second glance confirmed what he'd already known. The man wasn't Aubrey. He was a stranger, though his face was vaguely familiar from somewhere.

It wasn't important.

Teresa was.

'Teresa!' he shouted again, unable to withhold a massive, goofy grin. She was safe, and alive, and her boyfriend and family were not going to hate him forever and ever for being part of the council that had lost her. She still didn't smile or move. Her eyes were locked onto his, and she stood close against the other man. Had he helped her escape?

That was when Jadon noticed the man's hand in her hair. At first he felt a spark of annoyance – didn't this guy know she had a boyfriend, and a best friend who would kind of like to be the next one? But it wasn't an affectionate, playing-with-your-hair, tugging-your-hair kind of touch. The man's fingers were tightly entwined in her curly brown hair, near her scalp. Control. Domination. The annoyance gave way to fear, and fear was joined by anger.

He had almost reached the gate, had his key out and everything, ready to run to her and save her like he should have five nights ago, when someone collided with him from behind, slamming him into the gate and making him drop his key. Elijah? How did he catch up so quick? Stupid question, Jadon reflected as he grabbed at the chain hanging from his pocket. Elijah didn't *run*.

'Jadon, *no*,' Elijah shouted, struggling to pin Jadon's arms. It might have been the fiftieth time he'd said it, but it was the first time Jadon listened. No, what?

'It's Teresa!' Jadon exclaimed, unable to understand why Elijah couldn't see that.

'It's Lisandro!' Elijah answered, shoving Jadon away from the lock to the gates. Tian caught up, but Jadon ignored him. He only stared through the gates at his silent best friend.

'Are you quite finished?' the man on the other side of the gate asked politely. Lisandro. Jadon had never seen him before, but now understood why he looked familiar. His was a face ghosting in the thoughts of all the older councillors, tied up in feelings of fear, betrayal, bitterness and anger. He'd abandoned the White Elm and begun stirring the public against them, slowly, quietly, insidiously. He'd taken two councillors with him when he disappeared. Peter he'd murdered. Jackson was the other.

'Let her go,' Jadon demanded, ignoring Elijah's call for him to keep quiet.

'I wish I could,' Lisandro said with a sigh. 'Sadly, this lovely lady has put me in quite a foul mood, and I'm not renowned for releasing hostages on bad days. Maybe we can come up with a solution, so she doesn't end up like Peter did, hmm?'

Jadon made a move towards the gate again, and both Tian and Elijah stepped forwards to hold him back.

'Whatever you do, *do not open the gate*,' Elijah hissed. 'That's him, *really him*, out there. It's not an illusion. It's not a vision.'

'Neither is Teresa,' Jadon snarled. 'We three, we can take him.'

'No.' Tian shook his head. 'He cannot pass through these gates but we don't know who else is hiding out there. It could be three versus thirty.'

'Boys, please, focus,' Lisandro drawled, shaking the fist that was wrapped through Teresa's hair. She gasped, her bound hands reaching for her hair and trying to prise his fingers apart. 'Let's focus on getting your girl back. Don't you want to know why I brought her here, so tantalisingly close to your front door?'

'Do tell,' Elijah said, folding his arms. Jadon pressed himself against the gate, wishing he could slide between the iron bars and go to Teresa. It wasn't possible, so he settled for holding her gaze and staring at her. Lisandro's shield was strong, dense, but with eye contact and patience, a powerful Telepath could listen and speak through any magic.

'I had our dear friend Jackson and some boys pay a visit to your little girl here, as you would know,' Lisandro said, his tone conversational. 'Jackson was hoping to catch up with lovely Emmanuelle, but sadly it wasn't to be. He thought she might have something of mine, a ring, and perhaps he's right. In any case, he saw what he was looking for on this young lady's hand, so he brought her and her young friend back to my place to stay for a while. So I wonder whether you can explain this?'

He withdrew a black velvet ring box from a pocket and flicked it open. Empty. The illusion had worn off, and it had taken Lisandro and Jackson four days to realise they'd been duped.

Well done, Teresa.

'Perhaps Jackson misplaced it?' Elijah asked coolly.

'No,' Lisandro disagreed. 'It was there. I held it, I felt it. Then I tried to put it to use and it wouldn't work, and then it vanished. Where is it?'

'I told you,' Teresa said, and Jadon nearly fell over with relief to hear her voice. 'It was spelled to Displace at a false use. It could be anywhere. None of us could possibly know where it went.'

'You're very sweet, trying so hard to throw me off track, but not very convincing,' Lisandro told her, dropping the ring box back into his pocket and lightly stroking her cheek. Jadon wanted to kill him. 'I happen to know that you're a very established illusionist – in fact, I have a friend who tells me your work is the best they've ever seen. Isn't that nice? I'm sorry your phantom ring didn't last. It was extremely convincing. Your acting, not so much.'

The shield separating Jadon from Teresa was slowly giving as he worked to pierce it. Along the ring of consciousness that was the White Elm, he heard Elijah alerting Lady Miranda and Emmanuelle, wanting Emmanuelle to stay inside the house and out of Lisandro's sight. Teresa and Aubrey were still invisible on the ring. How was Lisandro blocking them from the council?

'Where is Gawain?' Lisandro asked, turning his attention back to Elijah and Tian. He paid little heed to Jadon, which was preferable, because he didn't need to know what Jadon was trying to do. 'I think I need to take my complaint to management. Is he inside?'

'He's not interested in talking to you,' Tian said coldly, and Lisandro smiled in response.

'I have a point to prove,' he said, yanking on Teresa's hair and pulling her close against him. She cried out, but with effort kept her eyes open and on Jadon's. Right then, with a final mental push, Jadon was past the shield, and connected his mind to hers.

Teresa!

Finally, finally, a small smile of relief on her frightened face.

Jadon, she answered, her voice desperate and terrified in his head. *You're alright. I thought... I worried he might have taken us all. They have someone else – was it Aubrey?*

'What point is that?' Elijah asked flatly.

Yes, they have Aubrey. But don't worry about him, he'll be okay. Are you?

So far, Teresa said. *I've just been alone.*

'That Lord Gawain is weak,' Lisandro said with a small shrug, as though this were obvious. 'Moments like this one highlight it. I want you to watch him struggle to make a decision between her life and the Elm Stone. He can't just *choose*; he'd hate to be responsible for something. He always wants it both ways, and in the end he falls in between and gets neither.'

'You talk so much garbage,' Elijah commented, but Lisandro shook his head.

'You'll see it,' he insisted. 'He has to do everything *his* way, and that means trying to weasel out of an ultimatum at any cost. He'll lie to me. Try to trick me. Fail. I'll have to prove I'm serious. Such a pity,' he added, running a hand down the side of Teresa's face to her neck, wrapping his fingers around her throat, and breathing in the scent of her hair. Jadon slammed a hand against the gate, fighting the urge to scream and bust through the gate and rip the stranger to pieces. 'You're a sweet girl, so talented, and you have such a pretty little face. But you're disappointing. I keep expecting a fighting spirit, a fire that just isn't in you. I like a girl with her own mind. Girls like Emmanuelle, or Ana Morrissey.' He looked up at Elijah and grinned. 'Where is Renatus? I want to talk to him.'

Was it him? Teresa asked of Jadon. *Did Renatus give us up?*

I don't know, Jadon answered honestly. *It's true it's his fault for putting you in this situation, but that seems to be all he's guilty of, and Lord Gawain and Emmanuelle are adamant he's innocent even of that.*

But who else knew we were going to be there? she asked.

'Why?' Elijah hedged around answering Lisandro's question. Lisandro didn't need to know that

Renatus was out of it, and newly bonded to an apprentice.

'Because as much as I might like you, I'm wasting time with you, Elijah,' Lisandro said over Teresa's shoulder. 'I want the ring; you want your girl. It's exactly as black and white as it sounds. Yet you're too high-minded to just *do it*. You think you're saving the world by withholding that stupid Stone from me? Please.'

'What do you want the Stone for?' Tian asked, arms folded tightly across his chest. Lisandro smiled.

'I wish I could share that,' he confessed. 'I'm sure you'd be much more pliable if you had a reason. But I'm afraid the truth isn't my truth to share. All I can say is I really, really need the Elm Stone, and I'm willing to kidnap a pile of orphans and feed them their own dismembered fingers if it gets me results.'

'Charming.' Elijah's smile was without feeling. 'You make the idea of giving you a wellspring of ancient, unchecked power seem so commonsense.'

'I know you think I'm going to take it and blow something up,' Lisandro said, 'and that to try to convince you otherwise would be pointless. Plus it would only undermine the reputation I'm relying on to get me what I want from people.' He flashed another quick smile. For someone so disliked, the man had no difficulty conjuring up a very genuine and cheerful expression. How stark his bright smile made Teresa's white, fearful face look. 'Listen, it's a fair trade: girl for the ring. If you don't want to be the bad guy who gave away the Elm Stone, call Renatus out here and let him take that fall. I've known

223

Renatus since the day he was born and I know he'll make the right choice.'

'What's that supposed to mean?' Jadon spat, both worried and buoyed by Lisandro's words. Was he saying that Renatus would choose to help the other side? Or was he saying that Renatus would value Teresa's life over a little ring? Did it matter either way?

'Just get him here and you'll see.'

'He's not coming,' Elijah said, moving to stand closer to the gate. 'Renatus isn't coming. Lord Gawain's not coming. It's just us.'

Lisandro sighed, expression closing down with frustration, and Jadon felt new tendrils of fear spreading within himself.

Jadon, he's going to kill me, he heard Teresa's voice in his head. She sounded scared.

He won't, Jadon answered firmly, refusing to believe he might have to watch such a thing.

Samuel – is he alright?

He's fine. Jadon didn't want to think of Teresa's adoring but simple boyfriend, but it was important that she knew he was safe. *You saved him. You saved me, and Emmanuelle.*

'How unfortunate,' Lisandro said, and suddenly there was a knife in his hand. Panic spiked through Jadon's body.

'*No!*' Jadon shouted, and again his key was in his hand and he was fighting against Elijah and Tian.

'Jadon, don't!' Teresa begged, starting to cry. *Just find Aubrey and take him back to Shell.*

She focussed on everything she remembered from Thursday night and since, and Jadon saw that she recalled very little, except waking up in a cold, dark room all by herself and being unable to perform any magic or feel her connection to the White Elm. She concentrated on a vision of her ankle from when she first awoke, on which a sparkling gold chain was wrapped. Was that an anklet?

'Very sweet,' Lisandro commented, tightening his grip on Teresa when she tilted her head to wipe her eyes on her shoulder, 'but very boring.'

'Don't hurt her! We'll...' Do nothing. The councillors as individuals had no right to agree to any sort of deal regarding the Elm Stone, the White Elm's oldest weapon. 'Give us time,' Jadon pleaded, unable to think of any alternative.

'Shut *up*, Jadon,' Elijah hissed. Lisandro considered this.

'What's your name again?'

'None of your business,' Tian snapped, but Jadon caved immediately.

'Jadon.'

'I'll tell you what, Jadon,' Lisandro said finally, and the knife disappeared. 'I'm not unreasonable. I know you have doddery Gawain to work over. Two weeks. I'll give you until the new moon. I can't use the Stone until after then, anyway, for the purpose I have in mind. That should be plenty of time to mull over what you want to do, and plenty of time for you all to watch Gawain fail your friends. Utterly. On the new moon, if I don't have the ring, she dies.' He nodded abruptly at Teresa. 'The next night, the boy dies. Then I start hunting, and someone dies every night until I get what I want. I'm not in the hugest rush, but I don't have forever. Are we clear?'

'Very clear,' Elijah said. 'Will you come back here on the new moon to negotiate the terms?'

'I don't think so. You're not smarter than me, Elijah. Do you think I'm going to tell you where I'll be ahead of time?' Lisandro smirked. 'You'll leave me a sign, and I'll get in contact. Talk soon.'

No!

Lisandro's shield dropped, and Jadon sensed a wormhole opening just on the other side of the gate. He saw the older man's grin as he dragged Teresa by her hair into the wormhole, but didn't care anymore whether it was a trap. He threw himself between his colleagues and pressed the key into the lock. Tian tried to pull him away and Jadon reacted as he rarely did, shoving with both his shoulder and his energy. Tian was flung back. The lock clicked and Jadon was through, ignoring Elijah's orders.

Lisandro stepped through the wormhole, pulling the tearful Teresa behind him.

'No, Jadon, go back,' she begged. Jadon's feet pounded over the compacted ground. Lisandro disappeared. Jadon reached for Teresa. 'Just find Aubrey!'

Then she was gone, too.

'Teresa!' Jadon screamed, pulling up, knowing he was too late. He felt Elijah rush past him and jump into the space they'd Displaced through. He disappeared as he fell between places, and Jadon waited, looking out for attackers, holding his breath. Was it possible that Elijah, world's most talented teleporter, had been able to trace and follow the wormhole?

Elijah was suddenly back, stepping backwards as though he'd been shoved.

'He didn't go far,' he said, sounding slightly out of breath. 'But I couldn't follow the whole way. He blocked the exit – I can't see where he went.'

Jadon closed his eyes and ran his hands across his short hair. He'd been so close, but for the second time in less than a week, he'd been unable to save his best friend from being taken. He had no idea where she'd been taken and no means of getting her back.

Worst. Friend. Ever.

chapter ten

'Jadon said he asked for you. Any ideas why?'

'How should I know?'

'He said he knows you better than we do.'

'Maybe he does. It doesn't mean I know where he is.'

Dimly, I heard low male voices. Where were they? Where was I? I felt disorientated and groggy, worse than most mornings. My head was swimming. My entire body ached.

What had happened to me?

Focus, I ordered myself, and tried to do so. It was easier thought than done. My thoughts and memories were blurry and all mixed up. I searched my head for familiar thoughts or memories but they weren't coming to me. What the hell was going on? My body and mind hardly felt like mine at all.

Focus.

I had a sister, Angela. I thought about her, envisioned her face. Her hair was always tied up, a ponytail that might have been either dark blonde or very light brown. Like gold. Her eyes sparkled when she smiled. She went for runs in the morning. She was a health freak. I liked everything about her. I remembered her braiding my hair when I was five. I remembered helping her to choose an outfit for a date when she was fifteen. I remembered the last fight we had – about two months after our parents and brother died. Images came forth with coaxing. Angela making pancakes; Angela and Aidan teaching me how to roller-skate; Angela going to work; Angela flirting with Aidan's best friend; Angela helping me clean Mum's carpet when I spilt red soft drink so I wouldn't get into trouble.

A vision of my sister lying dead in my arms, battered, bloody, unrecognisable, made me recoil and confused me. I shoved it away mentally, but slowly, curiously went over it again. This memory was not mine – was it? I felt the grief and horror of the moment, and the girl in the memory felt like my sister, but it wasn't Angela. The hair was too dark, the skin too fair, not that much of either was visible through the blood, gore and dirt. The ruined dress was one my sister would never have worn. This never happened to Ange, or anyone else I'd known. I'd never held a dead loved one in my arms. I'd never even seen my mum or dad or brother post-mortem. My aunt had identified the bodies and dealt with the funeral home. Was this some weird re-pressed memory sort of thing? Had I experienced this horrible moment and forgotten it?

Focus.

My best friend – Hiroko. She was a Displacer. She was Japanese. She was sweet and gentle but with a subtle attitude no one expected. She had a cool haircut.

I heard voices again. They were nearby, speaking softly. I struggled to open my sore, tired eyes.

'She's waking up,' a female voice whispered. It wasn't Hiroko or Angela, or even my aunt. If I wasn't with any of them, either in my dorm room or back in my house, where was I?

The room I was in was dimly lit, but the little candle flames burnt my retinas like spotlights when I looked at them. I raised my exhausted, heavy arms so I could rub my eyes. Ouch – my eyelids were sore to the gentlest touch.

What the hell had happened?

'Miss Aristea, are you alright?' the woman's voice said, worriedly. I felt her hand on my shoulder and cringed. It was a light touch, but felt like she was pressing down on a bruise.

'Aristea, how do you feel?' a male voice asked, speaking loudly and clearly. The volume hurt my ears. My every sense was over-sensitive.

'Horrible,' I muttered, not sure who I was talking to. My mouth was dry. I forced my eyes open and stared at the ceiling above me while my pupils struggled to adjust.

'That seems to be the consensus,' the man said, his tone joking, and despite the pain it caused to force my facial muscles into the expression, I frowned. What was funny about this? What, exactly, was funny about me waking up disorientated, hurt and unwell?

Somewhere in my jumbled mind, I felt a sort of acknowledgement. That wasn't me – was it? Was I acknowledging my own feelings now?

I heard a tap running, and started to pay attention to my surroundings. I turned my head to the right. I saw pots and pans hanging, copious bench space, a massive oven, and Fionnuala, the housekeeper, standing with her back to me at the sink. I recognised the kitchen momentarily as the kitchen in the basement of Morrissey House. I remembered being dragged through it only days before... I remembered sneaking in here as a lonely child and being given late-night snacks...

No. I didn't. *Focus*. Where were all these strange memories coming from? That wasn't my memory. I didn't grow up here. I grew up in a nice two-storey place by the sea.

Fionnuala turned and walked back to me with a glass of water.

'Here, sweetie,' she said softly, offering it to me. I was grateful for her quiet voice. She put the glass down beside me and, gently holding my shoulders, helped me to sit up. It was quite an effort, but a worthwhile one, because the drink was much-needed. I drank the whole glass in only a couple of swallows. I felt the cool water rush down my throat and down to my completely empty stomach. Fionnuala affectionately stroked my hair. 'That's better, isn't it?'

I nodded, and she took the glass and refilled it. I looked around, my eyes now much better adjusted. Sitting in a chair nearby with his head down was Renatus, and sitting opposite him looking twenty times more lively was Lord Gawain.

In a nauseous rush, images and memories of the previous night flooded into my mind. Ugh. That's right. *So that's why I feel so horrible.* I was grateful now for Qasim's warnings against eating beforehand.

'Welcome to the waiting list of the White Elm, Aristea,' Lord Gawain said, smiling broadly and making no effort to keep his voice down. I turned my head to limit the soundwaves reaching my ears. Fionnuala pressed the refilled glass into my hands. 'In just a few years you'll be eligible for your initiation onto the council. You'll be pleased to know I announced your new role to the whole school this morning, so that everyone is on the same page. Your peers seemed very surprised.'

I'll bet they did. None of them would have seen this coming. Following Sterling and Xanthe's gossip-fest, everyone had had their minds stuck so firmly in the gutter that the mere notion that something sacred and honourable was going on must have really shocked them. Losers.

Yes, I was feeling extremely spiteful in my exhausted, unsettled state.

'So, the ceremony worked?' I asked. Feeling this yuck, I would have guessed not, except for the strange memories that were not mine and Lord Gawain's welcome and clear excitement.

'Most certainly,' he said, beaming and speaking way too loud. I cringed as my ears rang.

'Talk quieter,' I said, rubbing my ear. He looked confused, and glanced at Renatus, who hadn't moved since I woke up. The headmaster looked up, and I stared at him. This was not the Renatus I was used to. He looked terrible, like he hadn't slept or eaten in a week, and beaten, like he'd argued extensively with every person he knew in that time and lost each time.

'It hurts our ears,' Renatus explained quietly. Slightly taken aback, Lord Gawain looked between us.

'Oh, I didn't realise,' he said, apologetic. After an awkward pause, he deliberately lowered his voice and continued. 'Well, so, yes, the ritual was a success, and I made the announcement to the school this morning. It is likely that your peers will be curious. I don't expect such news to remain in the grounds so don't be surprised if it becomes a matter of interest to complete strangers all over. You're the first apprentice of the White Elm in thirty years. Congratulations.'

I managed a pained smile. My muscles didn't want to do it. My body remained assertive that there was nothing to be congratulated for. My thoughts swirled around and around my head as I tried to sort out what was mine and what wasn't meant to be there. I felt horrible. Right then, if someone had offered me a ticket onto a time machine to go back a week – yeah, I would have taken it and told myself to stay well away from this situation.

I felt some strange sense of uncertainty in the back of my mind, and again, it wasn't mine. I looked to Renatus, wondering, and met his eyes for the first time since the ceremony.

It was him. These were his thoughts, his weird feelings, his memories – they were unfamiliar to me and I wasn't yet sure how to read them properly, which was why they were confusing me or getting mixed up with my own. What were they doing in *my* head? They belonged in his.

That clock chimed, distantly, nine times, and Lord Gawain lightly clapped a hand on Renatus's shoulder. The violet eyes closed briefly – apparently he was feeling just as delicate as I was – but he gave Lord Gawain no indication that the gesture was hurtful.

'I'm very proud of you,' the leader said softly, to Renatus entirely. The younger councillor angled his gaze up.

'Pleased it worked?'

'I knew it would.'

'But you still suspended me,' Renatus countered. Lord Gawain looked uncomfortable. Renatus asked, 'Am I reinstated? Do you trust me again?'

'I had my reasons for suspending you,' Lord Gawain said carefully, 'and they had little to do with suspicion or mistrust, Renatus.'

'Policy,' Renatus guessed. 'When do I return to work?'

Lord Gawain gave him the same look I chose this moment to cast him. *When?* When you look less like death, I imagined. He looked in no way ready to return to work, in any capacity. I didn't blame Lord Gawain for wanting to wait before making a decision on that.

'Not today,' Fionnuala answered in the White Elm leader's silence, voice firm. She turned her stern look on him. 'Lord Gawain, they need rest.'

'Take it easy, both of you,' the old man advised as he left the kitchen. I watched him leave, fighting the feeling of satisfaction at his departure. I was just tired and grumpy. Renatus watched me for a long moment, but didn't speak, even when I looked back to him. The weird feelings and thoughts that weren't mine were still in my head. I paid closer attention to them. Enquiry, curiosity, uncertainty... Now that I was listening to them, trying to read them, they *did* feel like him. Could he hear my thoughts and feelings in his head, too?

The next feeling I felt that wasn't mine was one of affirmation.

'Is it always going to be like this?' I asked. 'All mixed up?'

'No, it shouldn't be,' he said. 'I think it might take a while, but your mind and mine will settle back where they should be and we'll be able to access each other's minds at will, instead of at random like now.' He paused. 'In most of your childhood memories, there are two much older, blonde children. Is that your brother and sister?'

I felt a wave of possessiveness, very much my own, but I fought it down. I was replaying *his* private memories, too. I didn't know how I was going to get used to sharing so much of myself with someone else.

'Yes,' I said, finishing my second glass of water and placing it down on the bench beside me. 'They were really close in age, and I was born nearly six years after Angela. I was... unexpected.'

I didn't like to consider myself a mistake, but I knew my parents hadn't planned me. They had only planned, or really wanted, two children.

'But not regretted,' Renatus said with ease, saying the right thing at the right time as always in my experience. 'Often things happen that go against the best of plans, but it doesn't mean you regret those experiences. Not always.'

'I don't regret agreeing to be your apprentice,' I said, sensing his double meaning. 'I suppose on one level, I am, but it doesn't have anything to do with you. I just... feel horrid. Like I'm hung over.'

'It's worse than a hangover,' Renatus disagreed, letting his face fall into his hands.

I'd been drunk only once, not long after the accident, and the next day hadn't been pretty at all. Granted, this time I wasn't slumped over a toilet bowl with my sister sitting beside me simultaneously lecturing me about alcohol poisoning and holding my hair out of my sweaty face, but when I was *actually* hung over, my body hadn't felt like I'd been beaten up, and I'd not been able to think anything except *never drinking again*. I hadn't tapped into somebody else's head, watched somebody else's memories of their own dead family.

'Your sister was quite a bit older than you, too, wasn't she?' I asked. Fionnuala, trying to wash dishes very quietly, paused and glanced over at me. I felt her concern, but it was distant. My usual empathic abilities seemed dulled.

'Five years,' Renatus agreed. 'Old enough that she thought she was in charge of me, but she always looked after me, too, even when she got too old to want to play stupid games with me.'

I smiled, able to relate. Both of my siblings were looking for dates to school dances before I understood fractions. I'd inherited all of their toys and didn't have to share them with anybody, and I'd always been loved and looked after, but there were lonely times, too, knowing that my brother and sister were the best of friends and I was just the baby.

I suddenly thought of *my* best friend, and looked down at my wrist to check the time. My watch wasn't on me. Instead, I wore a tightly wrapped bandage. I glanced about for a clock.

'What time is it?' I asked hurriedly, spotting a large clock without numbers and finding it difficult to focus on the narrow, spindly hands. Renatus looked up at Fionnuala.

'Um, it's four minutes past nine,' she said, looking confused. Horrified, I pushed myself off the bench. My ankles weren't prepared to take my weight so when I landed I crumpled to the floor, only just catching onto the bench before my forehead smacked into it.

'Aristea, what are you doing?' Renatus demanded, reaching for me and starting to stand. I pulled myself up and waved away his assistance.

'My class is about to start,' I told him.

'You're not going to class. You're a mess. You can hardly stand.'

'I have to go,' I said, determinedly. 'It's Jadon's class.'

'So I'll have him give you a set of notes,' Renatus said, wearily standing up and looking down at me. 'I doubt he's prepared much for today's lesson, anyway, after last night's episode.'

I didn't know what he meant, but I didn't care. I started past him, heading for the door. He caught my wrist, stopping me. I looked down at his hand. He was stronger than me, even now. Vaguely, I noticed that my wrist, my left wrist, was bandaged the same way as was his right one.

'You need to rest,' he said, speaking softly. 'You won't learn anything sleeping at your desk.'

'You don't understand,' I said, starting to feel desperate. 'It's Jadon's class. Hiroko will be all alone, and Sterling and Addison are in that class.'

With a sigh, Renatus released me. He clearly still didn't understand, but he didn't need to.

'This is yours,' he said, reaching into his pocket with a wince. Everything hurt, every motion and every stretch of a muscle. He offered me back my watch, the second time in only days. I accepted it but didn't have the fine motor strength to buckle it on right then.

'Yes, it is.' I looked up at him. 'Thank you.'

I hurried out of the kitchen, unsteady on my feet, and into the reception hall. I shielded my eyes from the brightly lit hall, reaching unsuccessfully for the handrail of the stairwell. I half-opened one eye to find it, and quickly moved up the steps. Stairs are horrible things, especially when you feel like I did. But it was important to me that I get to class and sit with Hiroko, lest Sterling, newly informed about my status as Renatus's apprentice, decided to have a go at her. I could be too late, I reflected. I'd left Hiroko alone with Sterling and Xanthe all night, and she'd had to sit at breakfast by herself while everyone else was informed of where I was and why.

I didn't think about the fact that I had no books or whatever, and that I was wearing yesterday's crumply clothes. It didn't really matter. It was better to walk in unprepared than to just not go and leave my friend to sit in class alone and potentially be picked on, right?

Before I knew it, I was at the door of Jadon's classroom. It was wide open, and everyone inside was already sitting, so I hurried inside, seeking out my friend, my only friend, with my blurry eyes. There she was, sitting alone in the front row, the other three desks in that row empty.

No one was bothering her. She didn't looked harassed or upset. She was fine. I felt relief.

'Aristea?' Someone sitting further back stood up. His voice was tinged with concern. 'Are you okay?'

'I'm fine,' I agreed vaguely, feeling light-headed. I crossed the classroom and sat beside Hiroko.

'What are you doing here?' Hiroko whispered, resting her hand on mine when I slumped in my chair and closed my eyes against the brightness of the room. I heard someone approach, so I reluctantly opened my eyes again.

'You don't have to be here,' Jadon said, very quietly, leaning close so that no one else could hear.

'I want to,' I answered, and after a long moment he nodded and walked away.

'Sit down, Addison, she's fine,' he said, a little tightly, turning back to the blackboard. 'Who can tell me what part of the brain is activated when we perform sorcery? Come on, we covered this last week. Let's see who remembers. Willow?'

Her answer was loud and clear, but I didn't hear it. My ears ached from the volume of your standard, well-behaved classroom, and I tuned out. Hiroko shot me regular looks of concern but opportunities to speak to each other did not come up. I struggled to focus my eyesight when she pushed her book over to me.

Are you okay? was written in her neat, rounded script. I nodded, and she discreetly took her book back to write, *Did it work?* I nodded again, weary. I took her pencil.

Yes, can't you tell from my refreshed appearance?

It felt like the longest sentence I'd ever written and several times as I scrawled it I strongly considered just stopping mid-word, but I persevered and it was worth it when Hiroko read it and had to suppress a smile. She glanced back to check where Jadon was and wrote back to me.

Why are you in class?

The last sentence had taken so much out of me that I hesitated a long time before deciding to answer this one. I slowly took up the weighty pencil.

I couldn't leave you alone with these people.

That answer satisfied my friend, and she went back to taking notes. I focused instead on sorting out the crap inside my head, sort of mentally cataloguing.

Memories seemed the easiest. I mean, they either had me in them, or they didn't. I let the images, feelings and remembered sensations come to me, and mentally labelled them either mine or Renatus's.

His memories were so alien, I thought presently, as I reviewed a time in his early life when he'd been outside in the grounds, playing with a boy of a similar age. Instead of throwing a ball or riding bikes, they were lying very still on the grass and staring intently at a line of ants marching across a leaf. As young Renatus concentrated, the leaf began to levitate, and the ants on it freaked out, running any which way, disturbed, unable to find a way to rejoin their line. The other boy watched for a moment, then found a smaller leaf and concentrated on that. When nothing happened, the boy lost his cool and flicked Renatus's leaf out of the air in spite.

Most of the memories in my head were my own, but there were still some that surprised me. Seen through Renatus's eyes, reviewing them was almost the same as reviewing my own. A very pretty girl with curly red hair hitting on me – no, not me; Renatus. I saw a massive fight between his sister Ana and the man who had to be their father, Fionnuala kissing a bruised knee better, a banquet, a spell gone wrong, a city I'd never before visited, a wild storm in the orchard...

'Aristea, let's go.'

I blinked a few times, coming back to Earth when I heard Hiroko's low voice. Everyone was packing up and leaving the classroom. Walking beside Sterling, who was very pointedly ignoring me, was Addison, looking at me concernedly. He mouthed, 'You okay?' I nodded, and he left, practically pushed through the door by Sterling.

I hadn't brought any books with me, so I stood and shoved my hands into the pockets of my jeans, keeping my head down as my classmates walked past me. Once the room was emptied of my peers, Hiroko and I headed for the door. Jadon watched me closely as I left, but said nothing. Hiroko walked very close behind me as we went back to our room. Apparently she'd noticed how unsteady on my feet I was.

'Are you hungry?' she asked when I fumbled for my key. I shook my head. She let us in. I went straight to my bed and collapsed.

'I feel awful,' I complained. Hiroko placed her book and pen on her desk and sat down beside me.

'Lord Gawain told us this morning that it went well,' she said, settling back, 'but then I saw you and it didn't seem true.'

'Well, it worked,' I said, and told her everything that had happened the night before. As I relayed the story, I noticed that my wrist was slightly itchy underneath the bandage. Unconcernedly, I rubbed it against the denim of my jeans.

'Do you have the mark?' Hiroko asked, leaning forward eagerly and nodding at my wrist. I shook my head.

'I don't think so,' I said, still rubbing it subconsciously. It helped a little, but the itch wouldn't go away. I let Hiroko take my hand and begin to unwrap the bandaging. 'The council probably has to wait until I turn eighteen before they can tattoo me.'

Hiroko nodded agreeably but her eyes told me a whole different story when the bandage fell away.

'What?' I sat up and stared along with her.

The skin was reddish where I'd been scratching and rubbing, but that wasn't the chief concern. There was a dark, thin *drawing* on my skin. I scrubbed at it with my sleeve; it changed nothing. The previously smooth, virginal skin of my forearm was *marked*. With the tip of my finger, I traced along the shape. Was it meant to be some sort of letter, or symbol? I couldn't tell, but – was it my imagination? – it might have looked a wee bit like a capital "A" joined with a capital "R". Maybe. The upper shape consisted of two curved lines joining at a corner that pointed to my hand, like an arrowhead, kind of. I traced along the other stroke of the symbol, the swirly "P" shape that intersected the first, crossing the "A" and using the right leg of the "A" as the right leg of the "R".

Did I have a tattoo? Had they tattooed me while I was unconscious?

My sister was going to kill me, and then the entire White Elm.

Hiroko loved it, told me it was beautiful and explained how the mark was a symbol that had traditionally demanded the highest respect. I could only stare at it. I wasn't sure what I thought of it. I'd never really considered getting a tattoo. Now, whether I liked it or not, I had one, and Hiroko had started talking about how one day, when I got my own apprentice, my *other* wrist would also be marked, and then I'd have *two*. *Two*?!

I had better get married, and fast, before my sister disowned me and I lost my surname anyway.

'Jadon seemed unhappy,' Hiroko changed the topic finally. I glanced at her; I hadn't noticed.

'Did he?'

'I thought he was... he was...' She paused, looking around as she tried to work out what word she was trying to say. She muttered a phrase in Japanese, but of course that didn't help me. She shrugged. 'I thought he was only *trying* to seem happy.'

I thought back over the lesson, the part at the beginning that I'd paid attention to. Hadn't Jadon's voice sounded a little forced when he'd asked about what brains did? And hadn't Renatus made a comment about "last night's episode" to explain why Jadon's class might be disorganised?

What had happened after I passed out?

'I don't know why,' I said. 'Unless the ceremony took a lot out of him, too, and even that would be a farfetched theory, because Lord Gawain is practically skipping this morning.'

'He is in a good mood,' Hiroko agreed. 'He said you are now "direct agent" for the White Elm, which can mean that as your peers we must understand your new responsibilities and respect them. He said, "Aristea will return to classes when she feels up to it", so I was surprised that you came to class so soon. You do not look up to it.'

'I feel much better,' I said, only half-lying. My head felt clearer, and with the exception of my wrist, my body was feeling much less sensitive. The idea of eating no longer totally repulsed me.

Hiroko helped me up and I confirmed with my mirror that I looked utterly wretched. My cousin Kelly sometimes looked like this, on the "morning after" a particularly wild party. My skin was pale, and yucky to touch. My hair was lank and dull. My eyes were a bit puffy and sported dark circles. I looked completely drained. How surprising.

I showered. At first the needles of hot water stung my sad and sensitive skin but quickly I changed my tune as I was vividly reminded of why hot showers were pretty much my favourite thing in the world.

When I finished my shower and dried myself, the first thing I did was rewrap my wrist. Perhaps if I didn't look at it, it would go away... or something. I just didn't want to think about it. I dug my watch out of the pocket of my jeans and strapped that over the bandage, but it felt restrictive and weird so I moved it to my right wrist. Felt no less weird. Wrapped in a towel and with my hair dripping everywhere, I let myself out of the shower stall. Hiroko glanced at me in the mirror as she finished touching up her make-up. She only gave me time to get dressed in the loosest-fitting clothes I could find in my wardrobe before she attacked me with concealer and a hair-brush.

'This is a nice colour,' she commented as she brushed the concealer beneath my eyes. 'It suits you.'

'I thought concealers and stuff had to match your skin tone,' I said, eyeing the packaging of the product she was using. It looked vaguely familiar – had I seen her use it before? 'I didn't think we would match.'

'We don't,' Hiroko said. 'This is yours. I found it in your cabinet. It was never opened before.'

Of course – Angela had packed my bags. I didn't use make-up, mostly because it seemed like such a waste of valuable before-breakfast time, but Angela had been buying it for me for years, constantly trying to sophisticate me. Apparently she and Hiroko were in league.

Most people were nearly finished their morning tea when Hiroko and I walked into the dining hall, and our entry caught the attention of all. Feeling all of the stares on me, my instinct was to look down and away, but I forced myself to meet their gazes. *I didn't have anything to be ashamed of.* Most people now averted their eyes and pretended to go back to their meals. Sterling eyed me quickly and then snapped around to talk with Xanthe in a low voice. Whatever. Kendra and Sophia looked down at their laps, matching expressions of what looked like shame on their faces. What was that about? Did they think people would associate them with me because we used to be friends? I felt that sinking feeling start to develop in my stomach, but was buoyed significantly when my gaze moved to Addison and he smiled at me. *He* didn't hate me; maybe he would be able to talk his girlfriend around eventually.

'Hey, Aristea.' A male student I didn't really know sidled up to me as I walked toward the buffet. I slowed, slightly nervous, and Hiroko paused right beside me. She was tense, and I knew she was getting ready to defend me if she had to, but when I extended my senses tentatively to the boy, I couldn't sense any negativity or spite.

'Yeah?' I said, my tone cool as I worked on walling off my emotions in preparation for some sort of insult. I met his eyes challengingly. *Try me.*

He extended his hand. 'Congrats.'

I stared at his hand for a long moment before I realised what this was about. I shook his hand.

'Yeah, well done,' his friend, leaning past him, added. I knew his name – Daniel. 'Good on you.'

'Thanks,' I said, forcing a smile and taking my hand back. They were both cute, and seemed monumentally cuter now that I knew they weren't haters. I wished I knew the first guy's name, but I thought that now would be a weird time to ask. They moved on to grab seconds without a single nasty look or comment. They meant what they'd said.

It was a nice change.

Emmanuelle's Wards class was almost always a very practical lesson, and today was no exception. When I walked through the door she came over and enveloped me in a big hug.

'You shouldn't be attending classes today,' she scolded softly. She lifted my left wrist and checked the bandage. 'This will stop itching soon. Are you feeling alright? If you don't feel strong enough for anything today, just sit down.'

I nodded while she tugged the end of the bandage and tucked it under another layer, tightening it.

'Is it permanent? That?' I asked, nodding once at my wrist.

'You know it is.'

'I don't remember getting tattooed,' I said quietly, hoping she could fill in some blanks for me. Someone entered the room and went to stand with their friends at the back.

'You weren't *tattooed*,' Emmanuelle answered. 'It 'appens without our 'elp. It's part of the process. It was forming all night.'

I stared at my bandaged wrist. While I'd slept, out cold, a picture had been forming under my skin. Wasn't that sort of creepy?

'Thanks for what you did for me last night,' I said. She waved the thanks aside, so I added, 'And for my hand. I saw Renatus's palm – it was a mess.'

'Lord Gawain is a traditionalist,' Emmanuelle said, smiling quickly, 'and I am a Healer. Blood is not to be wasted.' She looked around and raised her voice to invite others to listen to her. 'Is everyone ready?'

She demonstrated the sort of ward we would be practising today. It was a cloaking ward, which were extremely difficult to sense through. They could be tailored to become invisible. I recalled the man in the shadows with an uncomfortable jolt, and my stomach jolted again when I remembered that he was dead now. I pushed those thoughts away – too much, way too much for right now. *Focus.* The ward we'd been working on for the past week was a personal one, the kind you just cast around your person and your mind, hiding just yourself and your energy from the attention of anyone nearby. This one, however, she inflated like a balloon around herself to include me and the person behind me. Briefly, Emmanuelle was energetically invisible, but as soon as the shimmery wall of magic passed over me, I was able to sense her again. We were on the same side of the ward, protected from the rest of the class.

'Work with the same principles as we 'ave all week,' Emmanuelle said, dropping her ward. It dissolved. 'It is the same magic, but you need to extend it beyond just yourself. 'ave a try.'

I made a couple of attempts but my magic wasn't really working. My wards fizzled out like Hiroko's normally did. It didn't take long for me to start to feel tired and overwhelmed, so I followed Emmanuelle's earlier instruction and just sat out, standing off to the side while my classmates tackled the new task. I was certain I'd be able to pick it up quick enough once my brain decided to be just mine again. Every now and then, a thought or memory would run through my head that wasn't mine, but it was becoming less frequent as the day wore on.

'Very good, Iseult,' Emmanuelle encouraged, stepping forward and checking her watch. 'That's almost four minutes. Keep it up.'

I glanced at Iseult and accidentally caught her eye. She'd been watching me. This time, I allowed myself to look away.

Iseult was, arguably, the best student at the Academy. She was driven, powerful and knowledgeable, and I knew for a fact that she'd wanted the apprenticeship I'd just taken on. I'd been granted her wish to become Renatus's apprentice and unlike everybody else, she'd actually deserved it.

I fidgeted with the edge of my bandage as Emmanuelle's lesson wore on. I didn't feel *bad*, but knowing you've got what someone else wanted isn't an entirely comfortable feeling, especially when the people who used to be closest to me were reacting decidedly negatively to my new position. I avoided Iseult's gaze for the remainder of the lesson and slipped out quickly at the end. The worst Khalida and Sterling could throw at me was mean words and nasty looks. I didn't know what a more established teenage sorceress like Iseult Taylor could do with a heart full of spite, and I didn't want to find out.

I found Hiroko and stayed well away from other people for the whole break.

People were so predictable, sitting in the same seats every day. I hadn't had a scrying class since I stopped talking to Xanthe, so I wondered what was going to happen with that. I mean, there weren't a lot of seating options. Eight students. Eight seats at this end of the room.

Constantine came in next, followed by Xanthe. Without even looking at me, Xanthe crossed the room and practically threw herself into the empty two-seater. Point taken. Always quiet, Constantine greeted Isao and sank into the seat beside him, discreetly glancing up at me. I looked away, reflecting briefly on his friend Jin calling out to me in the entrance hall over the weekend. Jerks.

Joshua and Iseult were the last to arrive. The whole room was silent as we waited for them. I heard them walk in, but kept my eyes firmly on the carpet. Great – another of my non-fans.

I felt the depression in the cushion as someone sat beside me. At least neither of them had opted to sit on the floor in favour of sitting beside me.

'Now that we're all here and *settled*, we can begin with our exercises,' Qasim said, quite pointedly, I thought. 'Start with one partner behind the other – no candles today.'

Since I was going to be working with him, I supposed I'd better at least *look* at Josh. I dragged my gaze up from the carpet.

To my surprise, sitting beside me with her hands neatly folded in her lap like a little fairy was Iseult.

'So the best witch won,' she said, extending a hand. Feeling a lot like I had at morning tea when

255

that guy had congratulated me, I numbly accepted her hand. 'Do you want to do the bunny ears first, or should I?'

Teensy-tiny, even elfin, Iseult Taylor had to be the smallest student at the Academy. Sitting on these old two-seaters, her little feet dangled well off the ground while mine were flat on the floor. Her size, as well as her thin and wispy white blonde hair, snowy skin and pale eyes, gave her a deceptively diminished look that wholly contradicted the intense aura of power she projected. Her power level, if I were to estimate, would fall somewhere between mine and Renatus's, and even without ever having had much to do with her, it was clear to me that she knew what to do with that power. She had knowledge and skills that other witches our age hadn't been exposed to. I knew she was local, like me, but beyond that I knew nothing of her upbringing. I assumed hers had been more "traditional" than mine, with magical study starting very early.

'Um, I will,' I said, standing and moving behind her. I waited until she closed her eyes and breathed deeply before holding six fingers above her head. The object of the exercise was for the seated partner to scry themselves and use that scried image to count the number of fingers being displayed out of their sight. I normally did this activity with Xanthe, and I'd taken the longest of anyone in Level 3 to catch on and really *get* it. It was tedious. It was time-consuming. It was boring. I felt eyes on me, and glanced up to meet Qasim's. I felt his presence inside my head and then heard his voice.

Are you up to today's lesson?

He did this sometimes, talked to my mind, but only here in this classroom. His facial expression did not change on his unmoving face as his voice addressed my thoughts, and there was little concern in his mental tone. I was still convinced he didn't like me so it was easy to add on the conviction that he didn't give a toss whether I was "up to" his lesson. Still, I told myself, he wouldn't have asked if he didn't care. And he'd told Renatus he wanted me for himself. So he had to care a *little bit*.

I nodded finally, and quickly hid my hands as Iseult turned her head to face me. So as not to disturb those people still getting "in the zone", she held up six fingers without speaking. She was quick. We swapped places. I felt a little apprehensive about playing with Iseult when I knew I was terrible at this exercise even at the best of times. I hoped I hadn't lied to Qasim.

I closed my eyes and tried to relax. This was going to take ages so might as well get comfy. My headache had greatly receded, and my mind was much more *mine*, so it wasn't so hard to focus now as it had been this morning. I searched my mind for my scrying talent. Would it still be in the same place? How much more effort would it take to bring an image up now? There... Would I –

Me, sitting on the two-seater with my head down and eyes closed... Iseult standing behind me... Both hands behind my head... Three fingers up on her left hand, one up on the right...

257

I opened my eyes with a sharp intake of breath. Where had that come from? I'd hardly even tried. Slowly, I turned to Iseult, and arranged my fingers the way she had. She smiled, approvingly, and we switched again.

It was a very successful lesson. Iseult was a great scrying partner. She made strange shadow-puppet shapes with her hands to force me to pay attention to detail, and one time even hid her hand behind her back so I had to work on changing my perspective. When Qasim gave each pair a small locked padlock, she and I were the only pair able to pick up enough impressions to work out the code without resorting to intrusive magic (using the mind to poke and prod at the workings of the lock to open it).

'Good work today, girls,' Qasim said when the bell rang and everyone stood to go. Khalida spared us an acidic glance when she realised who he was addressing. Xanthe strode out, shoving past Isao in her effort to be the first out. I ignored her. Instead I allowed myself to briefly bask in my hard-earned compliment from Qasim. I could barely remember the last of those I'd received and didn't know if it'd ever happen again.

'So, let's see your mark,' Iseult said, slowing as we reached the stairs and looking at my wrist. On the top step of the staircase, Dylan and Constantine hesitated, looking back in curiosity, and behind me, Josh and Isao paused their thumb war to listen. I turned my wrist over and held it out so Iseult could see easily. While she admired it, the boys leaned closer, unable to help themselves.

'Is it true that they use a knife to draw that?' Joshua asked, abandoning his game and moving so he could look over Iseult's tiny shoulder. I nodded, and he made a low whistle. 'Nice art.'

'Does it cut you?' Isao queried, also moving closer.

'No, it sort of floats, and draws the symbol in blood. Not my blood,' I added, when Isao looked shocked, 'Renatus's blood. I just got a little nick on my hand to get some of my blood to draw on his arm.' I stretched out my fingers to open my palm, but there was no sign at all of Emmanuelle's cut. 'It's really old magic.'

'And that mark lasts forever, hey?' Dylan asked, walking back with Constantine in tow. 'Just like any real tattoo.'

'I think so,' I agreed, turning my wrist back and forth. The idea that this weird little picture would last on my skin forever was going to take some getting used to. For now it was a novelty.

'Very cool,' Josh conceded. 'It's like that fancy writing... what's the word?' He clicked his fingers, trying to summon the elusive term. 'It's like an art form, with special pens... Calligraphy.'

'How do you even know that?' Isao asked, grinning.

'Do you do a lot of calligraphy in your spare time, Joshie?' Dylan asked innocently, and Iseult and I tried not to laugh at the annoyed look on Josh's face. 'I mean, when you're not scrapbooking and crocheting?'

'Shut your face,' Josh said, though reasonably good-naturedly. 'You know what I mean.'

'I hope I am chosen next,' Isao admitted, rubbing his smooth white wrist longingly. 'I only have nine months left before I turn twenty, and then I'll be ineligible.'

'Only seven months for me,' Dylan said, 'and I don't like my chances of Lady Miranda choosing me over Sophia or Willow.'

I looked away at the mention of Sophia. Isao tried to suppress a grin as he recalled a private joke.

'Maybe Emmanuelle will pick you,' he suggested. The boys shared smirks and Iseult and I glanced at each other knowingly.

'So the council isn't fussy about male-female apprenticeships?' Constantine asked me, speaking up for the first time. I half-shrugged, avoiding his gaze.

'Not all of them were happy about it, but the majority rules,' I said. 'And Fate gets the final say.' Iseult nodded knowingly while the boys looked sort of lost. The conversation was effectively killed. 'I guess I'll see you later,' I finished lamely, indicating the stairwell I was going to continue down.

Constantine hesitated.

'Hey, Aristea,' he said quickly, just as I stepped back into the stairwell. I looked back at him, and he made a shrugging movement, clearly embarrassed. 'Sorry about what Jin said the other day. He was just playing around. I'm sure he didn't mean it.'

I was sure Jin *had* meant it, but that was irrelevant. Constantine felt bad for his involvement, and I knew how difficult it was to admit it.

'Thanks,' I said, ensuring I smiled to convey how okay with it I was. He nodded once, apparently at peace with himself now, and walked away. I kept smiling for another couple of seconds as I turned away, too. There were people enrolled here who didn't think I was an epic waste of space. I jogged down the stairs and hurried to rejoin Hiroko in the library.

'You look much better,' she said when she saw me. She closed the book she'd been reading and laid a piece of folded red paper on top.

'Thanks,' I said, eyeing the paper. 'Garrett?'

She smiled and nodded. I sat down with her and she handed it to me.

Garrett standing right in front of Hiroko, struggling to hold her gaze while she smiles... 'Here. I made this for you.'... 'Thank you.'... 'It's a flower.'...

The exchange in which Hiroko received the origami came to me as an impression as soon as my fingertips touched the red paper. I turned the thing back and forth. It did vaguely resemble a flower, and was a much better attempt than the crane of a few weeks back.

'He said, "This is for you; it's a flower",' she told me, smiling uncontrollably. I started to nod, thinking she was repeating herself, but I quickly remembered that she hadn't told me yet – I'd just scried it from the origami. 'Then, he just walked away!'

Tapping into psychic impressions was a high-level scrying skill Qasim had only recently started teaching my class, and it was not one I was accustomed to performing without prompt outside of my familiar classroom surrounds. What was happening to me?

'He is so cute,' I said, giving her back the flower. 'He's getting braver, too.'

'It may be a week before he speaks again to me,' Hiroko said wistfully, twirling the paper between her fingers.

'Perhaps you should just take charge,' I suggested. 'Tell him you like him, too.'

'He may cry.'

We laughed. The idea of Hiroko scaring Garrett by being direct was a funny one, but I was pretty sure it would never happen unless he practically invited it. Despite her occasional complaints about Garrett's bashfulness and glacier-paced courtship, I strongly suspected that she was really enjoying the whole process, exactly as it was. As an observer, I was finding it both entertaining and sweetly romantic.

At dinnertime, Hiroko and I sat down in our new spot, and were soon joined by Iseult. I worried for a second that it would be awkward, but despite her frosty aura, Iseult fitted in with us well. Her presence made me feel a lot less like a couple of outsiders. Three's definitely a crowd, so there.

'What do you feel is the best technique for adjusting exit point?' she asked Hiroko when our conversation turned to the topic of Displacement.

Her tiny hands appeared on the tabletop as she illustrated her words with sharp gestures, and Hiroko's gaze was attentive as Iseult described her usual technique. I tuned out, somewhat disinterested. I was never going to be any good at that particular skill – I couldn't even *do* it, let alone consider best techniques or adjustments. I looked around and spotted my old friends. Addison was sitting with his male friends tonight, and the twins were sitting opposite my roommates, eating silently. The four of them looked like a small group now that Hiroko and I weren't there. It seemed a lifetime ago that I used to sit there and chat and laugh with those girls, but really it was less than a week. I looked over my shoulder at the staff table. Those few councillors who were present were sitting closely together, talking quietly over their meals. Jadon seemed to be getting frustrated with Lord Gawain, waving his hands passionately as he made his point.

As I watched, Lord Gawain shook his head firmly and gave Jadon a short and obviously unwelcome answer. Extremely pissed off, Jadon stood and left the table, abandoning his half-eaten dinner. Hardly any of the students paid his departure any mind. In the doorway, he almost walked into Renatus and Emmanuelle as they entered. Without stopping, Jadon slipped between them and stormed off. Concernedly, Emmanuelle followed, and with a quick glance after her, Renatus turned and looked straight at me.

'I'll be back in a sec,' I told the other girls, standing. They smiled their acknowledgement – they were quite absorbed in their talk. I crossed the dining hall to Renatus, attracting significantly more attention than Jadon had. Among others, I felt Sterling's gaze on my face. I glanced at her, and she switched her eyes to Renatus, which was probably where they would rather be, anyway. Would we be able to be friends again, once she realised that I couldn't have done what she hated me for, and that the way she and I thought of Renatus were totally different?

Renatus looked much better than he had this morning. He looked less tired (perhaps he'd been smarter than me, and actually spent the day resting), his eyes were less sunken and his skin was clearer. He looked much stronger and much more like his usual powerful self.

'How are you feeling?' he asked, his face turned to me but his eyes angling towards the councillors at the staff table. I resisted the urge to look over my shoulder.

'I'm fine. Well, better,' I amended, remembering who I was talking to. 'I'm seeing less of your memories and more of my own.'

'Same.'

'What's wrong with Jadon?' I asked, wishing my senses were working properly, so I could curiously extend them after the upset councillor. I had the advantage (or disadvantage, depending on how you looked at it) over anyone else on the estate of being Empathic and able to feel the feelings of other people, and right now I should be able to detect and decipher my teacher's emotions.

'Walk with me,' Renatus directed, turning and leading me from the dining hall. We stepped out into the entrance hall and immediately walked into sight of Khalida, who was just heading for dinner now. Renatus stopped and I folded my arms, irritable but more than prepared for round two.

'Khalida – exactly the person I wanted to speak with,' Renatus surprised us both by saying.

'Sir?' Disarmed by his casualness, and clearly liking the sound of her name spoken in his voice, she smiled.

'Khalida, please use our given names when addressing any of the lesser council members,' Renatus reminded her, referring to all White Elm except Lord Gawain and Lady Miranda. "Lesser" didn't seem the right word to use for people like him, or Qasim or Emmanuelle, or indeed any one of the councillors – the very reason they were White Elm was their remarkable singularity and conspicuousness. They were the best. 'It seems that you and I are experiencing a problem.'

Khalida's smile vanished. Renatus's expression didn't change. It rarely did.

'From what I have been told about this afternoon's scrying class, I understand that you are disappointed that you were not selected in Aristea's place,' Renatus noted. My older classmate struggled to control her blushing, and he continued. 'It's important that you understand my selection of Aristea was not entirely my own – Fate decides these things long before we think we do. Do you understand?'

Khalida nodded, unable to think of anything intelligent to say, unsurprisingly.

'I would ask that your behaviour towards my apprentice changes,' Renatus went on, and I looked away. 'Assaults on her, verbal or behavioural, are now assaults on me. The rumours you helped to spread about her also damage me, and I want it to stop. I hope this is clear.'

'It is.' Khalida's voice was small.

'Tomorrow morning after your first class, I would like for you, and your friends Bella and Suki, to please meet me in my office,' Renatus said, and Khalida looked down at her feet. 'I've read the events ideas you put together for me and, if you're still interested, I'd like to talk to you and your committee about organising some of your ideas.'

I watched Khalida's face light up as she realised that she was not in trouble, and that she was going to get to do her stupid committee thing.

'Yeah, we'd love to,' she gushed. 'Tomorrow morning, straight after Healing?'

'I'll see you all then,' Renatus agreed, nodding once in a clear dismissal. Khalida turned and passed us with an excited "thank you", and I walked through the front doors at Renatus's gesture. It was cool outside and I pulled my jacket tighter around myself.

'You have a way with people,' I commented as he closed the door behind us. 'Who knew that to get her off my back, all you had to do was tell her you liked her sparkly book?'

We walked in silence across the dark grounds. Clouds obscured the full moon. A breeze chilled me, and I shoved my hands into my pockets.

'What's up between Jadon and Lord Gawain?' I asked again. Renatus glanced to his right, at the gate.

'Jadon wants Lord Gawain to give Lisandro the ring,' he told me.

'What? Emmanuelle's ring?' I hadn't even thought of the thing in days. 'Why?' I stopped, an idea – a horrible idea – occurring to me. 'Is Jadon-?'

'A mole? I don't know,' Renatus said, still walking. I hastened to catch up. 'His motives for wanting to relinquish the ring seem sound and pure. Lisandro came here last night, to the gates, with Teresa. He knows that the ring she had was false, and has left us with the choice of the ring or her life, and Aubrey's.'

I stared at Renatus incredulously.

'Is that even a choice?' I asked. The idea that someone would kill two people just to get a piece of jewellery was frightening, but worse was the notion that anybody would choose to withhold that jewellery at the expense of two friends' lives. The right choice seemed extremely clear to me – it didn't even deserve consideration.

'It is for Lord Gawain.'

'Okay, so what's so special about the ring?' I kicked an apple core that someone had left on the grass near a tree. 'How could it possibly be more important than Aubrey and Teresa?'

'The ring is a massive storehouse of power,' Renatus explained. 'It's the council's weapon for times of terror and war. The *other* weapon,' he relented, when I glanced up at him. From what I understood of his position on the council, *he* was effectively a weapon, too; an academic of dark magic until such time as the White Elm needed to get its hands dirty and needed a warrior instead. 'It's called the Elm Stone.'

I brightened with recognition.

'I've heard of that,' I said. 'My aunt mentioned it.'

'Powerful White Elm sorcerers through the ages have spent centuries transferring energy into it. It could be extremely dangerous in the hands of someone destructive. Think of it as a bomb.' With his thumb he rubbed his right wrist. 'Do you know of the Trefzer Scale, about rating someone's power capacity from one to ten?'

'Yeah, Jadon taught it to us.'

'The ring on Emmanuelle's thumb would take Lisandro from an eight or nine up to at least twenty. Off the charts. Something we couldn't handle. He could flatten a small town if he focussed that kind of power the wrong way.'

I watched my feet as we started up a gentle slope. I now understood the dilemma. Renatus surprised me by asking, 'What would you do?'

I took a moment to think on that. I recalled, un-bidden, a memory of Renatus's – something Renatus had said to Aubrey just last week, something about seeing the difference between what is best for the one and what is best for all. I wondered what Aubrey would think if he were to hear that again, knowing that he and Teresa were the minority being considered for sacrifice for the good of many.

'I would give Lisandro the ring,' I decided finally, not caring if it was the wrong answer. 'I would save my friends. "Could" and "will" are different things. Lisandro "could" flatten a town, but if he doesn't get the ring, he "will" kill Teresa and Aubrey.'

Renatus nodded, but said nothing else. He only rubbed his wrist under his sleeve.

'It's itchy, isn't it?' I said, showing him my tattoo, and how the skin around it was still red and tingly. He glanced over, and pulled his sleeve up enough that his wrist was exposed. There, an exact match to mine but on the opposite arm, was a black symbol inked into his flesh, resembling our first initials interwoven. It suited him better than it suited me, I thought. He had this whole gothic dark sorcerer look going already, and a tattoo did nothing to disrupt that. It either didn't work as well with "eccentric schoolgirl", or I just wasn't used to being inked yet.

'Emmanuelle said it would stop, but it hasn't,' he confirmed, reaching his arm across so our marked wrists would be side-by-side. I smiled – the tattoos were totally identical. Finally, something I actually had in common with Renatus. Well, besides scrying, and being disliked by Qasim. And besides the deaths in our families, and the manner of those deaths. Something visible.

We reached the top of a grassy hill, and I could see the orchard. In the moonlight I could make out the gap in the trees that made the eerie path I was still dying to venture down. Renatus changed direction in what seemed a very conscious decision to avoid that path.

'Are your powers returned yet?' he asked, distracting me from my wonderings.

'Sort of. I did really well in Scrying this afternoon.'

'Mine are returning slowly. But I'm still not allowed to get back to work.' He scowled, an actual expression that I found very easy to read. 'My suspension is still in place. Lord Gawain says he is no longer investigating my part in Saul's death but has forbidden me to leave the estate until I am at full-strength.'

I glanced at him sidelong. When Lord Gawain forbade Emmanuelle from leaving the house, it didn't mean much to her. She'd been at my sister's house the very next morning. Renatus wasn't a particularly obedient man, yet Lord Gawain's word always seemed so final to him.

'Does he think you'll be targeted?'

'He is overly protective.'

I thought of my most recent interaction with the White Elm leader, when I'd woken up this morning. His enthusiasm and lack of empathy had irritated me. I wasn't sure that I would be as okay with allowing him to smother me and make decisions for me as Renatus was. I mean, he was our nation's leader and of course *I* would do anything he instructed me to do, but if I had the very strange, seemingly personal relationship with the old Seer that Renatus had, I wouldn't enjoy feeling indebted. Which was how Renatus seemed to feel.

'I have something for you.' He reached inside his jacket and tossed something weighty in my direction. Mid-step, I caught it, years of fielding for much older, sporty siblings to thank for quick reflexes.

Renatus, in his office... A smooth pinkish stone in his hand... He puts it in his pocket...

A day ago this stone would have given me nothing without concentrated effort. Now impressions came to me without prompt. I opened my fingers and admired the smoothed gem. It was a deep pinkish red – my experience at the little crystal shop I'd worked at before enrolling here told me I held a ruby, but we'd never stocked a specimen like this while I was employed there. It was the hugest one I'd ever seen, almost the size of a bar of soap.

'It's for scrying. I know Qasim has taught you with fire but it won't hurt you to try with a stone. It can be easier to focus with a tool and crystal is more meditative than flame. Steadier.'

'It's so beautiful.' I turned the stone in my hands.

'You can have it,' Renatus said. 'It's a Burmese ruby.' He labelled it so carelessly.

'No, it's yours,' I protested, trying to hand it back. It had to be worth a fortune. He wouldn't take it.

'It was never mine,' he disagreed. 'It was my sister's. She collected gemstones. You can have the others, too, if you want them.'

'But-'

'Take a look around you,' he interrupted, gesturing with both hands at the rolling hills of his estate. 'What am I going to do with a gemstone collection? I already have everything.'

He had a good point, but it wasn't *the* point.

'I'll rephrase,' he suggested. 'I'd like for you to have the stone.' It was harder to refuse, said that way. 'You'll have to get used to accepting – gifts, knowledge, advice... it's all energy. It has to move from one person to another.'

I thanked him, but it didn't seem enough. You say "thank you" to checkout person at the supermarket when they give you the receipt for your purchases. Can it really just be the same word for someone who casually gives you a fist-sized precious stone?

'Can I try something?' Renatus asked me, stopping and offering me his hand, upright like a traffic policeman. 'I'm not sure what will happen.'

It sounded like a completely unreasonable request, but no more unreasonable than his ruby giveaway. I pressed my palm against his. As always, it was cold.

'Alright,' I agreed. For a second, he just looked at me. 'What?'

The world tipped over. The night sky fell away, the hills dissolved and I was in a huge, bright but deeply familiar room. For a moment I thought I was back in my childhood bedroom – there were the pastel walls, the lacy curtains and the seashell wind chimes – but too many details were out of place. The room was much too big, and there were a few too many cardboard moving boxes and white-washed bookshelves filled with haphazardly stacked books and diaries, and the walls were nearly covered in picture frames displaying precious times in my memories. Shadows darkened a few corners, but I ignored those. I knew where I was. This was *my mind*, the way it had always been, except that now, at the back, there was a door. My hand was pressed against it, where Renatus's hand had been only a second before. Where had he gone? What had he done? Like smoke, thoughts and wonderings slipped through the space between the door and its frame, but the majority was kept back by the shut door. And I was being kept out. Compelled, I shook the doorhandle fruitlessly, but it made no difference. It was locked.

I looked around for a key, and saw one lying on a nearby table that hadn't been there before. How *Alice in Wonderland*. I grabbed it, and came back to the door. It slid into the lock and turned, but when I yanked on the doorhandle, it still wouldn't budge. A second lock had appeared, a latch with a coded padlock like the ones Qasim had tested me on just today. The subconscious really does take inspiration from life experiences.

On impulse, I turned the lock, matching the marker to the digits that made up my birth date. It clicked open, and I tossed it aside to unlatch the second lock.

Now there was a third one. A futuristic digital one, nothing I'd see here at Morrissey House. Again,

I simply knew what to do. The tattoo on my left wrist glowed golden, like Fate had. I swiped my wrist past the scanner. The door shimmered away.

Renatus was standing opposite me, on the other side of the door, his right arm extended. My mirror image, yet my exact opposite.

We both dropped our arms.

'Welcome,' he said, stepping back and gesturing for me to step through the door, 'to... Well, to *me*. I expect you'll find my memories much better organised now that things are becoming settled.'

I stepped inside his mind. This was nothing like mine. Darkened walls were lined with meticulously stacked bookshelves. Candelabras offered what light they could, but some shelves were obscured completely in shadow.

'It looks like your office,' I said, noticing that the wallpaper was the same.

'It looks like this to you because your imagination is ruling again,' Renatus answered, slightly amused. 'It doesn't actually look like anything. It's nowhere. But since I've brought your consciousness inside yourself and you believe you are experiencing this, your imagination fills in for your senses. You associate these themes with me.' He nodded behind me at the room I'd just left. 'You associate those things with yourself.'

I had no idea what all that meant, but I took his word. I approached the nearest bookshelf and opened a book. There were no words inside. Instead, the pages became like television screens, and I was viewing his memories. Fionnuala had three-year-old

Renatus on her lap and was reading him a story. I put the book back and found another one, this one from a shelf half-shadowed. This memory was from years later – teenaged Ana and preteen Renatus practising duelling in the orchard.

Present-day dream-Renatus closed the book in my hands, and the memory disappeared.

'Now that we have our own memories back in our own heads, we'll know when the other is viewing them,' he said, his voice odd. He put the book back and led me through the doorway back into my mind. It was so much brighter here, so long as you ignored those shadowy bits in the corners. I frowned when he headed straight for the darkest one. I followed. He reached into the shadow and withdrew a heavy photo album from the hidden shelves. I had a bad feeling about this. He flicked the cover back and held it to his chest so I couldn't see what was in it.

The first thing I felt was fear, cold fear, and then horror, shock and disbelief.

'What are you doing?' I demanded, trying to suppress the feelings. He held the book out so I could see. I watched as the tree fell onto my father and brother, crushing them, and felt it all over again. I snapped the cover shut.

'Whenever you access memories of mine, I'll know, just like you'll know if I'm in here viewing yours. Feel free to do so,' he added, 'but just be aware that on one level, I'll be revisiting them, too. Please be sensitive to the fact that there are some parts of my mind that I don't like to see.'

'Alright,' I agreed, keen to avoid feeling what I'd just experienced. It was only fair to do the same for him. I would let alone the books in the shadows, but I was dying to get at some of the others.

'You can,' Renatus said, and he was standing in front of me on the lawn of the estate again. The bookshelves were gone, the pastel walls, the seashell wind chimes and even that door through to *him* had completely disappeared. Back were the stars, the dark, the wind and the crystal in my hand. I blinked, all of my senses trying to adjust. 'My knowledge and experiences are at your disposal. Our minds are one now – it's one of the reasons apprenticeships in our world are so sacred and so sought-after. We share both power and knowledge. Whatever one knows, the other can know. Whatever I have learnt, ever, is available to you. My knowing it means that you, by extension, know it. You just need to find it.' He dropped his hand. 'Try this.'

He cupped his two hands together. They filled immediately with water, as though from an invisible hose. I watched as droplets trickled over his fingers.

'I don't know how.' I wished I did.

'But *I* do.'

The water evaporated and, hands now dry, Renatus gestured for me to copy him. I pocketed my new ruby and cupped my hands in front of me. Of course I didn't know what to do, but *he* did, and somewhere inside my brain a few unused synapses jolted to life as an electrical current surged between my intention and my action. Cold water bubbled into existence in my palms, filling my much smaller hands quickly and spilling over my fingers. Stunned, I laughed shakily and parted my hands. The water fell between my fingers in a rush and onto the grass between my shoes. I tried to memorise what I'd just done, the neural pathway, the feelings, but it would take a lot of practice before that pathway was fully developed.

Still. *I'd* done that. Me.

The water was gone now, more or less, and I was standing outside with dripping fingers. I shook them once and looked back up at Renatus with a massive grin. He was almost smiling too, at least with his eyes.

'Don't think this means you don't have to do classes anymore.'

chapter twelve

So it was done. Renatus and Aristea were bonded: for life, for better, for worse. It was a bond deeper than marriage. They were one and the same now, two halves of a whole, with the potential to complete or destroy one another.

That first night after the initiation, once all of the students were back in their dorms, the White Elm met in the ballroom. Lord Gawain could sense that the general feeling was one of displeasure and impatience, and that for the most part, it was directed at him.

Nobody was speaking as they waited on Glen, the latecomer. Jadon was glaring out the window, a statue. Even most of his mind was blocked off from the other councillors (despite their link, each councillor could still control how much of their mind was on display to the others – it was how Lisandro had betrayed them from within, and how one of them was even now playing both sides).

Renatus was sitting silently at the massive piano in the corner, noticeably different to even his self of a day ago. He'd always been stronger than anyone else on the council with an aura to prove it and last night's ritual had stripped most of that away, leaving him depleted and empty, but its crushing effects were so temporary. With every passing hour his energy brightened. At this rate he'd be back to his former strength by morning and from there, who knew? He would continue to improve until he reached his new potential. Even Aristea, who had spent the night unconscious, had attended her classes today, half-sleeping through the first, attempting the second and outshining her peers by the third.

The rest of the council stood or sat in pairs or as lone figures, and all kept their distance from Renatus. Lack of interest in his involvement by the Valeroans (despite Anouk's standpoint, her kin were determined that no one visible in the cell was at fault, and were doggedly investigating that theory) had kept the Dark Keeper from being officially trialled for the events in the prison, and so the free world's mantra of "innocent until proven guilty" had been silently and uneasily applied by everyone on the White Elm. No explanation for the execution was forthcoming but neither had Renatus been seen to capitalise on the death; the only thing for the uncertain councillors to do was watch their backs and warily continue with business as usual.

Lord Gawain had initially suspended the Dark Keeper for the window of opportunity such an action provided him with to investigate the situation, but now that Fate had spoken, indicating that Renatus's conscience was clean (for how could Fate bring itself to give Aristea a liar or a killer for a master? Surely it wouldn't) he felt reluctant to lift the punishment. He knew Lady Miranda disagreed – 'Either charge him or put him back to work; we're letting a resource go to waste if we're not using him,' she'd said – and he knew Renatus was frustrated with his unwillingness to discuss the matter. Lord Gawain couldn't really talk about it so he was glad when Renatus irritably gave in and left the topic alone. The future was a sensitive topic and in this case, Renatus didn't need to know what had been seen. He just needed to trust his leader, a Seer, to make decisions that brought about the best futures. He needed to stay put, stay *alive*, and house arrest ensured that, even if no one liked it.

The door cracked open, and Glen entered, looking slightly nervous when he noticed the atmosphere of the room. The door clicked shut and Lord Gawain got to his feet to face the music.

'It's time that we got some things out in the air,' he began, 'and we don't need a circle for that. We are friends – brothers and sisters. We can talk as brothers and sisters do, with honesty. First, as your eldest brother, I want to apologise for my lack of leadership. I have allowed personal matters to hold my attention when it was needed here, with the council. I regret disappointing you all.'

The level of resentment in the room decreased. Apparently, for most of them it was enough that he could acknowledge and admit his misjudgement.

'I, for my own part, accept your apology,' Qasim was the first to speak up. Lord Gawain and the others looked over at him. The most senior councillor under the two leaders was a powerful voice on the White Elm, and it was rare that anyone disagreed with him. Generally, when he spoke, he spoke the minds of the group as a whole, and even as he continued, there were small nods around the ballroom. 'Family takes many forms and yours has been at the forefront of our business as of late. Renatus's *timing* might have been better but your attention to Aristea's initiation was nothing short of expected in light of who was to become her master.'

There was a murmur of agreement and some more nodding. Lord Gawain allowed a smile. It was true; his relationship with Renatus was not like his connections with anyone else on the council. He'd met the last Morrissey on the worst day of his life – the worst day of *both* their lives – and couldn't account for anything the boy had done prior to that day, but had endeavoured to know, care for and guide the young heir ever since. His drive to protect Renatus blinded him at times, he knew; even now, his suspension of Renatus's White Elm duties was more in reaction to what he wanted for the boy than what the council wanted for him. Lord Gawain could easily understand why the others on his council would find the Dark Keeper difficult to like and trust but he could not bring himself to see him the same way. He was glad that at least the other White Elm could respect his affection for Renatus, even if they couldn't replicate or understand it.

'Thank you,' he said now to Qasim. 'I appreciate your words.'

'Two councillors are alive and unharmed but missing, and will be dead in two weeks unless we make a trade with Lisandro,' Glen said, eager to redirect the conversation. He looked over at Elijah. 'What exactly did he say?'

'He wants Peter's ring by the night of the new moon,' Elijah recited. 'If he doesn't get it, he's going to kill Teresa. If he still doesn't get it, he's killing Aubrey the next night. Apparently, after that, he's "going hunting". I assumed that meant us and our families, or something to that extent.'

'He said once we make up our minds, we have to leave him a sign,' Jadon added, still glaring out the window. 'What sort of sign would he be looking for?'

I don't think so, Tian said worriedly to Lord Gawain, who had been thinking essentially the same thing. Jadon didn't have the right to make this decision for the whole council and go summoning Lisandro.

'I'm not entirely sure,' Lord Gawain said finally. He looked around at the council. 'This is a more complex issue than it first appears, as you are all aware. The Elm Stone is our weapon and we must take care with it. Even we do not know the true damage it could do in the wrong hands. We were painfully lucky in the months following their desertion that Peter did not use the Stone or give it to Lisandro. Getting it back is an unlikely stroke of good luck and we need to think carefully now.'

'I think,' Jadon said, gritting his teeth in an attempt to retain a civilised tone, 'that my *best friends* are missing, and are going to be *killed* in two weeks if you don't swap them for a stupid ring.'

'What will Lisandro do with it once he gets it?' Susannah wondered aloud. 'And why does he need the Elm Stone? It's not like it's the only power source around, or even the strongest.'

The importance of her last comment struck Lord Gawain deeply, for she was absolutely right. Magic was stored in jewels and objects all over the world. Most old witch families had a crystal ball filled with magic in case of emergency. Atlantis had been powered by a stone pumped so full of power that the Elm Stone would pale in comparison. *That* would be worth the risk and adventure of tracking down; many had perished in the attempt, but there were thousands of other examples, smaller but less lost and less protected. Why was Lisandro so driven to obtain *this* particular piece when there were so many other, easier options? There were only two reasons the Elm Stone stood out: it was one of the few powered-up stones set into jewellery, and it had a very special method of inheritance. It could not be taken, only given. It would only give its power to its rightful possessor.

No one else's thoughts dwelled on this.

'He could use it to kill us all and our families anyway, or blow up a school,' Tian said. '*This* school.'

'No,' Renatus said, a little too sharply. 'He won't do that.'

'How do *you* know what Lisandro is going to do?' Anouk asked, tone cool. Energetically, Renatus seemed to back down, which he didn't often do.

'I don't,' he insisted, and then, more softly, 'I don't.'

'There's no known timeframe for demolishing this estate,' Emmanuelle spoke up. 'There is no special restriction on *any* destructive magic. Is there?'

'No. That doesn't make us feel any better,' Anouk reminded her younger colleague.

'It should,' the Healer shot back. She turned to Jadon. 'Tell them. Tell them what Lisandro said. About the moon.'

The youngest councillor looked unsettled to be thrown onto the spot by the firm-voiced Healer.

'He said we have until the new moon to decide because he can't use the Stone before then,' Jadon repeated.

'For the purpose he has in mind,' Tian finished.

'*Can't*,' Susannah repeated, frowning. Her mind was always at work, seeing futures and potentials that even Lord Gawain's gift could not touch upon. 'Is that the word he used?' The three who were present when Lisandro showed himself at the gates with Teresa nodded. 'He's got something specific planned for it, then. A spell, one that relies on moon energy, like the initiation we did last night. Something old.'

'Nothing good, if he wants to use the dark moon,' Elijah commented, but Lady Miranda shook her head.

'Not necessarily,' she said. '*After* the new moon it starts waxing again. New beginnings, growth. Attraction of luck and energy.'

'You don't think Lisandro has *noble* intentions for wanting the Elm Stone?' Qasim asked incredulously. 'If he wanted to do something righteous he'd have let us in on it. If he thought there was the *slightest* chance we'd agree with his premise he'd be selling it to us, trying to talk us around rather than threaten us for our compliance. He *knows* we won't like what he's going to do. Lisandro is electricity: his is the path of least resistance. If kidnapping two councillors from an unlisted residence in Italy and delivering threatening messages to Renatus's front gate is his plan, it means he thinks this is the easiest way to get what he wants.'

It was an uneasy truth and the room was silent for a long moment as everyone considered Qasim's words. Clearly, whatever it was, Lisandro's plan for the ring was one they would all prefer to remain unfulfilled. But likewise, Teresa and Aubrey's lives were hanging in the balance, and if their lives could not be saved, the lives of everyone in this ballroom and their kin were at risk, too, and that was not an outcome that anyone was prepared to face. Lord Gawain could see the futures flipping and twisting over themselves as the ten other councillors in the ballroom considered the implications of both choices. The decisions of these powerful sorcerers determined the fates of many, and until some of his brothers and sisters settled on a mindset regarding the White Elm's position here, the futures would remain murky. Beyond the choice that Lisandro had laid at his feet, Lord Gawain could not see much at all except the inescapable chances of failure that existed even before the choice had been made. There are always more opportunities for failure than for success, and it was easy to look into the future and see all the doom and misfortune and to drown in despair at it all. But just as life found a way to exist on a volatile early Earth, so too does Fate find a way to weave a single strand of success through all those dark possibilities. There was *always* a light at the end of any tunnel – the length, shape and contents of the tunnel, however, were a gamble one simply had to take.

Lisandro had given them a fortnight of grace to adjust their eyes to this particular tunnel, and Lord Gawain felt confident that it would be just enough time for more paths through the dark to become apparent. If neither outcome was acceptable, then with time, others must come to light. Surely.

'So, what are we going to do?' Glen asked finally. Jadon stared at him.

'I can't believe there's even a second option to be considered,' he muttered.

'We have two weeks,' Lord Gawain reminded him. 'We need to weigh our decision thoroughly. There may be more options that we haven't yet considered.'

'He said you'd do that,' Jadon said. His face was tight. 'Lisandro said you would try to find a way to weasel out, try to go *around* him. He said he'd kill Teresa if you tried.'

Lisandro had really said that? Lord Gawain looked away from Jadon's pained eyes, thoughtful. Having an enemy in one's former closest friend of eleven years was an unfortunate predicament.

'We'll hold a circle next week to make that decision,' Lady Miranda took charge. 'Each of us needs to have thought long and hard on it. Lives are at stake, either way we choose, so let's choose carefully.'

A few councillors nodded reluctantly. Emmanuelle, however, was still not calmed.

'In the meantime,' she said, 'perhaps we should talk about the fact that someone 'ere is a spy for Lisandro. Someone *here*, knowingly or otherwise, provided our enemy with Teresa's address, and with my location. Everyone's been thinking it, suspecting, wondering, but no one wants to talk about it.'

'Oh, people are talking about it, Emmy,' Susannah assured her, in a condescending tone. 'Just not around you, because you keep biting our heads off.'

'That's because you have only one suspect, and won't consider anybody else,' Emmanuelle snapped back, clearly defending Renatus. 'If you want to accuse someone, make sure you can back it up with something more convincing than prejudice.'

'Well, maybe it's you, then,' Susannah suggested. A deep and uncomfortable silence followed her words. It seemed, to most, like crossing a line to directly accuse anyone other than Renatus, and Emmanuelle was, well... she was Emmanuelle. Bossy, but clean.

'Me?' Emmanuelle repeated, clearly a little shocked. She gestured to indicate the other councillors, and said, incredulously, 'Of all the people in this room, none 'ave more reason to despise Lisandro...'

'Than you,' Susannah agreed. 'I know. But wouldn't that be a perfect cover? That's his style, isn't it? It's a bit like the way he undermined this council by turning our secret weapon against us. Maybe you've been in on it the whole time. After all, we'd never suspect *you*.'

'That's ridiculous,' Emmanuelle said, shaking her head slowly. Lady Miranda glanced worriedly at Lord Gawain. Susannah's theory seemed much too far-fetched, but in truth, it was no less difficult to believe than the guilt of any of the others.

'You're exactly Lisandro's type,' Susannah continued, on a roll. She turned to Jadon. 'Isn't that what he said last night to you, Jadon? Didn't he say that Teresa's not his type?' She spun back to Emmanuelle. 'He prefers girls like *you*.'

'*Pardi!*' Of course. 'Now we're back to typecasting, are we?' Emmanuelle snarled. She pointed at Renatus. "'e's guilty because of 'is last name, and if 'e's not, then *I* must be guilty because of 'ow I look? 'e said I'm 'is type? Well, *that*'s conclusive. I must be *so* flattered, because *no one else* 'as ever said that before, that I just decided to throw my future to the winds to pursue a life on the run with Peter's murderer. *That* sounds reasonable. Maybe it is me. *J'en ai marre.*' I'm fed up with this.

Lord Gawain sighed and fell out of the conversation as it became heated. They'd been over and over this for days and gotten nowhere. The facts were clear but insufficient to make a sound judgement. When Peter, the Elm Stone's elected keeper at the time, had fled with the power source, the council had chosen not to disclose this to the public. Only they, and whoever Lisandro had told, knew that the weapon was lost, and as such, only they knew that

Emmanuelle had come to inherit it. Lisandro and Jackson may have suspected her as the recipient but did not begin their attacks until the day after she shared her find with the council, indicating that it probably wasn't her (she could have given it back to Lisandro without the White Elm ever knowing she'd had it) but that someone else in their circle of thirteen had tipped their enemy off that she'd received it. Wasn't it something of a serious coincidence that after months of invisibility Lisandro had reappeared in that hotel lobby the same day they'd cremated Peter and learned he'd left them the Stone?

The situation at Teresa and Samuel's house was another too-huge coincidence in this world of no coincidences. Untrackable queen-of-wards Emmanuelle had somehow been tracked to the unlisted address of an unknown councillor. Maybe less-competent Aubrey or Jadon had been tracked there instead, but why would Jackson follow them? Nobody knew who they were, and if they did, no one had bothered to follow them anywhere previous to that night.

Some smaller coincidences were possible *real* coincidences, like Jackson's knowledge that Aubrey was in fact his replacement. Crafters were a rare Class. When Lisandro and Jackson were on the White Elm, it was the most to have ever belonged to the council at one time. They had almost literally struck gold to have discovered and enrolled not just one, but *three* Crafters in their Academy. So it was entirely possible that Jackson had simply inferred that Aubrey was the new Scribe.

Other coincidences were too disturbing to dwell on, like the fact that Saul had declared Renatus to be his murderer immediately before dropping dead, and that absolutely no one had entered the city other than White Elm. Follow-up carried out by Valero's very astute investigators had uncovered an unsettling problem: none of their highly trained security personnel and deeply sophisticated identification systems could accurately determine exactly how many White Elm sorcerers had passed through the city's magical barriers. Lord Gawain knew that normally those spells would work perfectly and track every soul to pass into the town, and that those men stationed atop their fortress-like walls never missed a single energetic flicker. Much like the wall beside Renatus in Saul's cell, the magic surrounding Valero had been warped and twisted to disguise another presence.

While it was possible that Renatus – everybody's favourite suspect – had warped the city's defences on his way in and while he stood in the cell simply to throw them all off, it seemed more likely to Lord Gawain (who, honestly, was desperately looking for a *logical* reason to pull suspicion off his protégé) that one of the other councillors had sneaked in to perform the execution before Saul could share too much information. But he couldn't say that, even to save Renatus from the council's doubts and fears, because where did that leave them except with the same doubts and fears, just redirected? Those who were not present at Valero would not take any more kindly to being accused than Emmanuelle just had.

Tian, Lord Gawain ruled out straightaway. He just didn't have the capacity. Of their thirteen sorcerers, Tian was the lowest-level, scoring roughly a seven on the old Trefzer Scale. It was a superhuman level for a Seer – Seers so rarely occurred in the upper bands of the Scale – but wasn't high enough to command the sort of energy required to do what was done in Valero.

Lady Miranda's innocence was above reproach. She had already attained the highest status and honour available to any sorceress in their world. Her mind was totally open and honest, always – she had nothing to hide. Lord Gawain often thought that he knew her better than he knew his wife and children. Qasim, likewise, was too high up the council's ladder to consider as having any sort of decent motivation for aiding Lisandro and had stood against the previous Dark Keeper when he'd asked who among the White Elm would leave with him. Qasim would be the next Lord.

But Lord Gawain had made the mistake of thinking Lisandro himself was above betrayal because of his position. It was unsafe to make the same assumption again.

Jadon adored Teresa and Aubrey. His priority was them. His reckless desire to rescue them, at any cost, had put Tian and Elijah in danger just last night. The idea that he would compromise his close friends' safety for personal gain was not one that seemed likely.

However... was it possible that Jadon *had* been working for Lisandro, and that Teresa and Aubrey were taken as leverage, to ensure Jadon played his part? That seemed very Lisandro-like, but Jadon was so selfless in nature that it still didn't seem to fit.

Elijah was more patient, compassionate and gentle than either of the present Healers. How could it be that a man who was so loving and soft with his sick wife could then betray his friends to their enemy, risking their lives?

Susannah had been on the council for over twenty years. Her service to council was indisputable, her talent undeniable, and her words always valued. But she had known Lisandro well. Living in the same country and on the same coast, they had met often as friends for coffee or lunch. Could it be that they still did? Was that why she had been so suspicious of Renatus and now Emmanuelle?

Anouk knew her city's defences and could most easily have manipulated them, but she had the most identifiable energy signature to the investigators and her mind was connected not only to the White Elm's ring but also to the collective mind of the whole of Valero. She couldn't have done this without someone overhearing her intentions. And she and Glen had worked together for so long that their minds were almost one; Lord Gawain doubted there was much by way of secrets between those two Telepaths. Glen could not have done this deed without Anouk knowing and being outraged. Could he?

Renatus, still sitting at his grand piano, was keeping quiet, avoiding being drawn into the conflict where he knew, as well as Lord Gawain did, that he would be painted as the perfect suspect. Sadly, that was exactly what he was. His lifelong ties to Lisandro were more incriminating than Susannah's lunches, as if his family's reputation and history weren't damaging enough. His secretiveness made the others suspicious. What did he have to hide? What did he *really* want an apprentice for? They were all torn between wanting to be right and wanting to be wrong – they wanted him gone, but didn't want to see him reappear on the other team.

Lord Gawain closed his eyes briefly, deliberately not thinking about the others in the room. Wondering only created suspicion. This was his family. He loved them all. Suspecting the wrong person could destroy those ties. He opened his eyes again and found that he was still looking at Renatus.

They are all wrong about you, he made himself think, very firmly. Renatus was theirs, not Lisandro's. He'd turned away from Lisandro seven years ago, on that first awful day, but only Lord Gawain had been there to see it. If only the others had seen, too.

Lady Miranda was the one to bring order back to the ballroom.

'We'll reconvene next week to decide our path in regards to the Elm Stone,' she said firmly in a raised voice, bringing the other voices underneath hers. 'While it seems that there is a chink in our armour somewhere, there is nothing we can do about that until further information comes to light. This blaming back and forth will get us nowhere.' She allowed her words to sink in. 'Continue as we have been – scriers seeking our enemies, Seers looking for changes in our missing friends' futures, Telepaths trying to make contact with them. Elijah, any leads?'

Lord Gawain turned to the Displacer and listened intently, because he'd only been briefed on Elijah's task.

'Not really,' the New Zealander admitted. 'I have a hold on most of the country. I'm focusing on big displacements, like international big. So far today there has only been one big enough to catch my attention – other than us – and it was just a guy going to Indonesia to visit his mother.'

Displacers at Elijah's level had such an amazing awareness of the fabric of space and time around them. It was so incredible that by putting his mind to it, Elijah could actually feel ripples and tugs on that fabric whenever anyone nearby teleported.

'Renatus, Aristea's formal training begins tomorrow,' Lord Gawain said. 'The sooner she can function independently as a member of this council the better. Her scrying ability has been helpful before, when we were searching for Peter. Maybe she'll be the key to finding Teresa and Aubrey.'

And if Renatus was here, training Aristea, he couldn't be anywhere else. It served a triple purpose, up-skilling the new initiate but also keeping Renatus in sight of the entire council where no one could accuse him of being up to anything and where, ultimately, he was safest. Danger would find Lord Gawain's favourite young councillor soon enough, and opportunities to prolong that were always opportunities he jumped on.

'That was Aristea?' Emmanuelle demanded, turning on Renatus. 'You didn't tell me that.'

'Lisandro is clearly working hard to block Qasim and I from seeing what he's been up to,' Renatus said, glancing at Emmanuelle but speaking to Lord Gawain. 'Whatever glimpses we receive are so late and outdated that they are almost useless, or are deliberately allowed to us at his discretion. Luckily for us, he doesn't know about Aristea, so he can't block her.'

'We can't know how long it will be before he finds out,' Lord Gawain said, slightly sad to think that someone here could destroy their advantage by trading secrets. Qasim shook his head.

'It doesn't matter,' he insisted. 'Lisandro can't block her specifically without knowing her energy, so until he actually meets her, his wards are all he has against her vision. Between the two of us,' he added, looking to Renatus, 'Aristea will have plenty of opportunities to improve in the next fortnight.'

The council dispersed.

A fortnight is a shorter expanse of time than Lord Gawain liked to consider. Days flew past without anything new coming to light. Councillors avoided one another as they privately deliberated their dilemma and started to take one side or the other. Most focussed on their classes to get their minds off the bigger issues. Qasim scheduled a Level 3 scrying class for almost every day and worked with Aristea alone for hours on the other days. Renatus took her into the grounds every afternoon to practise various skills she'd never attempted before. She was an eager and diligent student for him and he was a discerning teacher to her. He was still stronger than her and always would be, even though she was so much more now than she'd been on March first when Renatus had seen her from the study window, but that didn't stop her attempting every challenging task he set.

A week after their bonding, Lord Gawain stood in the ballroom, watching the pair through the tall windows. Renatus was casting illusions and showing his apprentice how to distinguish between what was real and what wasn't. She seemed to need some convincing at first that some of them were false realities. A rose bush erupted out of the ground; a hawk swooped down on her from the sky; a plastic bag fluttered across the lawn, blown by a wind that wasn't blowing. Aristea reached for the plastic bag, apparently environmentally conscious as well as gifted, and it dissolved into nothing at her touch.

Renatus was good at illusions, a talent Lord Gawain was thankful for, because it had allowed him to secure a place within the council for the youngest Morrissey in the first place. The previous Illusionist, a good friend and a confidant, had stepped down in the month following Renatus's twentieth birthday. There'd been no applicants as suitable for the role as Renatus, and so he'd earned his place among the White Elm, but he'd only been a fill-in. When Lisandro, Jackson and Peter left, and Renatus took on his current role, they'd found Teresa, who'd been just too young last time. Just as she was much better suited to the role of Illusionist, Renatus fitted better into his new position. He was made for it, Lord Gawain knew, as grim a thought as that was. Bad luck followed all of history's Dark Keepers and they almost always died young, but for now, Renatus flourished.

Lord Gawain knew that Renatus thought himself different to previous Dark Keepers, as all of them before him had believed, too. Maybe he was. Lord Gawain hoped so, every single day.

'Lisandro likes theatrics,' Lady Miranda commented as she came to stand beside him at the window. 'To be able to see through illusions would make Aristea quite an asset.'

They watched as Renatus showed Aristea how illusions were different from real objects. If they were near enough or small enough to touch, they would have no substance, usually, unless they were *very* good. He walked her around the rose bush and showed her how it lacked a third dimension, despite looking very full and real from her original viewpoint. Magical senses could often also pick up on this fact, able to sense right through them, and it quickly became evident that illusions of plants and animals lacked the aura and life-force of true living things. They felt like *nothing*, like air. Finally, Renatus drew attention to the very thin connection he had to all of his creations. No matter how real an illusion seemed, *that* was the giveaway. The hawk had no good reason to be drawing energy from Renatus unless Renatus was powering its existence.

'Qasim said Lisandro won't be able to hide anything from Aristea specifically until he meets her, so hopefully we can ensure it is a very long time before we get to test today's skills out on the real thing,' Lord Gawain replied, tentatively glimpsing into the futures and immediately disappointed. The very meeting he was hoping to put off would most likely occur in just a week. It was a Turning Point – one of the Stepping Stone events on which the paths of many lives could turn and be determined. If this event was allowed to occur, dozens of futures would disappear, unable to progress with its participants forever changed. Lord Gawain briefly followed the paths which forked from this decision but pulled back when he felt Lady Miranda's hand on his shoulder.

'Don't,' she advised, guessing what he'd seen. 'You've looked a hundred times. You can't save them. If they're to be saved, they'll have to save themselves. You can only guide.'

It was hard to suppress his helpless sigh, but he was spared dwelling on the morbid probabilities of the futures by an interruption no less concerning.

Shell's missing, Jadon told them all tensely. Lady Miranda closed her eyes, understanding the implications; outside, Renatus's illusions dissolved. *Lisandro lied to us. He's starting early.*

chapter thirteen

My life had become an unrecognisable tapestry of mystery, intrigue, intense study, massive ethical dilemmas and dire consequences. I'd known March first would be a fresh start for me, but I could never have envisioned *this*. I was learning so, so much, more at a time than I'd ever been able to absorb before. I was quite sure I wasn't any smarter, because I still spelt Welsh place-names wrong in Anouk's History lessons and still couldn't work out complicated mathematical algorithms in Jadon's class. I was just becoming quicker with those skills I worked on frequently. The development curve really was exponential – once I got some momentum, skills and knowledge started coming quicker and faster. I'd spent my life able to sense energies around people; upon coming here, I'd learnt the skills to *see* those energies with concentrated effort. Now, I could shift my focus as easily as the eyes focus for different distances and see shimmering outlines around each person around me, which generally sufficed, or change focus again (like looking further into the distance, just that simple) and view those nearby encased in deeply coloured eggs radiating metres from their bodies. Seventeen years spent on the base ability, two months getting small results with practice of the skill and now a week of connection with Renatus and switches flicked and I was there!

Now Renatus ended our lesson abruptly and turned away without a spoken word.

Lord Gawain needs to see us, I heard in my head as he retreated. I trailed after him, marvelling at this other incredible development. Renatus had always been able to overhear my most curious thoughts but now fully formed sentences moved between his mind and mine as clearly as verbal dialogue. He sometimes said nothing to me at all and instead I'd hear his voice echo around inside my brain. I hadn't yet mastered answering but I didn't think I was far off. He seemed to understand my disjointed responses of either vague affirmation or vague disagreement in the meantime.

I followed him inside. I ran to my dorm to use the bathroom before meeting him in his study. I hesitated at the door when it opened for me. My Empathic abilities had come back swinging within thirty hours of my initiation, and I could feel the very sharp emotions of the people inside. Several councillors were already gathered, crowded around the desk. Jadon seemed to be leading the conversation, explaining the significance of the items on the desk as he pointed to them. I couldn't see from where I was, so I strengthened my wards, braved walking closer and listened.

'The cell phone is Shell's,' Jadon was saying. 'I found it on the kitchen table. If she'd left by choice she could easily have grabbed it on her way out the door. The door was unlocked from the outside, with the key left in, which I thought was weird, so I took the key.'

'What about the envelope?' Lord Gawain asked.

'Ultrasound photos,' Jadon said without emotion. I could tell how difficult it was for him to hold back how he felt. He changed the subject as soon as he could. 'The magazine was on the floor beside the couch, like it had been dropped. It was the only thing out of place.'

'And the paperwork? Isn't that ours?' Anouk asked, leaning closer.

'Aubrey's,' Jadon agreed. 'I thought it was safer here than left there.'

'Good call,' Lord Gawain said, clapping Jadon's shoulder and turning to me. 'I'm sorry to cut your lesson so short. Jadon has brought some artefacts back from Aubrey's girlfriend's house. She's not been seen by any of her friends in days.'

Shell... Aubrey's pregnant girlfriend. Lisandro had started family-hunting early, choosing somebody whose disappearance he thought we wouldn't notice.

'Aristea,' Renatus said, beckoning to me. I squeezed between Lord Gawain and Anouk to reach Renatus's side. From here I could see the desktop, but most of the items in question weren't even on the desk. Floating at various levels above the desk were everyday objects encompassed in spherical bubbles of magic, similar to that ceramic shard he'd had a few weeks back. What were they?

'They're vacuum bubbles,' Jadon explained. 'It prevents contamination.'

'Contamination?'

'By picking this up and chucking it into a bag or pocket,' he said, pointing to the magazine, 'I would have risked dulling or removing any impressions left on it by Shell. So I've cast protective bubbles around everything I wanted to take, and that way I don't touch or damage anything.'

'Can you teach me that?' I asked, and Jadon smiled.

'Maybe next week.'

'Aristea, do you think you'll be able to divine any impressions from these items?' Lord Gawain asked, gesturing towards the bubbles. I looked at them. A week ago I would have been doubtful. Before my initiation I'd only tapped into very intense impressions, and only with effort. Now, knowing there could be a kidnapping involved, I was actually quite confident that the objects would carry enough emotional charge to give me a reading. This was one of several talents that had suddenly exploded into everyday existence this week. Now, an hour couldn't pass without it happening. When I rested my hand on the staircase banister, I tapped into a conversation between Suki and Isao in their native Japanese. When I used the edge of Anouk's desk to lean on when scooping a dropped paper off the floor, I overheard her discussing Renatus and I with Lady Miranda and Susannah.

'Lord Gawain just doesn't want to see it.'... 'He can't be blamed for caring too much.'... 'Something needs to be done, and soon.'... 'We should never have allowed him to have her. Her futures have sharply declined.'... 'How much

longer do you think Lord Gawain can keep Renatus prisoner here? Sooner or later, he's going to find an excuse to leave this house, and when he does, you know where he'll go.'...

It mostly happened when I wasn't paying attention to my surroundings – I guess that's when my mind was emptiest – but this meant that it was almost always a shock. I was getting better at reacting to the phenomenon internally rather than *externally*.

'Aristea?' Lord Gawain prompted. 'What do you think?'

He was *asking for my help*. Lord Gawain, leader of the unified magical community across the entire planet, wanted *my help*, and I was actually *capable* of providing said help. A week ago I would have been less than useless, just in the way in this instance. The idea that I'd grown in usefulness as quickly as I'd grown in capacity to learn was mind-blowing. My sister would be so proud of me if she could be here right now.

'I need to touch it,' I said, extending my hand towards the key. I kept my fingers a safe distance from the bubble of magic. I didn't know what would happen if I came into contact with it. 'I think I can do it.'

I had only to open my hand, for Jadon to pop the bubble encasing the key and for that key to fall into my palm to get my show.

Outside the house, early evening... A tall man with long black hair approaches the door, key in hand... Lisandro... He is alone... He knocks heavily... A flicker of fright from within... 'Shall I let myself in?'... He inserts the key into the lock and turns it, amused by this human act... A small voice speaks from the other side of the door... 'Is that Aubrey's key?'... 'Yes. He's alive, and perfectly well. He misses you a great deal. I thought I would do you both a favour and bring you to him.'... He pauses, key still in the lock, waiting for her response... 'Are you going to kill him?'... 'I hope it doesn't come to that.'... Another long pause... 'Listen, you had to know that this day was coming. Your boyfriend is White Elm – you didn't really think this life of yours was going to be all sugar and sweetness, did you?'... The door opens, revealing a girl a bit older than me and obviously pregnant, with dark red hair and a defeated look in her eyes, and Lisandro lets go of the key in the lock...

I took a breath as the vision ended, a tight feeling of suspense welling from deep inside. I looked up at Renatus, but his attention was locked onto Jadon's face as they communicated telepathically.

'Lisandro already had Aubrey's key,' I said, putting the information-rich item down. 'He told her he was taking her to see Aubrey. He said he doesn't want to kill him, and that she should have known that this would happen.'

Fear and worry for Shell stirred inside all of the adults in the office.

'Jadon, I need you to check on Samuel,' Lord Gawain said. 'The rest of us should improve the security around our own families.'

'Master, we're running out of time,' Renatus said pointedly, quickly turning his intense gaze on the council leader. 'There are people I can talk to.'

Anouk looked sharply at Lady Miranda, and Jadon's eyes flickered towards them, too. Something unspoken was being said between them, very loudly.

'Renatus, I don't want you in harm's way,' Lord Gawain said, somewhat lamely, I thought. 'Our enemy is dangerous-'

'I know what he is,' Renatus cut in, 'and you know as well as I do that I am fully capable of taking care of myself. I am stronger now than ever before. I have been patient for over a week, but now I need you to lift this ridiculous lockdown order. Let me do my job.'

'Renatus-'

'Why did you give me this role if you don't want me to do it?'

Renatus's question stopped Lord Gawain's stammering immediately.

'I... What?' he asked, sounding slightly shaky.

'Why did you bring me onto the council if you don't trust me?' Renatus pushed. I could feel the apprehension of the others in the room. 'Why did you choose me to take Lisandro's place if you didn't want to see me in danger?'

Lord Gawain stared at him for a very long, drawn-out moment. He looked... afraid? Resigned?

'I chose you for this role because of my eight options, your election was the only one which began a path to victory against Lisandro,' Lord Gawain said finally, very slowly. 'I – we,' he amended, 'Susannah and I foresaw that the selection of anyone else led inevitably to the downfall of the council. With you in his role... There is now a potential future in which we don't *all* die at his hand.'

The air was heavy as we all took this in. It felt like a massive admission to share first thing in the morning. Lord Gawain took a breath, which sounded so loud in the silence.

'I do trust you, Renatus,' he added. 'Alright. Do whatever you need to do.'

'What do you mean, we don't *all* die?' Renatus asked, slightly suspicious.

'I don't know yet,' Lord Gawain said, tiredly. 'The future is ever changing. Today, we all have futures, and that in itself is blessing enough. If Fate wishes me to know more, it will show me. Now that you have made up your mind, I see the outcomes of your visit to O'Malley. You are correct; he has information we need. Go.'

Renatus beckoned to me, not needing to be told twice, already circling the desk and heading for the door.

'She can't go to O'Malley,' Anouk protested when I followed after Renatus.

'She goes with me,' my master said as the door opened. He paused, and the other councillors filed out, not wanting to be locked in until his return. He met Anouk's eyes as she passed him. 'I don't suppose you'd prefer I go alone, unchecked and unwatched?'

Her return look was icy but she had no verbal reply. She might have responded telepathically, something spiteful and cold, but I didn't think so.

'Wait until your return before sharing anything with us,' Lord Gawain told Renatus. 'I know O'Malley was displeased with your decision to join the council, and I feel he will be less forthcoming if he senses you passing on everything he tells you.'

'Yes, Master,' Renatus agreed. The door closed, and he rested a hand on my shoulder, subtly urging me forwards down the hall. I looked back at the other three councillors as I headed for the stairwell. Anouk glanced at Jadon, catching his gaze for a millisecond, and I knew she was talking about us. Lord Gawain looked more than just a little bit worried, but I knew he was making an effort to feel calm.

As I led the way down the stairs, I felt myself being pushed to move faster, not physically but by Renatus's emotions. His eagerness to get outside the gates was infectious. Lord Gawain's order to remain on the estate had left Renatus feeling caged and useless, and the lift of that order seemed to have completely reinvigorated him.

We passed a couple of people in the reception hall and in the sunny grounds. Most gave us curious looks; some, like Sterling, simply looked away, although I knew that as soon as I wasn't able to see her, Sterling's eyes returned to Renatus's retreating back.

She still had it bad.

'Who is O'Malley?' I asked as we crossed the front lawn.

'Declan O'Malley,' Renatus clarified. 'He's an old... family friend, I suppose. Our parents were

307

friends. He is... well-connected... to some shady types.'

'I see,' I said. 'But you trust him?'

'Not really. Trust is a rare and precious commodity. Declan is dangerous in his own right, and a liar and a manipulator. I don't trust him, I trust his information. He's a talented scrier. He makes it his business to know everything he shouldn't.'

'Lord Gawain made it sound like he doesn't like the council,' I commented.

'Declan has no problem with the White Elm,' Renatus disagreed. 'He thinks I was stupid to so publicly choose a side.'

'You joined before Lisandro was a problem, though.'

'Even then, there were sides. There have always been sides. There is the White Elm, and all the lawfulness and light and leadership that it represents, and there is opposition. Not everyone agrees with what the White Elm represents. *I* did; I *do*.' He paused for a long moment. I knew he was reflecting on what Lord Gawain had said. 'Declan may not be affiliated with the council but neither is he affiliated with Lisandro, which makes him particularly unusual for someone like him. If we're against Lisandro, and Declan's not *with* him, that puts us practically on the same side. More or less.'

He had the gate open before us, and I walked through, following Renatus several metres away from the estate. When he seemed satisfied that we'd walked far enough, he grasped my upper arm and took one more step. He disappeared into another place, dragging me with him. My foot touched down on firm ground.

I pretended like I was perfectly comfortable and at ease with casually teleporting across the countryside, but really I was completely in awe of what had become commonplace in my daily life.

We hadn't gone far. The sun was in the exact same place, just peeking out from behind a cloud, and the temperature was the same. We had arrived at a house that was a lot like Renatus's, not as big but clearly from the same era. Unlike Morrissey House, however, this place had not been properly maintained. Broken windows reflected slivers of dull sunlight, vines had crept across the stone, and when we ascended the front steps, I was very careful, because some of the steps were broken and the handrail had collapsed.

The doors were battered but at least still hanging and locked shut. Renatus turned to me.

'Declan will try to offer you a drink,' he said. 'Decline it. Don't eat anything he gives you, don't let him touch you, and if you can help it, don't talk to him. He's our informant, not the other way around.'

'Okay,' I agreed. Renatus hesitated, looking like he wanted to say more but wasn't sure how, but after a moment turned away and rapped his knuckles firmly on the door.

We waited almost a minute in silence. I began to wonder whether the inhabitant was not home.

'He's in there,' Renatus assured me. 'He's just worked out I'm not alone. He's wondering who you are. Be on your guard.'

I nodded, starting to feel apprehensive. I wasn't on the best of terms with Anouk but she'd made of point of stating that I shouldn't come here. Presumably she had decent reason, and now Renatus was telling me to "be on my guard". Where had he brought me? A few seconds later I heard a scraping noise on the other side of the door as someone unlocked the door. It opened just a crack, and then was shoved open with a flourish.

'Oh, hello!' the man inside said brightly, as though pleasantly surprised to find us on his front porch. For the most part his emotions were neatly hidden from me so I couldn't know if this was the case but his tone dripped with falseness. He was a tall and thin man of Renatus's age, with messy dark hair and a tooth missing in his wide grin.

'Hello, Declan,' Renatus said, without cheer. 'Can we come in?'

'Uh, of course,' Declan agreed, trying to maintain a host's authority over the exchange. He stepped aside and held the door open for us, his eyes lingering on me way too long. 'And who have you brought with you this afternoon, Renatus?'

'Her name is Aristea.' Renatus didn't look back until he had reached the centre of the reception hall, where he stopped and turned to face Declan. 'You and I have some things to discuss.'

'Of course, of course,' Declan said vaguely, still looking at me. He smiled what I guessed was his most charming smile. 'Would you like a drink, sweetheart?'

'No. Thanks,' I answered. Renatus had guessed correctly.

'You know, I've never been introduced to any of Renatus's previous girlfriends,' Declan continued smoothly, 'so it's a real pleasure to meet you.'

'Thanks, but I'm not his girlfriend,' I said coolly. He feigned shock.

'Fiancée? Renatus, why didn't you tell me?'

'She's not my fiancée, and she's not a toy, so stop thinking about her like you are,' Renatus said, his tone cold. Declan pretended to be embarrassed, but I could sense that he was not in the least bit ashamed that Renatus had caught him out. He turned to me with that same smile.

'I'm sorry, sweetheart, you're just such a pretty young lady,' he said, his eyebrows coming together slightly as he finished the sentence. Something clicked in his head as he studied my face. 'A very young lady. You're younger than I thought.'

'That's right, she is, so don't even try it on, Declan,' Renatus said. He clicked his fingers irritably in the other's line of sight. 'Focus. I've got some questions for you.'

'Right,' Declan answered with eyes still on me. I could almost see the cogs turning in his head as he tried to work out why Renatus would bring a teenage girl into his house – one that was neither a girlfriend nor a plaything.

'Lisandro took Shell Hawke from her home in Baillieston,' Renatus said. 'I want to know where he took her.'

'But that was days ago!' Declan said, feigning disappointment. I gently brushed my extra senses over him and felt the falseness there that guarded the true Declan. We got what he chose to share and nothing else. Everything about him, from his casual and haphazard appearance to his overly friendly demeanour, was carefully selected and deliberately executed. I found that idea fascinating more than frightening, though certainly I could appreciate how quickly and easily this situation could slip out of our control. I knew I was underestimating Declan O'Malley and that was what he wanted.

'I know you know.'

'I have an idea,' Declan corrected. 'You're not the only person Lisandro is hidden from. I can't just pinpoint his exact location, you know. And anyway, it's not like I'm keeping tabs on him. It's not *my* job.'

The sparkle in his eye betrayed the cheek of his implication – it's not *my* job, it's *yours*.

'Why don't you share your idea?' Renatus suggested, not taking the bait, sliding a hand into his pocket and withdrawing a small cloth bag. Declan's face was impassive but his eyes strayed onto the bag.

'I suppose I could,' he agreed. 'We could talk over lunch?'

'No. Thank you.'

'Drinks?'

'Declan,' Renatus warned.

'Alright, fine,' Declan grumbled. 'We'll just stand here awkwardly, shall we? Like strangers.' His attention moved back to me, eyes flickering across the space around me. 'Loving the matching auras, by the way. Cute.'

I glanced up at Renatus, unnerved. Matching auras?

'Your idea,' Renatus reminded him, raising the cloth bag so it was more visible.

'My idea is that Lisandro might have taken up residence in an old beach house up north,' Declan said, picking at his nails as though bored. 'It's not anything flashy – just a place he might have used once to make some serious magic happen up there. It's designed so not everyone can find it, but you'll need to work that out yourself. This hypothetical beach shack would be closer to Portrush than to Portstewart. If you left Coleraine with a compass and went due north, you'd pretty much hit it. If it exists. That's just my idea, anyway.'

I hoped I didn't look too shocked. *I* had lived off a beach between Portrush and Portstewart. Would I know the beach? Would I recognise the house?

'Is he keeping hostages there?' Renatus asked, and Declan shrugged.

'*There* might not exist,' he reminded my master, which only annoyed Renatus.

'For argument's sake, say it does. Are they there?'

'I wouldn't know, although if you wanted me to take an educated guess, I would say yes.'

'Would you guess that he intends to harm those hostages?'

'I'm no more Empathic than you are. I can't know his intentions. I suppose that's why you've got

313

her,' he added, jerking his head in my direction. Renatus glanced at me, and I worked on building stronger walls around my mind. His mention of Empathy had inspired the thought *like me*, and somehow he'd heard it. I hadn't even felt Declan in my head, although now I felt him pull away. So sneaky. So *illegal*! Glen had taught us in, like, lesson one, what was allowed and what wasn't, and entering someone else's mind without announcing yourself was definitely not on. Declan was still talking. 'But again, if you're asking me to guess, then I would guess that no, he's hesitant to kill them. He's waiting.'

Declan's guesses seemed remarkably well-researched.

''Hesitant' wouldn't be the word I chose to describe how Lisandro feels about killing a White Elm councillor,' Renatus stated.

'It's the word I'll stick with,' Declan responded. 'It's not something he's done before. When he had Peter drowned it took days for that vision to reach you, didn't it? Because Peter wasn't White Elm any more. If he killed one of your people right now, you would all know; no blocks or wards would hide that, and you would all be on his back in an instant. His cover would be gone. I'll say it again – he's hesitant to kill them. He's waiting.'

'Is there anyone I can talk to who knows more?' Renatus asked.

'No one *knows* anything,' Declan reminded him, 'but I can think of a couple of people who might be willing to guess. Not for you, but maybe for me. You closed a lot of avenues when you took that oath, my friend.'

'I opened more.'

'I can see that. You're looking very *healthy* these days, Renatus – or maybe it's a new haircut.' Declan laughed at his own joke. 'I really wish you wouldn't block me from scrying your life. Then I wouldn't have to ask.'

'Stay out of her head, Declan,' Renatus warned, and I felt Declan's presence slip away so quick I had no chance to catch him. I instinctively touched my temple, as though I could physically cover any holes in my mental armour. I'd thought my wards were so good, but here was someone who knew exactly how to exploit my gaps and weaknesses. Declan was watching me again, like you look at a fountain, and I felt a burst of shock from him as his gaze slid from my face to my wrist. It was the first real emotion I'd felt him feel since I got here. He looked suddenly to Renatus.

'No,' he said, sounding startled. I knew he'd connected the dots. 'No – there's no way they'd let you.'

Renatus didn't answer, and I didn't have anything to say, so there was silence as Declan looked wildly between us. His attention was on Renatus when he next spoke.

'Well. Don't keep me in suspense. Let's see it.'

'You don't need to see anything,' Renatus said, tossing the cloth bag to his informant. Declan caught it with ease, his eyes glued to Renatus's right hand. The sleeve shifted slightly when he threw the payment, revealing the point at the top of his tattoo. 'You just need to keep your mouth shut. If Lisandro finds out about her, I'm holding you personally responsible.'

'Even if Lisandro has a spy in your council providing all that sort of information anyway?' Declan checked.

'How do you know about that?' I asked, suspicious. That was not common knowledge.

'Sweetheart, I hear things,' Declan said, speaking kindly. His emotional blockage seemed less solid when he addressed me, and I detected a fragment of genuine Declan in his demeanour. 'I don't know who it is; they don't use a name. They call this person "Friend". They don't talk about what the Friend is going to do – I'm not sure they know, although Lisandro might – they only talk about what the Friend has told them.' He looked back to Renatus, a pained look on his face. 'Renatus, seriously, did you *look* at this girl before you took part in that ceremony? You know what you've thrown away, don't you?'

'How is the information being passed?' Renatus asked, ignoring the last part.

'Clues, signals, hidden messages. Nothing direct. Why did the council let you have an apprentice? Why did you choose a *girl*?'

'Why haven't we seen who it is?'

'The Friend is too well buried in your council,' Declan said, slipping easily between the roles of compliant informant and curious inquirer. 'Someone underestimated and misunderstood. There is no contact with Lisandro or anyone else like him, to avoid suspicion. Did you at least try her out? No – of course not, it wouldn't have worked. I don't get it.'

'How surprising,' Renatus said, sarcastic.

'I think you're failing to grasp the fact that you can never, ever, ever have that,' Declan said seriously, pointing at me. 'I hope you're at peace with that.'

'I am,' Renatus agreed, coolly. Declan took a deep breath, clearly completely lost. He looked back at me for a long moment.

'Well-' he began, a smile breaking out across his face.

'And if you ever, ever touch her, your head will be above the mantle at Morrissey House,' Renatus added, cutting him off before he could start speaking. 'So don't try anything.'

'At least Morrissey House is nicer than here,' Declan said cheerfully, but he left it alone. 'Your secret is safe with me, so long as it is actually a secret.'

'How comforting,' Renatus commented.

'After that, well, it's just knowledge, isn't it, and knowledge should be free,' Declan rationalised. 'It won't take people long to work out what's changed with you, Renatus, and they won't need my help working out why you're dragging a teenage scrier everywhere with you. Lisandro has ears everywhere, and sooner rather than later he's going to find out that you're a master. He'll be so proud,' Declan added with that sparkle in his eye again.

'Go to hell,' Renatus snarled, with more anger than I thought the comment justified.

'Your master probably hasn't told you this,' Declan said to me, ignoring Renatus's glare, 'but he and I are related.'

'Yes, if you look back fifteen generations in both family trees, you might find a Morrissey and an O'Malley with the same nose,' Renatus agreed snidely.

In this one instance, I thought Renatus's comment might be more exaggerated than Declan's. Looking between them, I could see similarities. Their noses were indeed the same shape, they had similar hairlines, similarly shaped faces and the same colouring and build. Declan was plainer than Renatus, rougher, with much less defined features, and was not anywhere near as classically beautiful, but blood relationship was clearly a factor here.

'Yes, well, whatever,' Declan continued, unfazed. 'My point is that we go back quite a ways. And I know things.'

'Good thing, otherwise no one would have any use for you,' Renatus said.

'Harsh,' Declan commented, but his tone was bright and amused. He was not remotely emotionally invested in gaining Renatus's affection. This was just a game. 'Was there anything else?'

'You tell me.'

'I saw this and thought of you,' Declan said with false affection, reaching into his pocket and withdrawing something in his closed fist. He extended his hand and opened his fingers, but there was nothing there. He faked a gasp and turned his hand theatrically, as though searching for his lost object. I knew it was an act but I watched with interest as he played it out; Renatus, meanwhile, remained unimpressed. Declan looked over at me suddenly and smiled. 'Should've known.'

I didn't move as Declan stepped over to me, still captivated by the silly act and interested to see how he intended to wrap it up.

'I'm sure I don't have to remind you what will happen if you touch her,' Renatus said coldly as Declan reached a hand towards my face. He paused and sighed, dropping his hand.

'I guess you'll have to get it yourself,' Declan told me, looking pointedly at my right ear. Getting the hint, I reached a hand behind my earring. To my surprise, my fingertips touched something cold tangled in my hair.

Dark fear... dirty, blackened cement floor... grubby bare feet... golden chain wrapped around a skinny ankle... Teresa, sobbing silently, pulling herself upright against a wall, straightening her tatty skirt over her shaking legs... Trembling little fingers find a coin on the floor and turn it once... Door slams open, Teresa jumps, unprepared... Not more... 'Sneak that outta my pocket, did you, bitch? Think you should be paid, did you?'... A nasty laugh, a pale hand reaching for the money...

I withdrew a two Euro coin from behind my ear, meeting Renatus's gaze. My stomach was completely knotted in horror with what I had to assume that vision had meant. He advised me against thinking.

'I thought you'd like that,' Declan said proudly, beaming.

'Where did you find that?' Renatus asked Declan, his eyes still on me. Declan shrugged.

'Nowhere particular,' he answered indifferently. 'I know some people who met some people who heard some things and found some things. You know how it is. If anything further comes to light... well, you know where to find me, obviously. And you're always welcome back, too, Miss Aristea,' he added, much too warmly, 'whenever you like.'

'Thanks,' I said. This time, when he tried to venture into my mind, I felt him; just a faint, slippery, slimy little presence. *Not likely*, I thought as I blocked him. His smile widened, and I knew he'd heard me before he'd been kicked out.

'Aristea, we're leaving,' Renatus said pointedly, and I moved towards the door. Declan beat me there, holding it wide open for us.

'Always a pleasure, Renatus,' he said as we walked out, lightly hefting his little bag of coins and slipping it into a pocket. 'Best of luck, of course. Say hi to Lisandro when you see him.'

My master turned sharply, but Declan had already shut the door.

'Bastard,' Renatus muttered, clearly very annoyed, as he trudged down the steps. Declan, or perhaps just the frustration Declan created, had a strange effect on Renatus, I thought as I followed in silence. Frustration made him grittier and less elegant, both in the way he felt energetically and the way he acted. He walked heavier, less fluid, and his usually smooth, impossibly calm aura seemed spiky and rough now.

Frustration made Renatus more human.

'Renatus, is Teresa being... raped?' I asked, my voice unsteady. I'd expected her to be dead. Maybe isolated or otherwise tortured. I was struggling very hard with this new knowledge. If it was true it was so much worse to me. 'Who was that man? When did this happen?'

'I don't know,' Renatus told me truthfully. 'I hope we're inferring incorrectly. It must have been recent... She didn't mention this to Jadon last week.' He shook his head, jaw tight. He turned to me. 'You need to forget what you saw for now.'

'I can't forget,' I said in a small voice. Poor Teresa. For my first few weeks at the Academy, she'd been one of my teachers, and I liked her. The vision of her afraid, dirty and violated was incomprehensible.

'You need to,' Renatus insisted. 'We both need to. It's too painful, too awful, and there's nothing either of us can do. Save the disgust and horror for when Lisandro is standing right in front of you, charming and all-wonderful, and you need to remind yourself of why he's a monster.'

It was good advice, but shaking Teresa's clammy-cold emotions was easier said than done.

'What did you think of Declan?' Renatus redirected, starting to walk again.

'I can see why some might prefer not to be linked with him,' I agreed, following, choosing not to admit that I'd found Declan perfectly likeable, for all his faults. Yes, he was a complete creep, but at the same time, I was finding it impossible to dislike him on that alone. 'He is a bit... shady.'

'He's unfortunately necessary,' Renatus said, slightly regretful. He stopped and I handed over the coin. He pocketed it, gazing at the northern horizon for a moment. 'Let's go.'

He grasped my arm and pulled me along as he stepped forward, and then we were gone and we were somewhere else. But we didn't go home – not to his home, anyway. I smelt the ocean before I saw it, and my stomach flipped as I recognised the coastal road we stood on as a road I'd travelled a zillion times before.

Oh.

Ballyreagh Road, the road between Portsrush and Portstewart, off which ran the little road I'd lived on for the first fourteen years of my life. Renatus released my arm, and I slowly turned around, away from the caravan park that overlooked the North Sea. There was the sea that had lulled me to sleep as a baby. There was the beach, two hundred metres away from where I stood. If I squinted to the east, I'd surely be able to see the sandy stretch further along, where I'd collected my seashells as a little girl. And there, over that gentle hill, just barely out of sight, was the turnoff onto our old street.

This was *my home*.

The last place on the planet I wanted to be.

'I'm not sure how long it'll be before we're allowed out of the house again, so we should use this opportunity to investigate the area,' Renatus said over his shoulder as he began making his way across the grass towards the sea. Totally oblivious to the total mess he'd just made of everything.

I followed reluctantly. It didn't take us long to reach the water. I closed my eyes and breathed deep. There was something special about ocean air. It made you think life was beautiful and that nothing bad could possibly happen to you. The gentle waves sounded so calming and rhythmic, like they were agreeing, but *I* knew how quickly everything could change here.

'Which way?' Renatus asked, glancing to each side. His eyes lingered on the east and I felt a strange emotion in him. He felt... familiar. 'There's something-'

'West,' I said, cutting him off. I didn't want him to pick the east. I especially didn't want him to think there was something concerning and important that way that needed our attention.

'Can't you feel that?' he asked, apparently surprised. He had no idea. I stared at him, wishing we weren't here. I felt nothing here, mostly by choice. There was probably a lot of energy to tune into, but I wasn't ready to do that.

'No,' I answered firmly. I folded my arms in a childish attempt to hold my emotions in.

'There's a sort of taint on the energy somewhere up there,' he said, looking past me. 'It feels like... the orchard.'

'It should,' I snapped. 'My parents and brother died one kilometre up the road from here. I'm going west.'

I tried to shove past him, but Renatus turned with me and suddenly we were both walking west. He let me seethe in silence for several minutes, just keeping pace with me. I tried not to think about what he'd said. My old house felt like his orchard? I hadn't been back to my childhood home since the tragedy that had mostly destroyed it. The local council had demolished what was left, I'd been told. The site of remaining walls and cracked frames was unsafe and unstable. I avoided reflecting on how it had felt that day, standing in the rubble of the broken house while our neighbour stood nearby speaking shakily into a mobile phone. Had it felt dark? Was that why the orchard felt so familiar to me – because I'd felt it before? I couldn't or wouldn't remember.

'Declan, and Saul, both said that this house is spelled to make it hard to find,' Renatus said a few minutes later. I focussed very hard on what he was saying. Lisandro's house – special spells to protect it – somewhere around here. Right. 'Declan made it sound like a riddle to be solved.'

'Maybe's it's guarded by an illusion,' I suggested, kicking a rock.

'Perhaps,' Renatus agreed. I followed his thoughts with mine. He thought it was more than that. He thought Lisandro was cleverer than that.

'What more can he do?' I asked, realising a moment later when he looked at me that I had just done what used to annoy me about him – verbally answering thoughts before they were said aloud.

Apparently it didn't annoy him at all. I gathered from his feeling of satisfaction that he considered it a more effective and efficient means of communication anyway.

'Well, he could use spells like the ones guarding my house,' Renatus began, eyeing a section of very flat shoreline and extending his senses over it. I did the same. I felt nothing but air. 'Wards and worse. They would make it impossible for certain people to cross its boundaries. He may be using a variety of wards and illusions to hide the structure's presence from outsiders. I think he's gone further than your average ward or illusion, though. He likes to think outside the box.'

I closed my eyes and stood still for a moment, trying to tune in to the energy of this beach I knew so well. The natural energies were most prominent. I felt the waves race each other through the water, losing power as they approached the shore and finally washed across the rocky beach. I felt the salty, cold wind whip through the hardy grasses behind me, and I felt the energy of the small, hidden life forms braving this harsh environment. Across the road, I could feel the auras of those people staying in the caravan park. No one seemed to be out and about, or doing much at all, and nobody's emotions struck me as interesting or noteworthy.

When I dug deeper, I started to feel the alien energies left by magical actions. Sparsely around me, and more densely the further I extended my senses to the east, I felt what I had to describe as-

'Potholes,' Renatus agreed before I could finish the thought. 'Those are blocked Displacements. That's what's left when someone Displaces and covers the exit so they cannot be followed. They're very conspicuous from this end, but impossible to follow or trace from the entry point. Elijah should see this.'

In his head, I heard him sharing what we'd found with someone else.

'How long do you think Lisandro has been living up here?' I asked presently, staring into the water. I wasn't sure I wanted to know, but the question came out anyway. Renatus was pacing around one of the weird energy sinkholes, but looked up at me uncertainly when I spoke.

'This whole year, at least,' he said. 'I couldn't say for sure. Some of these cover-ups span back quite a while. Years and years, though, would be a stretch, I think. I don't think he was living here when you were,' he finished.

'Why is he here at all?' The demand burst forth without thought. Why would I ask that? Why would I want that answer? It kept coming. 'Why *this* beach? Why would he pick *this* place to hide?'

Renatus stared at me.

'It feels like the orchard,' he repeated.

'But what does that *mean*?' I asked, upset. 'Families die in car accidents at intersections and on highways all the time. Roads don't feel like the orchard. Is it just witch families? When witch families die all together in one place, does it leave that stain behind? Is that it?' I looked around desperately, and another inappropriate question that I didn't want to ask leapt from my mouth. 'Are there ghosts here, too? Are we going to see my brother covered in blood like I saw your sister in the orchard?'

'Lisandro chose this place to hide because the dark feeling appeals to him and makes him feel stronger,' Renatus answered only my first question, 'the same way the pathway in the orchard draws *you* in. Such places repel normal people, and especially the people emotionally linked to them.'

'I'm not normal?' I asked, trying not to sound hurt.

'No. That's why you're my apprentice,' Renatus reminded me. 'You fear the energy here because of what happened to you here, but the same – virtually the same – energy on my estate attracts you. Possibly even empowers you. Everyone else avoids that path.'

'Even you?'

'Especially me. The spot Lisandro has chosen will be a section of beach that everyone avoids.'

We both glanced to the east. Somewhere that way, maybe within eyeshot but invisible to my untrained eyes, Lisandro was hiding in a secret base. I could be standing less than a kilometre away from a killer and his hostages (assuming, of course, that Lisandro had Teresa, Aubrey and Shell with him and they were alive) and he could be watching me right now through a window I couldn't see. I shivered, and focussed on my wards. They had to be perfect. I had to be ready for anything.

'Come on, let's go back.'

Renatus reached for my arm; I pulled it away before he could grab me. He was worried about upsetting me – I got that – but was he really going to turn his back on this chance to find Lisandro's hiding place, and maybe Teresa and Aubrey? Why would he do that?

Because, I realised, he had no reason to think that I was up to this.

'He might have already seen us,' I argued. 'Lisandro could be watching us *right now*. Leaving now just to drop me off at home just gives him a head start if he thinks to relocate. This could be it – today could be the day you get Teresa and Aubrey back.'

'It's not,' Renatus said shortly. 'Susannah would know by now if I'd started down that path.'

It was so easy to forget that while I shared my thoughts with just him, Renatus shared his with the entire hive mind of the White Elm. That collective mind held incredible gifts, including the ability to know the consequences of actions long before the act was done. He never had to make decisions alone or without inform.

'But what if we've been spotted?' I pressed. 'Is it such a good idea to leave? He might not be here when you come back.'

'He hasn't seen us,' Renatus said. 'If he had, he'd have shown himself by now. He wouldn't hide from me – he's not afraid of me. Apparently he wants to see me.'

Renatus took me by the wrist and Displaced us both away from the beach. We arrived outside the gates of Morrissey House and walked the remaining few steps. A vague memory of the conversation I'd partially overheard when I'd awoken after the bonding ceremony surfaced, and I tried not to wonder why Lisandro would want to speak with Renatus and what made Renatus so certain.

How could he possibly know what Lisandro would do? Before my mind could wander, I dismissed the concerns – they were stupid. Renatus followed me through the gates. When I heard the iron clang shut, I turned.

'I can handle it, you know,' I said. When he stared at me, subtly sifting through my thoughts to work out what I was talking about, I added, 'The beach. I can handle the dark feeling.'

He still said nothing, and I realised that I hadn't finished.

'I can handle it, so when you go back tomorrow, and the next day, and whenever else, I don't want you to leave me here thinking I can't,' I said. My words were stronger than I felt, and that frightened voice in my head was once again begging for me to be quiet, but that voice was muffled now, slightly smothered by my determination to stop being a scared little girl and start acting like a White Elm apprentice.

'Aristea, you don't have to face down your demons to prove your worth to me or the council,' Renatus said, a softness to his voice. 'I've ignored mine for seven years. I don't expect any better from you.'

'*I* expect better from me,' I said with more strength than I felt. 'I can handle it. I *want* to handle it. I want...' I paused, struggling for the right words. They came to mind, and when I said them, I realised that although they didn't sound like it, they were all true. 'I'm not going to be scared of the past anymore.'

Renatus briefly rested a hand on my shoulder.

'You are much braver than I am,' he said. 'But I'm still going to leave you behind when I go back there. Not because,' he raised his voice over my protests, 'I think you can't handle it; because I don't think you *should* have to.'

chapter fourteen

I was not going to be afraid of the past anymore.

My new mantra took immediate effect, or so I told myself. When I met Hiroko in the dining hall for lunch a few minutes after first announcing those famous last words, I felt eyes on me, and looked instinctively to the door just as Khalida and Suki entered after Bella. It was Bella's superior kohl-lined gaze that I'd felt. I stared back at her, knowing they wouldn't say a word against me now. The three had avoided my presence and my gaze religiously all week. Khalida noticed and linked an arm through Bella's, nudging her and whispering something. When her friend looked away, Khalida lifted her chin in an acknowledging nod. It was the closest thing to friendliness as I was likely to get, so I took it with good grace, nodding back.

Suki, I saw, was clutching the sparkly pink notebook they'd dropped in to Renatus a while back. From their triumphant and satisfied expressions I gathered the trio had just enjoyed another events meeting with him.

'I wonder when they will be ready to expand their empire?' Hiroko said, glancing up from the drawing she was doing to look meaningfully in the direction of Sterling, who was glaring sulkily at the sparkly book. I remembered overhearing Sterling complaining that Khalida wouldn't let her help with their plans for student social events at the Academy. For goodness' sake – how many lives needed to be ruined in the name of that stupid notebook? Sterling and Khalida had a deep mutual interest in Renatus but apparently the older three girls hadn't been willing to adopt my roommate into their clique, and Sterling had been left out in the cold. I took Renatus's earlier advice and put it out of my mind. There was nothing to be done, and in this case, it had already been solved for me. Sterling could sort her own problems out.

I scoffed my lunch and made Hiroko do the same so I could drag her into Teresa's now-unused classroom and tell her everything that had just happened to me today. She made me practise Displacement while I talked, so we'd have an excuse if we were caught here unsupervised, and she sat back and cast simple little wards, quite adept now.

'That is horrible,' she agreed with me, looking like she'd swallowed something yucky. 'You must have misinterpreted. It is too terrible.'

'I hope so, too,' I said, 'but Renatus looked like he'd come to the same conclusion that I did.'

'But it cannot be,' Hiroko insisted. 'It is not done. It is not...' She struggled to come up with the appropriate word. She gave up after a moment. 'I never have heard of this. Magical people have protected women with laws longer than mortals have. There are ethics even bad sorcerers abide by. Lisandro is from the White Elm, he would know this... I am very shocked if he will condone what you think you saw.'

'What sort of ethics?' I asked, tossing pillows from nearby chairs at Hiroko's wards. She had a much more rounded understanding of magic and its systems than I did, and I loved getting her insight.

'Old ones.' Both cushions bounced safely away before they could hit her.

'Like what? What rules do bad guys follow?'

'Like,' Hiroko said, gesturing with one hand and in doing so losing focus on her ward. I lobbed my last cushion at her and hit her squarely. We both fell back into the nearest chairs, laughing. It felt good to laugh. My life had become so serious and it felt like I could only relax when I got to be alone with Hiroko. She started again. 'There are old rules, like, "don't kill little children", and "don't violate women". Even bad people follow those rules, because there are consequences. Fateful consequences.'

'What happens to them?' I asked with morbid interest, sitting forward. Hiroko shrugged uncomfortably.

'I do not know for certain. But my father tells me, Fate finds ways to punish those who break her laws. Those who remember the old ways are mindful.'

I took to making time for these sessions with Hiroko every day, slotting them in around my normal classes, my lessons with Renatus and my private tutoring hours with Qasim. My days were busy places to be. Renatus didn't take me back to the beach when he went back, but I kept myself in the loop as to what was going on. Elijah had found the beach lined with those Displacement exit points, becoming more and more concentrated the further east he'd moved and then becoming sparser after passing a certain inconspicuous point. The White Elm was concentrating its efforts there, but taking extreme caution – stumbling across Lisandro's hideaway would be a very *un*happy accident for them, especially if Lisandro was already watching them from inside, ready to announce himself and his million merry men as soon as he was discovered.

Elijah had also found the exit point Jackson had used after his initial kidnapping of Teresa and Aubrey. It, along with dozens of other blocked exit points of varying ages, was actually found in the surf. Every single one was carefully filled in. Elijah had added, amused, 'This place must be a huge secret if its frequent visitors still bother to cover their tracks when they screw up and land themselves waist-deep in the North Sea. The shock of the cold would probably reorganise anyone else's priorities pretty quickly.'

I imagined Displacing from a dry, warm place like Teresa's hometown in Italy and missing the dry rocky beach by mere metres. Not nice.

The coin Declan had left behind my ear was apparently circulated around the White Elm excepting only Jadon, for fear of how he'd react. Renatus maintained that I needed to try very hard not to worry about what I'd seen as there was nothing I could do about it, but that didn't make it easy to put my fears for Teresa away.

On the weekend I realised in horror that I hadn't written to my sister in *ages* and I felt like a deserter. Angela had written to me three times in the near-fortnight since I'd been initiated (each letter calm but steadily increasing in nervousness as she awaited my reply) and she didn't even know for sure if I'd survived the ordeal, relying only on a text message from Emmanuelle. I was a terrible sister. While Hiroko wrote to her elderly neighbour (*she* forgot no one) I grabbed this opportunity and poured words out onto a page.

Dear Angela,

I'm so sorry for how long I've left this letter! I've received all of yours but I have been busy, but that's just an excuse because I'm such a bad sister and I am sorry. My life has been so crazy lately, all starting with when Renatus asked me to be his apprentice, which is unexpected to say the least!

I stopped there, pen poised above the paper. *He broke tradition to ask me, no one on the council was particularly happy and there's a miniscule possibility that he's involved somehow in this little murder mishap in Russia, oh, and he's actually even younger than you* didn't seem like good things to put to down in writing. My sister was patient and level-headed but imagining her reading those facts made me cringe. She would flip. Slowly, eventually, I lowered my pen nib back to the paper and continued writing, neatly and deliberately.

I wrote about a page and a half, but the introduction was the only truly honest writing I allowed myself to put down. From the moment I'd agreed to work with Renatus, I'd said and done and seen so many things I couldn't repeat in a letter. One day, when I saw Angela again, I'd tell it to her straight, I promised my conscience, and I settled for a watered-down version of events that didn't include tattoos, bloodletting, people calling me names, Renatus lighting anyone on fire, Declan (I couldn't see Angela liking him any more than Renatus did), visions of sexual assault or our old beach. Instead I focused on my lessons with Renatus and Qasim, stuff Angela would love to read about, and the depth of the friendship I'd found in steadfast Hiroko. I ended the letter by suggesting that when this semester finally ended, and the guardians were allowed to pick the students up, Angela should meet Hiroko, and that I missed her hugely and loved her to the end of the world.

The end of the world could be nearer than any of us knew, I reflected grimly as I licked the envelope and left it on my bedside table. The White Elm was still deciding about the Elm Stone, but the deadline was getting very close and no one knew what the consequences of that decision could be. Lisandro could take the ring, release his three hostages into the estate as agreed and then just blow up the house, with all of us inside. There was nothing stopping him.

Qasim says your lesson is cancelled today, Renatus told me as I looked around the dorm for shoes. I looked up, slightly relieved. I was running late and one Mary-Jane was still missing.

'Good news,' I told Hiroko, who was sitting at her desk, still working on that picture. 'I'm free for an hour.'

'That is good news. We can work on your Displacement.'

'Oh. What are you drawing?' I tried, hoping she'd forget her suggestion. I leaned over her shoulder to see her work. She was quite an artist, I noted now, admiring the life-like illustration of a trees and a park bench.

'It is for Garrett,' she said. 'It is the park in Sapporo where I practise to Displace. Let's go.'

Displacement was a skill that had not been affected *at all* by my new power surge. I groaned but she would not be put off. She even located my shoe for me. We went to Teresa's classroom, which was always certain to be empty, we'd worked out, and I got a small reprieve in that she allowed that we would start with her wards study, as usual.

Hiroko was such a quick study, I thought with a twinge of jealousy as we got into it. She'd gained no recent advancement to her learning abilities – it was all dedication, concentration and willpower. Her physical wards lasted longer each time she tried, though after half an hour of practice, I noticed that she was unable to sustain the ward after an impact had distracted her.

'Focus more on the ward than on the threat,' I suggested, collecting our pillows back from the various corners they had been flung to. 'If there's a second shot, you mightn't have time to build a whole new ward. If your first one is still intact, better to keep that one going, I think, than risk being unprotected.'

I showed her a few techniques I used to maintain the shield after the initial impact. For the first few tries, Hiroko was able to create and hold a ward suspended in the space between us, but when I threw the pillow, it bounced off the shield of magic, which promptly dissolved. She was quick at making new ones but that wasn't what we were working on. I suggested she close her eyes.

'That way you won't know what's coming or when,' I added. She did as she was told, raising her wand again and casting the magic through it. The ward sprung into existence between us. 'Don't think about me or the pillows. Just think about your magic.'

She nodded, and I waited a few seconds before lobbing two pillows at her. They hit the ward almost simultaneously and tumbled to the floor while I grabbed for a third and threw that one, too. It bounced from the shaky but present remains of Hiroko's ward and landed back in my arms.

'You did it!' I exclaimed. The ward was gone by the time Hiroko opened her eyes, but she must have felt the three impacts and realised that her concentration, when shifted to the *magic* instead of the threat, was the main force keeping that ward going.

'It takes much effort,' Hiroko observed, collecting the pillows at her feet, 'but it is better. I can see that with practice it will become easy to maintain for long times.'

'Yeah, you've picked it all up really quickly,' I encouraged. 'You'll be making wards like Emmanuelle's in no time at all.'

Hiroko laughed and put the pillows back onto the plush two-seater.

'Perhaps,' she said. 'Let's see now if we can teach you to Displace like Elijah.'

Smart arse.

As always, we began with Hiroko Displacing partway across the room and then encouraging me to do the same. Like that was going to just happen. I closed my eyes tight, I concentrated, I wished, but I just couldn't feel what she felt in the space around me. To her, there was a fabric that could be folded, torn, and sewn back up. To me, there was air.

Renatus must have been listening to my thoughts then, or just browsing through, because I heard his commentary.

Do you remember when Glen showed you how to see auras? He taught you how to see something your eyes aren't used to looking for. This isn't far different.

'Try again,' Hiroko insisted. I nodded and tried to be where she was. Nothing happened.

This was entirely different, I thought irritably at Renatus. I was sure he only received a vague sense of annoyance. I was completely incapable of this, just like I was incapable of speaking back to his mind and just like I was incapable of flight. Displacers like Hiroko and Elijah were physically capable of seeing the Fabric of space around them, which enabled their gifts. Scriers like me and everyone else in the world had to only infer its existence, and some talented sorcerers learned to feel it and manipulate it, but we'd never see it.

'You aren't feeling it,' Hiroko said, walking back to me and waving her hand through the air. 'It is one layer deeper than the energy you are used to sensing. You must look beyond the surface energy to what is beneath. The Fabric. Try again.'

She's exactly right, Renatus said, hearing Hiroko's every word through my ears. *It's different for her because she can see what she's doing. You can't see it but you can still feel it. Think back to the beach when you felt those potholes. They went deeper than you knew. Think.*

I tried but got no immediate results. I frowned, frustrated.

Think, he urged again, and I felt my patience with him fraying.

I can't do it! I snapped at him, startling myself. I heard my response in my own head like a fully formed sentence. Did I just speak to him? I hadn't spoken aloud – Hiroko hadn't reacted. Perhaps I'd just thought it very clearly, but Renatus's smug tone when he answered convinced me he'd heard me perfectly.

Good, another thing you can't do.

I inhaled slowly, trying to put away my irritation with him being right. He was supposed to be right. He was the mentor. One minute ago I couldn't speak telepathically; now I had done it. That was reason to celebrate, not stew. I hoped it wasn't a one-off.

Can you hear me? I asked, tentative.

Like you're standing beside me, Renatus answered.

I paused, giving it a moment before trying again.

How about now?

It's not going to go away, if that's what you're waiting for.

I could do it. I squared my shoulders, feeling lighter. Under pressure I'd cracked my barriers to learning to scry. Under pressure I'd just broken through to my telepathic abilities. Apparently I worked best when pushed, so if I really wanted to Displace, I would need to push myself.

I did as he'd said, remembering the way the covered wormholes seemed to sink beyond the realm of my senses. The magic capping them was easy enough to feel, very present in the here and now, but the holes had gone much deeper, much further... somewhere else. Through this Fabric Hiroko was talking about.

I closed my eyes again and focused. Physically, I was surrounded by air, and beyond that, furniture and walls and floor. Reading between the lines, I could feel the energy that was present on and around the furniture and walls, like traces of the magic we'd been casting and places we'd touched. I'd never known what was beyond that, so when I finally *looked*, it was a shock to discover that there was indeed another layer of reality I'd never noticed before.

A delicate but iron-strong Fabric holding everything together, forming all matter and maintaining order.

It felt shockingly familiar, although I had no immediate memory of it.

The Fabric and Fate are inextricably entwined, Renatus explained, although I wasn't sure what he meant by that. *Elijah and Hiroko see the Fabric much the same way as you saw Fate during the bonding ceremony.*

I suddenly recalled the golden light. I remembered the incredible feeling as it flowed through me. That was the Fabric of the universe? What a beautiful existence we were leading, to live in a world made of the golden light. No wonder Hiroko found it so easy to believe that all things would work out perfectly in the end – she could *see* with her own eyes that there was a bigger picture.

Ask her to catch you, Renatus said, and I felt him leave my thoughts without an explanation and go back to whatever he was doing. He didn't respond when I asked for a clarification.

'Catch me?' I asked aloud without thinking. Hiroko had been tying her shoelace, and looked up at me, not with a look of confusion like I expected but a sparkle of inspiration in her eyes.

'I did not think of this!' she said. 'It is good to try.'

'What is?'

'I will catch you,' Hiroko said easily. 'It is a semi-assisted Displacement. You start it yourself and I can pull you through the Fabric to the new space.'

I had no idea what she was talking about, just that she and Renatus were on the same page and I was several chapters behind.

'I will go somewhere else,' she explained patiently. 'You will not see your destination – it is easier with some distance. You must find the Fabric and you will feel me holding a gap open for you. I will pull you through. You can feel the process and then you can learn to do this without help.'

'Sure,' I agreed, already convinced that this would not work. I couldn't do this when I could see the destination. How was taking my eyes away going to help matters? 'Sounds easy.'

Hiroko laughed at me, walking backwards. The first two steps were in the room with me, and the third was into another part of the house. She was gone. So cool. I extended my witch senses beyond the walls and floor, trying to pick up her energy. I found her almost directly below me, several floors down. First floor? I didn't think she was far enough away to be in the underground kitchen.

'Right,' I muttered, rubbing my hands together as if that could possibly help. I closed my eyes once again and concentrated.

All around me, there was air and other mundane features of the physical world. I looked harder, and came to notice the next layer of my world, the energies – the faint trace of magic left over in the air of this room from countless wards, the life force of two people at the other end of this floor. I focused on looking underneath all that, and felt it, dimly, all through the air and furniture and through the magic floating around me. The Fabric was everywhere and everything. I wasn't used to it, so I wasn't sure how to manipulate or use it. I waited, hoping something would change. Nothing did.

I focused more on the shape of the Fabric. The physical world had all its dimensions and depths and lines and curves, but the Fabric, for the most part, seemed consistent, smooth. It didn't jut out or curve or rise, like the physical world did with all its objects taking up varying shapes and spaces. It seemed to have only one dimension, or maybe thousands. It just... was.

Except in one place, right in front of me, where it seemed to sink into a dimension it didn't have. Hiroko had claimed that she would catch me – did I have to fall first?

I reached into the warped space with one hand. To my utter shock, I felt a hand grasp mine and tug lightly. I took a breathless step forwards. Either side of me, I felt a pulling sensation, as if I were walking through water or some other resistance. For a millisecond or less, the practice room dissolved into utter blackness, but the destination was well-lit and visible through a slit-like opening. I stepped through that gap into the new space.

I was in the reception hall, currently empty and quiet, holding Hiroko's hand. She was grinning.

'Good!' she said, dropping my hand and bouncing once on her feet. Her voice echoed. 'You found it on your own. You are here!'

'I Displaced,' I said, slightly uncertain. Did it count? Hiroko had helped a great deal. Would I have been able to get out of that blackness without her guiding me into the destination space?

'Now that you know what to look for, you will be able to find the Fabric on your own and you can follow me,' Hiroko said enthusiastically. 'Follow me.'

She turned away and disappeared. Displacers.

It was not as hard as I expected to do it alone. A pathway had been forged in my brain from that first experience. I felt my way through the layers of the universe, finding Hiroko's familiar energy pattern a few metres away in the dining hall, and then felt deeper until I felt the Fabric again. It was only the third time I'd experienced it, but already I was considering the Fabric as something familiar and real.

This time there was no hole held open for me. I had to do it alone. I had no idea how to judge distances with the Fabric – there were no bumps or features or "landmarks" to help me work how far away Hiroko was. I supposed I'd have to guess and practice would make perfect.

I remembered sitting with Hiroko in the library, well over a month ago, helping her to read a Displacement text. It had said to make a "furrow in the Fabric of space". A fold – I could do that. Maybe.

I didn't know how to handle the Fabric so I just had a go at willing it to fold slightly. To my relief, it did as I'd hoped. I felt it fold. It felt both gentle and monumental, like I was shifting the entire world. I supposed in a way I was. The Fabric was everything, and here was me, messing with it. Somewhere at the edge of my consciousness, I felt Hiroko's excitement. No doubt, she could feel or maybe even see the Fabric folding. I was doing this, all on my own.

On one level, my space and another space were now adjoining. I had to find a way between. Again I tried willing it to just happen. Power coursed through me – you don't get anything for free, least of all a manipulation of space – and a portal opened. I couldn't see it, but I knew it was there. Trying to be brave, I stepped through.

The epic nothingness of the void between spaces dragged on me as I passed through. What would happen if someone used magic to cover my exit? Had people been trapped in this void? Could I be trapped here? I forced myself forward and was somewhere again.

I was facing a wall. I'd been expecting to see Hiroko's face, but instead I was looking at a wall.

'*You did it!*' Hiroko practically shouted from behind me. I spun around. We were in the dining hall, as I'd hoped, but she was in the centre and I was in the corner behind the buffet table. Not bad for a first try, though, right? I felt an upsurge of excitement within me.

'I did it!' I called back, unable to wipe the grin from my face as I hurried towards her. 'It worked!'

My voice echoed in the mostly empty space. Only a couple of people remained, breakfast well and truly over. Sterling and Xanthe pointedly ignored me, but I couldn't care any less. What a rush!

'That is an excellent first try,' Hiroko commended when I reached her. 'You can be very proud and happy with that.'

'I *am* happy with it,' I agreed, still smiling. 'That's so amazing. I can't believe I went from there to here. It doesn't seem possible.'

'Some... people... experts,' Hiroko amended, 'think maybe it should not be. They suggest it is very unnatural.'

I could see why some people would think that. It was incredibly freaky.

'But it must be natural if roughly a sixth of the magical population are Displacers,' I said. 'Fate wouldn't give you the gift of being able to see it and manipulate it if it wanted you to leave the Fabric alone.'

'I agree,' Hiroko said, 'though there really are not that many of us. Displacers are almost as rare as Crafters.'

As there were six Classes of sorcerers, I'd always assumed that the split was roughly equal, with maybe a slight inconsistency for Crafters (people often said that they were rarer, but I wasn't sure by how much). Apparently I was wrong.

'How rare is that?' I asked. Hiroko shrugged.

'Elijah thinks our class of five may be the only Displacers in our age group anywhere,' she told me, looking uncertain. 'He isn't sure, but assumes that others would have been noticed by Qasim when he was seeking powerful young people. Displacers, like Crafters, must be high-power. Perhaps this is why these groups are so few?'

I didn't feel jealous, exactly, at this, but the rarity of Hiroko's gift and the rush of experiencing what was simply commonplace for her struck me with awe. Three months ago I'd fallen asleep on a bus out of Coleraine after a short shift at the New Age bookstore I worked at, and the most magical aspects of my life had been limited to recommending crystals and essential oils to eccentric weirdo customers who were concerned that spiritual dragons were watching them sleep. Really I should have been handing out business cards for psychiatrists. Few of my customers had been actual sorcerers, and my experiences in actual sorcery had been hugely limited. I was happily ignorant. Now my world had been opened up with Renatus, with scrying, with telepathy, with colourful characters like the White Elm and Declan O'Malley... and I had barely scratched away the surface of the massive iceberg of what was possible and happening every day in this universe. It made me feel extremely small and insignificant.

I leaned on the nearest chair as I considered this.

Addison, sitting at the next chair with one hand on the back of Kendra's and sitting sideways to face her... 'I'm not accusing you of anything. I'm just asking'... Kendra sighs, exasperated... 'This is unfair. I shouldn't have to explain myself to you'... 'No, and I shouldn't have to ask, but here we are'... Tension is high... Kendra laughs once, unamused... Sophia, sitting opposite, shoots her sister a dark look... 'Addison, don't take it seriously. They're friends; that's all'... Addison spares her a quick glance, and she smiles encouragingly... It seems to calm him, and he turns back to Kendra... 'I don't want to be the guy who gets jealous of your friends, so if that's not my right, just say so. Are you my girlfriend, or not?'... Kendra's mouth is set as she stands suddenly, upset... 'Yes, but you don't own me'...

I whipped my hand away, feeling slightly guilty. That wasn't any of my business. The twins weren't really even my friends any more, and neither was Addison, and the play-by-play of their spats were not something I should be seeing.

'Did you see something?' Hiroko asked with mild interest. I nodded, and something occurred to me with the suddenness of lightning.

'Nothing important,' I said. I could *see* things that were happening elsewhere or that had happened previously. Hiroko's gift was awesome and exotic and supernatural but so was mine, and it was mine that would get the White Elm its answers. Yes, the Fabric and Fate were all-encompassing and made me feel tiny, but I was part of that. The steep curve of development I'd hit this past week was part of Fate's plan. How incredible that something could make one feel simultaneously pathetic and powerful.

'I'll meet you outside,' Hiroko said with a tiny smile, disappearing before I could ask what she meant. Of course, more practice. I went through the process again, finding her on a hill in the grounds and trying to gauge how far away that was. I folded the Fabric and forced my way through it. I ignored the drag of the void and stepped out into the sunshine.

Judging distances and directions was going to be my next big lesson, I realised as I looked around and saw that I was nowhere near Hiroko. I'd landed myself in the orchard. The tall, still apple trees towered over me on either side, and beneath my feet, the ground was dry. No apples had fallen here, but littered the orchard floor just a metre either side of me.

There was only one place in the orchard where grass wouldn't grow, wind wouldn't breathe and apples wouldn't fall.

The path.

I was looking back along it to the brighter-lit grassy hills of the estate, a perspective I'd never encountered before. I'd only ever stood at the mouth of the path and looked uncertainly down it to the little gate at its end. I'd never been brave enough to walk it, always discouraged by uncomfortable friends or put off by the unsettling vision I *thought* I'd had of the girl in black, white and red standing between the trees. I didn't know how whether that was real, but I did know I no longer needed to deliberate whether or not to walk the path. The walking had been taken out of the equation and I was already here.

I spun around and stared at the low, old, cast-iron gate, so close I could reach out and touch it. I looked past it at twenty or so headstones of varying sizes, shapes and degrees of deterioration. The darkness of the place was intoxicating to my witch senses, like a drug making me feel powerful and brave. I'd never been this deep in the orchard, never walked along this path into the dark. It was inde-scribable.

Renatus, I said, reaching for his attention in wonderment. *This is incredible.*

I felt a lurch of horror and ill-feeling that was not mine; I felt Renatus block me out almost completely. He could feel what I could feel, through me, but he was having a completely different reaction. This was the final resting place of his entire family. He was feeling what I felt when we walked eastward on the beach.

Oops. Perhaps mildly insensitive of me.

Renatus? Nothing.

Had I unconsciously chosen to Displace here instead of to Hiroko, so attracted was I to Renatus's greatest source of heartbreak? Did the place of my parents' and brother's deaths appeal to Renatus the way his family's gravesite appealed to me? What was wrong with us?

He wasn't responding to my mental dialogue so I would have to go to him in person to apologise. I turned away from the graveyard and started walking back along the path. Strangely, though, the dark feeling did not recede. It got more intense.

When I was about twelve paces away from the gate, I reached the epicentre – my hair blew back in a blast of frigid air and the energy was so dense and packed with memory that for a second, everything went black, like a mini-blackout.

'Whoa,' I whispered, stumbling aside and gripping the nearest tree for support. What the hell? My eyes took a moment to readjust following that episode and my heart thudded. I felt like a current of electricity had just taken a joyride in my nervous system. But it wasn't a bad feeling.

Renatus had suggested that the dark energy of this place might not just appeal to me; it might also be a source of empowerment. I *did* feel stronger here than I ever had in my life. Uncertain but willing to give anything a try today, I reached into my pocket and withdrew the ruby that I kept there.

I only needed to look into its depths for an instant before the images came to me with incredible ease.

The beach...

A stranger arrives, alone, and is quick to wave his hands in strange movements, weaving magic into a cap to block the wormhole he has created to get here...

The tide coming in...

Jackson and some strangers, arriving together, dragging hostages... Aubrey, unconscious... Teresa, struggling against two captors, mouth covered... 'Knock her out.'... A hand on her forehead, and then she is limp...

The tide going out...

A house on stilts... Lisandro at the door, laughing, ushering someone inside as waves pound the walls...

I gasped as I realised our mistake. *Of course.* I reached to Renatus to show him what I'd seen but he was ignoring me with the expertise of Sterling or Khalida. Damn him, this was important. I sidled around the tree I was leaning against to avoid that dark epicentre, and bolted from the orchard, leaving the darkness behind. He had to know.

I passed Hiroko on my run and waved to her quickly, slowing only to exchange a quick explanation.

'You missed,' she said with a crooked smile.

'I saw something,' I replied between breaths. 'I need to see Renatus. I'll be back soon.'

Her smile dropped and a tinge of concern darkened her eyes at my serious expression. She waved me off and said, 'Go.'

I nodded gratefully and took off into the house. I had to dodge a few people on the stairs, but the higher into the house I climbed, the fewer people I saw. I reached the top step – finally – and raced along the top storey hall, breathing hard. Renatus was in his office, I could feel him there, but when I reached the door, it did not open for me. I practically collapsed against it, feeling shaky. What was he doing? He had to know I was here.

'Renatus!' I shouted, kind of pathetically, because I was breathing in gasps. I hit the door solidly with my palm. Ignoring me was totally uncool. 'Renatus! It's me! Open the door!'

I rested my forehead against the oak, struggling to get my breathing under control. It might have been as long as three minutes before I felt the door give, and I quickly took a step back, pasting an indignant look on my face as I did so. But it wasn't Renatus behind the door. It was Lady Miranda, and her face was ashen.

'Sorry,' she said as she stepped into the hall. She was followed by other councillors, and I realised that the entire White Elm had been gathered inside the office. 'We were in the middle of a very important circle. Letting you in would have disturbed the proceedings.'

She left without her usual smile. I stayed back, the urgency I'd felt just a moment before ebbing away in light of this new development. Nobody was speaking or looking at anyone else. Emmanuelle's lips were pursed tensely; Lord Gawain looked worn out; Jadon looked murderous but felt broken as his unbridled emotions washed over me. What had just happened? Renatus was the last one to the door, and wordlessly touched my shoulder and guided me inside.

'What was that?' I asked as soon as the door was shut. 'What happened?'

Renatus sat down at his desk before answering.

'We just voted on what we're going to do about the ring,' he said heavily, automatically beginning to straighten the row of fountain pens. 'Obviously, not everyone can get their way.'

'What was the verdict?' I asked, dragging my chair over to his desk and watching him closely. He always reorganised his desk when he was stressing or had too much to think about. So OCD.

'I have to find Lisandro,' he muttered, glaring at the pens, 'except of course I have no clue where he is.'

'I do,' I said, forgetting totally about the devastated expressions of the White Elm councillors. 'I know *exactly* where you can find him.'

'What?' Renatus looked up at me, pausing in his routine.

'You were right – the darkness gives me power,' I said, unable to contain my enthusiasm. A strange look passed over Renatus's face. I took it to be linked with his fear of the orchard and kept going. 'Hiroko taught me how to Displace, finally, and I tried to follow her outside but missed her by a long way and accidentally ended up in the orchard, on the path right in front of the gate.' I stopped myself, a thought from earlier reoccurring with more insistence than before. 'Was it an accident that I went there?'

'No,' Renatus said without hesitation. 'You were pulled there because you're Empathic and you feel it even when you don't think you do. Continue.'

He wasn't angry with me, then. Good.

'Well, I started to walk away from the graves but the energy just got stronger,' I went on, noticing the effort Renatus was going to just to hold back his feelings and to keep his face impassive. 'It's really intense about ten metres away from the gate. Like, really intense – I think I blacked out for a second when I walked through the middle of it.'

Renatus had to look away. He was still blocking me out as best he could. I knew I was ignorantly stepping all over an extremely sensitive and massive topic, but I had no idea what it was and my topic was huge, too.

'I used the dark and the ruby and I scried the beach,' I finished. 'I *saw* it, Renatus.'

Renatus sat back silently, blocking me from his thoughts and avoiding mine. I felt his inner turmoil and wondered why he wasn't already in my head, analysing what I'd seen.

'Don't you want to know where the house is?' I asked, confused. My master got to his feet and began to pace the length of his office, holding a hand up warningly when I opened my mouth to tell him anyway.

'Give me a minute,' he said, very firmly. I still couldn't see or hear what he was thinking, and he wasn't remotely interested in what I was thinking, but I could feel his emotions. What was so confusing and unsettling about finally getting the information he needed? Why was he worrying? What decision was he trying to make?

'Okay,' he said after nearly a minute of pacing. He came back to the desk and rested his palms on the surface, looking straight into my eyes. 'Okay. You can tell me what you saw, but first, you need to promise something.'

'Sure,' I said, raising my hands in a semi-shrug gesture. This was just so weird, but Renatus always was.

'After you leave this office, you won't think about what you've seen,' Renatus said. 'You won't tell anyone what you saw. You will not indicate to *any* of the other councillors that I know where to find Lisandro. This conversation *never* happened.'

I nodded immediately, sensing his seriousness. Two days left until Lisandro planned to murder Teresa and we were no closer to knowing who the White Elm traitor was. Thinking about this conversation could result in my thoughts overheard by the wrong person, tipping off Lisandro that Renatus was coming.

'This conversation isn't happening,' I agreed. Renatus nodded slowly, gradually dropping the defences around his mind and letting me back in. Trusting me.

'Okay,' he said again. 'Show me where he is.'

'You won't believe we missed this,' I said, opening my thoughts to him.

chapter fifteen

The moon, only two nights away from its darkest phase, was a narrow slit of paleness in the night sky. The harsh sea breeze whipped Renatus's black cloak about, so he held it tighter against his body as he strode purposefully across the beach. The closer he got, the more certain he felt that his apprentice's vision had been true. When he'd been here on each of the previous three days it was high tide, and the covered wormholes in the water had seemed to him and to Elijah as humorous accidents – Displacements intended for the pebbly part of the beach but missed by several metres, landing the sorcerer knee-deep in frigid waters.

Not so, Aristea had told him this evening. At low tide, this beach grew by several metres, enough to make most of those Displacements firm, dry, deliberate landings. How had they overlooked this very obvious, very routine, natural daily occurrence?

The hideout was a beach house at low tide, surrounded by sandy beach to walk or Displace onto. At high tide, the house would appear to be *in* the water – somewhere the White Elm had never bothered to look, until tonight. The tide was out, and Renatus was here.

A powerful scrier always knows when he is being scried, so Renatus briefly directed his attention inward, anticipating Qasim's furious demand.

What in hell are you doing?!

Qasim had seen him arrive at the beach, something Renatus had been hoping to do unnoticed. Damn. There was nothing to be done about it now, and in a few seconds, theoretically, he'd be too close to Lisandro's wards for Qasim to see him anyway. They'd long surmised that Lisandro had surrounded himself with magic that specifically blocked the White Elm scriers from sensing him and his surrounds, but this would be the first time any of them had any proof of that hypothesis.

My job, Renatus replied, still walking towards the place Aristea had seen. *Tell Lord Gawain not to be surprised*.

Qasim tried to ask something else, but was cut off suddenly. Renatus felt the resistance as he passed through the powerful illusions guarding this hideout and felt his connection to the White Elm deaden immediately. The image and sense of open beach dissolved into reality, and a reasonably-sized wooden structure on stilts materialised. This was it, and only Renatus was seeing it. He'd entered the dead zone of proximity to Lisandro, and the council had no access to his thoughts right now. For the first time in nearly two years, Renatus was all alone in his own head. Peace.

Almost.

Right at the back of his mind, paying him no heed whatsoever but only a mental nudge away if he needed her, was Aristea. His bond with her was stronger than he'd imagined it would be. Even Lisandro's magic could not dim their connection.

She was asleep, he realised as he brushed his thoughts past hers, unable to dream because of the magic enveloping the estate, deeply peaceful. In that moment he felt an immense surge of graciousness for his apprentice. She had trusted him enough to allow him into her mind, to share her visions with him today. She hadn't second-guessed his intentions. She'd just assumed he was doing the right thing with the information, which he was pretty sure he *was*, although not everybody would agree. She'd kept her promise and withheld her vision from the other councillors. And now, asleep, ignorant, she was still helping her master, unknowingly, simply by being present. It made the task seem much less monumental now that he knew he wasn't really alone.

Renatus felt a tiny flicker of magic – he'd just set off a magical alarm system, designed to let the occupants of that house know when somebody was approaching. Inside, a dozen or so people were moving about, worried. The door of the rough-looking beach house swung open, revealing Lisandro. The older man flashed a delighted grin at his approaching enemy and opened his arms wide in greeting as he began descending the stairs.

'Renatus!' he called in a cheerful voice. 'To what do I owe this pleasure?'

Without bothering to answer, Renatus continued to stride towards him. Lisandro reached the bottom of the stairs and tried to smooth his very long black hair back from his face. When the wind continued to catch it up and whip it about, he irritably waved a hand, like swatting an insect. Immediately, the wind around the beach house died down. His ponytail settled down his back; Renatus's soft black hair rested against the sides of his face.

'Controlling the weather these days, Lisandro?' Renatus asked scornfully. The former Dark Keeper grinned back at him as they stopped in front of each other.

'Always have, son,' he responded. 'I'd been wondering for a while when White Elm would send an ambassador, but, to be honest, I didn't think they'd send you.'

'Who did you expect to want to see you?'

'Not you.' Lisandro glanced over his shoulder at the beach house. A few of his minions had appeared in the doorway. They made a show of folding their arms menacingly but did not dare come any closer. 'How did you find me here, anyway? I've been watching you and your search team sniffing around in my front yard for days and I was just thinking how well I'd hidden myself.'

'Obviously not well enough,' Renatus answered. 'You must have forgotten who you were hiding from.'

'I never forget,' Lisandro said. 'You always know more than I'd like you to.' He grinned again. 'A little like our old friend Peter. I suppose you're one of the ones who found him. Unfortunate business, that. Sometimes we have to make sacrifices.'

'What would you know about sacrifices?' Rena-tus snapped. Lisandro surveyed him momentarily.

'More than you, I imagine,' he answered crypti-cally. 'Been keeping well, then, Renatus? Enjoying my old job? I heard you're in charge of looking for me.'

'Did your spy tell you that?'

'Ooh, another bingo,' Lisandro said delightedly. 'You're good. Yes, I've been kept updated by a good friend in White Elm. Have you figured out who it is yet? I suppose not – you wouldn't be here if you did.'

'I will.'

'I'm sure you will, Renatus, you seem to spoil all of my other surprises,' Lisandro agreed. He paused again, observing his young successor's gaze. 'Why did you come tonight? You find my hideout and turn up alone, unarmed?'

'You said to give you a sign when we made up our minds,' Renatus responded. 'Consider this your sign.'

'Hmm, I suppose I did say that,' Lisandro agreed. 'I'm still surprised, mostly that Gawain actually made a choice. Well, I'm glad, in any case. I've been looking forward to seeing you again.'

'Don't be disappointed if I say it isn't mutual,' Renatus said coldly. Lisandro laughed, always so enviably at-ease.

'Oh, don't be like that,' he said lightly. 'We've got so much catching up to do.'

'Why don't you start by telling me where the councillors are?' Renatus suggested. Lisandro smiled and gestured over his shoulder at the beach house.

'Your boy's in there,' he said, 'along with his little girlfriend. They're alive, and safe, you'll notice.'

Renatus extended his senses past Lisandro, not scared to turn his back on this man he'd known his whole life, and brushed over the wooden house. Fourteen unfamiliar energies, all male and nervous but trying to portray a sense of heroic bravery to one another, and two known energies – Aubrey and Shell – locked in a small room at the back of the structure. They did not seem to know he was here. Aubrey's mind was completely inaccessible. Supposedly he was wearing the same golden anklet that bound Teresa's magic inside her own body. At least he was safe, although Renatus had known this already. Declan had insisted that Lisandro was "hesitant" to kill either of his White Elm hostages. Did that mean Shell was not so safe?

'Happy?' Lisandro asked, amused. 'You don't look it.'

'Where's Teresa?'

'Jackson is taking good care of her at his place,' Lisandro said. He gazed inland for a moment. 'It's not far from here. Not far at all.'

'We must have differing opinions on "good care", Lisandro.'

'I'm sure we don't differ by much?' Lisandro's bronze-brown eyes narrowed momentarily, an expression that would go unnoticed by anyone who knew him less intimately than did Renatus. It was the only honest expression in his repertoire. He truly didn't know what Renatus meant, and was trying to determine the underlying meaning and its source.

'I want to see them.'

Lisandro paused for a very long time. It was an unreasonable request in this situation and Renatus knew he was pushing his luck. He had nothing to barter with – Lisandro had no reason to want to comply with such a demand.

'Alright,' the older sorcerer agreed finally, surprising everybody. He gestured to some of the men behind him and called, 'Bring out the pretty boy.'

Three figures disappeared inside and Renatus and Lisandro waited in silence for about half a minute. The men at the door parted as a small group came through and began shuffling someone forcibly to the front of the crowd. Renatus immediately recognised Aubrey and his stomach flipped over in shock. Their eyes locked briefly. To call him "pretty" was unfair of Lisandro; the young Crafter was no such thing tonight. His usually shiny copper hair was dull and matted against his forehead, his eyes were dark and sunken with exhaustion and there was dried blood under his nose.

A ripple of energy distracted Renatus briefly, but he was brought back to the present by Aubrey's voice.

'I wondered when I'd see you here,' Aubrey shouted bitterly. 'Has it been hard to get away from the council without drawing attention?'

His thoughts were still a total enigma, blocked by Lisandro's powerful magic. A glint of gold around his ankle betrayed to Renatus how Lisandro was doing this, but he didn't need telepathy to realise that Aubrey didn't trust him. He had felt no particular kinship with Aubrey until he'd gone missing, had even disliked him at times in past weeks and months, but now felt a wave of protectiveness and possessiveness. Aubrey was *his* colleague. Lisandro had no right to inflict the damage he had.

The physical damage truly shocked Renatus. He'd known Lisandro his entire life and never, ever known him to actually strike anybody. And the abuse of Teresa fell outside the realm of belief, too, though at least Renatus could tell himself that Lisandro probably didn't know about that.

'It was a bit,' Renatus called back, distracted once again by that same ripple. Something was happening to the wards and illusions, but they were not familiar enough to him to be certain of exactly what. 'But I'm here to negotiate your release. All three of you.'

Aubrey initially scoffed, but paused after Renatus finished.

'*Three* of us? Who was the third?' Aubrey demanded as Lisandro gestured to the men holding him. They began dragging him backwards into the house and he struggled against them, a frightened look in his eye. Of course he didn't know about Teresa – it hadn't occurred to Renatus previously, but Aubrey had been rendered unconscious before Teresa was taken. If he'd not seen her since, and he apparently hadn't, he wouldn't know about her capture. 'Renatus, who was it? Do they have Emmanuelle? Do they have-'

The door closed behind him and his panicked question was cut off.

'There. You've seen him. Happy?'

'I can't believe you struck him.'

Lisandro looked surprised.

'I've not,' he insisted, miffed. 'That would be like beating up a kitten. Have you met that boy? Softest substance about. No – that's what minions are for.'

'And what does Shell look like after a few nights in your hospitality?'

'Don't be frightened by your friend's messy appearance,' Lisandro answered. 'I'm taking much better care of the girl. She's getting all the necessary vitamins in her delicate state and she's not to be touched. She doesn't answer back.'

If each of Aubrey's injuries could be attributed to a moment of attitude, Renatus supposed it was probably for the best that Lisandro had only gotten hold of mild-mannered Aubrey and Teresa. Both Jadon and Emmanuelle, the two councillors who had escaped capture the same night, were mouthier and may not have lasted this long.

'Why did you take them in the first place?' Renatus asked.

'Uh-uh.' Lisandro smiled playfully. 'I've answered your questions. Now you answer one of mine. What are you doing here?'

'I don't know what you mean,' Renatus said coolly. 'I told you.'

'I know Lord Gawain didn't ask *you* to confront me and pass on his message,' Lisandro said slyly. 'No way he'd put you in harm's way to do his dirty work, and no way would he send you to me without a chaperone. So I know you're not here on official business as you say. That makes this personal, which is why I'm asking, what are you *really* doing here?'

Renatus glanced up at the steps of the beach cabin as a few of the men there laughed loudly. One in the middle, a wide man with a podgy face, was grinning, clearly the proud narrator of a most excellent joke. The urge to wipe the smug smile off that fat, stupid face was almost unbearable. Lisandro seemed to agree.

'Martin, why don't you come on down here and share your joke with our visitor?' he called back up the stairs. The laughing stopped abruptly. The wide man's smile died and a look of fear blossomed in his eyes. 'What's the matter? I thought you just said you "could totally take him"?'

When the students at the Academy were called on a bluff, their faces went red with embarrassment. When Lisandro called on Martin's, his face drained of all colour.

'I thought so,' Lisandro said after a long moment. 'It's easy to be brave standing behind me, isn't it, Martin? Next time think before you go about disrespecting my guests.' Shaking his head, he turned back to Renatus. 'Minions. Can't live with 'em; can't win without 'em.'

'They don't seem as impressive as the team you left behind,' Renatus commented. Lisandro grinned.

'Oh, this isn't a team of equals the way the White Elm is,' he said. 'I'm in charge here. Jackson looks after a little taskforce of the scummy ones I don't like having to look at. Everyone else is just a number. I like it better this way.'

'I bet you do.'

'They're not powerhouses like you or me,' Lisandro admitted, looking back up at his followers, 'but they are easily convinced and they have made vows to die for me if I ask it, which is nice.' He turned back to his young successor. 'If you try to harm me, they will step in, although of course they would be much too late, so their next instruction is to obliterate the scene – you, the boy with the nice hair, his pregnant girlfriend and themselves included. Blind loyalty: nothing quite like it, am I right? I've taught them how to combine their power to make it work. There would be nothing left. Now, I don't want that to happen,' Lisandro assured Renatus, 'but I know that you know I'm telling the truth. You know the lengths I'd go to for self-preservation. Therefore you're not here to kill me or take me in. You're not on a rescue mission, because you know you're outnumbered and I'd take *you* out. We've established you're not here for work. So it really begs the question – what the hell are you doing here?'

Renatus didn't want to tell the truth, because the truth was that he wasn't sure. He'd spent the entire afternoon debating with himself about whether this was the right thing to do. It was, wasn't it?

'I want to give you the ring,' Renatus said finally, trying to ignore that strange ripple through the wards around him. Lisandro didn't answer for a long moment. No doubt he was reading between the lines.

'*You* do,' he repeated slowly. He smiled thinly. 'Have I finally converted you, son? Have you finally seen what a spineless joke Lord Gawain becomes when he starts to feel any pressure to actually lead?'

'Don't try me,' Renatus warned, dimly surprised when a ball of black fire burst into life in his open palm. The verbal attack on Lord Gawain's character had elicited a stronger response than he'd expected. The men on the steps panicked and grabbed for their wands, but Lisandro waved a hand at them dismissively. Simultaneously, a tiny spell was cast. Renatus knew it wasn't meant to be noticed, but it would be hard to get something like that past him.

'Calm down,' Lisandro called over his shoulder. 'He's just pissed off.' To Renatus he added, 'Relax. You're going to scare them. I don't want one of them to accidentally blast you.'

'You wouldn't allow it,' Renatus said with certainty. He closed his hand; when he opened his fingers, the flames were gone and the air directly in front of him was glimmering with the thin, subtle ward he'd just uncovered. 'You need me. You're relying on the council's mistrust of me to keep your spy hidden.'

'Oh, that sounds so malicious and cunning, not like me at all!' Lisandro complained. 'How do you know I didn't cast that ward simply to keep you safe, because I care too much? You really won't believe that I just act out of love?'

'No.'

'What if I told you I do?' Lisandro asked, something strange about his voice. Renatus stared at him for a long moment, trying to read him. He got nothing.

'Then I would say that your love is twisted and soulless, which I knew already,' Renatus said finally, emotionlessly. 'You had me take the fall for your spy in Valero. I was nearly disavowed, thanks to you. Who was it, really, that killed Saul?'

Of course Lisandro wasn't that easily played, but he enjoyed the game all the same and grinned again.

'The little black angel on your shoulder, you mean?' he laughed. 'I was quite proud of my friend that day. *Valero*. Phew – can you imagine the creativity and power it would take to affect that city's magic so deeply and so fully that it actually protects *you* instead of itself? It was an impressive feat, no doubt. Inspiring, in fact.'

'Why did you have Jackson take our councillors?'

'When did you upgrade to a master?' Lisandro quipped.

Renatus tried not to feel annoyance that he knew already. He hadn't expected Lisandro to simply *not notice* the way his aura was brimming with power, after all. It was kind of obvious. Added to that was the fact that one of the White Elm was feeding Lisandro information, so of course he would know.

'A few weeks,' Renatus answered. Knowing when wasn't going to help Lisandro work out who his apprentice was, so it seemed safe to share.

'Aristea Byrne, isn't it?' Lisandro asked, pretending to be curious. Renatus held onto his unconcerned expression, his thoughts wild. How did Lisandro know that? Declan? No, Declan was scum, but reasonably loyal scum. It had to be the spy, the mole in the council, who had shared this information. 'Pretty thing, I'm told, and a scrier, although that doesn't surprise me. Quite shocking that Lord Gawain let *you* have an apprentice, at your age. A very unexpected but interesting turn of events. Congratulations.'

'How long have you known?' Renatus asked carefully, and Lisandro grinned back.

'About two minutes.' His eyes narrowed into a smirk. 'My friend doesn't think much of your alliance. Says she's too good for you.'

That meant that the spy was sharing with Lisandro right now, and Renatus, blocked off from the council by Lisandro's magic, was totally in the dark as to what everyone was doing. He had no way of knowing who it was, although if he could just get a few metres away from Lisandro, he could reconnect, he could know...

'Her grandad was Ó Grádaigh,' Lisandro went on, freezing Renatus's thoughts. How did he know that? No one knew that. Nobody on the council, anyway. Lord Gawain, maybe, but only because he was old enough that he might have actually known the infamous Crafter Aristea was descended from, in times past. 'It's quite ironic, really, that you would choose her. Her grandad was a friend of my mom's. Your grandad, too. You're a bit young to understand all that, though, I suppose. But you're a smart boy – have you noticed? That she's one of us?'

'I'm nothing like you, and neither is she,' Renatus snarled. He felt cold anger building at the mere notion that his apprentice shared any likeness to the monster of a man standing before him.

'You're a bit more like me than either of us would like to recognise,' Lisandro disagreed with a tight smile. 'And as much as you don't want to believe it, *she's* like us, too. Don't tell me you haven't seen the holes in her aura? Like you; like me. Damaged but not ruined. Tainted. *Scarred*. It's why you chose her.'

Scarred. Renatus didn't like the idea that past harms had already marked Aristea. She was *good* and innocent and she saw the good in all things and all people, and he wanted her to stay that way. He'd assured himself before he chose her that her path through life would be different from his, so it spooked him to hear Lisandro talking about her like he was. *She's like us. Damaged but not ruined. Tainted.*

When Renatus said nothing more, Lisandro looked out over the waves, and sighed. 'To answer your question, I had Jackson take whoever he could because it suited my plan for him to do so. Don't worry too much about it. You do your part, I'll do mine, and you'll get your people back. No sweat.'

Lisandro walked closer, a sly smile on his face. That ripple went through the wards again and suddenly it clicked in Renatus's brain – around them, magic was dissolving, tearing itself apart at Lisandro's will. For only two seconds, the magic blocking Lisandro from being scried was down, just long enough for him to say one thing.

'This is what you need to do,' he said, and then the ward was back up. They were hidden again, but Renatus knew he'd been played.

chapter sixteen

The quiet dark of sleep was interrupted suddenly and unexpectedly by a bright light source.

'Aristea. Wake up.'

I tried to open my eyes but it hurt. I struggled to sit up in bed; the blankets clung, holding me down. Feeling hugely disorientated, I ran a hand over my face, pushing my hair away so when I finally managed to get my eyes open, it wasn't hanging in my face. I blinked a few times, trying to focus on the tall figure standing beside my bed.

''mmanuelle?' I mumbled, squinting at her. I couldn't see her face properly but I imagined it wasn't a happy one, because the feelings rolling off her like water were serious, negative feelings.

'What's goin' on?' Sterling asked, speech slurred with drowsiness. I nodded once, hoping someone would answer her. My whole dorm was awake and confused. An explanation would be nice.

None, however, was forthcoming.

'We need to talk,' was all Emmanuelle said. I swung my legs out of bed, finally free of my blankets.

'About what?' I asked, totally lost. What needed to be discussed *now*? It was the middle of the night, or sometime in the early morning. I had no idea. The dormitory door was open to a darkened hall, and a key like mine waited patiently in the lock, a satiny ribbon dangling from the end.

'Where is 'e, Aristea?' Emmanuelle asked. Her tone was cold and grave and her aura felt the same. I got the impression that answering this wrong would get me into a lot of trouble, but I wasn't sure what she was asking or why.

'I don't-'

'Don't say you don't know,' she cut me off. She snatched for the satin ribbon and pulled the key from the lock just as Anouk appeared in the lightless hallway. The door snapped shut in the Telepath's face, apparently of its own accord. 'Just tell me where 'e is.'

'Emmanuelle, what's going on?' I asked, nervous. Anouk was knocking loudly and demanding to be let in. What did Emmanuelle have to ask that she didn't want the council overhearing?

'Aristea, I want to 'elp you but I need to know where Renatus is.'

'I really don't know,' I insisted. I had a good idea where he'd *been* tonight, but that could have been hours ago. What time was it, anyway?

'Find out, and quickly,' Emmanuelle said snappily. 'The council's been summoned and 'e is not responding. 'e is either in a lot of trouble, or 'e *is* the trouble.'

My stomach turned. What the hell did *that* mean? Why wouldn't he respond – was he hurt, dead, kidnapped? No; I couldn't begin to understand why, but the source of Emmanuelle's fear was

Renatus himself. Did she have a good reason? Should I be scared, too? Emmanuelle was my teacher and someone I trusted, but Renatus was my master. He was in my head. Surely if there was something off, I would know. Wouldn't I?

'Emmanuelle, *open this door*!' Anouk demanded.

'I *told* you, I'd get 'er!' Emmanuelle yelled back, making us all jump.

'She seems really angry,' Sterling commented uneasily as the heavy knocking continued.

'She *is* angry,' Emmanuelle confirmed tightly. She looked back at me intently. 'So will I be in a moment.'

'But she can't get in without the key, right?' Xanthe clarified, nodding once at the door. The knocking had paused momentarily and then started back up again.

'They could use the master key in Renatus's office,' Sterling said. She wrapped her blanket tighter around herself when Emmanuelle turned to her in exasperation.

'Renatus *is* the master key.'

I still completely didn't understand the situation, but for the first time in two weeks I met Sterling's gaze and she didn't look away. I suppose we were both a bit shocked by the fact that we hadn't worked that out sooner. Of course there was no super-special skeleton key sitting around in the office. Why would Renatus need it? The gates that we all needed keys to open swung aside at his touch. His office door responded to his will alone. This entire house was programmed to respond to *him*. The keys were just a formality, and a tool to make living here possible for the rest of us.

'Aristea,' Emmanuelle reminded me. I remembered that I was meant to be looking for Renatus. I reached for him with my thoughts.

Where are you?

Not far, he answered immediately. *I'll be back soon.*

Things are weird, I told Renatus, uncertain. *Please come back now.*

I felt Renatus browsing through my thoughts, reading my concerns, viewing my situation.

I'll be right there. Tell Emmanuelle where I have been and tell her it's not what she thinks. Get her onside. Rule of silence applies to everyone else. I want to tell them myself.

'Where is 'e?' Emmanuelle asked again.

'He...' I hesitated, looking around the room. This was supposed to be a secret. I looked over each of the girls who shared my room. Hiroko I could tell anything; I hadn't told her this yet because I'd promised I wouldn't think about it, but I'd planned to tell her later. Sterling and Xanthe – could I speak in front of them? After a moment's consideration, I decided it didn't matter either way. They weren't my friends, I didn't like them and they didn't like me, but they weren't enemies. In the grand scheme of what mattered and what was at stake, schoolgirl quarrels and name-calling were nothing. 'He went to find Lisandro.'

The other girls were still and silent as Emmanuelle closed her eyes briefly.

'Why was 'e looking for Lisandro?' she asked in a very soft, low voice.

'I... I thought it was for the council,' I said, confused. Clearly, from the look on her face, I'd been mistaken. 'I found the hideout. Renatus was going tonight. He... It's not what you think,' I finished lamely.

Emmanuelle stared at me, and I heard Renatus in my mind again.

A little more convincingly, please.

'He's coming back right now,' I continued, not sure how Renatus wanted me to convince Emmanuelle that everything was okay, especially since I didn't know that for sure myself. 'He didn't want me to tell anyone he was going. I... He didn't want for anyone to tip Lisandro off. That's why he didn't tell anyone.'

Still, Emmanuelle stared silently. I knew she wanted to believe me but was going to need something a bit more substantial than my weak insistence.

'He wants you on our side,' I added. She sighed.

'Aristea, I'm on *your* side. Whether that's *his* side, too, remains to be seen.' She grasped my wrist and turned to the door. She seemed to have made up her mind. I was still totally lost. 'Wards up; all of them. Every one I've taught you.' She turned her key in the lock and looked back at the other three. 'Not a word of what you've 'eard can leave this room, girls.' They all nodded mutely, because you just didn't argue with Emmanuelle. She pulled me through the doorway behind her and I glanced back once at

Hiroko's frightened face. I wished I could stay with her.

Anouk was silent as Emmanuelle locked the door and pocketed her key. I hastened to follow her instruction and build as many wards as I could. I barricaded my mind, blocked out all emotions, and then added a discrete, mushroom-shaped shield a foot or so in front of me.

'I told you,' Emmanuelle said again, very coldly, 'she's my responsibility – *I* will get 'er.'

'I know what you said,' Anouk responded, just as unfriendly in tone. 'But your loyalties might be considered *questionable* in a situation like this. *Biased* at least.'

'Save your questioning for the circle.'

Anouk's eyes glazed over briefly and she said, 'I can hear him again. He's coming back.'

Emmanuelle strode past with me in tow. She yanked me closer and leaned toward me to whisper in my ear as she hurried me down the stairs.

'You 'ad best be right about this,' she told me. I knew she was as terrified as I was.

'What's happened?' I whispered back. She shook her head and kept dragging me along.

'Wards up,' she reminded me as we reached the bottom floor. I focused on strengthening my barriers, although I wasn't sure yet what the danger was meant to be. I had a feeling that Emmanuelle wasn't sure, either.

As we strode across the reception hall, one of the front doors creaked and opened quickly. Susannah stepped through, looking angry. Emmanuelle dragged me straight past her.

'Make sure you keep her close,' Susannah instructed, her tone commanding and stressed at the same time. 'Don't let her be swayed.'

The whole council was gathered in their usual circular configuration. Susannah and Anouk took their spots. Emmanuelle kept me beside her, and I avoided looking at the other councillors. I could sense Renatus's proximity now, at the gates, walking up the path, skipping the rest of the distance, at the mansion doors, in the reception hall... Everyone seemed to hold their collective breath as the ballroom doors opened quietly for their master. The corners of Emmanuelle's nails dug into the skin of my wrist as she waited, petrified but determined.

Renatus entered the ballroom and looked straight at me.

Remember, you promised? I asked you to disregard anything you might hear about me and to make your own mind up.

He crossed the hall, heading towards me. Emmanuelle pulled me against her.

'Don't go near her, Renatus,' Glen instructed. He stopped immediately. 'She's Emmanuelle's charge until you can prove you're not a danger to her.'

A *danger* to me? Renatus stared at me for a moment, looking like he was going to disobey, but he turned away to take his place between Lady Miranda and Qasim. No one moved. I was glad Emmanuelle had warned me to block myself off. The tension must be as thick as butter. Feeling it as intensely as I normally did would probably have overwhelmed me.

'Blessed be,' Lord Gawain began, and I felt the subtle flow of energy that always started up when a circle was initiated. 'The Valeroans and a number of our other affiliated communities have contacted me with new information regarding the investigation into Saul's murder. It is deeply concerning and affects us all, as their conclusions will likely lead us to our own traitor.'

I saw many faces tighten in stress, and felt Renatus's concern in my mind. I wasn't sure what this was supposed to mean.

'Renatus, where have you been?' Lady Miranda asked, her voice so soft and deadly that I couldn't stand it. What was she saying behind that question?

'Wait,' I insisted. 'The guy that's dead – a bad guy, right? One of those ones we found at Teresa's? What's happened now?'

'Saul was murdered in a high security cell while several of us, including Renatus, were present, some time ago now,' Lord Gawain told me quickly, before continuing to address the council, his voice shaking slightly. 'The Valero security systems were again triggered about twenty minutes ago by a concealed sorcerer bearing the signature of the White Elm. Immediate investigation carried out by Valero sorcerers gifted in tracing identified the presence as Jadon.'

Most eyes turned suddenly to the youngest councillor, whose mouth dropped open in shock.

'*What*? But I didn't-'

'Jadon,' Lord Gawain interrupted, firmly, silencing the Telepath. 'I'm not finished. Far from it. Valeroan guards converged on the location of the trigger and your apparent entry point and found no one. They contacted Anouk straightaway, and she attempted to share the worrying news with me, but I was in communication with the MacCalyan Coven of Scotland, whose private meeting hall was just broken into by Glen.'

The council's collective gaze turned confusedly to the new accused.

'Then,' Lord Gawain said, frowning, 'there is a knock at my door and I find myself visited by the Steward of Avalon himself, affronted that I would send Elijah without first giving warning that we wanted access to their Great Library and wondering why he hadn't made himself known, and doesn't he know that there's no way inside without express permission?'

The New Zealander blinked blankly and the council's uneasiness increased.

'Meanwhile our closest allies among the Native American tribes alerted me that Teresa was not lost at all, but may have defected, because her trace had just been identified attempting to interfere as they took part in a ceremonial circle. Susannah came threateningly close to the sacred site of the Northern Druids; our friends in Massachusetts were upset when Aubrey triggered the defences of their leader's home; I myself apparently offended the Cymry of an all-magical settlement I once helped to establish by attempting to enter the town perimeter without contacting the people first. They couldn't understand why I would stand at the boundary long enough to alert them that I was nearby but then not wait around to be greeted.'

I'd thought Lord Gawain was telling this story to everyone, but I realised now that he was only really looking at Renatus. I was struggling to keep up. Now they were all spies?

'Twelve of our nearest allies tonight reported an attempt of infiltration by a different White Elm councillor. Obviously this is falsified,' Lord Gawain added, somewhat calming the circle. 'There were no sightings, only trace energies. Except in one case; the coven leader in Salem claims to have gotten to the trigger in time to hear the culprit whisper "murder".'

'Murder?' Glen asked, surprised.

'Are you sure?' Susannah added in a similar tone. 'That's an odd thing to just *say*.'

'Not murder,' Renatus piped up. '*Merde*. It must have been a close call.'

'So now it's me, is it?' Emmanuelle asked, annoyed when everyone else cottoned on to the language used and turned to look at her.

'No, I didn't say that.'

'It *wasn't* me. Besides, I don't pronounce it like that,' Emmanuelle added, and articulated her curse word slowly for everyone to hear the way she left off the "uh" at the end.

Lord Gawain frowned at her (I guessed that he didn't like swearing, regardless of the language) and resumed his story.

'Obviously whoever was doing this was covering all bases, going so far as to curse in French while impersonating Aubrey. Qasim assures me that Aubrey is right here in Ireland, I wasn't in Wales and none of the rest of you, when I reached for you, was in the location you were accused of invading. Twelve allies were targeted tonight by a White Elm who projected his brothers' and sisters' energies in order to cast suspicion onto them. Only one of our number was not implicated.'

'Me,' Renatus guessed.

Oh.

'I saw you with Lisandro tonight, Renatus,' Qasim said grimly. I looked between the two best scriers I knew and my stomach dropped. This wasn't a normal circle. This was a trial. His suspension had never been officially lifted and the investigation into him had never been officially dropped, and now the gavel was falling. The council had already pegged Renatus as guilty because they'd seen him with Lisandro, somehow, which was weird because I'd thought anyone within twenty metres or so of the man was invisible to the White Elm. What was weirder was that Renatus's *job* was to track and find Lisandro, and the council was hanging him for it. They wanted Teresa and Aubrey back, didn't they? How did they expect to do that without finding and approaching Lisandro?

Was there something I was missing here?

'It was important I go,' Renatus said, sounding careful. 'I understand how it appears.'

'You are not a law unto yourself, Renatus!' Lord Gawain shouted, scaring me. I jumped, and Emmanuelle's fingernails dug a little deeper into my wrist. I'd never seen the White Elm leader like this, and I assumed Emmanuelle hadn't, either. 'We voted! *We.* As in the council. Decisions like this are not for you to make alone. If you wanted to work alone, you should have declined my offer two years ago to join the White Elm. If you'd wanted to work for Lisandro, you-'

'Don't,' Renatus snarled, cutting the Lord off. 'I may not be who you wanted me to be, but don't lump me in with him. I am not like him. *You* are supposed to believe that, at least.'

Lord Gawain floundered with this, clearly disarmed by Renatus's words, as always. I remembered the night the council had voted on me, and remembered that while Renatus played the child and follower to Lord Gawain's mentor and powerful leader, it was Renatus who held the power in this relationship. He had Lord Gawain wrapped around his finger, and knew all the strings to pull to get what he wanted. The White Elm's leader was defenceless against the Dark Keeper's charm and influence, and I knew I wasn't the only one who wondered why this was.

Taking a deep breath, Lord Gawain pointed at Qasim, all the while holding Renatus's gaze as though trying to appeal to him.

'Qasim *saw* you with Lisandro,' he said, in a desperate plea. 'He *saw* you confirm to Aubrey that you'd sneaked off tonight only with difficulty. He *saw* you offer Lisandro the ring. He *saw* Lisandro ask you for a favour. Now suddenly all of our allies are offside and all of your brothers and sisters – including me – are accused of dishonest and underhanded behaviour. Please, please explain this.'

'He didn't ask for a favour,' Renatus corrected. 'He wanted to give me information. He told me what I needed to do to make a trade for our councillors.'

'After you were *told* not to!' Lord Gawain shouted, distressed. I couldn't begin to understand what he was going through, but when I lowered my wards slightly, I felt his overpowering grief, as though he was losing a battle he couldn't afford to lose. I built my magic back up, protecting myself. 'You were there this afternoon – we all voted. You voted. You lost the vote. I'm sorry it happened that way; I'm sorry we can't save them. But we cannot.'

'Wait, wait, wait,' I said loudly, stepping forward to get attention but unable to get far because Emmanuelle was still hooked into my arm. I settled for standing just in front of her. I stared at Lord Gawain. 'What do you mean, we can't save Teresa and Aubrey? Of course we can.'

'We voted, Aristea,' Lord Gawain said, his voice tight and regretful. 'The decision was made to keep the Elm Stone away from Lisandro at all costs.'

'*What?*' I demanded, my brain in overload. This eventuality hadn't occurred to me. It wouldn't compute. 'When did killing your friends for the sake of a ring become an option? You didn't vote for this, did you?' I turned to Renatus, horrified.

'No, I would have preferred to give Lisandro the ring, if those were the only two options,' Renatus told me, then looked back to Lord Gawain, 'but there are *other* options we have not fully explored.'

'None of them work,' Susannah snapped at him. 'I told you that already. We're a team, remember?'

'When your teammate tells you something like that,' Tian suggested coldly, 'and two other Seers confirm it, you could try listening, instead of running off and betraying us to your-'

'I betrayed nobody,' Renatus snapped back. 'I was not in Valero, Avalon, Massachusetts, Wales or the North American wilderness tonight. I didn't zap all over the world wrapped in false energies, leaving your calling cards at all our allies' front doors. I went to Lisandro because *it is my job*. It's the job *you* chose for me. All of you voted for me. The least you could do is trust me to do it.'

'Renatus, I told you, no more surprises,' Lord Gawain reminded him tightly. Renatus frowned.

'I told Qasim to-'

'To tell me not to be surprised, I know. How am I meant to interpret that when I don't know what you're thinking?'

'You can't seriously be planning to just let Lisandro kill Teresa and Aubrey?' I said, stuck on the impossibility of this situation. 'After them, he's going to kill your families, and then, isn't he moving on to you? Us?' I ran a hand through my hair, trying to get a grip. I looked to my master again. Another thought occurred to me. 'You let me believe the council had voted the other way and that you were *told* to find Lisandro.'

'I *was* told that,' Renatus said, slightly annoyed with me, 'a thousand times. It's my job. And I never said we'd voted the way I wanted. I didn't lie to you.'

It was his job, I reminded myself, trying to calm down. He wasn't the main concern here. The council was, although they seemed to think otherwise. They were condemning their friends, their families, themselves, and *me* to death. How could this be? Emmanuelle pulled me to face her.

'Aristea, you need to understand,' she said strongly. 'If Lisandro 'ad the Elm Stone, 'e could kill us all. It would be the same as 'anding him a gun with thirteen bullets and closing our eyes.'

'If he could be bothered picking us off one-by-one, like he says he will starting next week, he probably will succeed with a few of us,' Qasim told me. 'But his chances of defeating the lot of us before one of us overpowers him are very slim.'

I knew Lisandro would have his work cut out for him if he came up against Qasim.

'Unless he has the Stone,' Elijah clarified for me. 'With the Stone, Lisandro is something else entirely.'

'And giving him the Elm Stone does not guarantee Teresa and Aubrey's lives,' Tian added. 'Most likely, they will still be killed. Most futures are dark for them.'

I looked around. Jadon had his head in his hands. Most of the others were glaring at Renatus.

'That is why many of us voted to withhold the Elm Stone from Lisandro, at the second most terrible price,' Emmanuelle finished. 'We voted to keep it from 'im.'

'Lisandro is twisted and horrible, a dark shadow of who we thought we knew,' Susannah confirmed. 'He manipulates as easily as breathing. It is through his manipulations that we are gathered here tonight.'

'I think it can be assumed that the perpetrator of tonight's offences is attempting to distract us and redirect suspicion,' said Lady Miranda. 'Those named would not be likely to include themselves in the pool of suspects, which leaves us wondering why you are the only name not on tonight's list, Renatus.'

'I wonder that, too,' he answered.

'How do you know it wasn't Lisandro?' I asked, but Renatus overheard my thought and started answering it before I finished speaking.

'It can't have been. I was with him this whole time.' He cast a sharp look at Anouk when she shook her head knowingly. 'It wasn't me either.'

'Lisandro also wouldn't trace as White Elm,' Glen added. 'It's not a signature that can be faked. There are only thirteen people in the world who could have done this.'

'Please state for the circle the following,' Lord Gawain instructed the council. 'I did not enter the boundary of a Class 3 community tonight. I did not take the life of the prisoner Saul.'

'I did not enter the boundary of a Class 3 community tonight,' Lady Miranda repeated dutifully, her words ringing cleanly without any trace of a lie. 'I did not take the life of the prisoner Saul.'

Everyone turned to Renatus expectantly. He held Lord Gawain's gaze and spoke slowly.

'I did not enter the boundary of any Class 3 community tonight,' he said clearly. 'I didn't even leave Ireland. I did *not* take the life of the prisoner Saul. I did not feel your summons because I was with Lisandro, making arrangements to ensure we all survive the next week, and unfortunately his wards blocked my communication with this council. I came when summoned by my apprentice.'

'I did not enter the boundary of a Class 3 community,' Qasim told the circle. He looked sidelong at Renatus. I knew he'd felt what I and everyone else had felt – no lie. Everyone was waiting for the lie. 'I did not take the life of the prisoner Saul.'

The words moved all around the circle, excepting me and ending with Jadon.

'I was in Italy,' Jadon said after repeating Lord Gawain's words, his tone dull. I looked to him and noticed that one of his eyes was shadowed by a fresh bruise. 'I was doing something very dumb, but it didn't involve going to Russia and it didn't involve killing anyone.'

'Jadon, you're stronger than Samuel,' Emmanuelle admonished, finally releasing me so she could move closer to him. ''ow did he get that one on you?'

'I let him,' he replied, leaning away from her when she reached to touch his face. 'I deserved it. I told him about the vote. *Don't*.' He tried to push her hand away but she caught his fingers. For a moment there was a pale glow where their skin made contact, and the purpling on his face visibly decreased. He ripped his hand away from hers, but her work was done. 'I'm sure there are laws against that, you know. Even First Aiders have to ask permission.'

'Too bad for you that I don't care.'

'Renatus, nobody lied about their whereabouts,' Lord Gawain said, changing the topic back, 'and you're the only one whose story we can't confirm.'

'But he didn't lie, either,' I said, concerned. 'This isn't a fair trial. You can't just point at someone and say he's this or that without proof. Maybe it was someone else. Maybe there's a thirteenth town you just haven't heard from yet.'

'There won't be a thirteenth town,' Renatus disagreed, annoying me deeply. Whose side was he on? Certainly not his own.

'Why not?'

'Lisandro is playing us. There won't be a thirteenth town.' He looked at Lord Gawain. 'Make it formal. No more running in circles. If you really believe it, charge me.'

I felt breathless. The White Elm leader looked as he always did when challenged by Renatus – helpless and lost for words. Lady Miranda took lead.

'Renatus, you have been charged with trespass upon the territories of twelve of the council's allied colonies and with impersonating twelve White Elm councillors with the antagonistic intention of incriminating them with your own crimes,' she said. She had a businesslike demeanour but I could see that she was also uncertain and maybe a little bit scared. 'How do you plead?'

'I am not guilty of these crimes,' Renatus said, folding his arms. 'You'll see.'

'Then I summon the powers of Fate and Magic to oversee our circle and to-'

A breeze similar to the one that had presented at my initiation struck up immediately, but blew itself it out when Lady Miranda was interrupted by Glen.

'Wait, what about Aristea?' he asked, worriedly. 'If Fate rules Renatus a traitor it'll strip him of his title and power – will it affect her?'

Everyone looked at me. No one seemed to know the answer.

'What does it matter?' I asked finally. 'He's not a traitor so there's no problem.'

The eyes shifted from me to the floor or to other councillors.

'Aristea, we're so sorry that you had to be dragged into this,' Lady Miranda said to me. 'It isn't fair to you. I wish we'd seen that before. We never thought Fate would allow the connection if Renatus's past was not clean; we honestly believed your initiation ceremony would bring the truth to light and protect you from anything like this. We're very sorry. If you would like, we can arrange to have you disconnected.'

I felt Renatus's shock and horror in my being before I saw it on his face.

'*What*?' he demanded. Lady Miranda ignored him.

'It can be done,' she continued speaking to me, 'but it is a difficult and painful process. If you want a severance, we will, as a council, ensure it happens.'

'A severance?' I repeated, discomfort in my stomach. The word sounded harsh to my ears, and Renatus's feelings about it coiled inside me like they were my own.

'You can't do that,' Renatus snarled. 'Only Lord Gawain and Emmanuelle together get to make that call, and *only* if it's what Aristea wants.'

Lady Miranda glanced at the two witnesses to my initiation and waited a moment for their mental commentary.

'We've discussed it, and they're both prepared to partake in the ritual, if it *is* what she wants,' Lady Miranda said coolly. Emmanuelle held me closer, evidently frightened but determined also that she was in the right.

'No,' Renatus said, softer this time, looking between Emmanuelle and Lord Gawain with a cold, accusing expression. His two closest allies had suddenly turned on him. 'It's not a safe ritual... Half the time one of the parties dies. She'll die.'

'Aristea, it's up to you, at the end of the day,' Tian said, beside me. 'No one is going to force you to do anything you don't want to do.'

'They're just going to warp the truth and misdirect you,' Renatus agreed sarcastically.

'Don't be swayed,' Susannah reminded me, her tone too cryptic to determine the side she was on.

'He didn't lie,' I reminded the group. I felt like it was the only defence I had. I didn't want to think about what they were asking me to do. 'We can all feel lies here and Renatus isn't lying.'

'A lie only registers if the liar believes they're lying,' Jadon threw in for my benefit, 'so if he's being dishonest but it's how he believes it went down, you don't get that flicker. It's difficult because people all have their own version of events.'

'Not lying isn't the same as telling the whole truth,' Anouk added sharply. 'These are the facts. Someone here is sharing information with Lisandro, deliberately, it seems. Someone here murdered a prisoner only Lisandro would want dead. Someone here was in Valero again tonight, along with eleven other places, pitting us against one another but also distancing our closest and strongest allies. It follows logically that this person wants Lisandro in power, wants to give him the Elm Stone, and wants to be in a position to help him take over. *You* took on an apprentice to improve your power. *You* voted to give the ring to Lisandro. *You* knew that it would be at Teresa's that night because it was your idea. *You* were standing over Saul when he accused you of coming to kill him and *you* were standing in the exact place the lethal spell was traced back to. *You* went to Lisandro tonight, in secret, perhaps hoping we wouldn't notice. *You* are the one he asked after when he came here with Teresa. *You* are the one with the closest and longest relationship with Lisandro. *You* stand to actually gain something from him if he defeats us and comes into power. *You*,' she paused here for breath, and the breath seemed to echo in the silent ballroom, 'pretend to work for us, pretend to be sourcing intelligence, when we should be wondering how much of your information is just fed to us at the exact right time. *You* are the only logical conclusion to our question, Renatus.'

The silence grew like a swelling balloon, and Lord Gawain's soft, dead voice was what popped it.

'Renatus, you know Lisandro better than anyone here,' he said, like an apology and a goodbye at the same time. 'You know him better than me – and he was my closest friend. You can understand... why it seems logical...'

My heart seemed to have stopped, or at least slowed considerably, because after all, I was barely breathing. The pattern was extremely evident when put into words by Anouk. No wonder it seemed obvious to the council that Renatus was the one at fault here. I didn't know how or why Renatus knew Lisandro so well, but surely, it was just another irrelevant element here, because Renatus couldn't be guilty. He couldn't be a murderer. He couldn't be a betrayer. He couldn't be a liar, a manipulator, or the sneaking traitor they all said he was. He couldn't be. I would know. I would *know*. Wouldn't I?

'Sometimes information looks like evidence when actually it isn't,' I said, feeling like a stupid little girl again and not much like a White Elm apprentice, but trying to be one anyway. 'Sometimes you can read into things the wrong way. Sometimes... things that look related can just be coincidences.'

Renatus had blocked much of himself off from me, but I felt his gratitude. It bolstered me slightly.

'There are no coincidences,' Lord Gawain said, very sadly. 'You should know that.'

'There can be,' I pressed weakly. I knew I was fighting a losing battle here. I was the only one fighting for Renatus – even he seemed to have given up – so as long as we didn't lose *me* I would be okay.

'I've Seen how this ends,' Lord Gawain said quietly. 'I didn't want to See it, but Susannah and Tian have Seen the same thing, and I can't ignore that. There is no way around it now.'

'Well, maybe not how it *ends* but it least how it *goes*; except in the event that we remove your apprentice from you,' Susannah told Renatus. 'It's the only path to stopping you.'

'I don't understand,' Renatus said.

'Every future I can see is one in which you give Lisandro the ring,' Tian said. I knew he was sorry to say it, and he looked at me sideways, sorry to hurt me, but he had no idea. I wasn't feeling anything. I felt like most of my self had just shut down, overloaded with the task of processing this news.

'You will give the ring to Lisandro.' Lord Gawain was struggling to hold himself together. 'It is certain. Our only hope to avoid that future is to disconnect you from Aristea. It is not clear yet how, but that will alter the future and put our council on another path. I don't understand how it has come to this – I don't understand how I could have not Seen this earlier if it were so important. Fate directed me to put you on this path for the salvation of us all, but somehow it's gone wrong. I'm so sorry.'

'Sorry,' Renatus repeated without feeling. He was backing down. He was just allowing it.

'Don't apologise,' I snapped at him, frustrated. 'You didn't do anything wrong. Stick up for yourself.'

'Why?' he asked. He looked pointedly around the room at the unfriendly eyes of his colleagues. 'Who's listening?'

I had no answer. That the men and women whose decisions moulded our whole nation's existence were not open to truth was a worrying notion. Their minds were made up.

'It's our responsibility to protect Aristea from murderers,' Anouk said coldly. My stomach did some weird flip thing. The tension and fear building inside me was almost unbearable.

'He's not a murderer,' I told her. 'He's not. Tell them,' I added, glancing once at Renatus before turning back to address the whole council. 'My master is *not* a murderer. I would *know*.'

'Aristea…'

I looked to Renatus, scared. *Tell them*, I thought. I waited for him to explain, logically and clearly, exactly how all this incriminating evidence *really* fit together in ways they hadn't considered before. I waited for his smart reply, putting them all in their place, leaving them speechless.

'Tell them,' I said again. 'Tell them. Tell me.'

But he said nothing, his expression pained, and his thoughts were silent, too, blocked from me.

Fine. I turned to Emmanuelle, and looked past her to Lord Gawain. I waited for the French councillor to step in and say something harsh and slightly out-of-line in Renatus's defence. I waited for her to walk into the middle of the circle and glare at everyone and lecture wise and powerful sorcerers twice her age. I waited for Lord Gawain to say something positive and affirming. I waited for him to ask everyone to calm down and not jump to conclusions.

Nobody did what I expected tonight. Nobody did anything at all for a very long moment. I looked back at Renatus and he was still looking at me.

'Just tell me,' I said again, nearly a whisper. 'Tell me you're not a murderer.'

'If it's what you want to hear,' Renatus said, just as quietly.

'It is.'

'Then I'm not a murderer.'

And there it was; what everyone had been waiting all night for – the lie.

And then Renatus turned away, breaking the circle's energy flow and leaving the room with a flick of his black cloak.

The stillness that followed might have lasted a minute. I couldn't tell. I just kept trying to make sense of the way what I'd just heard and felt had contradicted.

What did that even mean? I knew what that meant.

This couldn't be happening.

'It's always been the Dark Keeper in the past,' Qasim commented grimly as the other councillors visibly deflated. Emmanuelle pressed her fingertips to her forehead. Jadon walked to the nearest window and let his head fall against the glass with an audible *donk*. Lord Gawain literally stumbled his way over to the grand piano and sat down at it, staring at nothing, like a person in shock. Was he shocked with Renatus, or shocked with himself?

I looked to Qasim once I'd allowed a few seconds for his words to process in my fuzzy, confused brain.

'What are you talking about?' I asked. His return look was level.

'You haven't read the book, then?'

I remembered with suddenness the book he'd insisted I read the night the prisoner had been killed. I'd never retrieved it from the library. I wondered if it was still there.

'I suggest you find it,' he replied. 'It might help explain a few things.'

I shook my head. I forced myself to take a deep, shaky breath. It wasn't possible. I would *know*.

'What does this mean?' I asked him. 'This has to be a mistake. Renatus – why isn't anyone following him, finding out what he meant? What happens with me? I don't understand.'

'It doesn't matter to us what he meant,' Glen answered. 'It isn't worth pursuing him over while he's upset. You, however, need to make a choice.'

He wanted me to make a choice – the choice to sever my connection with Renatus forever. I'd only been his apprentice a little while but I was so accustomed now to hearing his thoughts in my head and sharing memories and ideas with him. To spending time with him and knowing he was around. How would it feel to lose that? On the other hand, how would it feel to continue it forever, knowing I had a murderer in my head?

Renatus was a murderer. How could that be? How could I not have known? How could he have killed a man and then face me the same day and tell me he hadn't? *That* wasn't possible, because I'd detected no lie, and even he couldn't disguise lies as truth. And how could Fate have let me be bound to him if he was really this terrible person? It made no sense at all.

'Aristea-' Lady Miranda began, moving toward me, but I cut her off, a burst of determination and stubbornness erupting from somewhere within me.

'No, nobody is forcing me to make any decisions tonight,' I snapped, backing away from the circle and towards the door. 'I won't be *swayed*. I'm leaving.'

The doors didn't open for me the way they swung themselves aside for Renatus, so I shoved through. The force of my shove sent the doors swinging back against the walls, making a loud bang. It seemed an adequately dramatic exit.

chapter seventeen

I marched straight across the reception hall to the library and went to the shelf Qasim had accosted me at two weeks ago. Or a lifetime ago. I wasn't sure. It was dark but I remembered clearly the way he'd stuffed the book into the shoulder-height shelf on the left in the second row. I reached over the back and my fingers felt the tatty dust cover of *"The Facts Behind the Darkness"*.

I didn't really have any sort of plan. I just went to the most logical place.

I ducked past the ballroom, knowing that most of the councillors were still inside, and I let myself out of the mansion and into the cold, dark grounds.

It was early morning, I noticed as I crossed the lawn, not the middle of the night as I'd theorised. The clouds in the eastern sky were pale with the nearing light. It hardly mattered what time it was, though, because I was completely awake. There was no chance of me falling back asleep with all this craziness going around and around in my head. I felt like I'd had five energy drinks in as many minutes. I was buzzing, but not in a good way.

I wandered into the orchard and headed straight along the path. This was the perfect place to hide. Nobody would bother me here, least of all Renatus. I hadn't decided yet whether I wanted to keep him in my mind, and staying here would ensure he kept out until I'd had some time to think.

I sat down against a tree, less than a metre from the epicentre of dark energy I'd felt yesterday. This was the place I'd felt the most powerful in my life, but it was also where this problem had started, at least for me. If I hadn't come here yesterday and scried what I'd scried, this morning's circle wouldn't have taken place and I wouldn't be sitting here now, so confused...

I had kind of intended to sit here and think things through, but I found that thinking straight was a more difficult task than I had anticipated. My thoughts, when they came from my fuzzy, blank mind, were incoherent and disordered, leading nowhere. Every thought was chased by a disagreement, and then an argument against that, and so on, until I ended up back where I started.

Renatus killed a person.

But it was a bad person.

But that's what Lisandro would have wanted; just like the misdirection of falsified White Elm appearances all over the world.

But I didn't see or feel anything while I slept, and wouldn't the power needed for this trickery be of an amount that would register as abnormal? Wouldn't I notice him channelling that kind of energy? I noticed what he did when I was awake.

But Renatus was blocked from everyone else – he could have been blocked from me, too.

But he *said* he didn't leave Ireland tonight, and he wasn't lying.

But...

But he was lying when he said he never killed anyone.

And no one else lied during the circle.

Renatus killed a person.

Sensitive as I was to his mind, I noticed that my master almost checked on me at one point, but recognised the energy I was surrounded by before he could finish lowering his mental barriers. Immediately he turned his attention away from me. I suspected that he knew exactly why I was here – if he'd wanted to talk to me so bad, he would have gotten past his issues with this path and this energy to contact me.

No one else on the council came looking for me, either.

When the sun came up, I still had no answers, but at least I had adequate light to get them. I opened the book and let the pages fall to either side wherever they wanted. There were no random pages for people like us, Renatus had said. I was apparently to start at chapter three – "The Fall of the Dark Keeper".

The story continued from where my knowledge left off, in the 1500s, with a guy called Nathaniel Tynan taking the position offered by his cousin, Lord Philip, as the first Dark Keeper. He seemed like a pretty decent guy, protecting small towns and studying the darker magic performed by the council's opponents to be able to plan how to counteract them. He seemed like the ultimate medieval hero. He even got the girl – he married Anne, the White Elm's Healer, who in my mind looked like a previous incarnation of Emmanuelle. But then things went south. He was reprimanded by his cousin on several occasions regarding overuse or misuse of some of his newly learnt dark magic. The author claimed that Nathaniel had mostly ignored these warnings as silly lectures and continued to deepen his knowledge, determined to become stronger and cleverer as his opponents increased in both number and skill.

Though Lord Philip believed firmly in his young cousin's strength of mind and character, even he must have noticed that the Dark Keeper was becoming arrogant and increasingly reckless as his study took him deeper into the darkness. Records from Lord Philip's time, such as minutes taken during circles and the journal of Tynan's wife Anne, depict Tynan as a moody and self-absorbed man, driven to improve and obsessed with outdoing the power of adversaries. Anne's journal details at least five occasions on which Lord Philip privately chastised Tynan for his actions in battle. 'Philip's voice was raised, though he tried to speak softly... It seems my Nathaniel has done wrong once again, though I wish he would not disappoint his cousin, our Lord, so... Philip says Nathaniel's act today was inexcusable. I am glad I am not involved in these battles to see what he does. I am glad he guards his mind from mine'. Between them, Anne and Philip made many attempts to redirect Tynan's passion and obsession with power, but it was not enough. Much like an addiction to any drug, the allure of the darkness is much too strong to be overcome when the user is not truly committed to breaking the habit. By the time Lord Philip was aware of the damage he had done to his cousin, Tynan was too deeply involved in his darkness and was unable to draw himself – the self Philip had known and the self Anne had married – away.

I read through the details of Nathaniel Tynan's final days. Anne's diary detailed many meetings with shady sorcerers as her husband thirsted for the knowledge of those with souls darker than his own, and the mysterious disappearance of these characters immediately after their meeting. Following an explosive argument with his wife on this topic, the Dark Keeper had travelled to a nearby town the council had been monitoring due to reported sightings of wanted dark sorcerers in the area. The author inferred from Anne's diary that Nathaniel had been trying to prove to her that his path was a righteous and moral one, as was his cousin's intention by creating the role for him.

What Tynan did not understand, and what Lord Philip should have realised, is that dark magic cannot be used for righteous and moral purposes. By its mere nature, the darkness will twist and warp any good intentions to its own jealous will. While seeking out and obliterating those criminals hiding out in his chosen town, it must have occurred to Tynan to steal the power of his defeated opponents for himself. The method by which this was done will not be detailed here, for the ripping of one's soul power for the use of another is a most evil and heinous act.

However, the reckless desire for power was Tynan's downfall, because he did not properly prepare his body for the power he was asking it to absorb. Overwhelmed and overloaded, this was how the first Dark Keeper met his end, burnt from the inside out by his own insatiable, irresistible hunger.

I skimmed the last page of the chapter, not interested in how he died, or how this impacted on Lord Philip or Anne. Obviously they were sad. Obviously they learnt nothing from the experience and still voted someone else into the position following Nathaniel's death. My brain seemed to highlight the important facts Qasim had intended me to find in reading this book. Things like, since Lord Philip's time, there had been roughly three times as many Dark Keepers as there had been Lords of the White Elm. Things like, only one Dark Keeper *ever* had been deemed to have died a natural death. Things like, more than half of history's Dark Keepers had turned to dark magic before their end, and had either turned on the council or on themselves. Most had burnt out, too ignorantly absorbed in their pursuit of power and dark knowledge to understand their own limitations – like Nathaniel Tynan. Some had deserted the council altogether and tried to destroy their former friends and colleagues – like Lisandro. Some had taken on apprentices and later killed them as a means of gaining more power – was this to be mine and Renatus's story? All the other Dark Keepers had died young, either in battle, or by murder.

Where a Dark Keeper had been found to have been murdered, in about two thirds of cases, the one convicted for the crime was the victim's own apprentice.

I wasn't sure why I was still reading. It wasn't a nice book anymore. According to the historical data, Renatus was either going to burn out, kill me or *be killed* by me; then if I became the next Dark Keeper, I would face the same horrifying statistics. Dark magic was not to be messed with, it seemed. Lord Philip had been foolish enough to think a good person with a good heart could handle and redirect its power but he was wrong.

I turned to part two of the book, which listed the names of dozens of Dark Keepers. I looked for any familiar names but found none. These were not names the White Elm publicised. These were not heroes when they died, although many of them, I found as I flipped through the pages, had done many heroic deeds in their time before they'd folded and gone dark side.

I took note of the causes of death for each case – *burnt out trying to combat the rest of the council; murdered by apprentice; burnt out; burnt out; murdered – killer unknown; burnt out; killed by council as deemed necessary by vote following acts of unspeakable evil; consumed by own spell; suicide; died in battle...* How depressing a future I'd carved out for myself. I could see why so many of the councillors had so openly rejected my stupid determination to be Renatus's apprentice. I'd just been too dumb to see that they were smarter and more educated than I was, and that they had been trying to look out for me. After all, who would actually choose this future for themselves? What sick, crazy lunatic would read this book, see what this job did to people, and still want to do it?

People like Lisandro.

People like Renatus.

People like... me? Did I?

I put the book down, feeling even worse. If I let the council rip me from Renatus, I would probably die. I believed Renatus and his conviction that I wouldn't survive the process. Joining him had totally wrecked me; I could easily imagine that trying to reverse such a significant and soul-altering process might kill me if attempted. It didn't sound like something that was well-practiced and safe, like getting a filling or getting your legs waxed. It sounded like a radical, unregulated, rarely attempted procedure, more like stem-cell treatment in dodgy countries. I was pretty sure I didn't want to go there, but if I didn't, I was bound to Renatus – who had killed some guy – and I was bound to his future of death, darkness and reckless acts of evil.

This sucked. So hard.

Early rising people would be having breakfast in the mansion now. Hiroko would probably be one of them. I hoped Iseult and Garrett had taken her in for the day, and I hoped she wasn't too worried about me. If she extended her senses out really far, she might be able to sense me here, alive and vital.

For now.

What the hell was I going to do? I began running my hands through my hair, yanking on knots until they hurt and loosened. It didn't help distract me from my problems, and it didn't help me come any closer to a solution. What the hell, what the hell? Things had seemed bad plenty of times over the past few weeks, but now I could see that those problems were nothing. This was really, really bad. I was in a really bad position, with two really bad options, and I had no one to blame or to help me except for myself – the last person I would have wanted.

The logical thing to do was work out the pros and cons of each option. Well, that was easy enough. Follow the council: pros – escape this mess and start afresh somewhere; cons – probably will die or at least be extremely altered, and lose the future on the council I'd so badly wanted. For some reason, I was still in love with the idea of being on the White Elm, despite what I'd just read and despite what I'd experienced lately. Follow Renatus: pros – getting onto the council, keeping my mind intact; cons – certain death.

Then again, everyone in the world faces certain death. There can be no eternal human life. Certain death, then, wasn't such a bad con. A longer life with the probability of turning evil later was very appealing to the cowardly little girl in me.

I stopped yanking on my knotty hair. If I stayed with Renatus, he was going to have the power to finish his transformation into someone like the Dark Keepers of the book, because I refused to believe he was there yet. He'd fixed my watch, hadn't he? He'd been kind and honest with me. These were small things but someone evil wouldn't do them. Would they? I would know if he was totally bad. If I wasn't around, he wouldn't hand over the ring. The council would maintain control of him and of the power Peter had left them. What they were asking of me was for his own good – and for mine, although not so much. They were protecting me from him, and trying to protect him from himself and his horrible, inevitable future as Lisandro's twisted sidekick. Or deputy, or maybe his partner in crime? I wasn't sure what Renatus's connection to Lisandro was, but somehow I found it hard to believe that Renatus was subjugating to anyone, even Lisandro. Was it possible that Renatus was the one running the show, calling the shots, and that this "Lisandro is the baddie" thing was just for show?

I shivered, realising I'd allowed my imagination to get away on me. This train of thought was for the White Elm to worry about, investigate and judge. It was way too big and beyond me. If my master was an evil genius, I didn't want to know about it. I couldn't worry about that.

I could disappear.

If he couldn't find me, maybe the future would change enough that he wouldn't betray the council? If I just went away for, like, a day? I couldn't Displace very reliably but maybe I'd be able to get to a main road and then hitchhike back home...

It was a terrible idea, I knew, but it was the only one I had that didn't loop back on itself.

I hadn't noticed the low clouds darkening but I did notice when they began to rain on me. I tucked the book underneath my pyjama shirt to protect it from the fat raindrops that rolled off the leaves onto me. This would probably be a good time to return to the house, but it took me several minutes to gather the motivation. I'd spent so much time and energy worrying and stressing that I was starting to feel really tired, and the thought of going back to my problems and being forced to *do* something about them was very unattractive.

A shower, I reasoned, would be helpful, so I reluctantly got to my feet and started slowly back to the house. The further from the darkness in the orchard I wandered, the easier it became to ignore my concerns and blank my thoughts. Apparently the orchard stimulated my mind as much as it did my power. No wonder I had gone there to think, although without any obvious answer in sight, it hadn't helped much to think around and around in circles.

Having somewhat made up my mind and not quite able to believe that I was actually going to attempt it, the walk back to my room was kind of surreal. I quietly let myself in the front doors and walked to the staircase, probably dripping water all over the reception hall but failing to care. I also failed to care when some other students crossed the hall, heading for the dining room, staring openly at my appearance. I was, after all, still dressed in my pyjamas, with a book tucked under my shirt, and dripping, scruffy hair, but I couldn't be bothered even looking at anyone I passed. They weren't my friends; whatever they were thinking was totally irrelevant.

Besides, I'd be gone soon, and I was sure they'd all have a lot to think and say about me in my absence.

Once up the stairs and on my floor, I let myself into my room, ignoring the questioning looks of Josh and Garrett as they passed me silently. I supposed they had decided it best not to ask.

My room was empty, but I could sense Sterling and Xanthe in their bathroom. I dumped Qasim's book on my messy bed, still unmade from when I'd abandoned it last night. I grabbed an assortment of clothes from my drawers, unlocked my bathroom and went straight to the shower.

Life-giving hot water washed the rain and the problems away immediately. It was awesome. Straightaway I was a normal girl again, with normal problems like whether my outfit would match my shoes and whether I should tie my hair up or let it drip-dry.

I showered. I got dry. I got dressed. I brushed my hair, and decided to towel dry it and then leave it out. I checked my appearance in the mirror. I looked fine – wearing a lot of black again, but wearing it well.

A normal girl.

I wandered back into my room to decide what to take with me, overhearing as I did the last part of Xanthe and Sterling's conversation.

'I've just been going about this all wrong; he's *got* to notice this,' Sterling was saying, twisting deliberately to be able to admire her own outfit from multiple angles. Xanthe nodded appreciatively, and then they both noticed me and looked up suddenly.

I felt like I'd been hit. I stared at Sterling for a long moment. She was not dressed like she usually did. She'd adopted fishnet stockings, a freshly torn denim skirt, and a tattered t-shirt. She was wearing bright red lipstick and heavy eyeliner. The look screamed "bad girl".

I tore my eyes away and pretended to be looking for my shoes. I knew exactly where they were, but could hardly think.

Sterling was trying a new angle. She'd taken Emmanuelle's freak-out last night to mean that Renatus was a bad boy, but not in the way that I had. She was seeing an opportunity to make another try at what she thought she wanted. I was seeing an opportunity for her to walk into a big, big mistake. Renatus was *not* what she thought he was.

I was stupid to think I could run away and that it would fix anything. I was stupid to have considered outfit and hairstyle problems to be normal, safe problems. I quietly buckled my platform Mary Janes onto my feet. Renatus had no idea how many lives he was ruining. He had ruined mine. He was ruining the entire council's lives. He was going to ruin my sister's life, when she found out about this, and my aunt and her family's. He just had no idea and Sterling couldn't see it.

Suddenly I was so angry, I couldn't stand it. He was *so selfish*. He had no concern for how many hours Sterling had spent over these past two months carefully preening herself, trying relentlessly to get his attention. He wasn't worried about how upset she was going to be when she found out what he'd done. He certainly didn't care what *I* thought about what he'd done. He didn't care what the council thought or wanted. He didn't care what was best for the magical world. He only cared about what *he* wanted. Why had it taken me so long to see this?

Renatus was the bad guy here.

He had manipulated and tricked me.

He had killed someone. Maybe more people.

He kept claiming that he didn't know what Lisandro was thinking or planning, but his actions always seemed to contradict these claims. He was the one, obviously, to have been working with Lisandro this whole time. He might even be in charge of the entire operation.

I straightened and walked straight out the door, Sterling's bright eyes following me until I yanked my key free of the lock. I kept walking as I looped the key's chain back around my neck. I strode up the stairs, getting angrier with each step. Renatus had ruined *everything*.

When I reached his office, I was positively seething. I had no idea what I was doing, except being angry. I really didn't expect him to let me in while in this state, so I was slightly taken aback when the door opened for me. I paused, allowing a second for the anger to drown the surprise, and then entered.

Renatus was sitting in one of the comfy armchairs, which he'd dragged over to the window. It occurred to me that he had been watching me from afar the entire time that I'd been in the orchard. I decided I didn't care. It didn't mean anything, and if it did, it didn't mean anything good. I grabbed the door before it could close itself and I slammed it shut. He didn't react at all.

'I hate you,' I began, because it was what I was thinking. He turned his head to look at me, no emotion visible, so I kept going. 'You wrecked my life.'

'Yes,' he agreed, his voice a little scratchy. 'I'm sorry.'

'*Don't* apologise,' I snapped. 'That's not what I want.'

'What do you want?'

I floundered with that for a second. How should I know the answer to that? I settled for just being angry instead of delving into a self-reflection.

'You lied to me!' I exclaimed, furious. 'You tricked me. I'm meant to be on the White Elm someday, but you only chose me so you could be stronger and so you could leave them for dead and start afresh with Lisandro. You sold your friends to Lisandro. They trusted you. *I* trusted you! And you betrayed us all.'

'I did none of those things,' Renatus said simply. 'I've lied to you once only, last night, when you asked me to.'

'*Shut up!*' I shouted. I knew on one level that this was true – I'd never detected a lie of his before then. But maybe Anouk was right, and maybe he was just good at telling half-truths. 'You damned me. You never told me that all Dark Keepers turn evil or get murdered. You tricked me into being your apprentice so you could power up, and now I have the choice of dying now trying to get away, or dying later as an evil sorceress. Thanks so much.'

'You won't turn,' Renatus insisted. 'You and I are stronger than the previous Dark Keepers.'

'Oh, please,' I snapped. 'I'm sure that's what they all said.'

'I'm sure they did, but they were wrong and I'm not.'

This was exactly the attitude that was going to get him, and me, killed.

'I've spent this whole morning thinking,' I said, struggling not to shout and cry and otherwise fall to pieces. I'd been so *stupid*. 'There were so many warning signs. I should have known all along that you were an accident waiting to happen. I've just spent the last however-many hours sitting outside, thinking of all the ways you've totally screwed me over.'

'I know. I was watching you.'

'Whatever. I'm just collateral damage to you, aren't I?'

'I'm not answering that. I chose you because you stood out – you're special.'

'I'm special like you and Lisandro, right?' I spat. His otherwise impassive expression hardened.

'No. Special like my sister was.' He paused, watching my face as this sunk in. 'You remind me so much of her. You're strong. You're defiant, stubborn, determined... You're determined to believe yourself powerless and weak, of course-'

'You don't get to talk to me about self-esteem issues when you've got so many of your own,' I snapped. 'I know how you see you. You aren't happy. You wish you could be someone else.'

'Of course I do,' he snapped back, surprising me, although I shouldn't have been surprised. I hadn't expected him to deny it, had I? He stood, accentuating his own height and personal power and anger; accentuating the fact that for every way I felt powerful, he was still stronger. 'But I did the best I could with what I had. You can't undo all damage. You can't reverse every mistake. You can only try.'

'So, are you going to tell me how it is that you know so much about Lisandro?' I demanded, changing tact before I could calm down and sympathise, wondering how long this self-control would last. 'Are you working for him?'

'No,' Renatus answered, walking closer. He finally wore a confused frown for an expression; I'd expected him to look more upset, angry or caged.

'Then how do you know him? How is it that you know the way he thinks, where he'll be, and why?' I shook my head. 'I've been so stupid. I can't believe I just *trusted* everything you said without thinking about *how* you knew all this. Is he working for *you*, is that it?'

'No.' Still, he looked only confused, as though I were ranting without making a point.

'When you confronted him, alone, how did you know he wouldn't hurt you?'

'I didn't.'

'You did!' I insisted, upset. 'Somehow, you *knew* you faced no harm going to him. I should have guessed then.'

'Aristea-' Renatus began, but for once I interrupted.

'I understand why you'd want power – who doesn't? I understand why you'd sell everyone out if you get what you want. I understand how you'd justify ruining my one insignificant little life to better your own. I don't like it but I get it.'

More than just not liking it, I hated it. I'd been dumb enough to believe he cared about me, wanted me for family, enjoyed having me around, thought of me like a friend. I thought that what I felt was mutual. I'd been stupid to invest as deeply and as quickly as I did in this relationship, and now the most I could do was pretend like it didn't matter. But it did, secretly. It hurt. I drew a shuddery breath, feeling my self-control slowly slip from my grasp. Confronting Renatus alone had probably not been the smartest option.

'I just don't get…' I didn't really want to go on. It was painful. 'I don't understand *why* it's what you want. Lord Gawain loves you, lets you get away with so much. I just don't see why you would choose Lisandro over Lord Gawain, but I know there's some puzzle piece I'm missing. Lord Gawain said you knew Lisandro better than anybody, maybe even better than Lord Gawain himself. And they were best friends, so how could you possibly know him better than that?'

'Aristea,' Renatus said, in a voice that was both calm and curious, 'has no one jumped at the chance to tell you that I am Lisandro's godson?'

chapter eighteen

The council had been in deep deliberation for more than five hours. Since Renatus and Aristea had marched out, no one else had left the ballroom.

'We can't strip him of his title without absolute proof,' Qasim repeated for maybe the tenth time, because this conversation had probably gone full-circle about ten times. Susannah knew this would all be so much easier if just one person would make up their minds, but because everyone was so confused and worried, the futures kept changing, making a definite vote very difficult to make.

And she wasn't allowed to push anyone to any conclusion that was not their own. Though there were ways around this rule.

The mind most confused and most important was Aristea's. Until she settled on a decision of sorts, the council would not know what action to take next. The fact was that if Renatus had Aristea at his side on Monday night, the ring on Emmanuelle's thumb would change hands. They wouldn't get it back until... Well, a long time. And a lot of damage would occur between now and then, deaths and losses that Susannah wished she didn't know of. The obvious course of action to the council was to remove the girl from the equation, because trying to separate the pair by physical means such as distance or even locked doors would not work. If Renatus went to Lisandro as an emissary of the White Elm tomorrow night with an apprentice *anywhere*, she would find a way to be there, physically or just in conversation, and that was enough to ensure this path.

To some on the council, like Qasim, it seemed simpler to just leave both young scriers behind when they went to Lisandro. It was less drastic and Susannah personally preferred it over ripping the pair apart and killing a promising young sorceress, but she also knew that it wasn't an option. Renatus had approached Lisandro and arranged this meeting – if he were not present Lisandro would be suspicious and no deal was possible. But if they took Aristea from him, Renatus would no longer serve the White Elm and again, there could be no negotiation with Lisandro for the lives of the other two councillors.

To someone without knowledge of the futures, it seemed an impossible situation.

Rather than wait patiently for the seventeen-year-old to make the decision the whole council waited on, they had taken to discussing alternatives. No one wanted to hurt Aristea or risk her if they could help it, so the conversation seemed to keep coming back to the second-most extreme option, that of removing Renatus himself from the council.

'I think we got our proof when he said he didn't do it,' Anouk reminded Qasim.

'For all we know he's killed a thousand people, but one flicker of energy is not a good enough reason to rip him from the council,' Qasim insisted.

'It's all we needed to remove Peter and Jackson,' Glen said.

'*And* the fact that they both openly admitted to scheming against us and disappeared with Lisandro after 'e attacked me,' Emmanuelle said, folding her arms. 'Renatus 'asn't admitted to anything, and 'e never attacked any of us.'

'What about what you saw, Qasim?' Jadon asked. 'You said you saw him tell Aubrey he'd sneaked out tonight to be with Lisandro. Isn't it too much of a coincidence that he should say that and then someone sneaks around the world planting evidence that the rest of us – all of us except him – have been mistreating our alliance agreements? He's quick enough *and* powerful enough to have done it.'

'I know,' Qasim agreed, 'but now after some thought I'm uncomfortable with the theory. Lisandro has been hidden from my gift all year. The only times I've seen him has been when he's *let* me. The scraps of conversation I tapped into tonight were all very incriminating but also minutes apart. I wonder what was said in between? It wasn't Renatus that pulled those barriers down – it was Lisandro, which means Lisandro is the one who chose what to let me see and hear. Now I wonder... am I just playing along with Lisandro's script?'

Thank you, Susannah thought privately. A sound and rational voice, since she wouldn't permit herself to add her own.

'That's giving Lisandro a lot of credit,' Elijah said uncertainly.

'I don't think it's too much.'

'At the end of the day, Renatus wasn't meant to be there. He was betraying our trust and confidence to go,' Glen stated.

'We've known from the start that he's not squeaky clean,' Lady Miranda said carefully.

'Fine, I'll put it this way,' Qasim said coldly. 'Kick him out now, and you know where he'll go. You're giving him no other option. Am I right, Susannah?'

That future was cloudy, too, because everyone was terrified that Qasim was right. No one wanted to make the decision that ruined the whole council. Susannah had looked to that future many times before, trying to gain a concept of what a Renatus-less White Elm might be like, since it *sounded* like such a good idea.

No adequate replacement...

Picked off, one by one...

No call for help, until too late...

Councillors dead in their homes...

Susannah's eyes drifted to meet Lord Gawain's. She knew he'd seen the same. But now he was reflecting on these visions and wondering whether he'd misread them, while Susannah was not prepared to question Fate yet.

I don't think we should follow that path,' she said finally. As always, a strong ethical code bound her speech. It wasn't her place to share what she Saw, but she felt that Fate showed her what it did so she could help facilitate others in making the right choices. 'There are better options.'

People often said that Susannah was the best Seer of her time, and they were probably right. She had always known so much more than she should, and in her years had learnt the impact her knowledge could have on people and their lives. Sometimes, telling somebody something she'd Seen could make them extremely happy, but could prompt them to make foolish choices that consequently led them down paths that did not result in the future she'd seen. Knowing was not always a good thing. Sometimes people had to believe in an improbable future in order to create their ideal one for themselves. Sometimes, that included her beloved White Elm council.

'I never Saw this,' Lord Gawain was murmuring, still sitting at the grand piano and looking lost and upset. 'How did this happen?'

Lord Gawain was a powerful Seer as well, but his gift worked slightly differently to Susannah's. He tended to see things with a wider scope than she did. He would see how a significant life choice could result in a powerful consequence as much as a decade later. He often missed the smaller in-between things that Susannah saw so clearly. She was certain that when he'd first held the anguished and teenaged Renatus in his arms, he had Seen two things – his rise to the White Elm and his part in the survival of the White Elm at a crucial time in history. It was doubtful that he'd Seen the circumstances surrounding either consequence. He couldn't have known that

Renatus might actually be the reason for the White Elm needing help, and that his part in saving it might in fact be his selection of Aristea as his successor. She was many times better a person than he was. Her future was uncertain right now, but who knew? Well, Susannah did, but no one else needed to.

'This isn't your fault,' Lady Miranda told her co-leader consolingly, sparing a nasty look at Anouk when the Telepath made a noise of disbelief that was a little too loud. 'You did everything you could. This development shouldn't be seen as a reflection on you or your work with Renatus. He was damaged when you took him on; his prospects were never good.'

'That's right,' Glen agreed, trying to be encouraging, although Susannah could see that none of this was helping the Lord at all. 'Renatus's family – well, we were keeping a close eye on them for years up to their death. They were trouble. *And* he had Lisandro on his shoulder growing up. He never had a chance.'

'You did wonders for him in the time you had. You knew you might not be able to save him. You did everything you could,' Lady Miranda repeated when Lord Gawain covered his face with his hands.

'He's not *dead*,' Emmanuelle muttered. 'Can we stop speaking about Renatus in past tense, please?'

'Yeah, it's not very constructive,' Jadon added, sounding annoyed. 'He's not dead; he's perfectly alive and perfectly three floors above us and perfectly pissed off. You've all been so worried about how powerful Lisandro will be when he gets that stupid ring and how he could blow us all to pieces, but how about we start worrying about the angry powerhouse sitting on the top floor? Any ideas?'

'I'm not sure what you're Seeing, Susannah, but if Renatus is removed from the council, Lisandro never gets that ring,' Tian said hesitantly. A Seer as well, his skill was different again to hers, with a totally different scope. Tian Saw on an even smaller scale than she did, the very short-term, the major choice points and the definite, but with much finer details than she had ever known how to look for.

'Then that is what we must do,' Anouk said with certainty.

'It is not an ideal path,' Susannah reinforced, hoping Tian and Lord Gawain at least would take the hint. It was a *bad idea*. So far, all that had happened had happened *perfectly*. Trying to undo the past always backfired, and she needed her fellows to decide to look forwards instead of into the past.

'We're going to need to fix this, aren't we, Susannah?' Elijah guessed, perceptive as always. 'We need Renatus for this confrontation with Lisandro. We need to get him back onside.'

About time.

'What?!' Anouk asked, incredulous.

'He's not on our side, remember?' Glen added. Those two, always of the same mind.

'Well, we won't be able to defeat Lisandro without him,' Elijah said with a shrug. 'I don't care what you have to say about him. He's our key to defeating Lisandro. Lord Gawain Saw that when he elected him to the position of Dark Keeper. I don't believe that future has changed. Maybe he's not the man we want him to be, but more than likely he's the man we need him to be.'

Finally, words of wisdom. It was moments like these that Susannah craved in council circles – moments where her careful efforts were unnecessary and someone worked something out on their own.

'It's really not like 'im, is it?' Emmanuelle said now. "e's smarter than all this. Why would Renatus go to such lengths to upset our allies and redirect the blame in a way that so obviously points to 'im? It's very clumsy. It would make more sense to single one person out to take the fall.'

'He said he didn't leave the country last night, we didn't find any dishonesty and he was prepared to let Fate judge him – something the rest of us probably wouldn't be brave enough to allow,' Qasim said. 'He would have had to be extremely quick to visit all those places between the last time I saw him, with Lisandro telling him what he needed to do, and when he came back here. It doesn't sit right with me. I want to hear what he has to say, and *then* if he deserves it, excommunicate him for betraying us.'

'We shouldn't be discussing sentencing, any-way,' Lady Miranda admitted now. 'The trial was interrupted and inconclusive. We haven't formally charged Renatus with any crime.'

'Then let's get him back here and talk it out,' Elijah suggested.

'How do you suggest we get him back into this room?' Glen asked. 'You don't think he's going to come back willingly to be judged, do you? Even if we hadn't just completely alienated him, there's the added problem of him working for the other team.'

'Or *being* the other team,' Anouk added. Susannah tried not to sigh.

'Ask?' she suggested as nicely as she could.

'He'd never forgive us,' Lord Gawain said immediately. 'He'll hate me for what I've said.'

'Oh, cut it out,' Emmanuelle snapped at their leader, earning herself a surprised look and then a disapproving frown when she added, frustrated, '*C'est des conneries*! 'e would forgive you in a 'eartbeat. 'e's probably already forgiven your words. If you know 'im at all, you should know this much.'

'Do we *want* to get his forgiveness?' Anouk asked coldly. 'After what he has done?'

Susannah knew why this was so important to Anouk. It was her home town that had been infiltrated, despite its incredible protective wards and all the magic weaved around it. The murderer had been within a frightening distance of her family and friends, who she had always seemed to believe to be unreachable in their fortress. She was feeling shaken. Susannah could understand. However, at the present moment, her insecurity about this new near-attack was interfering with Susannah's careful planning, and swaying less passionate councillors in an unhelpful direction.

'We want whatever will help us,' Susannah said calmly. 'If you're really sick you don't worry if the medicine doesn't taste nice.'

'Since when are you pro-Renatus, anyway?' Anouk demanded. 'You've never trusted him before today.'

Susannah was unable to restrain her sigh this time.

People who were not Seers simply didn't get it. Yes, she disliked Renatus, and since Seeing a crime he was yet to commit (the vision had come when he was only a teen) she had found him impossible to trust. But at the same time, Fate knew everything, and blessed Susannah with the honour of Seeing snippets of what was in store. The fact that she disliked Renatus could not undermine the fact that he was instrumental in keeping them all alive.

And *they* were instrumental in keeping *him* alive and on-track.

'We need him,' she said finally, wishing they'd come up with this on their own, 'and we need *her*.'

'We should call her in,' Jadon spoke up. 'Find out what she's thinking, ask what she wants to do.'

'No,' Susannah said sharply. Aristea was unsettled and vulnerable right now. Surrounding her with frightened and powerful adults with their own agendas would only make her feel pressured and force her into making a decision that wasn't her own. She needed to choose without influence, or she'd back out of it later. 'We can't sway her.'

'We can't wait for her forever, either.'

'Susannah says we leave her alone,' Lady Miranda reminded the young American, 'so we leave her alone.'

427

'If we want them both, we need to wait, unfortunately,' Susannah told Jadon apologetically.

'Aristea might be enough,' Glen suggested hopefully. 'We might not need them both.'

Sigh.

'We either take them both or take neither,' Qasim said, slashing Glen's bubble. 'Aristea isn't ours. Renatus is right, the ritual will almost definitely kill her, and if it doesn't she'll be ruined and *if* she's still got any magic left in her, her trust in us will be broken. We either take them both as they are, or let them both go.'

'Aristea belongs to Renatus – not to us,' Elijah agreed. 'If we take her from him, we lose them both. They'll be irreversibly damaged. It would be a waste.'

'It could be the only way to save all our lives, and save them both from Renatus,' Lady Miranda reminded the group.

'I think Qasim and Elijah are right,' Emmanuelle spoke up. 'In trying to save our council we may be destroying it. This ritual – I don't even want to think about it – to separate Aristea from Renatus is very extreme. It would practically paralyse our strongest weapon, and damage one of our best resources and a very important-'

'Renatus is no longer *our* weapon!' Anouk burst out. 'Remember? The Dark Keeper was a bad idea from the very start. They work well for a few years but they can't last. With a train wreck like Renatus we were lucky to get the two years we did out of him-'

"e's not a faulty product!' Emmanuelle said, angrily cutting Anouk off the way the Telepath had just interrupted her. "e is not a broken appliance out of warranty. 'e's our brother and our team mate. I think Elijah made a valid point,' she said, glancing over at him, 'when 'e said that Renatus is exactly who we need 'im to be. Maybe 'e did kill that bastard we locked up in Valero. I notice that no one 'ere cared enough to attend the funeral the prison 'eld for 'im. Perhaps 'e has been feeding information to Lisandro, and perhaps 'e does want to overthrow our council and take over the world. I notice we're all alive. I *offered* 'im the ring once and 'e turned me down. I'm worried we're overlooking something incredibly obvious and making a massive mistake.'

Emmanuelle .vas another one Susannah disliked personally and yet respected for the part she was yet to play in history. The French councillor was impatient, defiant and forceful, three qualities that rubbed Susannah the wrong way but which made Emmanuelle an incredible sorceress. She always said it like she saw it, which often was exactly what needed to be said, and she was strong and confident, though she couldn't know yet what she was destined to do and be.

Susannah's dislike for Emmanuelle Saint Clair had made it easy for her to launch a verbal attack on her in last week's circle, redirecting the council's suspicions from Renatus. The actual accusation was meaningless. Catalysts always were. The result was Lord Gawain and Lady Miranda forced to consider the potential in each of the White Elm's members; to see how each of them could have committed Saul's murder, yet also, how none could have done it. For Susannah to just *tell* what she knew would not do. People, and especially leaders, needed to find truths for themselves.

Susannah's gift was useful but also a huge responsibility that she took very seriously. No one knew what she knew, and nobody should. She knew things even she wished she didn't. She was looking at Emmanuelle now, knowing the success the younger sorceress would attain, but knowing also the way in which she would meet her end. It was hard sometimes to feel like there was any point to life and to orchestrating the council's lives like she did when Susannah knew exactly how each of them was going to die, and when, and that she had no right to interfere because if she did, Fate would only find them somewhere else at another time. The bright side, if it could be called that, was that their lives and deaths were all part of a much bigger plan. Everyone had been chosen to play a role, some bigger and grander than others, but the play would always carry on regardless of who fell and how.

'We don't know why he's left us alive this long,' Anouk said, still pressing her point. Susannah tilted her head to the side, pretending to listen as the Russian continued her rant. Ah, Anouk. At least her end would be quick. Others weren't so lucky.

'He's left us alive because 'e doesn't want to kill us,' Emmanuelle said. 'I think that says something in itself.'

The future shifted quite suddenly; consciously or otherwise, Aristea had made up her mind, or had at least started to. She'd come into new information and her world view had changed forever.

'She chose,' Susannah said before Anouk could argue with Emmanuelle. 'Aristea chose. She won't be separated. So we need to take advantage of that.'

'If she won't be separated from him,' Tian mused, 'we can control him through her.'

'That won't be necessary,' Susannah said, seeing it already. As it set, the future unfolded for her like soft cloth, open and accessible. 'She will bring him back to us, then it will be our turn to do our part.'

'Are you certain?' Lord Gawain asked from his seat at the piano. His gift was great but his love for Renatus blinded him to many aspects of his council's and his own futures, which were all entwined.

'Don't concern yourself,' Susannah urged. 'Just do what you need to do to get him back. They'll come to us when they've sorted their problems out.'

This wasn't entirely true. Emmanuelle, she knew, would tire of waiting and would go and fetch the pair before they could decide to come on their own accord. But if she said this, Emmanuelle would leave too early, and interrupt a very important conversation; if she said nothing, Emmanuelle would not go at all, worried about the safety of approaching the Dark Keeper while he was upset. By telling her that they would come unsummoned, Susannah was playing on her French sister's impatience. At just the right time, she would lose interest in waiting and decide to fetch them herself.

'So what are we going to do?' Jadon asked. 'Just wait?'

'It'll be done and dusted in an hour, Jadon,' Susannah said. 'Teresa and Aubrey aren't going anywhere in an hour.'

'A lot can happen in an hour,' the youngest councillor mumbled, folding his arms and looking away. He just wanted things to get done. He didn't understand, like Susannah did, that everything *would* sort itself out with time and the right actions. They'd done everything right up to now – replacing Lisandro with Renatus, replacing the other two with Teresa and Aubrey, starting the school, Qasim driving Aristea to Renatus, Renatus taking a liking to the girl, Aristea agreeing to be his apprentice, Lord Gawain suspending Renatus from his duties to the White Elm long enough to ensure the Dark Keeper got stuck into training Aristea instead of chasing down his hated godfather... The future takes time to create, and Susannah was confident in the future they'd prepared for themselves.

'Susannah.' Tian walked over, looking very concerned. When he addressed her up close, his voice was very low, trying to avoid being heard by the other councillors. Most paid no heed; they were trying to console Jadon and assure him that his friends were fine, for now. Like that would help, when most of them had voted to let the pair die just yesterday. 'Susannah, what can you See that I cannot? I See that Lisandro is still going to get the ring.'

'I See that, too.'

'That's not the end we want.'

'Who said that's the end? There's a difference between a bump in the road and a dead end.'

'But this road... Are you sure it's the right road?' Tian checked, nervous. Susannah rested a hand on his shoulder.

'Tian, trust me,' she said, calmly. 'This is *definitely* the right road.'

chapter nineteen

After the long, tense moment it took for Renatus's words to sink in, I stepped backwards and cast a thick shield between us. It wasn't from fear; it was more instinctual.

I couldn't believe what I'd just heard. *Lisandro's godson.* I couldn't believe he would just say it like he did, like it meant nothing. Like he thought I already knew. This changed *everything.* Any uncertainty I'd felt about Renatus's guilt evaporated.

It all made sense now. I could suddenly see why the other White Elm had been so wary of him from the beginning. So many conversations came back to me, suddenly in context.

'You're his *godson?*' I repeated, horrified. 'And you just neglected to mention this before now?'

'Calm down,' Renatus said, raising a hand gently in an attempt to soothe me.

'No, I will not *calm down*,' I said harshly. 'I always calm down and listen; for you, for everyone. I'm over it. You've been trading information to you *godfather* all this time, screwing everyone over, including me.'

I snapped my mouth shut before I could add *you feckin' lying gobshite,* because my mother had never allowed my siblings and I to speak like that at home and my very proper sister had maintained that expectation when she'd taken over raising me, but I could tell somehow in Renatus's eyes that he'd heard it anyway.

'Aristea, I've told you, that's not the case at all,' he said. 'I didn't realise you didn't know my connection to Lisandro. I thought it was just common knowledge.'

'How in hell was I meant to *know*?' I demanded. '*You* never bothered to bring it up!'

'You never asked,' he reminded me, and his words shot me through with frustration.

'Why would I ask that? Nobody asks that! Did *you* ever ask *me* whether I had any deep familial connections to any infamous dark sorcerers?' I glared at him, seething. '*No*, you *didn't*. I could be anyone's goddaughter, anyone's niece, anyone's kid, and you wouldn't know. You don't know a thing about me, and I don't know a thing about you, apparently.'

I think this last accusation was more directed at myself in anger over my impulsive insistence on accepting Renatus's offer of an apprenticeship after knowing him all of a month or so and *despite* his general sketchiness, because in retrospect it was really, really dumb and I had no one to blame but myself. He hadn't forced my hand. Qasim had ensured that. I'd made my own stupid choices and now I was living with the consequences.

Renatus was Lisandro's godson.

'I didn't ask,' he relented now, 'because I wouldn't want to know. I know what I need to know and I'll deal with the rest when it comes.'

'What's that supposed to mean?' I asked, confused and trying to hide that behind bluster and attitude. It sounded like a veiled version of "I like you just the way you are" or "nothing like this would change my opinion of you", but that seemed too sensitive for the Dark Keeper.

'It means if your own murderous godfather turns up on the front steps wanting to kill everybody we know, I'll try to react a little better than you are right now.'

I narrowed my eyes further. 'You're a jerk.'

'I've been called worse.' Renatus looked away, clearly considering his angle, and looked back at me after a moment. His emotions were carefully tucked away from me, hidden like a hand of cards. He felt blank to me but I knew of course that he wouldn't be feeling blank on the inside. 'Honestly, Aristea, I thought you knew about Lisandro. I thought for sure Qasim, or Anouk, or someone would have told you before the initiation.'

'You thought I *knew* this about you and that I went through with it anyway?' I asked, incredulous. He tilted his head, regarding me without expression.

'Are you going for "hurtful" right now?' he asked. 'You're doing a good job of it if you are.'

'I'm going for *fuming*, because that's what I am,' I snapped. 'You're a liar and a traitor and you tricked me into playing a part in your stupid game.'

'Listen to me,' Renatus said suddenly, intense once again, taking a step closer to me, barely a pace away from my shimmery ward. He pointed at me with a finger that I noticed was bleeding. I stayed put. I wouldn't be the one to back down. 'I don't blame you for being angry. I don't blame you for any of the conclusions you're drawing, but that doesn't change the fact you're wrong. You can say you don't know me but that's a fucking lie.' I blinked in surprise; Renatus rarely cursed around me, always so articulate and refined, but he was definitely not refined in this moment. 'Go ahead: say it again and listen to yourself.'

I refused to rise to his challenge. I kept my mouth firmly shut, determined that I would not give him the satisfaction of being right. What if I *was* lying? He took my silence as a win and kept going.

'You *do* know me,' he insisted. 'You know enough. You know I didn't choose you so I could fill out my aura or steal your power or whatever. And you know I don't play games, so how could I have tricked you into one?'

Still, I had nothing to say. That he didn't play games was certainly true – he always got straight to the point, never beat about the bush... To call him tactless was probably fair. That I knew him, that I knew *enough*... I didn't know what to think of that. How could this new knowledge not matter? How could the events of the previous night just not matter? How could the council proceedings happening right now in the ballroom simply not matter? I couldn't grasp that yet. I needed more information to make sense of the scrappy fragments I had to work with.

Renatus withdrew, working to calm himself. He took himself a big restless step away, pushing his hair back with one hand. 'I'm not the mole, Aristea. I haven't been helping Lisandro and I don't want him to have the Elm Stone, and you know I didn't put you and myself through that god-awful initiation for a power trip.' His gaze on me was wrought with honest intensity, the kind that'd make you feel deeply guilty for even suspecting wrongdoing, except I was determined not to feel sorry for him. Not yet. He said, 'You were right – you were missing a puzzle piece. But now you're trying to force it into the wrong place in the jigsaw. I'm willing to give you the rest of the pieces... if you want them.'

Despite my insistence to the contrary, I felt myself calming down, too. Renatus was a bad guy and a powerful sorcerer I had no hope of defeating if I messed with him, but I couldn't bring myself to be scared of him.

'Alright,' I conceded. I shouldn't be giving him this chance to talk me over, but I couldn't help it. I wanted to know. 'Alright, fine. Start with yesterday. What happened yesterday?'

'The vote,' Renatus said, eyes softening slightly with relief that I was willing to listen. I nodded tightly.

'Yeah. I remember. You left me locked out in the hallway.' Keeping one hand outstretched to maintain my ward, I wrapped my other arm across my body, annoyed, but if I was waiting for an apology, it wasn't forthcoming. Which I knew to expect. 'What was the *actual* outcome of that?'

'The council voted against trading the Elm Stone for Teresa and Aubrey,' he said, 'and I wasn't happy about it but as Lord Gawain said, it was the council's vote that mattered, not mine. When you came to me yesterday I had no intention of defying Lord Gawain's order.'

'Then why did you go?'

'Fate, mostly,' he admitted. 'I'm told to give up, and seconds later you walk through the door with an exact location? No coincidences, remember.'

'No coincidences,' I muttered. 'I wouldn't be running with that one if I were you. Lisandro has a spy *and* a godson on the White Elm? Coincidence?'

'So there's *one* coincidence.' Renatus rolled his eyes and I felt a flicker of mild irritation within him. His guard was slipping. 'It occurred to me that someone in that vote was a spy for Lisandro, and if they went straight to him with news of our vote, he might murder Teresa and Aubrey on the spot. I'm still determined to save them, if I can, so I intended to approach him and convince him that we would make a trade.'

'You were going to trick him?' I clarified. Renatus nodded.

'I *did* trick him. He believed me. It was stupid of me not to tell Lord Gawain, but it bought our councillors an extra two days of life.'

I nodded once. It was a logical plan, and I had to admit, if he'd told me about his plan, I probably would have encouraged it. I didn't want Teresa or Aubrey to die, either.

'Okay,' I said, thinking. He'd gone to Lisandro to trick him, not to share secrets with him. He'd been trying to do the council's work for them. So far he was in the clear. 'And when Qasim said he saw you agreeing to help Lisandro? Offering the ring? Telling Aubrey that you had trouble getting away from us?'

'Lisandro said, "This is what you need to do", and lowered his wards so Qasim would see me there,' Renatus said, looking away in annoyance, with himself this time. 'He did it a few other times, too, but I was too distracted to take notice. He knew I was being watched. He's been playing with me this whole time, trying to put me in the spotlight, knowing how easy a target I make. I take the heat off his real spy – who, meanwhile, was teleporting about triggering our allies' security wards and falsifying other councillors' energy signatures to make it look like I was trying to shift the suspicion.'

'Whoever it was did a good job of that.'

'Honestly; if I wanted to pin the blame on some-one else, I would do a better job than this. This was clumsy. I'd pick *one person*.'

'So if he didn't send you off to do that, what did he tell you to do?' I asked. Everything was ringing true so far, making perfect sense, but the words *"he's Lisandro's godson"* kept running through my brain.

'He had me choose a place to make the trade. I told him about a middle ground I thought would be appropriate. We agreed on a time – Monday night at nine – and we discussed terms. When I heard from you, I left. I knew nothing of the trespasses until the circle. I didn't do any of the things they're accusing me of.'

Another banner of horrific words joined the first. Now my brain was screaming, over and over, *"he's Lisandro's godson"* and *"he killed someone"*.

I thought I'd blocked him out but I must have let my shields slip at some point during this conversation because Renatus overheard.

'I didn't kill him,' he reiterated. 'I swear to you. I told you that before, when I was first accused of killing Saul.' He met my gaze firmly. 'I didn't leave those fake traces everywhere. I didn't go to any of those places last night. I didn't even leave Ireland.'

I kept one hand outstretched to power my ward as I used to the other to run through my hair. He was telling the truth, every word. Now I had to calm myself and explain the frightening facts screaming around my brain.

'Tell me...' I began, trying to choose one impossible fact over the other. 'Why didn't you tell me your plan before you went? Why didn't you tell me what the council had decided and what you planned to do about it?'

I didn't want to ask it but the next question rebounded around my head instead and that was no less audible to him. *Didn't you trust me?*

'I thought...' He paused, hesitant. 'I shouldn't have thought it. I thought my plans mightn't be safe in your head. I thought someone might overhear.'

I frowned. 'I knew you were going and I kept that to myself. I could have kept the rest of the story secret, too.'

'I know,' Renatus said immediately. 'I should have trusted you. I thought I was trying not to complicate the situation for you by keeping you on a need-to-know basis but really I was being arrogant. I should have been transparent with you. You've trusted me; I should have known to trust you, completely.'

That little monologue went a long way in settling me down. I *did* matter to him. I wasn't wrong about that. I wasn't quite so much of an idiot as I'd thought. Still an idiot, but less of one.

'You're Lisandro's godson?'

'Yes.' So calm.

'How has this escaped conversation so far?'

'It's not something I like to advertise or even discuss, particularly,' Renatus admitted. 'We're not *close*. We aren't on speaking terms. My whole estate,' he added, gesturing to the window and the vista beyond, 'is woven with magic written specifically to keep him out.'

I ran my hand through my hair again, more agitatedly. There was so much to process.

'Start at the start,' I urged.

'Lisandro and my father Aindréas were childhood friends, as close as brothers,' Renatus said, speaking a little slowly, like he was concerned I'd get scared and run away. 'There was a third friend, but I never met him – he was made godfather of my sister Ana, and fell out with the other two before I was born. My parents asked Lisandro to be my godfather, and though he tried very hard, he never liked me, and I never liked him. He was always around when I was a child, always trying to do his role by teaching me new things and telling me about the world. He was on the White Elm and he would bring me things he'd found on his travels, but we never could just talk. We never became close.'

I pursed my lips, torn. I refused to lower my ward. The story seemed honest enough, and I'd detected no lie thus far, but it wasn't enough to convince me. Not yet.

'When I was fourteen, Lisandro... he took... he... he betrayed my father's trust, in a bad way,' Renatus said, looking hesitant to give details. 'My father ordered him off the property and forbade him to set foot on his land again. He wove spells around the estate to keep his former friend out, and for a year we neither saw nor heard of him. I was glad – he'd betrayed me, too. I never wanted to see him again.'

'But you did,' I said, surprised that I was being drawn into the story. 'You joined the White Elm alongside him.'

'I'd like to say it had nothing to do with him, but the fact that he didn't want me joining was definitely a motivator, and if I wasn't his godson, the rest of the council would never have let a *Morrissey* in. Lisandro vouched for me, insisted I'd inherited all the best qualities of my family, spoke great and positive and warm things about *Renatus Morrissey*, his beloved godson.' My master's usually smooth visage twisted with dislike at the memory. 'All of it polished and dripping with honey like everything that comes from his mouth. The council would never have accepted me without his declaration of approval.'

'So he helped you?' I suggested, but Renatus didn't like that way of phrasing it.

'I *hated* him for it,' he said bitterly. 'I *hated* that I needed his support to get something I wanted for myself, and I hated that I needed him because of my family's name. They were dead and they were still holding me back. I got the position and at my initiation I saw him smiling at me, like he was proud of me, and I decided I was never going to receive something just for being "Lisandro's godson, that Morrissey kid" again. I had Lord Gawain initiate me without my surname.' He paused. 'Lisandro was upset, to say the least.'

'You never sign off with your surname,' I realised now, thinking of the dozens and dozens of letters I'd watched him write. Always just Renatus.

'I don't have a surname. I dropped it. I was the last of my family and now there are none.'

I silently reflected on this. I didn't know of anybody getting about with only one name, except eccentric self-absorbed celebrities. I supposed Renatus could be grouped into this category, if we were being very general with parameters. It was a drastic move just to separate oneself from a reputation and a dependency, but then again, I couldn't know how bad it had been. I'd never been in those shoes.

'On my sister's twentieth birthday, the storm hit,' Renatus said now, his voice flat. 'She wanted a picnic in the orchard, like we did when we were children. The clouds rolled in... you know the next part... they were all killed.'

I nodded, but he paused, looking haunted.

'No,' he said slowly, 'I'm lying to us both.'

'How? They are dead, aren't they?'

'Yes. But letting you believe they died the way I told you would be lying to you.' He looked up at me with apologetic eyes. 'I told you I would give you all the puzzle pieces. If you want them. Do you want *all* the pieces?'

His tone implied I wouldn't want to hear some of them.

'Yes,' I said immediately, and he cringed, reluctant and torn.

'I told you I would tell you everything, but I also promised myself I would never speak of this,' he said, almost to himself. He turned away and began to pace nervously, like he had yesterday. I surprised myself by dropping my ward and approaching him. I stopped him by catching his arm. It was a really foolish move, especially if he'd wanted to fry my brains or paralyse me or something. If Lisandro was capable of it then Renatus certainly was, too. He could have pulled away easily but he didn't.

'I want you to tell me everything,' I said, very clearly, 'because I don't want to wonder about anything anymore. Downstairs,' I reminded him, pointing at the floor, 'are ten people who want me to leave you, and honestly, I've been considering it. You never told me what happens to Dark Keepers before you signed me up to be the next one. You didn't warn me about what I'd see in Italy. You didn't warn me what you were doing last night. For once, let me make an informed decision. Tell me *everything*.'

He stared at me for a very long moment, and beyond the barricades I'd constructed around my mind, I vaguely felt a change. When I lowered my defences, I found that his were gone – completely gone, like the time I'd upset him about his sister.

He was ready to be open with me, possibly realising that this was his very last chance to win my trust.

'This is going to hurt you a lot,' he apologised in advance, careful to avoid the "s" word.

'I'll deal with that. Just be honest with me.'

He didn't want to: that much was obvious in the tightness in his eyes and mouth. But he'd promised, and so he slowly started to speak.

'The storm... it hit so fast, I didn't know what to think,' he said. His eyes were looking through me at a time and place he usually avoided. My hand was still on his arm. I watched as a drop of blood accumulated on his fingertip and dripped to the floor. 'Everything just started getting ripped up. My parents screamed for us to run back to the house. I was running beside my sister and she was telling me to hurry and then she wasn't there. I couldn't see her anywhere, and when I stopped to look and reach out for her, I felt my father die...'

He was still talking, but I tuned his voice out and focused on what I was starting to *see* through him. Unconsciously, I'd dropped my own wards, all the protection Emmanuelle had insisted I build, and I found that as Renatus became more emotionally involved in his story, I was tapping into the memory.

Sharp grey rain whips about on wild winds... Branches are torn from trees and fly through the orchard, shattering on tree trunks... Teenage Renatus freezes suddenly, alone, and looks around... 'Ana!'... A branch ripped from its tree slams into his chest and knocks him into a broken tree trunk... Sharp, unforgiving wood slashes his shoulder... He screams... An unrelated, horrific pain rips through him... 'Dad!'... He shoves himself away from the shattered tree, cradling an arm as blood seeps steadily from the gash on his shoulder... 'Ana! Ana! Where are you?'... He stumbles as he feels the death of his mother... 'Ana!'... Another branch flies at him, with less force this time, and he blocks it with a quick ward... He runs for nearly half a minute, screaming for his sister, whose presence he cannot feel... In his mind there is a voice, terrified, unwelcome but familiar... 'Help! Quick! Please!'... All the while, the wind is dropping, perceptibly quieter and gentler with each passing second... Suddenly, he senses life, up ahead, and at the same time, he feels that which he has been hoping he will not – the end of his sister... 'No! Ana!'... He reaches out but that connection is gone forever... He pulls himself up to a sudden stop when he reaches the pathway that leads to the family graveyard... A man he has never seen before... This is the life he felt... But not for long...

I momentarily lost my channel, so to speak, my focus, and had to shake my head quickly. I felt my emotions welling up at the sight of what Renatus had seen, and had to make a conscious effort to tune myself back in.

I knew that the repercussions of this were huge for me, and everything I believed, but I couldn't think about that yet.

The stranger's expression at the sight of Renatus is one of fright and shock... He cradles the ruined body of a dead young woman in his arms... Blood and rain drip from her long dark hair... Her broken arm dangles at an awkward angle... Her shattered face is too bloodied to be recognised, but her hair, her complexion, her size, her clothes, are all too familiar... Young Renatus cannot speak... The stranger blinks through wet lashes and shaggy damp hair, clearly uncertain... 'You're not supposed to be here...' Renatus stares at the man who has destroyed his world and has the nerve to dictate where he should and shouldn't be... All around him, energy is building in a massive way... 'Neither are you...' His hands begin to glow... Suddenly afraid, the stranger drops the body, preparing to defend... Renatus can only watch in horror as his sister lands limply in the mud... The glow dissipates... The stranger's confidence returns in light of this child's dismay... Renatus looks up at the stranger, who has the time to hint at a cocky smile... The next instant everything happens at once... The stranger's very being seems to shudder all through, like something unnatural is happening on a level beyond normal understanding... The space around him briefly expands, compressing on him... Space folds in on him in a crushing, almost violent manner... The darkness is there, very present, and there is an almighty rip in the Fabric... And then the man ceases to be, and where he was, a dark, hateful wind bursts from nowhere, knocking Renatus into a crouch... When he looks up, the man who was is gone, and he races to his sister's side... He pulls her body against his, willing her to live, knowing on some level she will not... He wraps cold fingers around her broken arm and squeezes his eyes shut... 'Please, please, Ana!'... All his effort is not enough to mend the wounds... He hears his name shouted, and opens his eyes... Ana is dead and gone... He lightly releases her and backs up, standing and staring at his bloodied hands... Lord Gawain, another stranger at this time, appears in his peripheral vision... No threat is sensed, so he stands still as this new stranger envelops him in something of a hug and begins to drag him away, saying, 'Thank heavens you're alright. Come away from here, my boy...' The rain is softer now, and the wind has all but died... Closer to the house, Fionnuala is crying for him, hurrying closer with Lisandro at her side... His face is ashen, and tears run down even his face as he sees Renatus, coated in blood... Young Renatus shoves free of Lord Gawain's protective grasp and approaches Lisandro... 'Where were you? I thought you loved us?'...

I'd seen enough for now. I disconnected myself from that memory, shutting it out. Renatus's emotions were rolling over me, poorly contained. The most prominent were grief, guilt and shame. It was such a powerful, overwhelming snippet of Renatus's history, and I knew it had defined who I now knew.

And I did know him. I'd been telling myself I'd been tricked, as if he'd pretended to be someone he wasn't, but that in itself was a lie. I knew him. He was *me*, virtually, in some parallel universe in which I'd reacted to the same childhood trauma by going after it instead of closing down against it. Comparing our lives and states of mental health I had to take a biased perspective and suggest that my approach of accepting it and moving on without question was the healthier of the two, but he and I were both still young, with long roads of growing up still to travel.

My hand was still resting on his arm. I so badly wanted to tell him how sorry I was that he'd had to go through that, but that was a forbidden word here. I settled for changing the subject.

'I was wrong before,' I said finally. 'I don't hate you.'

'You can if you want to. I wouldn't blame you. You were right – I did ruin everything for you.'

'No,' I disagreed. 'I wish I hadn't said that.'

'You can leave now if you want to,' he said, slightly dully. 'I won't be mad with you. If you want, I'll consent to the separation ritual – it will probably be safer if I'm present-'

'I don't want to leave,' I said, very firmly, 'and I don't want to leave *you*. I just…' I paused, something occurring to me suddenly. 'Renatus, that stranger…'

'Yes, I killed him,' he said, immediately, tonelessly. 'Kind of. Worse, actually.'

'I don't think it counts,' I said, not as concerned as I might have been, my thoughts still focussed on my sudden – and frightening – revelation. 'You were young, upset and defending yourself.'

'It counts,' he said. 'I knew what I was doing. I was stronger than him. I could have incapacitated him in a second without doing a hint of damage. But… I was angry. I let it power me… and the result…' He took a deep breath, and I drew my focus away from my fears to pay attention to him as he shared this pain with me. 'I ended him in a way no one should have to go.'

'I don't understand.'

'I... I erased him. He no longer exists. Not dead,' he corrected, when I nodded. 'To die you must first be alive. Your body must expire, then your soul can leave for its next journey. I... sent him away. Into the Void.'

This was all beyond me, of course, but it didn't change how I felt about it. The image of Ana's battered body cradled in the arms of her killer was unbearable to me, and I'd never even known her. I couldn't imagine what it had done to her brother.

'You can't disgust me with descriptions of a horrible process I don't understand,' I said. 'If someone did that to *my* sister...' I trailed off, scared to ask what I'd just deduced. I swallowed and decided to be brave. 'Renatus... is this why the orchard has the dark feeling?'

'Yes,' he said. 'And the beach where your family died, and also the place I've agreed to meet Lisandro tomorrow night.'

'You said you had a theory about those places. I want you to tell me your theory now,' I said in a small voice.

'Places like these feel dark because several people were murdered there using dark magic,' Renatus said matter-of-factly, without emotion. I blinked, uncertain. Ana was murdered, I believed that much, and this brutal stranger, if his worthless life counted, but the Morrissey parents' deaths had been terrible accidents. Right? Just like my family.

'Several people?' I asked him, shakily.

'There was a storm, and my family was killed, but it wasn't the storm that killed them,' Renatus said. He looked conflicted, and I could sense him struggling to control his emotions. He didn't really want to talk to me about this. He knew where this was going. 'You saw him... It was *not* an accident. The storm was *not* an accident. It was a set up. It was murder.'

My head swam with the inevitable impossibility. Could this be true of my family's deaths, too?

'No,' I said finally, taking charge of my wayward imagination. 'Nobody can control the weather. Storms happen. Accidents happen.'

'I don't know anything more. I thought it was finished – I thought the sorcerer responsible was dead. But then I met you and learned that *your* family was attacked, and I realised that someone was still out there doing this, destroying families.'

Someone destroyed my family. It wasn't nature being its usual nasty, bitchy self.

'Why us? What's the link?'

'I have no idea at all,' he admitted. He tilted his head to the side. 'You're still here. I never expected this conversation, if we ever had it, would last this long.'

'So... you think both our families were targeted?' I said slowly. 'You're saying that my mum and dad, and my brother, were murdered?'

'I could be wrong,' he said doubtfully. 'The dark energy you and I both draw from so readily appears where someone has tampered very deeply with the natural flow of energy and drawn on something very evil. Like I did.' He looked away. 'I wish every day that I'd done better that day, been a better person.'

I shook my head.

'Renatus, I told you, we're not going to talk about self-esteem issues,' I reminded him. 'You're exactly who you're meant to be. That man... the stranger isn't worth all this angst.'

'That's only part of it,' he said. 'I'm a sad excuse for a sorcerer.'

'Don't be dumb,' I answered, and he shook his sleeve back to show me his hand. Annoyed when the sleeve didn't fall away, he yanked on the collar of his robe, unfastening it. The black fabric fell to the floor. I looked at his hand. Blood was dribbling slowly down his fingers from the fresh cut.

'When you left the orchard I tried to distract myself with work,' he said, holding the hand out to me as if I was supposed to be getting a really huge hint. I didn't know what the hint was meant to be, so I crossed the room to his desk, looking for tissues. There were none, but there was a conspicuously out-of-place letter opener. When I turned back to him, he twisted his fingers and a clean white tissue appeared from nowhere. Poor excuse for a sorcerer, huh? I took it and wiped the blood away while he continued speaking. 'The very first letter I opened, I sliced the letter opener straight through and into my own finger!' He shook his own hand, and I held it tighter, trying to keep it still so I could dab the new blood away.

'Yeah, that's really sad,' I agreed sarcastically, 'because *real* sorcerers never bleed.'

'Have you ever seen a sorcerer with scars?' he demanded, pulling away from me and tugging at the hem of his shirt. I took a step back, unsure.

'Whoa, wait,' I said, holding my hands up, the blooded tissue in one. 'Why are you taking your shirt off?'

It was already off, and he turned his back on me. The fact that my master was randomly undressing in front of me was immediately the last thing on my mind. My eyes were riveted to his shoulder. His otherwise smooth, pale skin was marred there with a knotted scar about twenty centimetres long, and about ten wide in the middle. In a flash I remembered the force with which he'd been thrown into a jagged tree stump during that storm.

'You're lucky your arm still works,' I commented. He turned around to face me.

'Tell me – have you ever seen another sorcerer with a scar?' he asked again. I thought about it, and realised with a start that I hadn't. Sorcerers tended to be exceptionally attractive human beings, with flawless skin and *no scars*. I looked all over my arms and considered the reflection I saw each day. No scars. I considered my legs and the number of times I'd nicked myself shaving. No scratch lasted longer than a few days before it completely healed over.

'I guess not,' I said. How amazing. Sorcerers didn't scar?

'Sorcerers don't scar because every sorcerer has the ability to heal, some stronger and better controlled than others,' Renatus told me. 'Every sorcerer in the world can heal themselves over time, and heal others in extreme circumstances... except me.'

I covered my mouth with my empty hand, realising now what he'd been trying to show me with the cut and the scar. Any other White Elm sorcerer would have healed their own stupid little cut. They would have healed their own muscle and skin from the inside out in the seven years since the injury. And most importantly, to Renatus, any other sorcerer would have had the power to heal their sister's fatal wounds and maybe revive her.

'I've never been able to,' he continued, looking away from me. I felt his self-loathing again. 'All my power, and I couldn't perform the most rudimentary magical skill when I most needed to.'

'Renatus, no,' I said, shaking my head. 'You don't really believe you could have saved her? She was already gone when you got to her.'

'I could have tried,' Renatus said, passionately. He pulled his hand free of his sleeve and scrunched the black shirt in his hands. 'I could have made a difference if I'd not been so useless. I could have-'

'But you didn't,' I interrupted gently, 'so maybe it wasn't meant to be.'

He stared at me.

'Lisandro heard me call for help,' he said, as though this were relevant. 'If he'd been quicker, he might have been able to save her, if he wasn't all twisted up in his own personal evil back then, of course. Dark sorcerers are the only others who can't heal, and that's only temporary, while they're practicing.' He glared at his hand. 'Lisandro was with Lord Gawain when the storm struck. He wasn't that far away. He didn't even know what was happening until Lord Gawain realised. What a great godfather.'

'There was nothing he could have done, either,' I said, hoping I was telling the truth. 'It was already too late.'

'*He* was too late!' Renatus hissed, resentment and bitterness flooding him. 'He failed us. All the things he taught me and he never showed me how to save someone's life.' He looked up at me, hatred for his past burning in his eyes. 'He knew. He knew he'd failed me and I'd, in turn, failed Ana, and he couldn't look at me. He sent me away to grow up somewhere else, out of sight, out of mind. Lord Gawain was the one who brought me back here.'

'Lord Gawain doesn't think you're a failure,' I said, hoping to pep him up with a new angle, but it backfired.

'Lord Gawain doesn't know the half of it. My sister's dead because I wasn't good enough to save her. I might as well have killed her myself for all the help I was.'

'That's not fair,' I protested. 'You didn't kill her. She died. Someone else killed her, and you were just there. It's awful but it's nothing at all to do with you and your choices. If it were meant to be different, it would be.'

'No, life's not fair,' Renatus muttered, turning away and beginning to pace again. 'If I'd been better, I could have saved her. She would have lived. I could have stayed here, lived with her...'

'You could have grown up totally different,' I continued.

'I would have not needed Lord Gawain,' Renatus added, less enthusiastically. 'I would never have joined the White Elm.'

'We wouldn't be standing here now,' I finished. 'You told me everything happens for a reason, to complete a bigger picture. Don't you believe that?'

He stopped pacing in front of his window. For a very long time he stood still, staring out over his estate to the orchard. I waited. I could feel his emotions rolling over each other as he weighed this up. There was some serious thought process going on. I chose not to follow his thoughts – they would be too fast, complex and reflective for me right now.

'Yes, I believe that,' he said finally.

'Then you know that sometimes bad things need to happen to good people,' I reminded him.

'It seems more frequent than necessary.'

'It's not for us to decide.'

Renatus finally looked back at me. He looked at my face, my eyes, my hair, my clothes, all the way down my body to the floor and then back up to my face. It was not the kind of objective, cheapening gaze of someone eyeing you up or imagining you in a compromising situation; it was a look of consideration, of comparison. I was sure I could hear the whispers of his thoughts as he mentally compared every aspect of my appearance with that of his sister. I had her height, and I was slim, but not shaped like Ana. I had long dark hair but mine had waves hers did not, and mine was distinctly brown while hers was more black. I had different eyes, in shape, in colour, in expression. My skin was darker. My face was different, softer in angles and less striking than either of the Morrissey children. I would never be mistaken for Renatus's sister, though he, who knew Ana the best, had seen something of her inside me, in my stubbornness, in my trusting nature, in my occasional bursts of ill-informed defiance and self-assurance, or so he'd said. I stood and said nothing as he looked at me and forced himself to know that for all the ways I was like Ana, there were an equal amount of ways in which I was dissimilar, and that unlike Ana Morrissey, who was receding further and further into the past with every passing moment, I was not going anywhere.

'It's not for us to decide,' he agreed finally. 'Ana's gone. You're here. That's how it was meant to be.'

'You wish it were different,' I said, understanding, but he shook his head and came back over to me. He closed his fingers over the tissue I held; immediately it was gone.

'No. I'm glad you're here,' he said. He took a long time to say the next part. 'If that means Ana can't be... I suppose I'm alright with that.'

chapter twenty

There was a knock at the door that interrupted the moment. Renatus didn't hesitate to open it. Emmanuelle stood in the hall, looking slightly apprehensive until she saw us. She raised an eyebrow, but didn't come inside.

'Am I interrupting?' she asked, folding her arms and leaning on the doorframe. 'Or do you enjoy being on suspension, Renatus?'

I hadn't realised until then how this might look to someone else – Renatus without his shirt, me standing very close – so I took a step backwards as I turned to Emmanuelle.

'Have you come to drag her screaming and kicking back to the council to have her ripped from me?' Renatus asked, slightly bitterly. Emmanuelle tossed her head to flick her hair from her eyes.

'No. I 'ave come to drag you both, screaming and kicking if that's what you want to do, back to the ballroom for a talk. I'd prefer you just follow, but I'll drag you if that's what you like.'

'What have we got to talk about? I thought you'd all made up your minds.'

'Did you kill Saul? Yes, or no?' Emmanuelle's tone was authoritative.

'I already answered that.'

'Well, tell me again,' Emmanuelle snapped. 'Humour me.'

'No, I didn't kill Saul,' Renatus said dutifully. 'I didn't go about last night upsetting those colonies. I haven't been out of the country since we were in Valero. I've been on house arrest. I didn't visit Lisandro with the intention of making any sort of trade. I haven't been sharing information with him. I am not his spy. Are you?'

'No,' Emmanuelle answered coolly. 'You brought another concern to our attention this morning.'

'I lied,' Renatus agreed. 'I wish that hadn't come out.'

'Hmm. I'm sure you do. Do I want to 'ear this?'

'I assume that's why you're here. Come in.'

Emmanuelle hesitated for a long time before reluctantly stepping over the threshold. Once inside, the door closed behind her. I felt her discomfort. I glanced at Renatus. He wasn't really going to tell Emmanuelle what he'd shown me, was he? What he shared with her became the intellectual property of the entire council if she allowed it. Some of the more old-school, traditional councillors probably wouldn't see his actions the way I had. I saw it as justified; Qasim or Lord Gawain would likely see it as an unforgivable crime.

'It's not what you think,' I insisted before he could start. 'He's too hard on himself.'

Emmanuelle's gaze flicked to me, and then back to Renatus, expectant. I knew she was scared but she wanted to know the truth. She'd dedicated herself to us over and over; I understood why she wanted justification for that. She wanted to hear something she could believe. She wanted to trust Renatus. That was a good start, I thought.

'As usual, I am misunderstood,' Renatus told her smoothly. She tilted her head to the side.

'But of course,' she agreed, slightly sarcastic. 'Do go on.'

'My family is dead because of me,' he said. His voice took on that flat tone again. 'I didn't kill them, but I'm at fault.'

'He's not,' I disagreed, protective, when Emmanuelle's folded arms tightened against her body.

'I have always considered the incident as my own fault,' Renatus said dully, 'because I couldn't save them.'

'Because you can't 'eal,' Emmanuelle guessed. Both Renatus and I stared at her, startled. I'd thought that this was a secret; apparently, he'd thought the same.

'How did you know?' Renatus asked, a little quietly. 'I didn't think...'

'You 'ave a scar on your jaw,' she said, pointing vaguely, 'and after your bonding ceremony, you didn't bother to 'eal your 'and. Most people wouldn't notice, but...'

'I suppose it's obvious to a Healer,' Renatus admitted.

'A little bit, once you're looking.' Emmanuelle eyed him critically. 'As nice as you look without a shirt, you manage to look extremely mortal with all those scars.'

I looked back at my master. I hadn't noticed before how lean and well-built he was, and even now, I found it hard to appreciate. It was like looking at my brother.

I could see that Emmanuelle was right about the scars. Somehow, Renatus had managed to get several long, thin scars across his chest. I wondered what they were from.

'A sword fight,' he told me, as if I'd asked aloud, 'in Avalon.'

I waited for him to say the obligatory "you should see the other guy", but Renatus didn't have a conventional sense of humour. Emmanuelle seemed to have lost her fear, because now she was circling Renatus, shaking her head when she saw the mangled scar on his shoulder.

'*Incroyable*,' she murmured. 'You're the only one I've ever met that is literally *unable* to perform one of the basic magical skills. 'as it been this way your 'ole life?'

'Always.'

'Do you think it has something to do with the fact that your power is channelled so intensely into other areas?'

Renatus looked over his shoulder at her.

'I've wondered that, but I don't know.'

'Why didn't you 'ave this seen to when it 'appened?' Emmanuelle added, sounding annoyed about the scar. 'It's too old to erase now.'

'I was... depressed,' Renatus answered, and I sensed that he was being careful with his words. 'I didn't want anyone connecting to me to be able to heal me.'

I figured by that he meant he'd avoided the connection because he didn't want his thoughts read, and his shameful secret discovered.

'So you were stupid,' Emmanuelle said, as though confirming her own suspicions. She pressed her fingertips to the knotty scar, and I hurried around to stand beside her and watch. The point of contact glowed slightly, and before my eyes, the white edges of the scar began to recede and smooth out. She dropped her hand away and sighed. The scar had lost a third of its size, and was less lumpy. Her gift was so amazing. 'That's as good as it's going to get. The others should be smoother, too.' I followed her as she moved to stand in front of my master. Many of the white lines had shrunk and taken on a more natural colour.

'Thank you,' Renatus said, softly, looking down at her work. Emmanuelle didn't look as impressed.

'It would be better if you 'ad just swallowed your pride and let someone 'elp you at the time,' she reinforced. 'It's lucky that you have an apprentice who is learning 'ealing.'

Her words implied that she didn't think Renatus and I would be better off without each other. I glanced at him hopefully. Maybe the council had calmed down and changed their minds? I myself had been of so many mindsets in the past hours. Surely others had had time to reconsider their perspectives, too.

'Emmanuelle, Aristea,' Renatus said suddenly, turning away and going to his desk. He dropped his scrunched black shirt on the nearest armchair. 'Do you remember, when the White Elm was voting on whether Aristea should be my apprentice, who refused to give their support?'

He found a sheet of paper and snatched up one of his fountain pens. I glanced uncertainly at Emmanuelle. What was this about?

'Uh, Qasim,' I recalled, walking over to stand at his side as he wrote the other scrier's name. 'And Anouk.'

'Susannah refused,' Emmanuelle said, leaning against the desk and watching as Renatus etched the names quickly. She looked to me for inspiration. 'Glen... Tian...'

'I think that was all,' I said, going through all the councillors' names in my head. It had been a close vote. Would it have swung our way if Aubrey and Teresa had been present? Neither had ever seemed to be fans of Renatus.

Renatus held his completed list up for us to see.

'One of these people is the spy,' he said. 'Lisandro was communicating with his mole *while* he was talking to me. Whoever it was must have chosen last night to visit those colonies, knowing where I was and how easy it would be to pin it on me, the same way he, or she, stood behind me while he killed Saul and almost had me take the blame. Lisandro knew way too much about Aristea, and he said that his *friend* was someone who was unhappy about the alliance.'

My stomach twisted slightly when he said my name. Lisandro knew about me?

'Right down to your name and heritage,' Renatus confirmed grimly. He allowed Emmanuelle to take the list and pen from him. 'I want to know who this traitor is before I face Lisandro again on Monday night.'

'Wait,' Emmanuelle said, waving the pen. 'Wait, wait. We all agreed – we won't be making the trade. And you still 'aven't told me why you went to see 'im in the first place.'

She frowned. I suspected that some of the annoyance I felt from her was directed at herself for not getting this issue sorted out before she caved and began to trust Renatus again.

'I went to him because I think we still stand a chance of getting his hostages back,' Renatus said patiently. 'I'm smarter than he is. I have a plan.'

'Oh, *imbecile*,' Emmanuelle retorted irritably. 'You think you're smarter than everybody.'

'My plan can work, Em.'

I'd never heard Renatus shorten anyone's name before but it didn't sound strange and Emmanuelle didn't seem put-off by it.

'You'd better be able to articulate that plan very nicely to Lord Gawain and the rest of the council,' Emmanuelle said sharply, standing up straight. 'They've been convinced to give you a chance to explain yourself.'

Renatus nodded once, gracious, guessing that she would have been one of the drivers of that decision.

'We should 'ead back down,' she added, dropping the pen onto the desk and ripping the paper in half, and in half again. Renatus reached out as though to take the paper bits from her, and made them disappear like he had the tissue. His finger was healed, I noticed as he discreetly nudged the haphazardly dropped pen back into its place. A by-product of Emmanuelle's quick treatment. 'I've been gone a while. Someone will probably come looking soon, thinking you've tortured and slaughtered me.'

Obviously, Emmanuelle had been cured of her fear of Renatus, because their tight friendship was back in full-force. She crossed to the door, which Renatus opened for her, and as we followed, she glanced back.

'You may like to dress yourself, unless you want to give some of your young fans something new to look at,' she advised. Immediately Renatus went back for his shirt and robe. Emmanuelle ushered me through the doorway, touching my shoulder briefly, affectionately. I was glad to have her on our side. Renatus clearly felt the same.

'Thanks for this, Emmanuelle,' he said as he stepped into the hall, pulling his shirt on roughly.

'Don't thank me yet,' she warned. 'Your name is very dirty downstairs. You will 'ave to work to win them all back.'

'Well, I managed to convince you,' Renatus said. 'Four hours ago you were ready to string me up from the ceiling and leave me there.'

I remembered how Emmanuelle had kept me close and not allowed me to go to my master.

'I was doing my job,' Emmanuelle replied. Her tone made it clear that she was not apologetic. 'I took a vow to protect Aristea if you couldn't.'

Renatus didn't push it. I could sense his apprehension building as we walked down the hall, descended the staircase and neared the ballroom. Emmanuelle stopped us at the doors. She glared at Renatus.

'Do *not* mess this up,' she instructed. 'Understand that this is your last chance. You will walk out of 'ere either forgiven or renounced. If you go down, I am not coming.'

'I understand,' Renatus said quietly. 'I wouldn't expect you to.' He reached over her shoulder to touch the door. It opened at his will, silently swinging on its hinges, and Emmanuelle cast him one last loaded look – she needed him to climb out of this disaster almost as much as I did – before entering ahead of us. Renatus looked at me, catching the door lightly as it swung back to close. 'Ready?'

'Almost,' I agreed, 'and I'm sorry.'

'Aristea-'

'I know the rule. And I stuffed up. I promised to listen to you, and I promised to ignore what I heard and not let it colour my opinion of you. Susannah told me not to be swayed and I was. I broke my promise. I'm sorry. It won't happen again.'

Renatus regarded me for a long moment, and then nodded. His face showed nothing as he pushed on the ballroom door, but I knew he was glad to have me back one hundred percent.

He was in the process of opening the door when I grabbed the doorhandle and pulled it back shut, needing a moment longer. Renatus had me and he had Emmanuelle, but we were only two allies in a big world. Beyond the door and at the edges of my barricaded auric field, I felt stirrings of negativity, and knew that Emmanuelle was right: Renatus was going to need to work to regain the trust of many of his brothers and sisters.

'Renatus,' I said. 'Are you sure about this? After what happened before?'

'About what?' he asked. 'I have to go in and be judged.'

'Do you, though?' I pushed. 'Do you need their approval? They were going to kick you out and take me away. Are you sure you still want to be part of the council if that's how they treat you whenever something goes wrong?'

Renatus had to think about how to word his answer, but I saw in his face that he didn't have to think about his *answer* at all.

'Everywhere I have been, in my entire life, I have been unwelcome,' he said slowly. 'It is not unfamiliar to me. In most cases I have been unwelcome and similarly disinterested in being there, and have been only too happy to leave. But the White Elm is Lord Gawain's council. There is good work to be done through being one of them. There are countless opportunities to do good, be better, do right, and I have a lifetime to take them.' Atonement, I realised. 'Yes. More than anything, I need their approval, because I need to stay on this council.

There is nothing else for me in this world if I am excommunicated. I'd be back to where I started.'

'There's me,' I commented in a small voice, not even knowing why I said it. *You'd still have me.*

Renatus looked at my hand on the doorhandle rather than looking at me. I turned my wrist so he could better see the inky black symbol that marked my skin. He pulled his own sleeve back to gaze at his own tattoo. Identical, except on different arms. Kind of like an "A" and an "R" interlinked.

'I'd be better off than where I started,' he amended. 'But let's not go back to where I started.' He finally looked at me. 'Let's try going forward instead.'

We opened the doors and stepped into the ballroom together. The White Elm was gathered in its usual circle, with the now-familiar gaps for Aubrey and Teresa, and the waiting space for Renatus. He didn't go there. He walked to the middle and stopped. I hesitated beside him, feeling like we were on show – as usual.

The entire council was on edge, as it had been this morning. Their emotions were more organised now, however, and they all seemed to have steeled themselves for this... whatever this was.

'Aristea, please join the circle,' Lord Gawain said, glancing pointedly at Renatus's usual place. I glanced at my master, unsure. 'You are Renatus's apprentice, which gives you the responsibility of standing in for him during his absence, and the right to a voice when we make a judgement on him.'

Absence? Judgement? I nervously left Renatus's side and took his place between Lady Miranda and Qasim. Neither of them looked at me. That was fine with me. I glanced around. Nobody was looking at me. All eyes were on Renatus.

'Renatus,' Lord Gawain began, clearly being careful with his words as he went on, 'earlier this morning, many things were said. Some, perhaps, should not have been. I myself should not have made any accusation against you without giving you the chance to explain your actions.' He paused for a long moment, and then added, 'I apologise for my words.'

'I should have shared my plan with you,' Renatus said immediately, the closest Lord Gawain was going to get to an apology. 'I wish I had told you. I know you said no more surprises. I just thought... you'd try to stop me.'

He looked away, out the ballroom windows at the rainy estate, and the hint of vulnerability in this action was evidently enough to melt Lord Gawain, who sighed.

'Tell me now what you should have told me,' he said, but I knew from his tone that he'd already been won. I wasn't the only one thinking it. Anouk and Glen shared a subtle look. I wondered what they were saying to each other that no one else could hear.

'Someone at the vote yesterday is feeding our every word back to Lisandro,' Renatus said bluntly. 'My concern was that their next move would be to inform him that we had no intention of giving him the ring. To him, this news would render his hostages valueless, and there would be nothing to stop him killing them on the spot. I wanted to lead him astray, give us an extra few days to explore other possibilities to save them. So I found him, I spoke with him and I have convinced him that we will make the trade on Monday night. It gives us some time.'

'Did you really see Aubrey?' Jadon asked. His question was quick, with a hint of desperation. 'Are they alright? Is Teresa alive? Shell?'

'Aubrey and Shell are together, alive and guarded personally by Lisandro,' Renatus reported. 'Aubrey is a physical mess. Apparently Lisandro's men have taken to him whenever he speaks out. I didn't see Shell but Lisandro claims to be treating her properly and to be aware of her needs.'

'And you believe him? How do you know he's not beating her, too?' Jadon demanded, his voice rising. Renatus stayed calm.

'He had no reason to lie to me, nor the ability,' he said. 'Lisandro is not the one who has hurt Aubrey – I have never known Lisandro to strike anybody – and he told me that Shell is "not to be touched".'

'Renatus, my biggest concern is how you came to be in Lisandro's presence in the first place,' Lady Miranda said. 'You and Qasim have been looking for him all year, with no success, and suddenly, yesterday, his location simply occurs to you?'

'I saw nothing,' Renatus answered. 'The vision came to Aristea, and she passed the information to me. I instructed her to keep this a secret, in case the spy within our council tipped Lisandro off that I might be coming by.'

Now all eyes were on me. I wasn't sure what to say, but I was spared having to speak by Qasim.

'Lisandro has blocked himself completely from the White Elm,' the Scrier said. 'Sometimes, snippets come through, like last night, but usually these are timed by Lisandro. Since Lisandro has never met Aristea and she is not yet a councillor, he cannot block himself specifically from her sight. Information has a way of reaching those for whom it is intended.'

That seemed to answer everyone's silent questions, because their eyes moved back to Renatus, expectant.

'So where was he?' Elijah asked, curious. 'There were so many Displacements to that beach.'

'His hideout is well-hidden, but it was there,' my master told him. 'There were more than a dozen men there-'

'A dozen? We could take on a dozen,' Jadon said recklessly. He glanced around the circle for support.

'They'd be gone by now,' Tian disagreed.

'And we don't know anything about them, it would be stupid,' Anouk added.

'They're not special,' Renatus said. 'He and Jackson would be the strongest and best his side has to offer. The men are weak but loyal. Lisandro admitted that himself. He's gathering numbers, not skills.' His eyes flicked to Tian. 'I doubt they're going anywhere. He's not afraid of us, and it didn't concern him that I knew where to find him.' He turned his attention to Jadon. 'He knows he's safe where he is because we won't be attacking. Every man following him is a suicide bomber waiting for a chance to go off.'

Lady Miranda and Lord Gawain shared an uncomfortable look.

'My agreement with Lisandro is that I will meet him on Monday night in Glasgow,' Renatus finished, 'so we have until then to devise some sort of strategy.'

'Why Glasgow?' Lady Miranda asked, confused.

'It's... a sort of middle ground,' Renatus answered, carefully.

'Details are wonderful but let's solidify the future before it changes again,' Susannah said, tiredly.

'Yes, you're right,' Lord Gawain agreed. 'Renatus, we must continue with the trial. Your willingness to allow Fate to judge you is commendable but as we don't know what effect that may have on Aristea as your extension and successor we must consider other ways of proceeding.' He paused. 'Do you have evidence you would like to present to the circle that may prove or otherwise support your claim of innocence?'

Renatus turned his attention to Qasim, and everyone followed his gaze. I had no idea what this was about.

Wait. Was he suggesting...?

'Qasim?' Lord Gawain asked slowly, clearly as confused as I was. Renatus ignored him and spoke only to the older scrier, whose expression remained unreadable.

There were five people on Renatus's latest list. He couldn't possibly have worked it out already.

'You have been waiting for this moment for a very long time,' he said coolly. I felt my heart shudder in my chest. Qasim? The man standing right beside me? One of the best scriers in the world? 'The truth. Everything out on the table.'

'That would be a good day,' Qasim agreed guardedly. I struggled to inhale. No, no, it couldn't be Qasim... Not the Scrier...

'Renatus, what are you trying to say?' Lady Miranda demanded.

'I want a Trial by One,' Renatus answered, 'and I nominate Qasim as my interrogator.'

The older councillors exchanged surprised looks; the expressions of the younger members looked only confused.

'A what?' I was thankful when Jadon finally asked this.

'It's an old alternative to a trial within a circle,' Anouk said eventually. 'The sixth Dark Keeper, Adam, was accused of vulgar crimes and requested his trial take place in the mind of one his fellow councillors, whose purity and loyalty to the White Elm were above question.'

This short history lesson was followed by another awkward silence. No one else asked for clarification but I saw on Jadon and Emmanuelle's faces that I wasn't the only one still unclear.

'How does a trial happen inside Qasim's head?' I said.

'He is granting me access to his whole mind,' Qasim said, as though this were obvious. I released the breath I hadn't known I was holding. Renatus wasn't accusing Qasim. He was showing him the truth. But how much truth was safe to share?

Anouk went on, unable to help herself, 'Adam carried secrets that would be divulged in a circle but could bring dangerous consequences for those who knew them. Rather than compromise his work or the lives of his brothers and sisters, he requested the first Trial by One. His interrogator gained access to his whole mind but it was shared only in a private space in the interrogator's mind, so no other councillor would ever see the truths for themselves. His guilt was still determined by the council as a whole, but weight was given to the judgement of the nominated interrogator.'

I could hardly believe this. All those secrets he'd just shared with me – out in the open, on the table for Qasim to pore over? How did he expect Qasim to react when he saw some of the things Renatus had done?

Trust me, Renatus begged of me, his eyes not moving from the other scrier's face.

I trust you, I assured him, but I was hard to say when I was so worried.

'Qasim, do you consent to investigate Renatus on behalf of the White Elm council?' Lady Miranda asked, taking charge. Beside me, my scrying teacher was standing very still. He hated Renatus. I wondered what he was thinking.

'Only if he means it,' the Scrier said gruffly. 'Trial by One means *everything*. Any roadblocks and walls, and I'm throwing you back to the circle.'

'Nothing hidden; nothing barred,' Renatus promised. He opened his hands and knelt down, submissive. I felt all of his wards dissolve. 'I'm not going anywhere.'

Arrogant and powerful Renatus on his knees at the mercy of his colleagues was a sight both unfamiliar and uncomfortable. Considering the fearsomeness I'd seen in them collectively in the past few hours it was not a position I would like to be in personally. These were great people with vast capacities for compassion and loyalty but just as swiftly as they might respond to an S.O.S. call, they would throw overboard whoever had ripped holes in their sails.

Their ruthlessness both scared and impressed me. There had been definite moments of overcautious crab-stepping around major issues – such as the questioning of their prisoners in Valero – in the weeks since I'd been introduced to this council but their dealing with an internal threat certainly didn't qualify as one of the things they'd mucked about on.

'Then your request is granted,' Lady Miranda told Renatus. 'Qasim, you may proceed as you see fit.'

Silence settled over the ballroom again, but this time it was deep, expectant.

'Do not blink,' Qasim instructed my master, finally. He squared his shoulders, as though preparing for some sort of onslaught, and met Renatus's gaze intensely.

I looked around the circle. Every pair of eyes was on the two scriers.

There was more silence, such a huge, deep, long silence. Nobody moved, least of all the scriers. I knew that everything Renatus was and had ever been was being passed between the two in this long silent minute. Then it was done. In a tense, dramatic moment, Renatus's eyes shut and his head fell forward; Qasim took an unsteady step backwards, rubbing his eyes with the heel of his palm. They both breathed deeply, as though they'd been short on air for the past minute.

'It's not him,' Qasim said breathlessly, shaking his head roughly. 'It's not him. He's not the spy. He's not the killer.'

His words were convincing, but the look he cast over at Renatus was one of fear and shock at what he'd just witnessed.

'Qasim, are you sure?' Glen asked from his other side.

'I... I am certain,' Qasim said. I looked up at him, shaken. I'd never seen him like this. 'Renatus is many things, but not a traitor. He is not Lisandro's. His commitment is to us, to Lord Gawain and to Aristea.'

Everyone was looking to someone else, silent and bewildered. Was that it? Did Renatus have only to open his mind to Qasim, and the trial was over?

'And the murder?' Tian asked, eliciting several nods around the circle. 'He said he'd murdered.'

'The murder,' Qasim said slowly, still staring at Renatus as though trying to decide how he felt about what he'd seen. 'Renatus is not responsible for the killing in Valero. He...' There was a heavy pause. 'He holds himself responsible for other deaths... however... his part in these deaths does not fit the White Elm's criteria for murder.'

My heart leaped. Could such a loophole be possible? At only fifteen at the time, Renatus was not an adult when he'd taken that stranger's life. And Renatus had said himself that he hadn't really killed him, it was more of an erasure. Was Qasim really willing to take that into account?

'What does that even mean?' Jadon asked, raising his hands, lost.

'It means the charges are empty. From what I have just seen, we have bigger problems.' Qasim looked at me, worried, and then turned his gaze back to Renatus. 'Is she really? Who even knows that?'

'Me, and now you, and obviously at least one other,' Renatus answered.

'What can he do with that kind of information?'

'Probably more than I can. I have no idea what it means.'

'What are you talking about?' I asked, uncomfortable with being the topic of this mysterious conversation.

'*About* you,' Qasim snapped, leaving the ending, *not to you*, unsaid but evident. I felt annoyance well inside me.

'*Excuse me*, I am not a *problem*-'

'No, you're an asset – as long as Lisandro knows nothing about you,' Qasim cut me off. 'It looks as though our window of opportunity is closing.' He stepped into the middle of the circle, where Renatus was still kneeling down. He offered a hand, and when it was accepted, he pulled Renatus to his feet.

Qasim dropped the younger scrier's hand as soon as he was standing, but the gesture itself was clearly significant to those councillors watching. Through my wards I felt their reluctant approval, and their acceptance of Renatus's innocence. The vision of Qasim, who liked Renatus the least of all of them, offering his hand to the Dark Keeper as a brother, was a powerful and influential one.

It was a relieving image for me, because I knew that Renatus's split-second decision to let Qasim inside his mind was both stupid and reckless and could have gone so differently.

'We have spent too much time worrying about this "spy" within our ranks,' Qasim said, turning away from Renatus to face the council leaders. 'We have turned on one another, thrown accusations and burnt bridges. Lisandro had only to take two of our people, fake a few energetic prank calls and leave us to our own wild imaginations, and see how we have almost destroyed ourselves. We are stronger together, even with a weak link, than we are divided. It really doesn't matter at this point who the spy is.'

'He or she will be revealed in due time,' Susannah confirmed.

'What matters,' the Scrier finished, 'is that we stop seeing the spy in the eyes of every brother and sister we have.'

'Wise words, Qasim,' Lady Miranda said. 'For now, we proceed as though the leak does not exist. If our plans and words make it back to Lisandro we will only have more evidence as to who his puppet is. In the meantime it is both all of us and none of us: we have only tried and tested one councillor.'

She glanced at Lord Gawain, and he inhaled deeply, standing straighter and looking more relaxed than I'd seen him in a long while.

'Renatus,' he said, 'you are cleared of all charges. You are reinstated, in full, to the position of Dark Keeper. And we will hear your suggestions for a rescue of Teresa and Aubrey.'

chapter twenty-one

By midday it was obvious to Qasim that Aristea was exhausted but was just too proud to admit it. She'd only slept half the night, had experienced a dozen emotional ups and downs in the hours since being woken and had missed breakfast – a dangerous mix in any adolescent – then he'd subjected her to four or five hours of intensive concentrated scrying instruction, and she was just running out of steam.

'I still can't see anything,' she said tiredly, rubbing her eyes with her fingertips.

'So try again,' Renatus said before Qasim could. Aristea shot him a resentful look but did as she was told, taking a deep breath and focusing her gaze into the orange flame burning away the candle in front of her.

The three scriers had chosen the usual scrying classroom to work in. Aristea felt comfortable here, and there were so few energetic distractions. Qasim's assumptions had been right – Renatus and his family had been betrayed here, in this room, and in disgust and horror Renatus had erased its every energy trace, scrubbing the space cleaner than Qasim had ever encountered before.

He discreetly glanced backwards to where Renatus sat in one of the armchairs. The Dark Keeper's whole life swarmed through Qasim's brain like angry bees and he redirected his gaze to Aristea's candle in an attempt to calm his thoughts. It was too much. He hadn't had time to fully process all that he'd seen – twenty-two and a half years is a long time, after all – and for most of it he still couldn't identify his own opinions and feelings on it.

A few important memories stuck at the forefront of Qasim's mind. The erasure of that stranger's life, for one. Had Renatus ever just admitted to this, Qasim would have been the first one to slap him in irons and throw him out of the council. But now the older scrier had been inside the younger's head, into every shadowy corner and every darkened alcove. Now it was like he'd *been* there beside Renatus when he'd lost his family and seen a man carrying Anastasia Morrissey's brutalised body. Qasim didn't have a sister but had a wife and four children, and if he saw any of his own in the same state, he knew he'd have reacted much as Renatus had.

Still, it was not pity or empathy that had driven Qasim to defend Renatus's actions at the trial. There had been no death, no intention to *kill*, only to make the offender go away. Fifteen was also too young to be charged with murder in their world; although, Qasim reflected, it was certainly old enough to do frightening things to other people and to know it was wrong. For the better part of a decade Renatus had carried around the heavy burden of guilt and the unspoken terror of his shame being uncovered by the people who still retained faith in him – namely his nanny, and his hero and mentor, Lord Gawain.

Qasim had known immediately that it didn't matter how shocking the truth was to him. It would be worse for Lord Gawain. This particular truth wasn't pertinent to the charges Renatus was being trialled for – and he'd seen, amongst everything else, that Renatus had never acted to endanger the council or to benefit Lisandro, least of all done what he'd been accused of – and it really didn't need to come out in the middle of an already tense circle.

Trial by One had been the right choice.

Elijah had been right to say that Renatus was exactly what they needed. The White Elm didn't need to know any more than that. More importantly, *Lord Gawain* didn't need to know. Renatus's efforts to keep the moments before they met a secret had initially been for selfish reasons but over the years and as he'd matured his intentions had changed to centre on protecting those who had invested love and care into him.

Aristea sighed loudly and sat back against the winged armchair's tall back.

'He's probably just blocked me too now that he knows who I am,' she announced. Qasim looked away, frustrated. She didn't know how blocking worked. Lisandro *couldn't* block her without knowing the signature of the particular scrier. She just wasn't looking properly. On purpose, without knowing. Renatus or Qasim would have been through the defences in minutes if they were not actively blocked. Aristea was not blocked; she was afraid, which was worse. She had seen O'Malley's coin, Qasim now knew from Renatus's memories, and she was quietly terrified for Teresa. Rightly so, because if its meaning was being inferred properly, the young Healer was being grossly mistreated, but without Aristea's gift of scrying the White Elm might never know where to rescue her from.

'He hasn't blocked you,' Renatus told his apprentice. 'Try again.'

'I can't see anything!' Aristea insisted, narrowing her eyes. Qasim felt his frustration spike again – perhaps Fate had struck him a very good deal when it gave Aristea to Renatus instead of him. He really didn't have the patience for the mood swings of teenagers. Heavens help him when his children hit this age.

'You don't *want* to see anything, Aristea,' Qasim corrected coolly. She turned her unimpressed gaze onto him. 'You're not open. Do you want to save Teresa or not?'

She looked shocked.

'Of course I do!' she said, angrily.

'Then: you need to start thinking of her, not yourself. You,' he raised his voice over her objections, 'are afraid of seeing what's happening to her. I'm sorry if it's awful. It may well be. But you are an agent of the White Elm and this is the job. Are you up to it?'

Aristea's mouth tightened into a thin line.

'This is *my* job,' Qasim amended, considering another angle. 'This is what the White Elm's Scrier does. Providing Renatus lives out the decade in his current position and Lord Gawain steps down in that time, this will be *your job*. You are prepared for it?'

Aristea glared at the candlelight, clearly thinking hard. She was only seventeen, Qasim reminded himself in an effort to stay calm, and she'd only been scrying or practising any serious magic for a couple of weeks. She'd experienced some terrible losses in her short life but unlike Renatus she'd come out of them relatively unscathed. Remarkable how upbringing could have such a significant impact on a young person's ability to process trauma. She'd not seen her sister mangled and murdered and she'd been cared for and protected in the years prior and following. She was very innocent. It was a strength in that it allowed her to view the world in simple black and white. It was, however, now a barrier to her greater abilities. Her innocent nature knew what she would see if she scried Teresa – brutality, degradation, humiliation – and knew these to be wrong and to be avoided. The mind will always seek to protect itself.

'I... I'll try again,' she said eventually, quieter now. She inhaled deeply and settled deeper into her seat, focusing her eyes first on the flame and then beyond it, looking for whatever the universe wanted for her to see...

Aristea's concentration snapped immediately when a bird fluttered at the window, struggling to land on the windowsill, its wings beating against the glass. Renatus stood abruptly and killed the candle flame with his fingertips.

'That's enough for now,' he said. 'Go and get something to eat. Come back when you're ready.'

Qasim only barely managed to refrain from disagreeing, and stared at his hands as Aristea nodded and left. He knew she had it in her to do it and he knew she was close to breaking down those barriers of hers, but she was Renatus's student. Qasim had had his doubts about their pairing but could see now, from Renatus's point of view at least, that he shouldn't have been so worried. The Dark Keeper really did have the girl's best interests at heart – whether he was capable of meeting these interests was a different issue – and if he thought she needed a break and a meal, Qasim shouldn't interfere.

'We're wasting our time until she's recharged,' Renatus said as soon as the door closed behind her.

'You negotiating with Lisandro has bought us some but generally speaking, time is something we don't have,' Qasim responded, shifting in his seat to better see the younger scrier. A few hours ago he'd seen his worst nightmare confirmed when visions of Renatus and Lisandro together suddenly started coming to him without prompt. *I wondered when I'd see you here; has it been hard to get away from the council without drawing attention?* Aubrey had demanded. *A bit*, Renatus had answered, in that expressionless tone that was his. And no sooner had Qasim told Lord Gawain about it, he'd been contacted by Egypt's biggest all-magical community, convinced that Tian had been in their temple, furious that the White Elm would enter their territory without permission. The reports had rolled in, mostly to Lord Gawain but at least two others had come to other councillors. Renatus had looked so guilty – and Qasim, who had been waiting for this evidence for almost two years, had eaten it up exactly as Lisandro had intended.

He'd thought he knew Lisandro, but with Renatus's memories and experiences he realised he'd only ever known half of the story. Maybe less. Lisandro the Dark Keeper was a different man from Lisandro the godfather, and who knew how many other faces he wore? Every man is a complex weave of traits, values and motives that sets him apart from anyone else, making him distinctive but also unknowable.

Qasim was starting to understand this about Renatus. There were so many versions of the young scrier. He'd known already the sullen, quiet, arrogant, know-it-all Renatus, or thought he had; he now knew the life experiences that had forced this persona to evolve.

Renatus moved closer and sat in Aristea's now-vacant spot, bringing the flame back with a click of his fingers.

'We have thirty-two hours,' he said, staring intently into the flame. 'She'll see something before then. She has to.'

'She said she was Cassán Ó Grádaigh's grand-daughter,' Qasim brought up, and knew from the shift of focus in Renatus's eyes that he'd distracted him, 'but you never checked.'

'As soon as she told me I realised it was too poetic to *not* be true.'

'And you're sure no one else knew?'

'Not for certain – she might have told someone.'

Obviously, Qasim thought, whoever knew about Aristea's ancestry should be regarded with extreme suspicion at this point, because Lisandro had only mentioned it while communicating with his mole in the White Elm.

'I'd have to confirm with Aubrey's notes, but when I was asking after her – as I suppose you were doing at the same time – I'm sure he said Aristea was quite mediocre at Crafting. Isn't that odd, with those genes?'

'It might come out later,' Renatus suggested. 'Or that talent might have gone down another genetic line.'

It was true that with magic, it was often observed that talents and gifts were passed genetically, but were passed either fully or not at all. Qasim had four children, but only one, his third, showed any aptitude for scrying. And she was going to be amazing, he knew already, another Aristea, probably the scrier who would replace Aristea on the council when, inevitably, Renatus died some way or another and Aristea had to take his cursed chair. The other three had inherited from their mother a much lower capacity for magic and the gift of telepathy.

'Probably it's with the sister,' Qasim agreed. He paused. 'She's on Peter's list, too. And Ó Grádaigh.'

Renatus nodded, scrubbing his face tiredly with his hands. How many times had they pored over that apparently useless list, left with the Elm Stone by Peter in his final days? They had determined who many of the names belonged to (even without surnames, "Renatus", "Aristea" and "Lisandro" were a little too obvious to bother wondering about) but were no closer to understanding what Peter had meant to tell them.

The two scriers stared into the candle flame for several minutes in silence, allowing information to flow from anywhere the universe felt they ought to direct their attention.

Glen's ex-wife, glancing over her shoulder at the wall clock... Shaking her head at her daughter... 'He's just busy, darling... His work is very important and he doesn't get to choose when it gets busy'...

Two figures, hooded, running through the rain...

Peter's grandmother, taking her vitamins...

'Tomorrow night, if we succeed,' Renatus said finally, 'what do we do with Lisandro and Jackson?'

Qasim looked up from the flame. Before today he might have considered this a sarcastic remark, but his new insight into Renatus's personality and motives gave him pause. It was an honest question. The Dark Keeper was skilled and competent, but like his apprentice, he was young. Reality is a cruel thing. One does not get to stay young for long in its presence.

'Tomorrow night, if we succeed,' Qasim answered calmly, 'you'll confront Lisandro and Jackson, and you will kill them.'

Renatus looked away; Qasim almost felt pity for him. It was such a strange thing, to be sitting opposite a man he'd disliked so intensely for so long and to be talking like close friends; to understand one another for the first time. To see him standing on the precipice of his own destruction and knowing it would do no good to pull him back. Renatus had to fall for the rest of them to survive. No one had said it but it seemed clear. It had always been the curse of the Dark Keeper. He protected the council two-fold. He took the chair and studied the magic their enemies would use against them so he could do battle and stand a chance at winning, but in doing so he also sacrificed his own soul so that the other councillors wouldn't have to. He killed so they could keep their souls clean.

Despite what he'd done as an anguished child, Renatus's soul was still relatively clear. That would change when he killed Lisandro or Jackson. Lord Gawain had done what he could to prolong this but he'd made the decision for Renatus when he'd put him on this chair.

'I don't-' Renatus began, quickly cutting himself off. He blinked, expression gone, obviously scrying something. Qasim wasn't receiving it so he took a guess and assumed it was something to do with Aristea. A quick check showed him a vision of the girl striding determinedly across the lawn. She was intrigued by the orchard, Qasim noted from Renatus's memories, and Renatus hated the place, for reasons that were evident. His discomfort with her growing closeness to his past was becoming apparent on his face and in his aura. They'd talked about this, Qasim knew, and Aristea was quite aware of how any visit to Renatus's unpleasant memories affected him. Yet here she was, trekking across the estate with a destination now in clear sight.

'She is becoming less... sensitive, tactful, the better I come to know her,' Renatus admitted. 'I suppose it's part of the bond – Lord Gawain said there was often a transference of traits, so this could be my acting out, not hers – and I suppose I deserve it.'

Qasim leaned forward to extinguish the candle and then got to his feet, displeased with the idea of Aristea becoming any more like her antisocial, secretive master.

'Yes, you do,' he said coolly. 'Imagine the pleasure she'll be by the time she makes it onto the council.' He moved to the door. 'I'll get her.'

Renatus didn't respond as Qasim left him there and started through the house. Ugh, to even imagine a Renatus-like adult Aristea had him shaking his head. Lord Gawain was right: apprenticeships in their world *did* often include transference of personality traits between the two parties. Qasim subconsciously ran his fingers over the black mark on his left wrist. At the time he hadn't believed it, but now, an older and wiser man looking back, he knew he'd been changed by his connection to the previous Scrier. Changed for the better. He'd learnt so much in those years, but he'd also slowly absorbed his master's patient and rational nature. He had shunned responsibility before meeting the Scrier, had even run away from his oppressive Saudi family and the future they'd planned for him in the non-magical world, so he must have received his ambition from Joseph, too. Had Joseph taken on Qasim's impulsivity, his anger, and just been well-adjusted enough to deal with it? He'd never seemed to change, always quiet, always insightful, always patient.

Qasim had first been inducted into the White Elm at the age of twenty-four. Gawain and Miranda had been two other junior members of the council, and another Lord and Lady had presided over them. Back then, the White Elm had consisted mainly of elderly sorcerers from the UK, some of western Europe and the USA. White men. Miranda had made history as the first black sorceress on the White Elm – Qasim, an apprentice of a councillor (the common path onto the White Elm in those times), joined her on the council as the first sorcerer of Middle Eastern origins to be accepted. Sadly, his American master died before seeing his talented apprentice take his place on the council.

The circle had changed so much in thirty-two years. The White Elm had since seen two gifted sorceresses take up the role of Lady before the title was passed to Lady Miranda; the former Lord had lived a great many years before passing away peacefully, leaving Lord Gawain to take his place. All other councillors on the White Elm had either died or retired in that time, leaving positions to be filled. Qasim had been quietly ecstatic with the huge variety of applicants who came forth in those times – Chinese sorcerer Tian, for one, and New Zealander Elijah for another. Though the council had always been strong and successful as a council of elderly Anglo-Saxon sorcerers, Qasim had known that diversity was a necessity for the future of the White Elm.

Today's White Elm was one their predecessors would not have recognised. It was more female than ever before with five sorceresses, more varied in ethnicities and younger than any previous incarnation of the council, with a massive count of eight members under forty. It had a twenty-two-year-old Dark Keeper, for heavens' sake, and he was the only one with an apprentice. Not so long ago, apprenticeships and family connections were the only ways into the White Elm. Qasim would have stood no chance without the luck he'd struck in being discovered by Joseph as a teenage runaway.

He was outside now and halfway to the orchard and to Aristea. She was probably not the one the council, in any of its forms, would have picked out of the Academy's pool of potential to be groomed for a position on the White Elm. She was unconventional in manner, under-skilled, and her pedigree was not widely known. It was lucky, then, that she'd stood out to the two scriers – lucky for her, and lucky for the council, whose own processes might have had them otherwise overlook her.

He didn't feel it immediately upon coming in sight of the orchard, but by the time he could make out Aristea's black outfit in the dim of a path through the trees, a discomfort had begun to emerge. The closer he got, the more uneasy Qasim started to feel. He might have wondered, except that he now knew everything Renatus knew, and knew that this was the place it had all happened.

Aristea was sitting against a tree about halfway down the path, staring into something in her hands. She looked calm, unaffected – a moment's focus on her aura told Qasim what Renatus had already known. Far from unaffected, Aristea was highly strengthened, while Qasim knew that he was weaker here than he'd been inside the house.

He called her name, ignoring the desire to lean tiredly against a tree. He was *not* tired. His voice jolted her from her trance. She hurried to her feet and almost ran to him, deliberately rounding the exact place Ana Morrissey had been dropped seven years before. She held out the pinkish stone she'd been scrying with.

'I knew I'd scry better here,' she said breathlessly. 'I saw her, in a dark room all by herself, the floor is cement and there was this chain-'

'Wait,' Qasim interrupted, raising a hand to stop the barrage of information. He took her arm and pulled her a dozen metres away from the orchard. It was far enough away that he didn't feel unwell anymore. 'You've seen Teresa?'

'Yes,' the apprentice confirmed. 'In my ruby.'

Qasim didn't ask how a seventeen-year-old from a modest background had happened across a fist-sized ruby.

'Do you know where she is?' he asked instead, taking the stone from her extended hand. Aristea's face fell a little.

'No. But she's underground somewhere. There's this little window at the top of the wall and I could see grass outside...'

Teresa's foot, bare... the gold chain, wrapped tight around the ankle... cement floor... nondescript door, locked... small window, up high, out of Teresa's reach, overgrown grass obscuring most of the weak sunlight that dared peek through... Teresa, underfed, curled in a corner, speaking softly to herself in her native Romanian...

The ruby provided everything it had been kind enough to show Aristea. Normally this was impossible, but Qasim was not an amateur scrier. His master had called this particular skill "cheating"; essentially hacking into someone else's vision. Just like impassioned moments in time left impressions of memory on physical objects for scriers to tap into, scrying tools retained memories of the visions they'd channelled. If one was timely, the tool could sometimes be prompted to repeat these. It was much like checking a computer's browser history or putting a removed DVD back into the player.

It was because of Joseph that Qasim was, and always would be, a better scrier than Renatus. The Morrisseys were all self-taught, while Qasim had enjoyed nine years of explicit tuition under a White Elm Scrier. There were some skills you couldn't just teach yourself.

'Qasim,' Aristea said, her tone questioning, 'why do you think Lisandro is keeping Aubrey and Teresa separate? Why bother guarding two prisons? That's twice the chance of a break-out, twice the chance of being discovered, and it's splitting the workforce.'

Qasim began walking back to the house, figuring that Renatus would open back up once they got further away from the path and see the vision for himself. Aristea trailed behind.

'Demoralisation, I suppose,' said Qasim. 'It is easier to be hopeful when you have someone with you. Probably he expects they would plot an escape together. I gather that Aubrey is the one Lisandro is guarding personally because he regards him as more of a threat than Teresa.'

'Qasim,' Aristea said again, uncertainly this time, 'what... I mean, uh... what sort... uh... I, um, I touched Declan's coin, and I saw... I saw what's happening to Teresa.' She reached out for her stone; Qasim returned it silently, waiting for her question. 'Is that what sort of *person* Lisandro is?'

Armed now with Renatus's lifetime of knowledge and experience with Lisandro, Qasim didn't feel any uncertainty in shaking his head.

'I don't think so. I think that's who Jackson is, and we somehow didn't pick up on it in all the years we had him on the council. Without our code to bind him, his moral boundaries seem to have severely blurred.'

They walked in silence the rest of the way to the house. Only at the steps did Aristea stop him.

'Qasim,' she said. 'Renatus was really stupid this morning.'

The Scrier turned to her, his curiosity piqued. He absolutely had to hear this.

'He risked both our futures by trusting you in his mind. I know it was the only way, the best way, because you couldn't possibly think any less of him than you already did, but anyway... thank you, for taking the stance you did.'

She looked extremely uncomfortable to have to say this, and Qasim repressed a sigh. Pride – he could try to blame it on Renatus and say she was just getting it from him as a result of their bond, but he knew that she'd been suffered from this trait long before she'd come to Morrissey House and that Qasim himself was no better. Pride was an inherent fault in all scriers, along with scepticism, difficulty trusting others and secretiveness. Aristea was only new to scrying and to her own magic. For now she was a proud sceptic. The privacy and trust issues would come later, undoubtedly, as she exposed herself more and more to her gift and saw the ways in which human beings betrayed one another on a daily basis.

'I didn't choose a stance,' Qasim answered finally. 'The evidence was clear. Your master was trying to do right by the council and its councillors and knew nothing about the prank visits to our allies.'

In retrospect, Qasim should have known immediately that it wasn't Renatus. Egypt was visited *before* Lisandro seemed to be giving his successor instructions. He'd just been so prepared by Lisandro's careful planning to catch Renatus out.

'But, the other stuff, too,' Aristea said, braver now. 'You've seen what he's done. I'm just glad...' She paused as some students opened the front door and came down the steps, then quickly added, 'that you think about it the same way I do. Thanks for standing up for him.'

She slipped past to go inside. Qasim waited a moment as the small crowd of teenagers passed him, heading out for a walk in the grounds before the impending rain could come down, pretending not to be extremely interested in whatever had transpired between the two scriers.

Slowly, Qasim headed in after the apprentice, deep in thought. She was only seventeen, and not a grown-up seventeen at that. She was still all those things he'd thought about her when she'd first come to the Academy. But she was not the only child in her relationship with Renatus, only the less capable one, and already she was stepping up, recognising his weaknesses and protecting him.

Distantly, Renatus touched Qasim's thoughts. Qasim showed him what Aristea had seen and what she'd said.

You may not be a traitor or a murderer, Qasim said, *but she's still much too good for you. You don't deserve her.*

Renatus was not the least bit offended.

I know.

chapter twenty-two

What a whirlwind of a day. It was only early afternoon and already my personal position regarding Renatus had jumped from naively positive to bitterly resentful and back to positive, though arguably more informed now. Likewise, my feelings towards his council had also shifted between the same extremes.

'You're back!' Hiroko said when I fell exhaustedly into the seat beside her in the dining room. 'I was worried.'

'Everything's alright now,' I told her, plonking my ruby down on the tabletop and sparing a smile for Iseult opposite us. Both were totally not allowed to know any of the things I had to say, and though I'd long since decided that Hiroko was well above such rules, there of course remained a code of public silence between us. 'Some things were just confused.'

Iseult didn't seem interested, and nobody else gave me funny looks (no funnier than normal, anyway). Could it be that Sterling hadn't told the whole school about our midnight wake-up call, and therefore nobody was wondering about it? I glanced around the room but couldn't see either of my other two roommates anywhere.

'Sometimes I'm not sure why the White Elm even have timetables,' Iseult complained. I watched as she dismantled her chicken and salad sandwich and then delicately remade it, neater than it had been to start with. 'They're never here. I wanted Lady Miranda to look over my draft today but she wasn't around. I hope she gives us an extension.'

I noted the hand-written essay at Iseult's elbow. Hiroko reached over and nudged the corner so that it turned enough that we could read it. It was a discussion piece on medical uses of chakra knowledge.

'Lady Miranda do not set this sort of work for our level,' Hiroko commented dubiously. 'I hopes she will not start to.'

'Unlikely. She told us that whoever she selects as an apprentice will also be expected to study a full medical degree at university, so we might as well get used to the workload. She probably doesn't have the same expectations of your level.'

It sounded harsh but I knew Iseult meant no offence. I dug into my lunch, contemplating the various costs of joining the White Elm. For Lady Miranda's as yet unchosen apprentice, study and career options had been preselected. For me, possibly, a dark end awaited. What would others here at the Academy pay, ultimately, to achieve this dream? How would we ever know if it was worth it?

I glanced over at the staff table. Emmanuelle caught my eye and offered me a small smile. I returned it. Probably I would never know if it was worth it, because I was never going to know any different. Like Emmanuelle, who lived and breathed this life and loved it passionately. I tried to imagine her sitting in a lecture hall somewhere, or sitting at a sewing machine in a factory, or handing out brochures to tourists with a bright fake smile, or scanning groceries and packing them into bags. I couldn't. I couldn't imagine her as anything other than the strong and driven White Elm Healer she was.

Likewise, upstairs was Renatus, and I couldn't picture him out in the mortal world. Even in this world, the magical society in which he'd always lived, I had no clue what he'd be doing right now if he wasn't working for the White Elm. His skills were perfect for the council's purposes, and I couldn't think of anywhere else his particular skill set would be remotely useful. All that money and power but without purpose: I considered he would probably be just sitting around this house being miserable or causing trouble, driven mad with his own uselessness, if Lord Gawain hadn't guided him onto the council. He was right this morning – he *needed* to win his way back into their graces, because it was where he was meant to be.

Did that mean that the council's members were *fated* to end up where they were; that there was actually no other avenue for them and this was always what they were going to end up doing? Was it the same for me? Out in mortal society I was a misfit, unremarkable, useless. I walked out of it two months ago and I had more fingers than people who'd noticed. Gearing towards my future on the White Elm made me feel real. Like I mattered. And it made me feel like I couldn't, really, be anywhere else.

'Should we go now to get that book I have told you about?' Hiroko asked when she saw I was finished eating. I got the hint.

'Yes, I've been looking forward to reading it,' I agreed, standing and pushing my chair in. 'We'll be back soon,' I added to Iseult, but she waved the words away.

'I won't be here; I'm meeting Josh soon,' she said, looking towards the door.

Iseult was so easy to lose. Hiroko and I walked in silence to our dorm, and locked ourselves in our bathroom. I told her everything, but it came out all over the place, out of sequence, because even I was having trouble keeping up with the events of the last few hours. As always, Hiroko was the perfect audience.

'They were going to separate you?!' she demanded, horrified, when I was halfway through. 'That is very serious. I think that is always bad. Someone is always... hurt.'

'Renatus said that,' I agreed. We stood side-by-side, looking at ourselves in the mirror, styling and restyling our hair over and over. 'He said I would probably die.'

'The White Elm must have been very concerned.'

'They really believed it was true.'

I told her about the trial, the lie that had come out and the inherent truth in that, the hours spent in the orchard, what I'd read, then skipped to how I'd gotten the book and what I'd talked about with Qasim, and then resumed my story with what I saw

Sterling wearing – 'She is so *hopeless!*' Hiroko interrupted with a long-suffering sigh – the resulting confrontation with Renatus and what I'd learnt.

'So... Renatus actually thinks his family was attacked,' I said, by now focusing on Hiroko's hair only, because hers was so silky and dark and straight and I loved the feel of it. She held a twisted lock in a complicated spiral while I pinned it. 'There was definitely someone there. But how can that storm be somebody's fault? And he also thinks that the same thing happened to my parents and brother. If that's true, I can't think why, because my family and his were completely different. We didn't know any of the same people. Mine wasn't rich or anything.'

'I do not understand either how a storm can be a person's fault,' Hiroko offered. 'Perhaps the stranger foresaw the storm and so arranged for the family to be exposed to it? But you cannot know that the people will stay outside, or who will be hurt. It sounds...'

She struggled for the right word.

'Implausible, yes. But can people, like, *organise* weather patterns?' I asked curiously. Hiroko shrugged.

'They can in old stories,' she said, 'but in life, I do not know. Have you heard of it before?'

'No.' It sounded dumb to even be talking about it, especially while standing with another seventeen-year-old girl in front of a bathroom mirror. I dug around in the pencil case Hiroko used for hair pins and found another one to secure the style we were working on. 'I guess there's the possibility Renatus is paranoid and slightly crazy.'

'Hmm,' was all Hiroko said about that, and redirected the conversation by asking what had happened next, possibly wanting to spare me the useless effort of thinking on this issue. Doubtless, Renatus was slightly crazy.

Though the main event for the weekend, Renatus's trial, was done with, the tension within the White Elm did not let up. My dessert that night of cupcakes and caramel slice was cut short when I was summoned to help strategise with the council in the ballroom – 'Just go,' Hiroko said good-naturedly, and she, Josh and Iseult happily divided up my remaining cakes between them – where agreements and compromises were few and far between.

I was tired and grumpy: I didn't want to be there, and barely listened as Lord Gawain outlined to me the plan to split the council into three teams to each target different... well, places, I wasn't paying attention... and this would all happen in a timely fashion upon a signal... or something... while Lord Gawain and Renatus had Lisandro distracted with the false promise of the ring, and did I have anything to contribute or any comments? What?

'Uh, no,' I said, realising that it was my turn to talk and shaking my head harder than was necessary, trying to wake myself up. 'No, it sounds good.'

And then the polite disagreements would break out again. Qasim's wise sentiment that morning had convinced the council to act cohesively as a team and to pretend like Lisandro's spy wasn't among them, but it was clear that this fact remained at the back of everybody's mind. At any given point I could only consider our progress to be marginally successful, with many tensions erupting between councillors over what seemed to me to be very unimportant points, like who would belong to which taskforce.

'There should be a Healer in each of the rescue groups,' Tian said, folding his arms and frowning at Emmanuelle. 'Teresa and Aubrey are alive but we don't know the true nature of their condition. They are, at the least, injured.' He chanced a look at Jadon, the only one present who did not know how badly. 'Skills should be where they are required.'

'Teresa *is* a Healer,' Emmanuelle reminded him. 'She probably doesn't need me. My other skills would be useful against Lisandro.'

'They would be useful against anyone guarding Teresa, too, or against the suicide bombers guarding Aubrey,' Elijah said. He had been easy to place – as the only Displacer, they needed him available to follow wormholes that might lead them to Teresa if Lisandro didn't give her up. 'I would personally prefer you to stay with me. I could use your wards.'

'No, there's too great a chance you'll meet with Jackson,' Lady Miranda disagreed. 'She's to watch the beach house and step in *only* should an opportunity to reclaim Aubrey become apparent.'

'The do-nothing group,' Emmanuelle said irritably.

'We're not the do-nothing group,' Jadon responded. 'We're-'

'Going to do nothing unless instructed otherwise,' Lord Gawain finished firmly. 'Do not jump into situations without thinking, Jadon. Do not get yourself killed tomorrow night.'

'Why would you even say that?' Jadon demanded. He narrowed his eyes. 'What do you know?'

'The two of you are not the best decision-makers.'

'We have three Seers and three Telepaths,' Elijah said loudly, trying to redirect the focus. I thought he was fighting a losing battle. 'Does that mean one per team?'

'Yes,' Lord Gawain said, at the same time that Glen and Anouk said, 'No.'

'Anouk and I want to be on the same task,' Glen explained. 'We work best that way.'

'Well, alright,' Lord Gawain agreed tiredly, sounding like I felt, 'but there should definitely be one Seer with each group to ensure everyone stays informed.'

Jadon glanced quickly at Emmanuelle.

'In that case,' he said, 'we want Tian.'

It was at that moment that Renatus turned to look out the ballroom window.

'Excuse us,' he said, beckoning to me as he headed for the doors. I followed, with no idea what had caught his attention. No one really paid us any attention, for once.

'What is it?' I asked quietly as I slipped through the doors after him. He strode across the reception hall and out the front doors that opened for him.

Outside, it was dimly bright, the way only a rainy evening can be.

'Declan,' he answered, nodding at the distant gate. I looked, and saw a tall figure waiting in the rain just outside the estate. 'He must have found something.'

I wondered what Declan could possibly have discovered that would prompt him to turn up here unannounced, considering that his parting words last time had implied that Renatus would have to come to *him* for anything further.

'Wards, remember,' Renatus reminded me as we trekked across the lawn through the drizzle.

Declan might have looked out of place outside on a sunny day, so indoorsy did he seem, but he looked very comfortable standing around in the rainy twilight. Droplets clung to his scruffy dark hair and his long eyelashes. He ignored us as we neared the gate, staring bemusedly into the grey distance until we'd let ourselves out of the gate and were standing right in front of him.

'Good evening, Renatus,' he said pleasantly. He smiled widely at me. 'Good evening to *you*, Miss Aristea. I was really hoping to see you again. You're looking lovely, might I add.'

'Don't even start,' Renatus said impatiently. 'Why are you here?'

'Always so mean,' Declan noted. 'I'm here to help. Why else would I be here?'

'I don't know. Stalking?'

I glanced at Renatus sidelong, feeling very much in agreement with Declan. Renatus *was* mean to him.

Obviously I didn't know their history but I didn't think that there was much justification for my master's blatant rudeness and distaste for his informant.

'No, I am not stalking; although, it is a real pleasure to see your beautiful apprentice again,' Declan said, shooting me his big smile. He quickly returned his gaze to Renatus's unimpressed one. 'You are being watched, though, I hope you realise.'

'By whom?'

Declan jerked his head towards the hills.

'Various persons, at various times,' he said vaguely. 'Contractors. I happened to cross paths with one such person.'

'Did you really?' Renatus asked, his tone sarcastic, but I could tell he was interested.

'I did indeed,' Declan agreed, withdrawing something tiny from his pocket. I squinted at the chipped blue glass ball he held.

'Is that a marble?' I asked.

'Not just any old marble,' Declan corrected, showing it to me. 'A marble I lost eleven years ago. I found it under an armchair. Amazing, the things you find when you don't concentrate. I miscalculated a Displacement across my own parlour, landed too close to the chair, knocked it over and what should I find but this old thing!'

I really failed to understand the significance, so I looked up at Renatus for explanation.

'Maybe you should clean your house more often,' he said coldly, 'and you might find all the other things you've lost. Though it seems poetic that lost marbles should be the first thing you stumble across.'

'Renatus, cousin,' Declan said, pleasantly, 'don't you recognise your own possessions? It was your marble we lost. Now I'm returning it to you, with interest. Am I not a most excellent friend?'

'Very excellent,' Renatus said, frowning. I could sense that he felt like his time was being utterly wasted. I wished he could be more patient – I was sure that Declan was leading somewhere with this, although I had no idea where.

'I know, I know,' Declan said with a smile. 'I'm wonderful. I know how hard you've been looking for this.'

Standing closest to me, he dropped the marble into my palm.

The dark cement room where Jackson has been keeping Teresa... Jackson and a stranger stand over Teresa, kneeling on the grubby floor... She is dirty and her hands are bound together... 'She doesn't look like much,' the stranger notes... 'Don't worry, she's quite the little prize'... Jackson waves a hand and a silvery disc shimmers into existence, floating in the air... Images begin to appear in it, shifting, changing focus... Teresa watches... The mirror settles on a vision of Aubrey, sitting in a corner with Shell huddled against him... Hands grab at the couple, pulling them apart... Shell cries out as a carving knife is thrust against her partner's throat... The image is confronting, and Teresa swallows as Jackson laughs... 'Now, my friend's payment, please'... Teresa glares up at her captors... 'That's not real'... 'Do you want to risk that?'... The anklet is removed, and in the mirror, Aubrey struggles... The hilt of another blade strikes him across the head, and he is still again, the knife remains at his throat, a threat... Teresa hurries to her feet... 'Alright, alright!'... A sapphire, the size of a milk bottle cap... The stranger picks it up in wonderment... 'If you're hoping to sell that, you had best do it in the next hour,' Jackson warns... 'I already have a buyer lined up'... Teresa tosses her messy hair behind her shoulder... 'I've done what you asked. Get out'... Jackson laughs, and the stranger chuckles... 'You think this is the only man we've got to pay? Do you know what kind of manpower it takes to keep watch on your council? Or should we pay them the other way?'... Teresa looks away... Jackson claps the stranger on the back... 'I'll call on you later in the week. Go get your money'... The door behind them creaks open, and Lisandro enters... The stranger's eyes widen, and he bows his head... Lisandro frowns, Teresa glares... 'How'd she get so messy? Renatus suggested you weren't taking care of her'... 'I don't know'... A lie... Lisandro looks unconvinced... Eventually smiles at her... 'Oh, good. You're in the illusion-making mood. I was hoping to catch you before you got bored with it'... All eyes slide to the magic mirror, which still displays Aubrey held at knifepoint...

As abruptly as the memory had opened to me, it ended and once again, all I could see was what was before my physical eyes. I turned to Renatus, my mouth already open to discuss what I'd just seen, knowing he'd seen at least some of the vision through me, and certain that he was just as concerned about this information as I was, but he quickly covered my mouth with one hand and spoke loudly.

'Declan, you're right,' he said, very clearly. 'I didn't want to admit it but it will be nice to have the set all together again. Thank you for thinking to give this to me.'

'You're welcome,' Declan said, still smiling pleasantly, although with a knowing glint in his eye now. 'I knew you'd be happy to get it.'

'Offhand, when exactly did you find this?'

'Hmm... It happened early this morning. Maybe three?' He winked at me. 'Don't Displace in the dark, lovely.'

'I see.' Renatus looked at me now, lowering his hand. I resisted the urge to look around. They were still speaking as though the marble itself was the object of interest, but what Declan had really been delivering, the vision, was too important a topic to openly discuss, especially when they both believed they were being watched.

'I'll be going now,' Declan said. He turned to me with his massive smile, the missing tooth glaringly obvious. 'It was delightful to see you again, Miss Aristea. I might have to make a habit of turning up here in bad weather. It's certainly worth the chill to see your gorgeous face – and there's something very appealing about a pretty girl standing around in the rain-'

'Goodbye, Declan,' Renatus said firmly, dragging me back through the gates into the estate. I glanced back over my shoulder as Declan waved once and Displaced. My master shook his head, clearly annoyed and frustrated, and said, 'He never ceases to disgust me.'

'I noticed.' I pulled my arm free of his grasp. 'He's really not that bad, though, you know.'

Renatus just seethed, and I tried not to think about how flattering it was to be called "pretty" and "gorgeous" after all the negative attention I'd received lately, even if the admirer was a little bit creepy. He was the harmless sort of creep, though, the cutely amusing type.

In silence I followed Renatus back to the ball-room, which was at least as tense as we'd left it. Whatever they'd been arguing about, though, ended when we walked in and handed the marble over to Lord Gawain.

'Teresa is creating illusions for Lisandro?' Jadon repeated sceptically once Renatus had explained Declan's findings. 'That's ridiculous.'

'Is it?' Lady Miranda asked suddenly, looking as though she were surprising even herself. 'Is it crazy that we've never suspected either of them?'

'You're crazy if you do,' Jadon retorted. 'It's a bit hard for Teresa or Aubrey to trade information on us when they have no connection to us.'

'We have no connection to them,' Anouk countered. 'It's possible the block works only one way. They might still be able to read and feel *us*.'

'No. Teresa told me she felt cut-off from the council,' Jadon said. 'They have no way of knowing what we're doing or thinking here.'

'And if they were traitors, they might have negotiated a better deal,' I added, agreeing completely with Jadon. Lady Miranda, I suspected, was looking for options that meant that no one here was her enemy, even if her other options were completely preposterous. 'Neither of them are happy or even clean, or showing any other signs of reaping any sort of reward.'

'She's not sharing her talent by choice,' Lord Gawain said now, handing the marble on to his co-leader, having already witnessed the vision it held. The council's Telepaths stared at him intently, essentially downloading the memory from him directly. 'Why would Lisandro need Teresa to create an illusion for him? Other than the stones? His aren't bad.'

'Hers are better,' Renatus said. 'It must be something important.'

'Whatever it is, we won't know it from the real thing,' Susannah said slowly. 'He could be replicating a whole person, or people. It could double the appearance of his army, or he might be replicating one of his hostages so he doesn't really have to hand anyone over.'

The situation really just seemed to be worsening. With each new snippet of information, the White Elm just became more aware of how uninformed they were.

By Monday I was over spending time with the council and glad to attend classes, even if I knew I would mostly just sit by myself.

This Displacement class was the best one I'd ever had, because now, I realised when Elijah encouraged us to have a go at the beginning exercises, I actually knew how to do what was being asked of me. Beside me, Willow closed her eyes and started concentrating. I did the same, reaching for the Fabric that Hiroko had shown me. It took a few long moments, maybe half a minute, to find, so I was glad that there was absolutely no performance pressure in this class of fellow failures, but when I did find it, I was able to manipulate it with relative ease. I folded it, just a tiny bit, parted it, and moved through it...

'Aristea!' Elijah shouted in delight, distracting everybody from their deep concentration. 'You just Displaced.'

I looked back over my shoulder and saw that I was about four metres ahead of where I was before. Willow was staring at me from where I'd left her. Elijah's face was brighter than I'd seen it in weeks. One of the boys – the one I'd been sitting next to on my very first day, I recalled uselessly – clapped enthusiastically for a second, then stopped, realising that he was the only one doing so.

'Aristea, well done!' Elijah said, beaming as he approached. 'Is that the first time you've done that?'

I shook my head.

'Um, no, I did it on Saturday,' I answered, trying to stop myself from looking around. The others in my class were staring at me openly, not that this was unusual these days, but it was still discomforting.

'Well, it's good to hear you've been practising.' Elijah smiled around at the others, seeming not to notice their intent stares. 'See what happens when you keep working on something?'

'Is that really from practice, or just because of Renatus?' asked a boy I'd hardly spoken to before. I felt a twinge of irritation at his arrogant tone.

Nobody was content to let me take my victories at face value.

'Renatus didn't teach me Displacement,' I said shortly. 'Elijah and Hiroko did.'

'They're just jealous,' someone said boldly, and I turned quickly to the speaker – the boy who had clapped, who I'd sat with on the very first day, who had that very young face. Noah. 'Everyone here wanted to be the first one to display some trace of Displacement talent, so they're just jealous.'

'I'm sure everyone is very pleased for you, Aristea,' Elijah insisted, ever the peace-keeper. 'They're just surprised! Can you do it again?'

I pretended to try, pretended to fail. I shrugged helplessly.

'Maybe not,' I apologised to my nicest teacher, hoping he'd let it go.

'I'm sure it'll come back to you when you need it,' he said with a knowing smile. He redirected the attention of my classmates, but I was worrying about his words. *It'll come back to you when you need it... When you need it...* Tonight was going to be a massive deal – I didn't remember much of what was said at the circle last night but I recalled that timing and position were paramount. Was my Displacement skill, so new and fresh, reliable enough for whatever tonight was going to throw at me? I still wasn't even sure what *I* would be doing tonight, or perhaps I'd been told but couldn't remember, so I assumed I'd been lumped in as an extension of my master and I was to stay with Renatus, who was to confront Lisandro with Lord Gawain. Nobody seemed sure what would happen tonight. I might get hurt. I could die. I might never see my beautiful big sister again. I was really missing Angela now. I'd sent the letter but wished I could go and see her, and talk to her about movies and cleaning my room and Orlando Bloom. Who even knew how long it would be before I got to do that? I hadn't even mentioned any of that stuff in the letter.

I moodily scuffed at the lawn with my shoe. My life was a terrifying mess and I had nobody to blame but myself.

chapter twenty-three

The day whizzed past in a blur, and suddenly it was dinner time and I was sitting at the dining table with Hiroko, sipping steaming hot tomato soup.

'Do you expect it will be very dangerous?' Hiroko asked, very quietly. I shrugged lightly.

'The entire council will be there, so I don't think I'll be in any more danger than they've put me in before,' I said, also keeping my voice down. Nobody was listening to us, but our conversation wasn't meant to be happening, so we didn't want to risk being overheard. The students weren't supposed to know that anything was happening tonight, and technically, I wasn't meant to tell Hiroko anything about the plan, but naturally by this point she knew about as much as I did.

'And they will protect you,' Hiroko added, nodding as though confirming her own question. I nodded, too.

'Renatus always stays close,' I agreed quietly. 'He won't let anything happen to me.'

Hiroko silently sipped her soup for a little while, looking thoughtful. A few times she put her hand into her pocket, as though checking that something was still there.

'I think you are very brave,' she said finally, putting her spoon down and looking at me.

'I'm not that brave,' I said.

'You are. I wish I were as brave like you.'

Hiroko's pretty eyes slanted their gaze past me for a second, and without looking, I knew that Garrett was somewhere behind me. She'd finished her picture over the weekend and given it to him, I knew. Apparently, predictably, he'd blushed, mumbled thanks and all but ran away. Hiroko hadn't spoken to him since. When she looked down suddenly, I knew it was because he was walking this way.

'You *are* brave,' I told her, very firmly, and at that moment a crumpled paper shape fell to the table between us. More of Garrett's origami, this time something resembling a butterfly. Hiroko looked up at me, and I looked back at her and said again, 'You *are* brave.'

'Garrett.' Hiroko stood and turned quickly. Garrett, and Addison walking beside him, stopped and glanced back at her. Garrett's milky cheeks flushed bright red and his eyes struggled to meet Hiroko's as she grabbed the butterfly and walked over to him. She held up his handiwork. 'This is very good. How did you learn this?'

Addison and I watched on in mild amusement as Garrett squirmed, uncomfortable with being the centre of Hiroko's attention. He'd hoped to impart his paper token without having to endure any actual interaction.

'I... I found a book, taught myself,' Garrett muttered, looking away.

'I keep them all,' Hiroko said, stepping a little bit closer. 'I like them.'

Addison moved away slightly, and for a moment I caught his eye. I smiled in a "our-best-friends-are-cute-together" kind of way, but when he looked at me, his grin faltered. I tried not to feel hurt – I'd thought, or at least hoped, that Addison had been one of the few people who didn't hate me. I'd thought we were cool. Apparently I was wrong, and I expected he would quickly look away, but he did not. He kept staring at me, an awkward, uncertain expression on. I didn't know what that was about, so I turned my attention back to Hiroko and Garrett.

'That's good,' Garrett was mumbling.

'I like you, too,' Hiroko added simply.

'That's g-' Garrett stopped himself in the middle of his automatic response, suddenly realising what she'd really said. 'Oh.' I expected his cheeks to get even redder, but by this point they could not, and instead they began to drain of colour. He stuttered silently for a few seconds while Hiroko waited patiently for a response. It was quite painful to watch. It was enough to break Addison's stare and drag his attention back to the real action. 'Uh... Well... Uh... Um... Uh, me too.'

Hiroko smiled. Disgusted, Addison slapped a hand roughly into Garrett's shoulder.

'What he *means*,' he translated clearly, 'is that he thinks you're hot.' He beamed at Garrett, who was dying of embarrassment. 'Isn't that what you meant to say? Or were you going to go the nice-guy angle and tell her she's cute? That always works.'

Garrett couldn't even speak.

'I think you're cute, too,' Hiroko said, stepping closer again. 'I like you a lot.'

'What's that, Garrett?' Addison leaned close to his humiliated friend, pretending to listen, though of course Garrett was saying absolutely nothing. 'You want her to know how much you like to watch her, especially when she's wearing those jeans, which make her look so freaking sexy?' Addison raised his hands innocently when Hiroko gave him a look. 'You heard him – his words, not mine!'

I covered my mouth, trying to stifle a laugh. Addison glanced over – he always did like to have an audience – and again, his grin faltered when our eyes met. I looked away, focusing instead on the Hiroko-Garrett cuteness.

Hiroko took one of Garrett's hands lightly in hers. He finally looked up at her and properly looked her in the eyes. For the first time, he didn't look like he just wanted to melt into the floor. For the first time, he didn't look like a scared little boy. He looked like a guy holding hands with the girl he was into.

'You can kiss me, if you want to,' Hiroko said quietly.

'Whoa, Hiroko, I don't know,' Addison said, shaking his head. 'This is just too soon for me–'

'Addison!' Both Hiroko and Garrett spoke at the same time, Hiroko good-naturedly and Garrett less so. The moment adequately lightened, Addison obligingly moved away, coming to stand almost right beside my chair. He looked down at me quickly.

'Hey,' he whispered, clearly uncomfortable being this close to me. I couldn't understand why, then, he was choosing to speak to me.

'Hi,' I replied shortly, otherwise ignoring him. Hiroko half-stepped forward, closing the remaining distance between herself and her guy.

'If you want to,' she repeated kindly, giving Garrett an easy escape if he wanted to take it. For a long moment he just looked at her, then he nodded quickly and leaned down to press his lips against hers.

There was a whoop from further up the table – Joshua was watching on, too. Garrett pulled away, and Hiroko smiled like she'd won something.

'So... I'll see you later?' Garrett asked, shy again but at least able to produce full sentences. Hiroko nodded brightly.

'I will see you later,' she agreed, letting his hand go as Addison stepped forward to reclaim his mate. He slung an arm over Garrett's shoulders and steered him away, shaking his head lightly at Hiroko.

'Now you've done it,' he said soberly. 'Corrupted him, you have.'

He started towards the door, hesitantly glancing back at me. He looked like he was going to say something.

'What?' Garrett asked, trying to look back as well to see what was making Addison pause.

'Nothing,' Addison insisted, and they left the hall. Hiroko sat down next to me, her eyes dancing and a big smile left behind where Garrett had kissed her.

'That was *very* brave,' I said, and we both broke into giggles.

'I thought...' Hiroko struggled to get her laughter under control as Joshua shouted down the table, '*Go* Hiroko!' She took a deep breath and tried again. 'I thought he wanted to run away.'

'I think he may have considered it,' I agreed. 'I'm impressed he stood still so long.'

Hiroko grinned and went back to her soup. Positive, excited emotions rolled from her in pleasant waves, so when I saw the White Elm councillors stand and file out silently after Qasim, I was able to easily ignore the butterflies that came to life in my stomach.

'I've got to go,' I said quietly, arranging my cutlery neatly.

'Wait,' Hiroko said, shoving her hand into her jeans pocket again. This time she withdrew something little and shiny. 'I have been making things also.'

She extended her palm so I could see two tiny silver rings.

'They are friendship rings,' she said, slightly embarrassed. I stared at them.

'You *made* these?' I asked, incredulous. They looked store-bought. 'How?'

'Magic,' she answered. 'I have been practising creating things with magic.'

'They're amazing.' I tilted my head to see them from another angle. They were plain and unadorned, but very shiny, like brand new jewellery. 'I can't believe you *made* these.'

'It is...' Hiroko struggled for the right word. 'When it is silly? A silly present.'

'They're not silly,' I disagreed, accepting the one she handed me. It was really very tiny, and looked too small for my fingers, but I tried it on my pinky and it fitted perfectly. 'They're fantastic.'

I stood as she slid her ring on the same finger of her own hand. I smiled, holding out my hand to admire it from various angles beside hers. Now our friendship was official. Nothing officialised a friendship like matching jewellery.

'You're the best,' I said, leaning down to hug her tightly. 'I'm so proud of you right now. Making jewellery out of nothing; kissing boys.'

Hiroko giggled again and gave me one last affectionate squeeze before she released me.

'I'm proud of you, too,' she said, smiling up at me. 'Joining councils; saving the world. I'll see you tomorrow?'

'For sure,' I agreed. I waved as I left her to finish her dinner.

The White Elm was gathered in the reception hall, ready to leave, looking very impressive. Tian was dressed in a traditional Asian outfit I had no name for, consisting of tightly wrapped layers of dark material. Emmanuelle looked ridiculously amazing in black leather pants and a corset – probably the first time I'd ever seen her in anything but a full-length dress or robe. Qasim looked even more imposing than usual in a high-collared black suit. Renatus was absolutely the warrior in residence, heavy combat boots on, cloak gone. Everyone else was dressed in dark colours, many in jeans.

Lady Miranda was going over things one last time with Qasim's team – Tian, Emmanuelle and Jadon.

'You three, and you two in particular,' she was saying, speaking mostly to the youngest two, 'are to keep in mind that Qasim has seniority. This is his taskforce. What he says, goes. I hope that's clear.'

'Of course,' Emmanuelle said coolly, while Jadon jerked his chin once in arrogant agreement.

'Too much is at stake and too much is unclear for us to rush into anything,' Lady Miranda reminded everyone. 'Elijah, you go first. We'll be in touch.'

The Displacer nodded and started out the door, but paused when he saw me.

'Aristea?' he said, sounding surprised to see me there. How many times had I heard my name said like that in the past month? Straightaway, all eyes were on me.

'Yeah, what?' I responded, trying not to sound too rude. Was Elijah annoyed about my fake-out today? Apologising would probably be a good start, I supposed. 'Sorry about today.'

'Oh, forget that,' Elijah said dismissively, waving a hand. He still looked confused. 'I didn't realise you were supposed to be here.'

'She's not,' Anouk said shortly, twisting her long hair into a bun and securing it. I frowned.

'Where am I meant to be?' I asked. 'What am I even doing tonight?'

Renatus glanced at Lord Gawain, and Lady Miranda frowned back at me.

'Aristea, you're not coming,' she said. 'We discussed this.'

'What? No!' I said, indignant. 'Why not?'

'It's too dangerous,' Lady Miranda answered, as though this were obvious.

'Everything's too dangerous,' I snapped. 'On the weekend you were going to have me ripped from Renatus, knowing I'd probably die. *That* wasn't too dangerous, but this is?'

'Aristea, you know what I mean,' the high priestess sighed. 'We're not having this argument. You're staying here.'

'No, I'm coming,' I argued anyway, folding my arms determinedly.

'We've spoken,' Lord Gawain said firmly. 'The White Elm's leaders have ultimate authority over its members-'

'Maybe so, but I don't belong to the White Elm,' I reminded him, knowing I was totally out of line but so caught up in my irritation at being ousted. 'I belong to Renatus, so I only have to stay if *he* tells me to.'

I turned to my master, who hadn't spoken until now. My heart pounded with the unsettling thrill of confrontation. He looked at me for a long time, and I started to feel a bit stupid. I'd backed him into a corner, which was really unfair of me. He now had to choose between me and Lord Gawain, and he had no good reason to pick me after my immature outburst.

'She's coming,' Renatus said finally, and I breathed a sigh of relief. How embarrassing if he'd chosen otherwise.

'She's-'

'She's my apprentice, which means where I go, she goes,' Renatus told Lady Miranda, who was shaking her head.

'It's too dangerous,' she insisted, looking to Emmanuelle. 'Tell him. He's putting her in danger. He's putting *himself* in danger. You can stop him.'

'Only if 'e is being unreasonable,' Emmanuelle said, 'which I don't believe 'e is. What's the point in 'im 'aving an apprentice if 'e 'as to leave 'er behind every time something scary 'appens? She wants to come; 'e wants to bring 'er. I can't step in. And I don't think I should.'

Susannah closed her eyes.

'Aristea, you can't come,' Qasim said calmly. 'If Lisandro meets you, he'll be able to start blocking your visions. Not as well as he blocks us, but at the level you're at now, you won't be able to see much of anything he does.'

I understood his logic, but wasn't about to relinquish my win.

'I'll just have to work harder and get better,' I said boldly.

'You will indeed,' Qasim agreed. 'Much better.'

I wasn't sure what that meant, but Tian was speaking now.

'Renatus, she can't come, because if she's there, we'll lose the ring,' he said, folding his arms. 'It's that simple.'

Hmm, I'd forgotten about that. It seemed that I was the only one who had. Others looked away, confronted once again with this frightening certainty. Renatus sighed impatiently.

'Emmanuelle, don't give me the ring, under any circumstance,' he directed. 'And don't lose it just because Aristea is out of the house. Please.'

'Swallow it,' Jadon advised, earning him a half-annoyed look from Emmanuelle. He turned back to the rest of the council. 'I guess Aristea's coming. Can we go now?'

'She's *not* coming,' Lord Gawain disagreed, 'if it means I lose Renatus to Lisandro. She can stay right where she is.'

His use of the pronoun 'I' instead of 'we' was not missed by anybody, but no one mentioned it. Renatus was his personal project, a broken and ruined thing he'd nurtured, loved and supported into what it was today.

Susannah shook her head suddenly, as though coming around after a brief moment of unconsciousness.

'No, she has to come,' she said. 'Her presence is necessary. There is information... that won't come to light for anyone but her. She must come.'

'What sort of information?' Anouk asked suspiciously. Susannah paused for a little bit too long before answering.

'Where to find Teresa, among other things.'

'But if Lisandro meets her...' Qasim began, not needing to finish that sentence. Susannah nodded.

'I know. But it'll be worth it, believe me.'

Susannah's advice always seemed like a final word amongst the council. I felt everybody's feelings towards my presence smooth out. Renatus approached Lord Gawain.

'Master, you don't need to worry,' he said, an expert at working the emotions of the leader. 'You will be with me. Aristea will be with me. What you've seen will not happen. It has to have been a misinterpretation.'

'Yes, it must have been,' Lord Gawain agreed doubtfully. He looked over at me, concern clouding his grey eyes. He gathered himself together. 'Elijah, go. Lady Miranda, take your group and wait with Elijah until we give a signal.'

Susannah, Anouk and Glen followed Lady Miranda out the door and into the cool night.

'Qasim, take care to stay hidden,' Lord Gawain said by way of dismissal to the next group, and they slipped out, too.

'Nobody will be here to watch the students?' I asked Renatus.

'The idea was that you would be here to do that,' he answered in a low voice.

'Well, thanks for the heads-up,' I replied in the same tone. 'If someone had told me that earlier I might not have rocked up and caused this big fuss.'

'You could have *listened* yesterday; but it doesn't matter,' Renatus said. 'Fionnuala and the other staff can keep the estate safe, and Elijah or I can be back here in seconds if we have to be.'

'Let's go, then,' Lord Gawain said, holding the door open for us.

'Aristea.'

Renatus paused in the doorway when I stopped and looked back at the person calling my name. Addison.

'What?' I asked. *Now* he had something to say? He looked even more uncertain and nervous than he had before, but he was standing resolutely in the centre of the reception hall, alone. Waiting for me.

'What?' I said again. He looked around.

'Look, I have something to talk to you about,' he said. I raised my hands helplessly, so confused by his way-weird behaviour. This was not the Addison I was used to.

'Like what?'

'I... I'm not sure I'm really meant to say this-'

'Addison, I can't do this right now,' I said, turning away. I'd barely taken a full step when I walked straight into him.

'Sorry, a bit close,' he apologised, taking my shoulders and stepping back to put an appropriate distance for speaking between us. He dropped his hands. 'Kendra saw something. She said it was unethical to tell you, but-'

'Then don't tell her, Mr James,' Lord Gawain said, opening the door a little wider, a big hint.

'I know, I know,' my Australian classmate said, running a hand through his hair, clearly agitated. 'She was going to come talk to you but she thought you wouldn't listen if it came from her, and then she said it was probably best you didn't know at all, but she wasn't sure because she said the vision was *for* you, not *about* you... not sure what that's meant to mean, funny Seer-talk I guess. But anyway,' he said hastily, seeing Lord Gawain's impatient expression, 'I see you're busy. What she said was, "Trust him only to the door, but no further. Outside, you hold the torch. He's in the dark".' Addison eyed the men standing in the doorway. 'I don't think she meant *this* door.'

'Probably not,' I agreed. I glanced back at Renatus. 'I've got to go, but... thanks, Addison.'

He forced a smile, the most Addison-like interaction I'd had with him all day.

'Just take care,' he advised, stepping aside so I could leave. I hurried through the doors, his words – well, Kendra's words, really – repeating themselves over and over in my head. From what I understood about Seers, the visions they received were rarely literal like my scried ones. The information was rarely in context and required a lot of careful interpretation. There were a lot of metaphors, half-truths and fragments of truths to sort through. I wondered what the significance of the door would be. And the torch? It was unlikely that there would be a real torch involved. *Outside, you hold the torch.* It sounded like a leadership metaphor. *He's in the dark.* Was *he* Renatus?

'Don't think too much on it,' my master advised as we crossed the lawn to the gate. Lady Miranda and her little team were waiting on this side of it, and Elijah was on the outside, ready to Displace at any moment's notice. 'Messages from the future are difficult to make sense of without knowledge of the future.'

'When that future becomes your present, you'll understand what Addison James meant,' Lord Gawain agreed, nodding once to Lady Miranda as he passed her and went to unlock the gate. Renatus leaned past him to press his hand to the iron, and it opened quietly.

'No movement there yet,' Elijah told us quietly as we filed through and let the gate clang shut behind us. I assumed he was focussed on the Fabric around the beach house. 'He must be waiting for something.'

'Qasim arrived unnoticed?' Lord Gawain checked.

'As far as we know. They're keeping back, like we talked about. I don't think Lisandro has the resources to detect them from that distance.'

'Resources?' I asked, thinking of money and tools.

'Displacers like Elijah,' Renatus filled in.

'Is it time?' Lord Gawain asked, looking first at his own and then to Renatus's left wrist, looking for a watch. Neither of them were wearing one – I wasn't sure Renatus even owned one, because I'd never seen him with one – so Renatus reached for my arm to check mine. I was still wearing it on my right wrist, though my tattoo had long stopped feeling itchy.

'As good a time as any,' he said. He tightened his grip on me and pulled me closer. He extended his other hand to Lord Gawain. 'Let's go, then.'

The White Elm's leader paused for way too long to be just thoughtfulness. He was scared. I could feel it all around him, though he tried to hold it in. He slowly took the offered hand, and before he could change his mind, Renatus opened the Fabric and pulled us both through.

I felt my new surroundings before my eyes adjusted to the deep blackness enough to see anything. The darkness was not only visual.

'Renatus...' Lord Gawain's voice betrayed his uncertainty. My master released my arm. A sudden bright light sparked into existence, and I shielded my unsuspecting eyes as the ball of sunlight in Renatus's hand illuminated the area. He dropped his hand; the ball stayed in place, suspended by magic I wasn't sure I'd ever understand.

I drew a deep breath, empowered by the dark energy that permeated this place so deeply, looking around. It was a confusing picture. We were in a sort of clearing, sparse forestry all around what had once been a home and its garden. The home was now a wreck, uninhabitable. Its roof was caved in and many internal walls (visible because much of the outer brickwork had been smashed away) had collapsed under the weight. The windows were long-since shattered. Nature had claimed the rotten front porch. Clumps of hardy grasses were growing through holes in the broken floorboards and a thick layer of moss and dead leaves coated what was left of the porch.

The garden was in no better state. The deteriorating trunks and branches of long-fallen trees lay scattered about. One rested against the busted gutter of the house, an unstable ramp. If there had ever been flowers in the neat beds beneath the windows, they were long dead, replaced by rampant weeds and an out-of-control vine. In places, mostly hidden by weeds and grass, I could see stacks of broken old furniture.

'Renatus, why did you choose this place?' Lord Gawain asked, clearly very uneasy. I looked over at him, feeling sure and prepared. What was wrong now?

'It's a middle ground,' Renatus reminded him, lightly kicking at a broken brick beside his foot.

'I don't understand. Can't you feel that? This energy... It gives Lisandro strength, and makes me weak. It's death. It's darkness.'

'I know what it is,' Renatus said, turning to face Lord Gawain fully. 'It makes me strong, too.'

Lord Gawain nodded slowly in the silence that followed. I glanced between them, wondering how this would play out. The old Seer was freaked out enough about me being there; I wasn't sure he could handle this new information. His eyes changed focus as they analysed first Renatus and then me.

'It makes you both strong,' he noted. 'Your auras... are changed.'

It took a moment for my eyes to remember how to see auras, but before I could shift my focus, Renatus had already looked me over and started speaking.

'The holes are gone,' he murmured, extending his own arm and glaring at the air above his skin. I frowned.

'Holes? *My* aura has holes. Like birthmarks, Glen said.'

'So does mine,' Renatus said vaguely, turning back to Lord Gawain. 'What does it mean?'

Lord Gawain didn't answer; just snapped his head to the side and raised his wand.

'Wouldn't you just love to know?'

chapter twenty-four

Lord Gawain's breath caught. Renatus caught Aristea's arm as she jumped in fright, and yanked her backwards and behind him, blocking her from his predecessor.

If Lord Gawain had been observing Lisandro with his physical vision, he would have seen that his former friend looked as he always did, tall and impressive with his long black hair secured in its usual slick ponytail. However, looking at him through his ability to perceive energy, it was hard to remember a time he'd ever seen Lisandro like this. More powerful than usual, Lisandro seemed immensely more threatening than Lord Gawain had hoped. He felt his heart sink. Renatus had made a mistake, choosing this site.

Lord Gawain, too, had made a mistake, bringing with him the prize he had in his pocket.

On the other hand, Renatus was also overfilled with power Lord Gawain had never before seen in one person, and Aristea on her own was glowing with enough energy to take on Lisandro if only she knew how. Energetically, in terms of firepower, their side had the advantage, although, reluctant though he was to admit it, Lord Gawain's weakness here could really hurt that advantage. The energy of mass magical murder was so unhealthy and draining – no wonder nobody had ever wanted to get close enough to this virtual bombsite of darkness to clean it up and rebuild. People had tried to burgle it and take what hadn't been destroyed, but their efforts had clearly been short-lived, because the furniture and watches and other bits and pieces had been abandoned metres from the front door, lying askew all over the property.

Lisandro took a deep breath, closing his eyes as though savouring fresh mountain air.

'Thanks for choosing this spot, Renatus. Brings back memories.' He smiled fondly at the broken shell of a house behind him. 'Makes me feel like a powerhouse. I suppose you feel the same. Wouldn't you like to know why?' Lisandro asked again, staying where he was, beside the shattered front steps.

'I would,' Renatus answered eventually, guardedly.

'I can tell you what I know,' Lisandro said. 'It's a very rare phenomenon. I'm still researching exactly why *us*, but it seems to be genetic. They represent the segments that are missing from our souls.'

Aristea frowned, upset by this news, and Lord Gawain forcibly avoided looking at Renatus. *Rare... genetic... segments missing from our souls...* Could that mean...? A horrific notion had just occurred to him, but he immediately dismissed it, realising the holes in his half-baked theory. Renatus was the son of Aindréas Morrissey – he looked every bit his father's son, except for the softer features of his beautiful mother. His parentage was without doubt.

'I know it sounds bad, but I'm yet to discover a downside,' Lisandro continued. 'The dark fuels us because we have those holes. Not sure yet how or why, but when I know, I'll be sure to let you know.'

He always spoke as though everyone present were on speaking terms with one another, which was of course a part of his ruse, distracting his prey from their immediate danger by lulling them into a false sense of security. At an instant's notice, he could change.

'Thanks,' Renatus answered sarcastically. 'So you don't know anything more than I do?'

'What I know and what I suspect are two different categories, and I said I'd share what I *know*. I suspect that *I suspect* more than you do.' Lisandro smiled between the two councillors. His attention fell on Aristea and clung to her. 'How rude of me to just come in and start lecturing without even greeting everyone, and without introducing myself to your newest friend, Renatus.'

Renatus tugged Aristea a little closer, keeping her mostly hidden.

'This is Aristea, then?' Lisandro pressed, starting forward. 'I've heard so much. "Sees through illusions", Saul claimed, or so he told a mutual friend... before he was electrified.'

Lord Gawain struggled to keep an impassive expression. He couldn't give Lisandro that little victory of hurting him whenever he was reminded of the spy within the council.

'Well, don't be shy,' Lisandro coerced, smiling as he moved slowly towards Renatus and Aristea. 'I want to see you. I want to see who you look like.'

Aristea pulled against Renatus's grip, not breaking it but loosening it enough that she could step forward into Lisandro's vision.

'Who should I look like?' she demanded. Lisandro stopped to look her over. Lord Gawain knew the face he was looking for, and knew he wouldn't find it on Aristea. It was her reckless impulsiveness, her loyalty and her stubbornness that had reminded Renatus of Ana, not her face.

'Hmm,' Lisandro said, clearly realising what Lord Gawain had. 'You have replaced your sister with a beautiful apprentice, Renatus.'

Aristea flinched, probably from the explosion of anger beside her.

'I replaced nobody,' the Dark Keeper replied frigidly. Lisandro was still looking at Aristea.

'Yes, Ana was irreplaceable.'

'I'm sure you've managed just fine,' Renatus said harshly.

Lisandro ignored Renatus's remark. He gave up looking and he changed tact, looking to Lord Gawain.

'So, Renatus said there would be something of a trade to make tonight,' he said. 'I'm very surprised to see you here, actually. I really thought that this was my boy just being rebellious. I didn't think you knew anything about it. Maybe you don't. I hope you know why we're all here.'

'I do,' Lord Gawain agreed cautiously, hating Lisandro for calling Renatus *his* boy. 'I'm here to get my councillors back.'

'And I'm here to get a certain little ring of Emmanuelle's, though I see that both she and it are not present,' Lisandro commented. 'That doesn't put me at ease, boys.'

His response put Lord Gawain at ease, though. Lisandro was referring to the prize inside Lord Gawain's pocket, concealed in Emmanuelle's strongest wards, its energies hidden to all. It had been Lady Miranda's idea, and Emmanuelle was the only other one who knew of the swap. As the ring's guardian, including her was unavoidable, but her outstanding ability to produce wards had proved the decision worthwhile. Lisandro had no idea it was in his presence.

'She'll be along, once we've agreed to terms and we're happy that you'll be holding your end,' Lord Gawain assured, getting a scoff in response.

'Please!' Lisandro almost laughed. 'You really think I'll try to double-cross you? I may have done some things you don't agree with, but really. Have I ever been dishonest with you? Alright, bad example,' he backtracked with that falsely apologetic look, that easy casualness that let him slip under everyone's defences. 'Better to ask, have I ever *not* done something I said I would? I said I'd pull the council apart – I did. I told Peter I'd kill him, so I did. I said I would trade your people for the Elm Stone. So I will. Teresa and Aubrey – unharmed, mostly, and alive and intact and all that – in exchange for that ring. I have no reason to keep them after tonight. You only have one thing I want. I think it's a pretty good deal you're getting – two for one, you can't do much better.'

'How can we know you won't take it and kill them on the spot?' Lord Gawain countered. 'Or us, on that note.'

'Please,' Lisandro said again. 'I hardly have motive to do so. Killing them doesn't help my cause – it would make future transactions with the White Elm very awkward, and I don't need that extra effort. And I'm not sure I could kill all three of you simultaneously without blowing myself up in the process, so I'd have to kill you one at a time and I can see that ending badly for me, too. There's really no point in me deviating from our agreement.'

Lisandro talked a good talk, logical and honest as his words were.

'So. What exactly are your terms?' he asked now.

'First, you give us Teresa,' Renatus said, as planned, calmer now. 'Once we have her secure, we'll give you the ring. Once you're assured of its authenticity, you give us Aubrey and Shell. When they're safe, we part ways. Those are the terms.'

'Interesting terms,' Lisandro said, eyes narrowing briefly in that way of his. It was so brief that only people who knew him as well as Lord Gawain or Renatus could possibly have noticed. He was uncertain. 'Why that order?'

'Because those are the terms,' Renatus answered firmly. 'We don't even know that Teresa's alive, and the sooner we get her back from Jackson's *care* the better.'

Lord Gawain waited for Lisandro's response, hoping he didn't guess the council's motives. They had all agreed that Teresa was the priority: they had no clue where she was being held, so if Lisandro gave them Aubrey and then realised he wasn't getting the ring, he could just disappear, and their chance at finding Teresa would be lost. Aubrey was in a known location; there was a possibility of being able to storm the beach house and reclaiming him and his partner, which was Qasim's team's job, should that future eventuate.

Teresa had also apparently created an illusion for Lisandro. If they were able to recover her before Lisandro asked for the ring (and the ensuing conflict when they did not give it up) they might have a chance at disabling this illusion, whatever it was, and carrying out the second phase of their plan – to have Teresa create another fake ring.

There were so many holes in the plan, Lord Gawain knew, but he'd also seen a future in which it played out perfectly. There were just so many milestones between Now and Then, and every time a milestone was missed, that future became less and less likely.

'Fair enough.' Lisandro folded his arms and smirked. 'I agree to these terms. Jackson,' he added, turning his head to the side. Instantly, a fourth man appeared on the scene, tall, dark and bald with a wide, white smile. He was bigger, more muscular than Lisandro, and slightly younger, still in his late thirties. His arms were muscled and bared by rolled-up sleeves, and they were scooped under the knees and shoulders of an unconscious young woman.

Teresa.

Renatus's mind, connected with Lord Gawain's through the network of the White Elm, went briefly blank with horror at the scene.

'Don't you drop her,' Renatus snarled, and the Fabric of the clearing seemed to flex briefly. Aristea, whose mouth had dropped open at the sight of the arrivals, yanked on his arm, trying to bring him to his senses. He visibly struggled to get his emotions under control. Jackson smirked, but, just like Lord Gawain, it was clear that he was missing something very significant to the young scrier.

'Wasn't going to,' he answered, kneeling down to lay her at his feet. 'You good, Renatus?'

Lord Gawain looked over his most fragile young councillor, both relieved and terrified for her at once. Her knotted curly hair obscured a lot of her grimy face and her eyes were closed, but from first sight she didn't seem to have sustained any head or facial injuries. Her limbs rested at normal angles, so hopefully nothing was broken there either. Her fingertips were brown with dried blood, and many of her fingernails were broken. Her long skirt had a tear in it, revealing smeared blood on her knee and the golden chain on her ankle. Her aura was in tatters, her hope, resolve and confidence stripped away.

She was a mess, and Lord Gawain saw his planned future shrinking away. Even *if* he could get her back to the house and wake her up before

Lisandro demanded the Elm Stone, would she have the strength to recreate her best illusion to date?

'*Focáil leat*,' Renatus told Jackson forcefully; the first time in a long time that Lord Gawain had heard him speaking, or rather cursing, in Gaelic.

'Language, son,' Lisandro chided, catching his ally across the chest when Jackson made a threatening movement towards the Dark Keeper. 'That's no way to speak to the man who just brought your friend back to you!'

As satisfied as he could be with Teresa's state of health, Lord Gawain turned his attention to Jackson. Like Lisandro, the big American had hardly changed, although, it had been only six months or so since they'd last interacted. It only *seemed* like years. His aura was darker than before, frayed at the edges, tell-tale signs of wrong-doing. Unlike Lisandro (and Renatus and Aristea), Jackson wasn't relishing this darkness. It probably wasn't hurting him like it was hurting Lord Gawain, but he definitely wasn't as strong as usual.

'Don't try and tell us to be grateful,' Aristea spoke up, angrily – her outburst was enough to pull Renatus's own rage under control as he tried to keep her quiet and out of sight. 'The White Elm didn't sexually assault Saul, so there's no excuse for this. And anyway-'

Renatus covered her mouth, blocking the end of her sentence.

'Sex what?' Lisandro asked, lost. He turned to frown at Jackson, who shrugged, unfazed.

'The White Elm *incinerated* Saul, I heard,' he defended to Aristea, before adding to Lisandro, 'and it wasn't me, it was the boys. I told them to cut it out.'

'You told them to cut it out,' Lisandro repeated after a beat. 'Cut *what* out?'

'Look, I wasn't there *all* the time,' Jackson diverted carelessly. 'Anything could have happened.'

Lord Gawain tried not to scowl with disappointment. Jackson had, not long ago, been one of his White Elm brothers. Compassion had never been a strong trait of his, but this blatant disregard for a young woman's violation while in his care was repugnant. That this heartlessness could have existed in his personality all along was also frightening – how many other councillors did Lord Gawain "know"?

Lisandro was regarding Jackson with a similar expression to how Lord Gawain felt. Displeasure, maybe even bordering on contempt.

'Tell me again what you told the boys who could have done "anything" to our guest?' he prompted. Jackson looked irritated.

'To cut it out,' he said shortly. 'Wh-'

He was interrupted by his own sharp yowl of pain as he whipped his hand back quickly. Renatus and Aristea were similarly startled by the outburst, and two shimmery shields of magic sprung into existence between the pair and their enemies. Lord Gawain kept his attention on Lisandro, who was just the type to use this kind of distraction, but the previous Dark Keeper did not act on this opportunity. He only tutted condescendingly at Jackson as the other Crafter winced and sucked on a wound on the back of his hand. The skin had split open on Lisandro's mental command and a welling of blood had spilled forth from the cut, at least ten centimetres long but not very deep. Theatrics; all part of Lisandro showing the White Elm how powerful he was over his underlings in this new role of his, a show enhanced by Jackson's lack of response. No sharp words, no push or shove, no retaliation of any kind. Jackson was always quick to anger but he was unwilling to challenge Lisandro's attack on him.

'I think you and I need to have a discussion about what kind of operation we're supposed to be running here,' Lisandro told him. 'I'm not sure we're on the same page.' He turned apologetically to Lord Gawain. 'I'll investigate. In the meantime, let's get this show on the road. I think we all know each other here – except Aristea, of course,' Lisandro said, gesturing to her to direct Jackson's attention. The other glanced up at her, mouth still sealed over the skin of his hand. 'Aristea, this Jackson; Jackson, that's Aristea. She's Renatus's apprentice.'

'Pleasure.' Jackson checked his hand and confirmed to himself that the injury, though no doubt smarting, was only superficial and wasn't even bleeding enough to develop into droplets. He bowed theatrically. He eyed the teenager when she didn't react. 'Something wrong, pretty?'

Aristea was ignoring him totally. She had just nodded vehemently at her master, though neither of them had spoken aloud.

She says Teresa has no feelings, Renatus told Lord Gawain. *Even sleeping people have emotions*.

'You don't get to talk to her,' the Dark Keeper informed Jackson crisply. 'Elijah is coming for Teresa. We expect that he can come and go without interference.'

'Like we could stop *him* if we wanted to,' Lisandro agreed jovially. 'Call him, take the girl, sounds like she deserves the escape; but then, we expect to see Emmanuelle and the Stone.'

Fragments of possible futures streamed through Lord Gawain's mind, but for the most part he ignored them. Maybes, potentials... No certainty yet. Except the haunting image of Renatus's long fingers dropping the ring into Lisandro's open palm. It had not yet been avoided, but at least Lisandro still thought Emmanuelle had the ring, which was relieving, because it was necessary that he believe this in order for the White Elm's plan to work.

Something's off.

Lord Gawain heard Renatus's comment but called for Elijah anyway. A lot was off – the whole situation was wrong – but without specifics it was hard to do anything about it.

Elijah appeared exactly at Lord Gawain's side with the kind of stillness and suddenness that only natural Displacers could manage. They didn't need to take steps or walk through gaps in the Fabric. They had a level of control that allowed them to pull the gaps in the Fabric *to them*. It was the truest form of teleportation.

'Elijah.' Lisandro greeted the New Zealander with genuine cheer. Everybody liked Elijah, whether they were on the same side or not. 'We meet again, and so soon.'

'Apparently we do,' Elijah agreed, coolly, stepping forward to get a closer look at Teresa. She lay still at Jackson's feet, her chest rising and falling very slowly and shallowly. What could have happened to nullify her emotions? Trauma? Or was this a side-effect of her spell-induced sleep? Elijah met Jackson's eyes. 'Back up, will you?'

'Why? Scared?' Jackson laughed, but stepped back at a look from Lisandro.

'Oh, yes,' Elijah said sarcastically. 'Very scared, of an ex junior councillor.'

Jackson folded his arms moodily as Elijah knelt by Teresa. In the days when Jackson had still belonged to the White Elm, his place had been the position immediately below the Displacer.

Renatus's hand visibly tightened on Aristea's arm.

Master, we're being fucked.

It was only Lord Gawain's determination not to sound like Lisandro that prevented him from calling Renatus up on his language choices tonight.

Look, Renatus added, *look what she saw*, and shared the vision that was the source of his stress. An image of Teresa, fading in and out against various other images, the chain around her ankle... The high, narrow windows, like she was partly underground... Her grubby cheek... Broken fingernails... The heavy door, locked... The other side of that door, some kind of abandoned basement... The dirty concrete steps up and out... A concrete slab, the remainder of a house long ago knocked down... The shattered tree stump...

The image was blocked abruptly by what looked like a dark wash of sudden heavy rain. Aristea, from whom the vision was evidently coming, shook her head determinedly.

'No. That's... not right. That can't be it,' she insisted, looking up at Renatus. 'The whole thing was meant to be cleared.'

Lord Gawain realised with a slightly sick feeling exactly where Teresa was held, the real Teresa, because that was why the woman that Elijah was gathering up lacked feelings... *She* was Teresa's illusion. Lisandro was trying to do exactly as they'd planned to do and trade in a ghost. It would have worked, too, were it not for luck and Aristea's unusual gifts. Lord Gawain watched as Elijah stood with Teresa cradled in his arms, saw the way every strand of hair fell naturally across her face, the way her arm swung as Elijah moved and the way the slack in the anklet hung towards the ground, doing exactly as gravity asked. And he'd thought the false ring was her best work. He opened his mind to Elijah.

Don't react, but that's not the real Teresa. Take it to Lady Miranda in case he's watching you, then go to-

'My house,' Aristea murmured, upset. 'You've been using my old house as a prison?'

'She's not slow, is she, Renatus?' Lisandro said, apparently impressed. Elijah and the illusion seemed to evaporate on the spot, gone.

'You had no right!' Aristea exclaimed, her voice and temper rising.

'It suited the purpose,' Lisandro asserted, smiling at Lord Gawain. 'Aristea's place feels like this place. Nasty, isn't it, the way it makes you feel, old man? Tired, weak, queasy…' He smirked and turned back to the girl. 'You forget, Aristea, how completely *yuck* this delicious dark energy feels to normal people. Mortals hate it. They cleared the house itself because it was unsafe, but even the people *paid* to be there couldn't stand the worksite, so they left the foundations… including your old basement.'

Go, Lord Gawain told Glen, hoping it was the right thing to do.

'A bit like this place,' Lisandro continued, turning to admire the old wreck of a house. 'It does have an interesting history. A family used to live here, quite a nice family, probably – Kenneth Hawke, and his wife and their child. I suppose that name sounds familiar?'

He was speaking to Renatus, but the name rang a bell for Lord Gawain, too. He couldn't for the life of him place it, though.

'Kenneth Hawke was Ana's godfather,' Renatus said after a moment. 'I never met him.'

'You never will.' Lisandro tipped his head towards the house, drawing attention to its destruction. 'Mother Nature dealt to him, too.'

Another storm, another witch family gone. Lord Gawain let his eyes drift over the shell of a house, thinking briefly of the storm at Morrissey House.

'So, does that make you next?' Renatus asked Lisandro. 'Karma seems to be taking its time.'

'Me, next? I hope not,' Lisandro answered, looking briefly confronted by the idea.

Aristea was still scrying, and Renatus was streaming it straight to Lord Gawain.

Teresa, filthy and barefoot, sitting against a wall, grinding at the anklet with a stone... Making no progress... Outside the door, Elijah is already there, working on removing the enchantments blocking everything, from noise to intruders, from reaching her... A brief conflict outside... Feet on the concrete steps... Susannah, then Glen... 'What have we got?'... Anouk follows closely, dabbing a cut across her face with tentative fingertips... 'A bit of everything, I think.'... Teresa, inside, continues with her impossible task, oblivious...

'So, you have your girl,' Lisandro said now, when no one responded. 'I believe that your terms dictate that I should get my ring now.'

That ideal future was dissolving as quickly as the events that would have made it possible were missed. If only they could get Teresa out of that basement, away from that draining energy and remove from her ankle the forsaken chain designed to cut her off from her magic, they could get a false Elm Stone from her and complete their original plan. She was conscious, at least, which was a step up from the illusionary Teresa, but not necessarily in any better state for creating convincing illusions.

Elijah and Anouk carefully but quickly dismantle layer after layer of magic... Lady Miranda arrives from scouting the property... 'There's magic lying around like cobwebs, but no illusions, except the one I left on the ground. I can't believe it's not really her'... She heals Anouk's face with a touch...

'Elijah and Lady Miranda are taking her up to the house.' A lie, but not one that registered because Renatus didn't consider it one and because in the near future they probably *would* be doing exactly as he said. 'You remember what a walk that is. What's the hurry?'

Renatus frowned and his godfather smiled.

'Just eager to get my new toy, son,' he said pleasantly.

'Why? Whose lives are you going to ruin with it?' Renatus pulled Aristea minutely closer.

'That's really not my intention for that ring, and besides, I don't need it for that. I'm quite capable of dealing with my problems without delving into the savings account.' Lisandro delicately brushed an escaped lock of long black hair behind his ear. 'It would be such a waste of that ring's potential.'

'What do you want it for?' Renatus asked, and Lisandro shook his head.

'Son, that's a secret, and not my secret to tell you, although often I wish I could. Things might be easier if you knew.'

'So tell me,' Renatus tried.

'I told you, I can't. Not my secret. Now... if you will.'

Glen slices through another spell... Inside, Teresa looks up suddenly as their muffled voices become audible... 'I've nearly got this one... Glen, can you take care of the ward crossing the end of it?'... Teresa stands... Anouk waits for

Glen to remove the spell pinning down the one she is working on and then dissolves it... 'Got it. Which one have you got?'... Teresa hurries to the door and begins to shout... 'Help! Help, I'm in here!'... Outside, the more senior members of the council pause... They continue, faster now...

Maybe, just maybe, it could all still work out. Maybe they'd get her out before Lisandro or Jackson noticed. Maybe she'd have the strength to cast the illusion they needed. Maybe Lisandro would fall for it. Maybe he really would release Aubrey and Shell to them, or maybe he wouldn't, but maybe Qasim's taskforce would successfully seize the beach house and evacuate the pair safely while Lord Gawain and Renatus did battle with Lisandro and Jackson. Maybe tonight really would be the end of all this, with Lisandro and Jackson killed or otherwise incapacitated.

And Renatus ruined.

Teresa, standing at her door, shouting... 'Help!'... Glen, Elijah and Anouk on the other side, wands carefully, delicately, precisely picking apart dozens of spells... 'This one's stuck!'... Glen pauses, waiting for one of the others to lift the spells above his... 'Thanks'... Teresa smacks her hands on the door, frustrated that she cannot help... She shrieks and jumps backwards, cradling her hands against herself... Palms burnt... Anouk freezes, hearing the sound... 'Teresa?'... 'Don't... Don't touch the door! It's cursed!'...

Lord Gawain turned his attention away from Aristea's vision and looked instead to the futures, which were shifting once again. The window for success in their original plan was almost closed, but another path was writing itself.

'Call Emmanuelle,' Jackson commanded, the eager look in his eye chilling Lord Gawain. What was Jackson's fixation with Emmanuelle? Could it interfere with the plan? It had been apparent when she'd first joined the council that he was attracted to her, as was the case with most men when they first saw her, but she'd not accepted the advances and Lord Gawain had assumed it had ended there. Apparently for Jackson it had not.

'Call her,' Jackson repeated. The future was opening up for Lord Gawain, not all of it pleasing, but its result was his goal – all White Elm, Aristea and Shell out alive.

The maybes were gone. This was the way. This was the only way.

Lord... Emmanuelle just disappeared without a word, Qasim said uncertainly. *Elijah came for Jadon and then she went too. Did you call for her already?*

'I did,' Renatus insisted, but Lord Gawain knew he hadn't.

'Hold on, just one second,' Lisandro said, raising a hand as he began to pace before them. 'Forgive me for my suspiciousness, but really? What's taking her so long? Am I detecting the scent of White Elm treachery here?'

'This is coming from the man who gave us an illusion in place of our councillor,' Renatus commented coldly. Lisandro paused in his pacing, right in front of Renatus, and shrugged sheepishly.

'Touché,' he agreed. 'Caught me. I guess that's game over, huh?'

chapter twenty-five

Connected to Renatus through our minds and physically where he held my arm, I had access to everything he scried and he saw everything I got.

I was really wishing at this point that I'd not been such a stubborn, stupid girl, insistent that I had some right to be here or that I really had any good reason to be here, because now I was ridiculously scared. Both Lisandro and Jackson were clearly great sorcerers who could wipe me out in a blink and probably wouldn't hesitate to do so if given half a chance. Their confidence scared me, too. Anyone who could stand opposite Renatus with no fear was someone *I* should fear, I thought.

Elijah unpicks a spell and stands back... Anouk and Glen struggle briefly with the last one... 'That's it! Remember, don't touch the door'... Anouk points her wand at the handle and attempts a spell... It is unsuccessful... 'How do we get through?'... Teresa, blowing gently on her hands to test their sensitivity... Lady Miranda, on the other side of the door, tries another spell... Nothing happens... Elijah disappears... Susannah throws a ball of power at the door... Sparks fly, everyone ducks their faces... No change... Elijah returns, his hand on Jadon's shoulder... 'I thought we could use some firepower'... Glen and Anouk stand back... Jadon stares at the door... 'Is she in there?'... Teresa looks up at the sound of his voice... 'Is that

Jadon?'... Emmanuelle hurries down the stairs and pauses at the bottom... 'I need that ring!'... Susannah's grim smile... 'The window's closed on that one. Time to think of a plan B'...

'Call Emmanuelle,' Jackson said in a commanding tone, and repeated himself a moment later. I inched closer to Renatus, too scared to be angry with myself. *Dumb, dumb, dumb...* I shouldn't be here! I inhaled deeply, trying to get a grip. Two of the greatest sorcerers in the world were here with me, and Emmanuelle was on her way. Things were, doubtless, about to get messy, but if they were, I couldn't think of three people I'd prefer to have around me, except maybe Qasim.

'I did,' Renatus said, while Lord Gawain looked to the side, as many of them often did when communicating telepathically. He looked worried.

Lisandro had begun to pace before us, but now raised a hand in a "stop" gesture.

'Hold on, just one second,' he said. 'Forgive me for my suspiciousness, but really? What's taking her so long? Am I detecting the scent of White Elm treachery here?'

Oh god, oh god, he knew! I barely recalled the plan but I knew it depended on some sort of trickery, a bit similar to the way he'd just tried to trick us with the fake Teresa. It had taken me several minutes to work out that she wasn't real, because she'd *looked* exactly like a sleeping person. She'd even given the illusion its own aura and energy. Teresa was officially the most incredible, most talented witch on the White Elm if *that* fell within the range of her abilities.

In my constant stream from the basement – *my old basement* – I saw all of the older councillors shield their faces as Jadon's spell blasted through the door. And so I think I was the only person who saw that when Jadon pulled Teresa into his arms, and she threw her arms around him, and she went to hurriedly kiss his cheek, and he turned his face to kiss her cheek, their lips met accidentally. Before either of them could think better of it, Jadon pushed closer, deepening the kiss so it was unmistakeably *that* and not something so brief and vague that they could pretend it never happened.

Both open their eyes... They step back from each other abruptly, evidently surprised... Lady Miranda enters... She saw nothing... 'Are you alright?'... Teresa turns to her... Relief... 'Aubrey? Have you got Aubrey?'... 'We need you to-'... 'They made me replicate us both. Lisandro can power the illusions without me so I have no connection to it. It could last and last and I wouldn't know'... Concern... 'Where's the real Aubrey?'... 'I don't know. He could be dead'...

'This is coming from the man who gave us an illusion in place of our councillor,' Renatus rebuked coldly. Lisandro's pacing paused, right in front of us. He shrugged, sheepishly.

'Touché,' he agreed. 'Caught me. I guess that's game over, huh?'

He was so quick. He feinted towards Lord Gawain; Renatus read his body language and stepped forward to block him, but Lisandro had already changed tact, much too quickly, and was moving back the other way, towards me. I had lost focus on my wards and they had lost their power. Renatus realised half a moment too late, and I felt his panic as he reached for my arm. I didn't know what was happening until I felt fingers wrap around my wrist and a sharp pain in my elbow as I was spun around, my arm was twisted upwards behind my back. I think I called out Renatus's name but I couldn't be sure. I stumbled a little as I was yanked backwards, and then I was against a body I couldn't see, with a hand around my neck and Renatus standing in front of me with a tiny glint of horror in his eyes.

Lisandro had me.

My instinct was to throw a deflective ward out around myself, but it never materialised. I tried again, heart beating wildly. Nothing. My powers were neutralised. I grabbed at the forearm across my shoulder with my free hand but didn't have the strength to pull it away. I was useless.

An instant later, Renatus had his wand out and pointed past my face at Lisandro's throat. It took a whole, massive, loaded second for me to realise what a dire situation this was.

I was between two angry, driven super-sorcerers. I was about to die.

'No!' I pleaded, wrenching forward to no effect. 'No, don't!'

'*Stop!*'

Everyone froze for an instant, processing the command from the unexpected voice. Emmanuelle strode over, hands out.

'Too far, Lisandro,' Renatus snarled. Behind him, I could see Lord Gawain with his wand out, too, looking between the Dark Keeper and his predecessor. He looked like he wasn't sure what to be scared of.

I knew what to be scared of. I was the new hostage. I was in danger. I'd told Hiroko I'd be fine, but I'd lied. I wasn't fine. I was the furthest thing from it.

Help me, I begged Renatus, our telepathic link the only thing I still had control over. I wished I sounded less pathetic but I was so frightened. *Please, please, don't let him hurt me! I'm sorry, so sorry, for making you bring me...*

Renatus shook his head. He seemed unable to articulate what was going through his head. It would have been difficult. I heard mostly curses and incoherent threats. I closed my eyes, realising fully what position the White Elm was now in. It was me or the ring. My death or maybe fifty deaths. How could I possibly ask them to pick me? Even if Lisandro wasn't going to use it to commit mass murder – what use could he possibly have in mind that was *preferable* to the loss of one little person? And I was just one little person. One little nobody.

Lisandro tapped his fingertips on the skin of my neck like he was tapping on a steering wheel. I shuddered.

'Maybe, but we'll see whether this approach gets results,' Lisandro said cheerily. His hand was not tight around my throat, but the idea that he could choke me and didn't even seem like the sort of person who would be terribly remorseful kept me in a heightened state of panic. I struggled, leaning away, but he pulled my wrist higher behind my back and beneath his hands, my skin seared. I gasped and Renatus's eyes flicked to me briefly. The skin of my neck and on my wrist, wherever Lisandro's skin had contact with mine, heated up quickly to the point of stinging, and then the pain would slowly recede, the way it felt to touch a hotplate or to catch your fingers under the hot tap unexpectedly.

He was *burning me*.

'Don't hurt her,' Lord Gawain called. 'You're burning her. She's just a child.'

'Whose stupid fault was it to bring *a child* along?' Jackson sneered.

I'd been so stupid. I'd screwed up. I was going to die. I'd never been this afraid before.

'Let. Her. Go.' The crystal in the end of Renatus's wand was glowing, pent up with energy. I tried again to pull away, and my neck burned. I yelped, pitifully, and Renatus snapped at me, 'Don't move.'

Like I could move even if I wanted to!

'Yes, sweetheart, don't move,' Lisandro agreed, massaging my neck, fingers rubbing over the raw-feeling skin he'd just burnt, reactivating the pain. I flinched and tried to lean away. The motion upset Renatus more than it upset me – he was losing it. I could see it in the way his expression contorted and his aura fluctuated. 'Surprisingly, I like having you this close.'

'Let go of her,' Renatus commanded, his voice tense, ground out like stones underfoot.

'You're too young for me, obviously,' Lisandro went on behind me, clear and confident voice in my ear, sending shivers down my spine, 'but the reaction your absence sparks in my boy Renatus is an attraction all in itself. Maybe I can get past the age thing.'

'I'll kill you!' Renatus shouted. Enraged, frustrated, the glow of his wand's crystal tip swelled in brightness and either side of us I heard a swift cracking and bursting sound. I squeezed my eyes shut against the shower of shards that pelted us from the three rocks Renatus had just exploded around the clearing. Just barely, he contained himself from directing this same destructive energy through the wand and into Lisandro, where it would surely give similar results; both Lord Gawain and Emmanuelle shouted his name, a warning.

'Don't try it, Renatus,' Lord Gawain begged. 'You know you can't control yourself. You could kill us all.'

'I can control it.'

I heard the conviction in his voice and I believed him.

Do it.

'Renatus, calm down,' Emmanuelle instructed, firmly like always. She moved closer to the rest of us. 'I'm sure this can be resolved easily. 'e just wants 'is stupid ring.'

'Finally, somebody sensible arrives on set,' Lisandro said with exaggerated relief. 'Do you have it?'

'What do you think?'

'I've been looking forward to seeing you again,' Jackson mentioned. 'I've been looking for you.'

'Is that supposed to be flattering?' She rolled her eyes and turned back to Lisandro. All eyes went to Emmanuelle's hand as she slid the plain old ring from her thumb. It positively glowed with power. She held it up.

'I'm afraid I need you to assure me of the girl's safety,' she said. 'I've sworn oaths that would force me into battle with you if you 'urt 'er.'

Thank you, thank you... Emmanuelle was here, she had the fake, and we were all going to go home, safe and sound... The White Elm now outnumbered Lisandro's side.

'Naturally, I'll have no reason to hurt her if I have my Stone,' Lisandro agreed. He uncurled his fingers from my neck and extended that hand. The French sorceress eyed him.

'You killed Peter.'

'Yes. I'm sorry for the way that hurt you. It was just business. It's what happens to people who try to cross me.'

Emmanuelle's eyes slid from his face to mine and then back. She tossed the ring to Jackson.

'It's a fake,' she said abruptly, and looked over her shoulder at the White Elm leader. 'Lord Gawain 'as the real one.'

The moment following was still and silent. Renatus slowly turned his head to stare at Emmanuelle, anger simmering away in light of shock; Lisandro blinked; my mind was in overdrive. I didn't remember this part of the plan.

'Emmanuelle...' Lord Gawain murmured finally, and a huge smile spread across Lisandro's face.

'That'a girl,' he said affectionately. 'Trying to trick me, was he?'

'Trying to,' Emmanuelle confirmed. Without expression she met Renatus's accusing gaze, and from the look on his face and the thoughts flying about his head, I knew that this was not part of any plan he was aware of.

'Em, what the hell are you doing?' he demanded. 'You said-'

'I said a lot of things, and so 'ave you,' she replied shortly. She pressed a hand against his cheek; his face contorted with hurt and fury. 'Don't even try. You're not getting back into my 'ead while you're in this mood.'

She'd blocked him from her thoughts, I gathered. I was so scared, and in such a panic from the pain, that I couldn't think of a reasonable excuse for this. Why would she want to hide something in her head from Renatus?

Because...

Because the impossible had proven true.

Grey, swirling skies... Thunder crashing...

I squeezed my eyes shut. How could I think about stuff like that while I was trapped here? Was it a weird trauma thing? Think back to the last time you were genuinely afraid for your life, and this awful situation might not seem so bad?

A gentle breeze lifted the ends of my loose hair. For the weather to change now would really just ruin what remained of my spirits.

'You bitch,' Renatus spat, and I opened my eyes. Emmanuelle grabbed him by the back of the neck to yank him close, and whispered in his ear, loud enough for us all to hear.

'As usual,' she purred, 'I am misunderstood.'

She shoved him away, pushing him several steps away from Lisandro and me. My stomach clenched. I wanted him back, close to me. Two days ago I'd stood with my supervisor at Renatus's trial, trusting *her* to keep me safe from my master, but now I needed the reverse. Emmanuelle, beautiful, strong Emmanuelle, my hero, was the danger. We'd all misunderstood her.

Flashes of lightning... Branches torn from trees...

Go away, traumatic memories.

'Emmanuelle, you little treasure,' Lisandro said, 'would it be too much to ask to get your assistance in removing the Elm Stone from Lord Gawain's custody?'

'I don't think so,' the Healer answered. I swallowed, afraid and confused. What was she going to do? Was there going to be a fight? The idea of Emmanuelle attacking the elderly Seer was revolting; the knowledge that Renatus would defend his leader with all he was, against anyone, and that Emmanuelle couldn't possibly survive this and that I would watch her die tonight, was too much. I pulled against Lisandro's grasp and was rewarded for my disobedience with a brief burn.

'Emmanuelle,' I cried, desperately. She'd supported my decision to join with Renatus, she'd been to my sister's house, she'd taken part in my initiation and only cut me a little bit, and healed me straight after. But the attacks for the ring didn't begin until *Emmanuelle* came to obtain it; she was present when Teresa and Aubrey were taken and Jackson had asked for her; the White Elm prankster upsetting the council's allies had cursed in French. Lisandro had claimed she was his *type*. Her name had come up almost as often as Renatus's but it hadn't been taken seriously. I couldn't believe it. 'Emmanuelle, don't!'

I screamed as Lisandro's hand began to burn again, and my skin blistered and seared. I clawed at his fingers but they were like vices, unmoveable.

'Stop,' Renatus demanded. It didn't. I kicked backwards and hit a shin. It didn't seem to have any effect. 'Stop! Emmanuelle!'

'Renatus, the damage isn't-'

'I don't care! Just stop him!'

'I don't take orders from pretty French girls,' Lisandro said, tightening his hold on me. I went still. The burn died away but the stinging remained. My heart thudded and my breaths came hard, fast and erratic. Emmanuelle turned back to him, hand on hip.

'Maybe for tonight you can make an exception.'

'Emmanuelle, are you the spy?' I asked. I tried to keep back the tears. The heat in my skin hurt, all over my neck, on that wrist, everywhere Lisandro had touched.

'Shh,' she replied. To Lisandro she said, 'You're treading very close to the edge of my patience. I told you, I took oaths. I can't stand by and watch you 'urt 'er.' She was taller than me, and leaned down a little to look me in the eyes. She reached out and stroked the side of my face, ignoring my attempts to pull away in horror. 'I'm quite fond of 'er. Will we be taking 'er with us?'

'You wouldn't dare,' Renatus retorted. He was standing back where Emmanuelle had pushed him, wand still aimed at Lisandro but inert, afraid of making another sudden move now that his allies had been halved and things were less certain.

Emmanuelle's words finally processed in my brain. Taking? Me?

'No!' I shouted, and sobbed tearlessly as the burning started back up and the anxiety inside me swelled. The physical pain, at least, stopped almost immediately, and Emmanuelle's voice was in my ear, her hand still on my cheek.

'Aristea, be still,' she advised, looking me in the face. I couldn't believe this was happening, or that she still looked on me with concern or care. 'Don't make this any worse for yourself.'

She withdrew her hand, and it felt like she took something with her, although I couldn't imagine what. My hope? My faith in my own instincts, because I'd trusted her so implicitly?

'I suppose we will,' Lisandro said eventually, 'but I think before we steal a treasure from each Renatus and Gawain, Gawain at least should know what's going on here.'

'He's not the only one confused,' Jackson agreed. Emmanuelle ignored him and looked to the council leader.

'Lisandro 'as Aubrey,' she said simply. 'I want my cousin back alive. This was the only way. *N'est-ce pas?*'

Lord Gawain nodded once, almost imperceptibly. He reached into his jacket and withdrew a misshapen, pearlescent blob. It completely lacked energy. I knew it had to be the ring, wrapped in wards and spells to keep it safe and hidden.

'Take me to Aubrey,' Emmanuelle told Jackson, 'while Lisandro finishes up 'ere. We can take Aristea with us, too.'

'Done,' Jackson agreed, extending a hand to her. She gave it a disgusted look but took it anyway, and Jackson smirked at Lisandro. 'Should we take the kid, or do you want to hold onto her until you're done here?'

'Give 'er to me,' Emmanuelle said in her usual instructional tone, flicking her fingers authoritatively at Lisandro. Demanding he hand me over. Like I was a *thing*. 'Jackson and I will get 'er away from 'ere, where Renatus can't snatch 'er back.'

'She's not going anywhere with you!' Renatus contended, so angry but so helpless. He could have blasted Lisandro away, I knew it, but he wouldn't because he was afraid of overdoing it and hurting me. I wished he wouldn't think so hard, because I was already hurting and I couldn't imagine him managing to worsen my situation.

'Renatus, for once, just *shut up*,' Emmanuelle ordered.

'You can't take her away from me!' My master was adamant, furious.

'*Tais-toi!*'

'Renatus…' Lord Gawain called, resignedly, but it went unheeded.

Frustrated, Renatus turned his wand on Emmanuelle. 'What are you doing? Answer me!'

'Don't point that at me,' she snapped, shoving it away with her free hand. 'I told you, forget about getting inside my head until you've calmed down, and then maybe, we'll talk again.' She shot Lisandro an impatient look. 'Come on. Give 'er to me. Let's do this.'

No, no, no… The former Dark Keeper stared at her for a long moment.

Wind whipping leaves from trees… Sharp raindrops pelt the family as they streak towards the little house…

The breeze I thought I'd felt earlier had definitely picked up. I could see Renatus's long dark hair rustling in the wind, and Emmanuelle's very long golden hair reflected the clearing's artificial light as it moved about.

'To answer your earlier question,' Lisandro said kindly to me, finally, 'no, Emmanuelle was not my informant, so I'm just as confused as everyone else. Dear Emmy, I think it's time you explain yourself.'

That awkward silence was back. Emmanuelle was the first to recover from the shocking revelation.

'Your spy and I go a long way back,' she said finally. 'Perhaps further back than you realise. I was brought onboard a few months ago.'

'Oh, I know exactly how far back you two go,' Lisandro countered. 'I find it hard to believe he wouldn't tell me something as significant as *you* signing up.'

I hadn't moved but I was breathing like I'd just sprinted to the road. Emmanuelle wasn't the spy – the spy was male – so what the hell was she doing?

''e doesn't *belong* to you,' she scoffed. 'We're White Elm first. There's a certain degree of self-respect linked to that, and it doesn't just *go away*. We're our own people, even if we 'appen to agree with you. Not everyone is like Jackson.'

The black giant looked taken aback, not sure how to take her comment. Lisandro paused for another long moment.

'Divide and conquer, was it?' he asked. 'Separate me from my back-up, take my leverage, team up with her at the destination to overpower Jackson?'

Emmanuelle looked for a long time like she wasn't going to answer. She held his gaze over my shoulder without falter. When she did speak, it wasn't with shame or hesitation.

'More or less.'

Lord Gawain closed his eyes. I held Renatus's gaze, the restrictive feeling of panic around my chest loosening slightly at this news.

Emmanuelle's not the spy, she's playing a part, she's not the enemy.

'So you're another Peter,' Lisandro said, shaking his head. 'I should have known. No wonder he left the ring with you; no wonder he died still infatuated with you. Another idealist, and quite the actress. I nearly bought that. Why do you have to make things so hard?' He sighed, running a hand along my arm.

568

My throat began to burn again, and wherever his hand went, my sleeve burnt away and my skin began to redden and blister. It *stung*. I couldn't hold in the sound of my pain.

'No!' I screamed, trying with all my physical strength to pull away. It was worthless. I was just a kid, tall but skinny and weak and Lisandro was bigger, stronger, older, and I was hurting. Nowhere I wriggled or writhed to gave me an escape. I choked on a breathless cry.

Trees bent unnaturally in deadly winds... Rain slashing at windows... Frightened faces inside...

'No, stop it!' I shrieked. Panic was drowning me. 'Stop it, stop it, it hurts!'

'Just stop!' Renatus's voice sounded shattered. 'She's not yours!'

'I told you to leave 'er,' Emmanuelle said angrily. She ripped her hand out of Jackson's, and Jackson was knocked from his feet by an unseen force as she rounded us to stand at Renatus's side. My master seemed bolstered by her returned presence and squared his shoulders.

'You say a lot of things,' Lisandro reminded her, moving his hand from my neck to my chest, immediately above my heart. 'As do I.'

His hand grew warm. My thudding heartbeat noticeably shuddered and my next breath caught.

'No, stop!' Lord Gawain shouted, hurrying forward. 'Don't. Don't kill her. It's not worth all that.'

Kill me?!

'Finally. Progress.' Lisandro's hand slid back to my neck. My injuries still stung like crazy, but the damage was done and wasn't, at present, being worsened.

'Are you sure now? Sure you don't need to put the kid through any more before you make up your mind?' Jackson asked snidely as he got to his feet. Lord Gawain stepped forward. He looked so old and so tired.

'He's a Seer, Jackson,' Lisandro reminded his friend. 'Of course he's sure.'

'I'm not sure that it's the right thing to do,' Lord Gawain admitted, holding the blob out while Emmanuelle carelessly unwound dozens of different wards from it. Slowly, its incredible power became apparent, even from this distance. 'I just...'

'You don't want to see Renatus lose something else precious to me?' Lisandro guessed. He smiled apologetically at Renatus. 'I have been quite an irresponsible guardian, I suppose. I've taken much more than I've given.'

'*Let her go*,' Renatus said through gritted teeth. Any second now, I half-expected him to actually pounce on his godfather and tear him to shreds with his hands.

'You seem genuinely worried about her, Renatus,' Lisandro noted. He looked over at Lord Gawain. 'Did you know he had the capacity to care this much? Is that why you kept him in the first place? Or are you just realising now, and feeling guilty because you've always thought him cold and heartless? Is that why you were able to suspect your favourite little boy of being my puppet?'

Lord Gawain just shook his head.

'Lisandro, let her go,' he requested, bordering on begging but not quite. 'She has nothing to do with this. Your problem is with me.'

'Too true,' Lisandro agreed, releasing my arm from behind my back to extend his hand for the ring. One dangerous hand still around my throat, I dared not move.

Trees uprooted... One life lost... Regret...

It suddenly occurred to me that *his hand was on my skin.* I'd been trying to block the confronting memory of the storm, something I'd not had to deal with since living at Morrissey House because I hadn't dreamt about it, but now it crashed over me in full force, like a vision scried from Renatus. Except this wasn't from Renatus, and it wasn't from me, either. I was scrying from Lisandro.

Branches smashing windows... Screaming... A life extinguished...

Storms brewing... Lisandro, standing on the roadside, guiding the storm with his hands... Face grim... Regretful...

Lisandro at the beach house... Waves buffeting the walls... Thunder rumbling... A death, such a waste... My mother's death...

And then I knew.

Lord Gawain gave the ring to Renatus.

'It's meant to be you,' he said, defeated. 'You give it to him.'

My first instinct was to cast a ward around my body to push Lisandro away, but as soon as I did that I recalled that he'd neutralised my magic. So I was immensely surprised when it worked. As

Renatus dropped the Elm Stone into Lisandro's waiting hand, my magic burst from me, pushing Lisandro's body forcibly from mine, briefly unsteadying my captor. Just barely, his fingertips remained on my throat. My neck burned severely as a punishment, and I screamed, but it was as much from anger and grief as it was from pain.

'Renatus, it was him!' I shouted, scratching at the hand with my sharp short nails as it regained its grip around my throat. 'He made the storms! He killed them!' The burn intensified and I could barely speak over my own screaming. Did my neck have any skin left? Did it even matter? 'You killed my family!'

Lisandro's fingers closed over the ring in his palm.

'Thanks,' he said cheerfully, and dimly, I felt an opening in the Fabric.

'No!' I struggled and fought and wrenched away with all my weight but Lisandro had only to step to one side to move through the wormhole and pull me with him. Emmanuelle reached for my master's hand and Lord Gawain disappeared. I saw the fear in Renatus's eyes. He was losing me. He was losing me and he wasn't able to stop it. *I* was being lost.

Then *I* was no longer there.

chapter twenty-six

When my shoes hit wooden floorboards, I became aware of two things at once. The first was my new surroundings. I was in a dingy, sparsely furnished bedroom with just Lisandro for company. The second thing I noticed was the lack of restriction on my power. Lisandro's spells were gone. That was why my ward had worked. I realised that this was what Emmanuelle had taken away when she'd touched my face.

How could I have suspected her? She'd just risked her life for me – risked being killed as a traitor by Renatus, not to mention the risk she'd taken by lying to Lisandro – and constructed this whole farce just to get close enough to me to disable Lisandro's magic and get me out of that clearing.

On impulse I gathered together all the magic I could and a force field burst from me, bigger than before. The hand released my neck and I turned quickly as Lisandro was blasted backwards and into the wall behind him. I raised my hands and a pearly mushroom ward formed, protecting me from pretty much anything, I was sure.

Lisandro had to grasp at the wall behind him to avoid stumbling to the floor, and I felt a surge of satisfaction when he looked up at me with honest surprise. He'd not expected a fight from me.

'Stay back,' I ordered. My voice was so strong, but inside I was quaking. Why had he brought me here, to the beach house? To kill me? To hide me?

'Aristea, you-' he began, in that easy, casual tone of his, but I wasn't interested in hearing his next line.

'Don't move,' I interrupted, unsure how I would enforce that. He slowly got to his feet and stepped away from the wall. He was thinking the same thing. He didn't think I would know enough magic to be able to protect myself, and he wasn't far wrong. With a lurch of my stomach, I realised that I didn't know any offensive magic at all.

'You killed my family,' I confirmed with Lisandro, struggling with this new information. 'My mother, my father... My brother. You killed them. And you killed Renatus's whole family, and that Hawke family?'

'Those were all accidents, I heard,' Lisandro said loftily, though a strange tone in his voice told me he hadn't wanted all of this to come up. 'Bad weather. How could it have been anything to do with me?'

'That's just it. You can't have done it. Weather control is...' Unimaginable. Incredible. 'Ridiculous. No one can choose the weather.'

'No one?' His eyes glittered as he smiled, unable to help himself from teasing, from playing with me. He didn't need to glance at my still-throbbing, still-stinging neck to remind me of what his other capabilities were. I was alone here with him, all alone, with only a thin thread of consciousness joining me to Renatus, and I was barely aware of that right now, so focussed was I on what was happening here in this little room.

'It's impossible,' I said, adamant, then, less certainly, 'but you were *there*. I saw you there, watching each storm... Guiding the clouds...' The vision I'd channelled from him was still clear in my mind, and I knew I was telling the truth. 'I know you did it.'

'Then perhaps I did,' Lisandro replied. Nothing seemed to faze or distress him. He scared me. I kept my ward up, trying to control at least my wild imagination, since I couldn't control anything else about my situation.

'You can't have done the Morrissey storm. You were with Lord Gawain when the Morrisseys died,' I insisted, shaking my head, trying to be reasonable. 'Renatus told me.'

'Ever preset a VCR to tape a show? Maybe you're a little young for that technology... Still, same deal. The Morrisseys were organised well in advance. Only way I was going to be able to make myself do that one. Yours, on the other hand,' Lisandro added to me, delicately running fingers through the ends of his ponytail, 'was an impulse thing. Easy. Didn't hurt at all.'

I was too numb to feel pain at that remark.

'Renatus said you cried when you saw the damage the storm had done to Morrissey Estate,' I remembered. 'It hurt you.'

'They were my family, too,' Lisandro agreed, his voice soft.

'They loved you.'

'I loved them. But it was necessary. Sometimes you have to choose between what you *love*, and what you love. It's not an easy choice to make. After tonight, though, with this ring, it'll finally be worthwhile.'

'You found it in your heart to end a family you loved, just like you found it in your heart to destroy my family.' I stared at him, and he said nothing, so I added, coldly, 'Why not me? Why not Renatus? Did you miss a few?'

'No, that would imply a mistake,' Lisandro stated. 'I don't like to think that I frequently make those. I deliberately left you and your sister. I deliberately left alive Asheleigh Hawke.'

'And Renatus?'

'That was a promise.'

He was Renatus's godfather. He'd undoubtedly sworn oaths to protect Renatus through his child-hood. I wondered what punishment Fate would deal Lisandro if he broke those old oaths.

He stepped closer, sending my whole being into alert, and I channelled some power and threw something at him, not sure what it would be. It came from the back of my mind, something I'd never seen or done. Renatus knew it; therefore I knew it, too, like that first spell he'd shown me with the water. This spell took the form of a red ball of lightning, and struck a ward just centimetres from Lisandro's face. It sizzled and dissolved as it burnt a hole through his ward. He paused.

'He's been teaching you bad things, sweetie,' he commented. 'As much as I love that boy, he's a bad influence.'

'No thanks to you, I'm sure,' I spat, throwing a second ball of power at him, larger this time. He waved a hand, forming a new, stronger ward in time to deflect my spell. It bounced off and hit the floor, and began burning through the wood like acid.

'You think he's so sweet and cuddly, do you?' Lisandro asked with a harsh laugh. 'You think that he loves you? Let's see if he comes for you here. Let's see if he chooses you over a chance to chase me down. *You* are a substitute. You're a project, just like he was to Gawain.'

'You don't know Renatus like you think you do,' I snapped. I reached out for my master with my mind but felt our connection sever immediately. 'He's-'

'He was "rescued" by Gawain, which is enough for me to know he's ruined,' Lisandro said flatly. He opened his palm and finally took a moment to admire the ring, slotting it onto a middle finger. 'Well, sit tight. No doubt we'll meet again.'

Lisandro turned away, disappearing completely and unexpectedly, leaving me alone in the small locked room.

Renatus! I shouted with my mind's voice but felt, again, that feeling of severance, like someone was closing a door between him and me and blocking the sound. As afraid as I'd been with Lisandro, I felt a different kind of fear now. The fear of being alone, and of no one knowing I was here. My senses were dulled by the enchantments over the structure. Could anyone sense me inside? Would Renatus come looking for me?

I raced to the walls to look for a way out. The windows to a darkened and roiling seascape were locked, and there was no other door but the one right in front of me. Keeping my wards tight around me and well-powered, I raised a shaky hand and covered my eyes with the other, blasting the door with the biggest and brightest ball of lightning yet. It exploded against the wood. I chanced a look, ready for the equal possibilities of failure and conflict. I received neither. I'd put a decent-sized hole through the middle of the door, just big enough that I would be able to squeeze through, and there was no immediate threat on the other side. Cautiously, I approached the door and peered through my escape hatch. The beach house was quite nice inside the living space, spacious and open-plan, with a dozen fold-out sofa beds and camping cots awkwardly taking up all the space. The place was currently empty of occupants. It was brighter out there than in my little cell, lit as it was by just one dim, bare light bulb.

I slipped through the gap in the door, singeing my fingers a little on the overheated splinters around the edges, but that hardly compared to the rest of my injuries. I looked around. The living space seemed to have been abandoned abruptly, and outside, I could hear shouting. I wondered whether anyone even knew I was in here. Beside my door was another one, apparently to a small space the same size as the room

I'd found myself in. Aubrey and Shell, maybe? The real ones? I couldn't sense anything or anyone through the walls. I felt lost and disorientated without my usual magic.

I tried again to reach Renatus but my attempt was cut short. I tried once to Displace, thinking it would be best to get some help, but the Fabric was completely unresponsive. I recalled Elijah telling our class that there were some places where the Fabric had already been manipulated and pulled taut, making Displacement impossible. So I couldn't Displace. I couldn't communicate with Renatus. Could I at least scry?

I thought first of Renatus, and saw glimpses of him on the beach outside, shouting and firing energy at people I didn't know. He was coming for me.

I ran my fingers across the other door, hoping to pick up impressions, but they were all the same – unhelpful. *Lisandro, locking the door... A stranger, locking the door... Lisandro, opening the door, pulling Shell to her feet and marching her out... Aubrey begging... 'Be careful with her, please!'... Lisandro, locking the door...*

I knocked twice on the door with my fist, and waited. After several seconds, I heard the same knock in return.

'Stand back,' I called, hoping they could hear me and no one outside could. I couldn't see the beach house's front door from here and I wasn't sure how deep this house was, so I couldn't know whether my voice would carry. I took a breath, gathering power and nerve, and cast my newest spell.

I got better at it each time. The door was half gone, and little splinters of wood continued to drop onto the floor, smouldering with extreme heat.

'Aubrey?' I asked, looking in. My room had been brightly lit by the hanging light bulb. This room was dark.

'Who is that?'

I squinted, trying to see my former teacher, made more difficult because the lights behind me flickered then. Was he alright? Was he hurt? I could sense human life inside but I couldn't tell whether he was intact or even real.

A sudden boom made me leap backwards and press myself against the wall, hands and wards up. I looked around in terror but there was nobody around.

A storm was nearing.

'What the hell is going on?'

I turned to Aubrey, finally seeing him as he clambered through the hole. He looked so perfectly real that I immediately forgot that he might not be. Roughly Renatus's age, he looked aged with the tiredness and discomfort experienced in captivity. He was wearing the same clothes he'd been kidnapped in, I realised. They were dirty and there was dry blood on a sleeve. His usually shiny coppery hair was dull and matted on one side with what looked like more blood.

'This was supposed to be a rescue,' I told him. Distantly, I heard raised voices. He ducked down, eyes wide. 'It's alright, they're-'

'Shh!' he begged, looking around. He continued in a frightened whisper. 'What are *you* doing here? And what happened to you?'

I remembered then just how long he'd been here – how much he'd missed.

'I'm Renatus's apprentice,' I said, turning my left wrist over. My jacket's sleeve was burnt away, and I got my first proper look at the damage Lisandro had done to me. My tattoo was untouched, but from the back of my hand, curling around to the underside of my forearm and underneath my elbow, my skin was ruined, peeling and red. Judging from the relative pain levels and the way Aubrey's eyes remained on my throat, my neck looked much worse.

My tattoo blurred, and I thought that seemed very strange until I realised that it was my vision that was slipping out of focus. I reached for the wall, something to lean on, feeling unsteady. I'd never been this badly injured before. Would it heal? Did the no-scarring rule apply even to magical injury?

'You're what?' Aubrey asked, as though certain he hadn't heard right. '*Tu es folle*. He sold us out. He set us up. He's working for Lisandro.'

He still believed as he had that night he'd been captured. He hadn't seen all the evidence I had that demonstrated the contrary. He hadn't believed the same thing about absolutely everybody in the past two days.

'Well, somebody did sell you out, but it wasn't Renatus, I promise you.' I could still hear the distant shouting, all male voices. What was happening outside? My wooziness passing, I pushed away from the wall. 'We don't know yet who it was. Everybody is working together tonight to get you two back.'

'Three,' Aubrey corrected, leaning against the wall in my place and pulling the leg of his grubby jeans up to reveal his anklet. 'Renatus told me Teresa was captured, too.'

Of course, he thought of Shell as the second person rather than Teresa. I kept forgetting about his girlfriend.

'Where is Shell?' I asked now, looking around. His face darkened.

'You mean she's not out yet?'

'No, we've only got Teresa. We thought Shell was with you.'

'Lisandro just walked in and took her, not five minutes ago. Can you get this off?' He gestured at the chain around his ankle. I knelt down to examine it, still listening as he continued. 'Do you think he's hurt her?'

'I don't know,' I said, twisting the chain in my fingers, trying to sense a weakness in its complex magic. 'I hope not. I didn't know before tonight what a complete psycho he is. He controls storms.'

A massive thunderclap made us both jump nervously.

'Like this one, I suppose,' Aubrey murmured, looking up at the low ceiling. 'Quickly, help me get this off so we can get out of here. I think we're on the sea, or very near to it. I saw the beach.'

He had no idea where he was.

I found a gap in the magic that was wound around the anklet, and focused on it. Like a clasp, it clicked open and the chain fell away. Aubrey breathed a sigh of relief and I stood.

'Let's go,' I said, heading for the front of the house. He hurried to keep up, limping slightly. What had Lisandro done to him?

'Are you sure this is a good idea?' he asked nervously. 'They're going to see us.'

'I think Renatus is out there,' I answered, reaching again for Renatus's mind. Again, the connection was suddenly cut off.

'What are you doing?' Aubrey demanded, catching my arm and stopping me in the middle of the living room. A flash of lightning accompanied a dimming of the lights, and a second later the whole house shuddered with the thunder. I tried to ignore the fear rising within me. I hated storms. When he could be heard over the rumblings, he continued. 'Lisandro will notice any telepathic communications from inside this house, I'm sure. You'll get us caught; he'll know you're here.'

'He already knows I'm here,' I said, pointing at my neck. Aubrey seemed unwilling to look. I was sure it was unpleasant. 'And we're already caught.'

I tried again to speak to Renatus, and again my communication was blocked off.

'Haven't you been listening to me?' Aubrey asked, still stage whispering. 'Renatus sold us all out. He's not ours.'

'He's my master, and he's not a traitor,' I responded, snatching my arm back. 'Are you blocking me?'

As soon as I asked, I realised that it didn't matter. He could block me from talking telepathically with Renatus, but my link with my master was deeper than telepathy between two minds. Our minds were, in some ways, just one but in two bodies. While I couldn't share words and thoughts as long as Aubrey was going to be paranoid, I could still share feelings. Empathy was a talent he wouldn't be able to block. I concentrated on how I was feeling – a bit scared, but okay, no longer in pain – and sort of *sent* it to Renatus. I felt a faint acknowledgement in reply.

'I'm not going back into that cell because you can't keep quiet,' Aubrey hissed. We both turned as one of the distant voices became nearer and clearer.

'I'll just check,' someone called. I glanced at Aubrey, afraid. Before we could think to hide, a heavyset man appeared from behind the wall dividing this living space from the next room. He walked several steps into the room before he saw us, and then he froze, clearly shocked.

Aubrey raised a hand suddenly, something black and translucent springing from his fingertips to strike the stranger in the chest. The intruder immediately lost consciousness and fell to the floor in silence.

'Nice,' I commented, relieved.

'I'm better with my wand,' Aubrey said, looking around again. 'No time to find that. We need to get out.' Another flash of lightning almost killed the lights, and the thunder was less than a second in delay. Through a window, I could see only black and grey as waves lashed the sides of the beach house. I became aware that the house was continuing to shake even after tl.under finished rumbling. The water was absolutely pounding the outside walls. I hoped the structure was stronger than it looked from in here.

I hurried over to the still form on the floor and went through his pockets.

'Renatus teaching you to mug people, sorcerer-style?' Aubrey asked coolly. I stood, silently thrusting the wand I'd found into his hands. The cold *you're welcome* was heavily implied.

I started towards the room the stranger had come from, hoping it would lead to a front door, and peered cautiously around the corner. The next room was really a kitchen and a dining room, but again, had been filled with sofa beds. Apparently quite a few people were camping out here.

The front door was open, and through it, I could see that it was raining. Flashes of light illuminated the doorway, not all of it lightning. Some of it had to be magic.

I ran forward, ignoring Aubrey's calls for me to wait. I had the sense to stop in the doorway, steadying myself by grasping the doorframe as the house was given a mighty shake by the elements.

Aubrey grabbed me again, turning me away from the unknown scene outside and pulling me down into a crouch so no one would see us.

'Do not go out there,' he whispered, desperate. 'You're going to get killed. We've got to find another way. I think we should try a window. If we get into the sea we should be able to swim to shore unseen.'

'That's stupid,' I hissed back, annoyance with his paranoia coupled with the fear that was steadily increasing within me with every crash of thunder putting me in a very unwilling mood. 'We'd drown.'

I tried to stand; he kept me down.

'You don't know what you're doing!'

I had a sudden vision of Addison's face. *Trust him only to the door, but no further. Outside, you hold the torch. He's in the dark.* I had trusted Aubrey to here because I knew him and he was a White Elm councillor, and he had probably saved my life by knocking out that stranger, but beyond this door, I couldn't trust him. He didn't know it, but he was completely useless. He was traumatised and paranoid. His escape ideas were insane and were good only for not being seen – which happened to directly oppose *my* escape plan, which involved getting seen by as many people as possible so they would know where to rescue me from. Aubrey didn't even know who he could trust. Once we stepped outside, I would need to become the leader. I was the one holding the torch. He was in the dark.

'No,' I said, pushing him away with a quick shove, '*you* don't know what you're doing.'

I got up and stepped through the door.

Outside, the most incredible sight was mine to behold. Against a backdrop of tumultuous dark sky and pelting rain that had come in out of nowhere, two dozen sorcerers were facing off against the White Elm. Magic was flying – flashes of light, balls of energy, balls of fire in Renatus's case. Streaks of magic bounced from wards all over the place. Every now and then, someone on this side would cast a spell and be hit by its rebound off a White Elm ward, and he would drop to the gritty, wet beach, and the ever-nearing waves would threaten to claim him.

It was a battle.

In the middle of this side, I saw a huddle of forms. The tall one being protected by the others I recognised as Lisandro, and beside him was Jackson. I saw that despite much of the White Elm's attention being focused purely on them, neither bothered to retaliate or cast magic back in return. Instead they held two hostages, one male and one female. One, I knew, had to be Shell, and the other...

'Aubrey, it's you,' I murmured, glancing back at him, uncertain. Aubrey was here with me, just inside the door, but also outside, struggling as Jackson held him in a headlock. One was a lie. Frowning, the Aubrey I'd rescued stepped forward to stand nervously at my shoulder. He surveyed the scene.

'Shell,' he whispered. 'Do you think they'll be able to get to her?'

'You're not worried about the fact that there's another *you* down there?'

'That's not me.' Aubrey squinted. 'Who is that?'

He didn't know about the illusion Teresa had been forced to create. Either that, or he *was* the illusion.

Remembering the way I'd worked out the false Teresa for what she – it – was, I gently extended my senses over this Aubrey, feeling for his emotional state. It was mostly guarded, a common reaction to shock and trauma, apparently, but I detected his frustration and worry simmering away below the surface.

This Aubrey was real, or realer than the Teresa Jackson had given us.

At the front of the White Elm, Renatus, Qasim and Emmanuelle were really pushing forward, with Jadon working towards them from their left. But for every step they gained, Lisandro only moved sideways. He was edging towards the water, I noticed. What could his motive be for getting to the sea?

Jackson suddenly dragged his Aubrey behind the crowd and began moving quickly through the rising tide. Emmanuelle and Jadon most certainly noticed; they refocused their efforts on the men to their left, to clear a path. Renatus had his eye on Lisandro, but glanced up as a massive wave buffeted the house. I grabbed for the doorframe again, but my grip slipped and I was thrown out onto the landing. I clutched the handrail, looking up as the spray and rain quickly soaked my hair. The salt stung my burns like crazy. I hardly noticed. In the midst of the battle, Renatus was looking straight at me. He knew where I was. He was going to come and get me, and take me away from the violence and the storm. It was almost over.

Right then, the other Aubrey managed to struggle free of Jackson's hold, and made a run for it. Emmanuelle's wards held off the attacks while Jadon froze to watch. Aubrey bolted through the turbulent surf, ducking to avoid blasts of dark energy, running as directly as he could towards Susannah at the edge of the White Elm line. Jackson reached for his wand but he didn't have it. Apparently frustrated, he whipped his hand through the air, flinging a black disc of power at Aubrey's retreating back. It struck the escapee in the shoulders, which seized as his body failed, and he fell into the waves with his aura fading into nothing.

'*No!*' I heard the scream from both Shell and Emmanuelle. Jadon's magic and resolve seemed to return to him instantly, and every spell he cast seemed suddenly bigger and stronger than before. I struggled to breathe, wondering whether I'd just seen a murder.

'What happened?' Aubrey asked worriedly. I glanced back, and saw that he was crouched in the doorway, clinging to the frame. He hadn't seen himself die, which was probably good. Most likely, I'd not seen him die, either. I'd probably just watched Jackson destroy an illusion. Why he'd bother to kill it, I couldn't guess, though it occurred to me that maybe Jackson hadn't known that he'd been handling the fake Aubrey. Maybe only Lisandro knew which was which. It was his psychotic plan that we were all playing out, after all. Or maybe I was with the illusory Aubrey, and maybe they really had just taken the life of a White Elm councillor, here on this same beach that they used to murder Peter only a month ago.

A thunderclap coincided with a huge wave slamming the side of the beach house, and I heard a terrifying crack. The house obligingly swayed in the direction it was shoved in by the wave, but did not sway back. It continued to lean, and I realised in a rising panic that one of the supports was broken.

Lisandro pulled Shell free of the crowd, too, and Jackson hurried back to meet him. The sobbing girlfriend was exchanged and Jackson dragged her by the hand into the waves. Jadon shouted her name, but she followed her captor, too grief-stricken to fight back. When they were deep enough that the waves were almost crashing over Shell's head, Jackson pulled her close and Displaced with her.

'No! Shell!' Jadon screamed, uselessly, abandoning magic and throwing himself into the huddle of Lisandro's guards, literally fighting tooth and nail to get through. The White Elm was clearly overwhelming the crowd of brawny hired hands, having pushed them back almost as far as the steps up to the landing I waited on, but they were no closer to reaching Lisandro, who had weaved his way back through the group and appeared on the other side, slipping further and further away. Only Renatus's eyes didn't lose him in the tight crowd. He left Emmanuelle and Jadon, slid past Glen, shouldered past Tian and ducked beneath Lord Gawain's hands as his mentor reached for him to wait. He appeared on the far edge of the council's line, opposite to where Aubrey's clone had been lost to the waves. He raised his wand, ready to strike, and I watched in anticipation, hoping that he would end all of tonight's horror with one clean spell.

Lightning flashed through the sky, brightening the low, dense clouds, and a bolt of electricity zapped between the storm clouds and the house. It struck just below the landing, much too precise to be anything but Lisandro's intention, and I felt the support snap and give. I smelt the sharp scent of energy frying the air particles and old wood singed.

I screamed as the house buckled, grabbing at the handrail. I felt rather than saw Renatus's look; I felt the way his stomach flipped over because the same thing happened to mine. He was scared for me. He was going to come and get me. But doing so would rob him of his chance to confront Lisandro, who was waiting patiently in the surf, smirking.

Kill him, I said, and knew that he heard me. Aubrey was distracted and the blocks were gone. He and I were about to plunge into the sea and probably drown.

The house collapsed, and for some reason I knew what to do. I let go of the rail and stumbled to Aubrey. I grabbed his hand and pulled him up, and ran down the sloping landing as the house fell into the sea. At the edge of the landing I jumped, pulling Aubrey unwillingly with me, and grasped desperately at the Fabric. Here, above the sea, outside the boundary of Lisandro's house, the Fabric was untouched, and it parted at my request. I had no particular place in mind – anywhere would do, honestly.

We landed solidly and my shoulder smashed against unforgiving, hard, wet ground. I felt completely ill – I'd never experienced this nausea following a Displacement before. Groaning in pain, I rolled onto my back and clutched at my throbbing shoulder. Had I broken it? It certainly felt like it.

The deafening sound of a thunderclap directly above shocked me out of my thoughts. I opened my eyes and sharp raindrops spiked my eyes, so I quickly closed them again. Where was I? Had I even left? The storm was going strong here, too.

'Aristea, quick!' Aubrey shouted, barely audible over the incessant rumble of thunder. Through my damp eyelashes, when I dared open them, I could barely make out his silhouette against the flashing lightning. He was already standing, if you could call his hunched, frightened posture that, and he was gesturing for me to follow him. 'There's a basement over here!'

I rolled onto my hands and knees as I retched violently, but nothing came up. I knew now why I felt so sick. I knew where I was.

The street was the same. The O'Leary house over the road was still painted an obnoxious shade of green. The gardens either side were different now, updated or overgrown. The house I most expected to see was long gone, as Lisandro had confirmed, but its foundations had not been ripped up. The wooden trap door my parents had expressly forbidden us to play near when we were children had not gone anywhere and the old basement it opened to was still here. I could scarcely believe it but here I was. Proof.

'Come on! Quick!' Aubrey called, further away now. I heard a loud, tearing crack, which sounded too familiar, and when I struggled to my feet, something struck me hard in the stomach, knocking me back down and forcing all the air from my lungs. I blinked through my lashes at the branch beside me. It was happening all over again. Same place, same fear, same things...

Lightning struck the ground not fifteen metres away – once, when I was four, my dad had filled a blow-up pool there on a summer day – and I shuffled up and away, petrified. Lisandro had a sick sense of humour. If he'd wanted to kill me, he could have done it three years ago, and then again a hundred times already tonight, but he preferred to wait to do it like this?

He'd killed my parents. He'd killed my brother at the prime of his life. Here. *Right here.* And now he was going to kill me, too. It terrified me and incited in me an anger I'd not felt before. The anger of injustice. It wasn't *fair*.

I had to get away. I was too exposed. Most of the trees I remembered from my childhood had been cut down since I was last here, and I was *not* going into that basement. I could hardly run into a nearby house and endanger the lives of all my old neighbours. I began to jog cautiously down the street, away from what I knew. Feeling like being sick, I drew on the dark energy that was all around me (mildly surprised that it served to empower me energetically just as the orchard or the Hawke house) and reformed my wards. The sharp leaves caught up in the winds were deflected as they flew past me, and a frail stick shattered centimetres from my elbow. The rain still poured through. Expending energy on staying dry at this point seemed ridiculous, even to my panic-stricken logic.

Where are you? Renatus demanded. I looked around, sensing that he was close. What was he doing here? He was meant to be over the hill at the beach. He was meant to be getting justice for our families.

'What are you doing?' I screamed, not sure he would hear me but so scared and angry about *everything* that I didn't care. 'Kill him!'

I already made my choice.

I started to cry, running wildly to my right as another lightning strike exploded the ground less than ten metres away. I was going to die. Lisandro was just playing with me, because when he decided to end me, no way would my wards deflect a zillion volts of electricity and no way was I fast enough to outrun it. Renatus had messed up. He'd chosen to find and save me instead of going after the person that was about to kill me anyway.

I kept running, down the street, thinking of a covered patio area built onto Mr Beatty's place after he inherited that property from his mother and renovated it extensively. If I got there I might have a chance, I told myself, knowing it was a lie. I wasn't going to get there. Intuition told me to dodge left, so I did, narrowly missing a bolt of lightning that would otherwise have fried me.

A horrific crack accompanied the strike that hit an electrical post just ahead. I saw it begin to fall and realised that it would fall across my path. I turned quickly to change direction but lost my footing on the slippery road and fell onto the harsh road surface. I tried to push myself up but my injured shoulder gave way. I fell back into the puddles, my cheek grazing on the stones. Three months ago, on another street near another home of mine, I'd found a pebble in a puddle and it had changed my life. Now that life was practically over, so soon. Was there any use in trying to get up and keep running?

My sense of self-preservation was what compelled me to struggle back to my feet and look around to get my bearings. The big wooden post, with its live, sparking wires flailing about, was still falling, and was due to land right where I stood. This was exactly like how my dad and brother had died, except that their killer had been a tree. There wasn't really enough time for me to get out of the way, not really. Had they thought the same thing? I was going to die in the same street as the rest of my family had three years before. My poor Angela, all alone...

My shoulder seared with pain as a cold hand closed around my upper arm and yanked me out from under the falling post. The massive old wooden column slammed into the ground exactly where I'd just been standing, and a cable whipped towards me. I instinctively fortified the wards I'd lost focus on, hoping it would be enough, and Renatus flicked a small, intense ball of magic at the offending wire. The wire, sparking menacingly, bounced uselessly from my ward, and upon impact of the spell, the cables and the post glowed white-hot and dissolved into nothing. Illusions? No. Just obliterated by Renatus's spell.

'You've got what you want!' Renatus shouted at the clouds. I followed his gaze, breathless. The clouds moved like water, fast and swirling. The lightning strikes had ceased. Lisandro couldn't get me without hitting Renatus, and he had no intention of killing Renatus, at least not tonight. 'Take it and go.'

Almost immediately, the rain lightened, the clouds softened and rose, the thunder quietened and the wind died down. That was it. Lisandro had apparently relinquished control of the storm, leaving the weather to disperse it naturally. It continued to rain, it continued to rumble, but it was nature now, and nature was kinder than Lisandro.

Overwhelmed, I choked back a sob and half-collapsed, holding myself up by grabbing my knees and locking my elbows so I didn't fall over. I felt Renatus's concern as he tentatively touched my shoulder. I surprised myself by jerking away, almost losing balance.

'What's the matter with you?' I demanded, still crying. 'Didn't you hear me before? Lisandro killed my parents. He killed my brother. *Here*. And he killed your whole family. You were meant to kill him.'

'I know,' Renatus said, quietly. I knew he'd wished he had. He'd wanted to.

'It's *your job*.'

'I know.'

'So?' I drew a shuddery breath and felt my chest heave with the effort of controlling my sobs. 'So why didn't you?'

'Because I had to make a choice,' he answered, speaking over me when I tried to argue, 'and it was *my* choice to make. Previous Dark Keepers have fallen apart because of choices like these – I don't want to be another one who chose vengeance over protecting what family I have left.'

For a long moment, I stared at him, processing his words. When I realised what he was saying, I burst into fresh tears and stepped forward to bury my face in his shoulder. Renatus wrapped his arms tightly around me in something of a hug – the most affection I think he'd shown anybody in a long time – and I finally felt safe and secure. He cared about me. I was his family. His desire to protect me outweighed his hatred for Lisandro.

I gathered myself together quite quickly after that, taking deep breaths and forcibly calming myself down. I was safe. Nothing could happen to me when I was this close to Renatus. He wouldn't let it.

After a minute, I felt the movement as he looked to the side. In his mind, I recognised that he was speaking with someone on the council. He relaxed his hold on me, extending one hand out to the side like he was trying to catch the raindrops in his palm. I shifted slightly, turning my head to look just as Emmanuelle appeared, one hand in Renatus's. He'd caught her the same way Hiroko caught me.

'Aristea, *je suis désolée,* I'm so sorry,' she whispered, her bright eyes skating over my various injuries like she was looking straight under my skin. I straightened, fortifying my emotional barriers. I already felt like an idiot for falling to pieces in front of Renatus. Emmanuelle didn't need to see that, too. She mistook my shutting down as mistrust, and hesitated before touching me, her hand extended to my face. 'I'm sorry. The Seers told me it was the only chance we 'ad of success.' She looked at Renatus, slightly less apologetic. 'I couldn't let you in. They said if you knew, Lisandro would realise. It made no difference, it seems.'

'I nearly killed you,' Renatus told her. 'Don't ever do that again.'

'I'm sure Lisandro won't give me the chance,' she answered, still examining my injuries. 'Such a mess. I'm sorry I let it go on so long – I thought if I could get you back with me, we could take Jackson together and I could 'eal you then. I'm sorry I stood by.'

'You're not the one who hurt me,' I said, uncomfortable with the apologies. It wasn't her fault. It was mine. I should never have been here. And I was the one who should have apologised, for being so quick to lose faith in her when she'd been working so hard to keep me alive. She obviously had a deeper faith in me – she'd expected my help in a surprise attack. She took my face in her hands, locking my gaze into hers.

'I'm still sorry,' she said, and I felt her hands warm up, though not cruelly as Lisandro's had. I could feel the subtle flow of energy from her skin into mine as she healed me. 'This shouldn't 'ave 'appened.'

No, because I shouldn't have come along to-night. I'd been stubborn and stupid and I'd nearly gotten myself killed as a result. I'd not helped out in any way. Well, I'd done one thing right.

'Someone's got to check out the basement,' I said. My shoulder tingled as it was fixed up. I tested it by lifting my arm carefully to push my sopping wet hair out of my face. 'Aubrey was hiding in there.'

'Aubrey?' Emmanuelle glanced sideways at Renatus. 'Aubrey's dead, Aristea. Jackson killed him.'

I heard the grief in her voice. Aubrey was her family. Tonight, she thought she'd watched him die. I shook my head.

'No, that was the illusion. Aubrey's alive. No, he is,' I insisted when the pair of them offered me sad looks. 'He was with me. I brought him here. He's really... paranoid. Thought Renatus was the enemy, kept blocking me from talking to him, suggested jumping into the water to avoid being seen...' I was rambling but couldn't stop. 'He didn't know where Shell was and reminded me that we needed to find Teresa, and knocked out some guy who came back to check on us and I gave him a wand and I saw Jackson kill the other Aubrey, but the one with me didn't see it-'

I bit my tongue, trying to end the nervous chatter that was pouring from me. I became aware that I was shaking all over, from cold or shock or both. Lady Miranda, Qasim and Elijah appeared nearby and approached briskly. Emmanuelle dropped her hands but her eyes stayed on me.

'I can't sense 'im,' she said doubtfully. 'Are you certain that the Aubrey *you* found was the real one?'

'Pretty certain,' I answered, keeping my dialogue to a minimum, looking at Renatus and thinking of the emotions I'd felt from the Aubrey I'd rescued. He nodded, seeing what I'd done.

'It's him; he's alive,' he told the others. Glen and Jadon appeared next.

'What do you mean, "he's alive"?' Qasim asked with a frown. He'd obtained an impressive gash across the temple, and the rain had diluted the bleed, making it look many times worse than it was. Lady Miranda reached for his elbow, and where she touched glowed palely. The open cut visibly sealed itself. 'Are we talking about Aubrey?'

'The basement,' Renatus said by way of explanation. Elijah took Jadon and they Displaced up the road just as Lord Gawain and Anouk arrived.

'What a disaster,' Lord Gawain muttered as he approached. 'Half of them went and drowned and the rest disappeared. We've got nothing.'

'We've cleaned up as best we can,' Anouk reported to Lady Miranda. 'The bodies will look like fishermen. We've positioned a boat wreck nearby.'

So much to think about, like, how to make a supernatural battle scene look like the scene of a natural tragedy?

Would they have needed to think about this if I hadn't insisted on coming along? Anouk overheard me – I had to learn to stop thinking in questions.

'Aristea, I personally didn't want you with us tonight,' she said bluntly, 'but Susannah said your presence was necessary for the best outcome, which is all I need to hear to know this is exactly where we're supposed to be. You found Aubrey, alive?'

I nodded, still feeling ridiculous. I should have stayed at the estate. Surely, there would have been another way of getting Aubrey out of there without me getting kidnapped.

'No.' Anouk shook her head firmly. 'If there was another way, a better way, Susannah would have led us down it.'

'Perhaps he died in the storm,' Renatus said quietly. He was looking back the way I'd come running. I couldn't look yet. I would see my old property. 'I still can't sense him.'

'No, we would have all felt that,' Tian said, appearing beside him. He wiped a bloodied knife on the grass. I so didn't want to know how it got like that, especially when I saw a neatly carved symbol on the back of his left arm. He'd done it to himself, clearly, though for what reason, I couldn't imagine. There was a lot of magic I was not yet aware of. Tian stood, sheathing the knife alongside his other ones. He looked confused. 'Aubrey's future is still completely hidden from me, like he doesn't have one.'

'Like he's dead,' Emmanuelle guessed.

'Yes.' Susannah now arrived, looking pale. 'Just *like* he's dead.'

'Aristea,' Renatus said suddenly, 'did you say that Aubrey asked after Teresa?'

'Aye. He said you told him about her, that she was the other hostage.'

'I didn't tell him that.'

I couldn't guess what this meant. Jadon and Elijah returned, shaking their heads. Was I wrong? Had the real Aubrey died on the beach?

I felt the pang of shock as Renatus looked suddenly over at Qasim, and from the looks on their faces I knew something, somewhere, was very, very wrong.

epilogue

The weather at Morrissey Estate was so different from the weather just a few hours north. Everything was still, and though the sky was hidden behind cloud, there was no rain here.

Aubrey dug through his pockets for his key to the estate. He hadn't expected to ever need it again, and couldn't be sure it would even work now. If the White Elm had been smart, they would have thought to disable Aubrey and Teresa's keys immediately after they'd been taken. What if the keys had fallen into the wrong hands? Well, this key had been in the wrong hand to begin with, but still.

Relieved to hear the lock click lightly when the key turned, Aubrey slipped through and hurried away from the gate to a distance where its magic wouldn't warp his Displacement to the front door. He didn't have time to run. The council could return at any minute, and he couldn't be here when they did. He was supposed to be dead.

Everything had gone to shit. There had never been a specific plan, per se, but Aubrey still couldn't help but feel as though it had all backfired and now it was *his* neck on the line, which had never been part of *his* plan. All he'd done was fall in love with a girl who turned out to be Lisandro's favourite pet. Without ever actually meeting the man, he'd been handpicked by Lisandro in the months before his departure from the White Elm to serve as a plant within the council. Knowing how his colleagues thought, knowing what they would be looking for, Lisandro had found ways to quietly pick off the competition, paying people off and scaring others, so that when the time came for the White Elm to choose three new councillors, Aubrey would be a certainty. Even *that* had come close to blowing up, when Jadon and Teresa had popped up unexpectedly as applicants.

Aubrey pulled open the front doors and came face to face with Teresa. He froze. She froze. What did she know?

'Aubrey!'

She threw herself at him, hugging him tightly and turning her head away very deliberately. She knew nothing. Good. No, perfect.

'Teresa.' Aubrey hugged her back, surprised by how relieved he felt to see her alive. He had worried constantly about how she would be treated, knowing she was being kept by Jackson, who was at least as cruel as Lisandro but with much less restraint. As long as Asheleigh Hawke remained loyal to Lisandro, convinced as she was that he had rescued her as a child, Aubrey's loyalty would lie there, too, but that didn't mean that the friendships he'd formed with Teresa and Jadon this year were not just as real and meaningful to him. They'd befriended him while the rest of the council had treated him like the new kid. Teresa had cooked dozens of fantastic meals for him, compassionate as she was, and she'd fought at his side the night they'd been taken, prepared to go down with him. She was such a good person. She didn't deserve any of this.

Aubrey turned his face to look at her. She was in a bad state. She'd clearly been shoved around a lot more than he had. His bad treatment had been for show; hers had been real.

'*O, Doamne*; I was so worried about you,' Teresa was saying, speaking so fast against his shoulder. 'I was scared that when I saw you, I'd just be looking at my own work – they made me make copies of us both, and I thought maybe they'd try to give us the copy instead of the real you. They did it with me.'

'Hmm,' Aubrey said, unable to say much without telling her things she couldn't know. 'Who else is here?'

'No one. Lady Miranda patched up the worst of me, and Elijah brought me here and then left. I'm still struggling to really connect with the council. Can you feel them?'

'Not yet,' Aubrey said, knowing he never would again. He was supposed to die tonight. Everyone was meant to think him dead, and in order for that to be possible without him *actually* dying, his connection to the White Elm had been forcibly and permanently severed. Because he'd already been blocked from them by the chain on his ankle, they wouldn't have felt his departure from the council early this morning when he'd undergone the difficult ritual with Lisandro. When the illusion had been struck down by Jackson, "Aubrey" was supposed to have died, allowing the real Aubrey to continue his life in secret without worrying about being looked for. Lisandro had organised this kind of thing before and it had worked perfectly. There were people serving Lisandro who had been "dead" for years.

Aubrey was meant to become one of them – his reward for the danger he'd put himself in these past months, a chance to start over – but it had all been ruined by Renatus's stupid apprentice. No one was meant to have seen him. No one was meant to know. And it had to be *her*, an underage, uninitiated witch... Someone he couldn't kill without scarring his own soul beyond salvation.

'I can't believe this is finally over,' Teresa murmured. 'I can hardly believe we're both alive! There were so many times, when I was alone, and when I wasn't... I thought I would never see you or anyone else again.' She took a deep breath, fortifying herself. She was so weakened, emotionally, by this experience. Aubrey didn't want to know what had happened to her. 'I'd lost hope. I was losing my mind. I think I already lost it – I kissed Jadon!'

'What?' Aubrey asked, shocked into a laugh. He wanted to hear all about this, and almost started teasing her, when he realised how much time he was wasting. This was a relationship he couldn't salvage. He'd betrayed Teresa the moment he'd joined the council and smiled at her. He'd betrayed her again when he'd left her address on Shell's dining room table – the same place he'd left news of the ring, lists of the students' names and all sorts of other things Lisandro had asked Shell for.

'I know, it's crazy,' Teresa groaned, shaking her head and pressing her face into his shoulder, embarrassed. Aubrey laughed, gently weaving his hand through her messy curly hair so that his fingertips touched her neck.

'It's pretty crazy,' he agreed, lowering his other hand a few centimetres to her hip, where her shirt had lifted slightly. 'What came over you?'

'I have no idea,' she muttered, clearly annoyed with herself. She didn't notice as her energy started to drain, slowly but steadily. 'It was mainly him but I just let him. God, I'm so stupid.'

'Offered the choice between Jadon and Samuel, I would personally take Jadon, so I wouldn't have said you were stupid,' Aubrey disagreed. She gasped.

'What am I going to tell Samuel?' she whispered, partly from fear and partly because she didn't have the energy to speak any louder.

'Tell him nothing,' Aubrey answered, shifting her hair and shirt with his hands so that more of his skin touched hers. Her energy drained faster, and then he was holding her upright and she was blinking drowsily. He held her close and whispered in her ear as she lost consciousness, 'Tell them all nothing.'

She was out, and Aubrey stopped taking, unwilling to bring any real harm to her. He'd committed his first murder just this month, and wasn't prepared to make her his second. He took her into the library, where he laid her gently on a two-seater.

Someone would find her here, and it might seem as though she'd just gone to sleep. A few quick spells later and her memory of this exchange was blurred enough that it might have been a dream, and all energetic traces of him were gone from her and from the scene. There was still a chance that he might get out of here a "dead" man.

Unlikely, he thought dully as he hurried up the spiralling staircase. Aristea had seen him, so unless Lisandro had succeeded in killing her and she hadn't had the chance to tell Renatus what she'd seen, it would be her memory against theirs. On top of that, there was the fact of what he was still about to do.

At the second floor, Aubrey heard voices and froze in the stairwell, whipping out the wand Aristea had stolen for him and pressing himself against the wall. This sneaking around reminded him forcibly of Valero, not that long ago. He'd gotten into the fortress-like city easy enough, his connection to White Elm still apparent in every fibre of his being. With councillors coming and going all the time and with several of them already inside, the security systems had barely registered his arrival. Still, it hadn't hurt to muddle with the spells and distort them, making accurate measurements of White Elm presence impossible.

Entry to the prison had been just a few memory charms and distractions. The true challenge had been moving around the place. The White Elm were not idiots – far from it, and the cream of the crop in terms of magical ability – and the staff of Valero's prison were in a similar category, so finding them in a huge stone fortress without *being* found had presented him with a rather epic test of his own abilities. The prison walls were entirely coated with cloaking magic, interwoven with wards and other magical blocks. Aubrey had warped it enough that the spells actually treated him as part of the wall, unseen unless by his choice, unheard unless by his choice, undetected in every sense.

From there it had all been too easy, sneaking in, feeling around for Emmanuelle's familiar energy, slipping into the cell behind her and listening to Renatus's interrogation of Saul... until it had come time to kill him. He had recalled Jarvis's plain face from that Thursday night, and recalled the deliberate memory wipe he'd performed on that one. Jarvis was not a threat to Lisandro. He knew nothing that could help the White Elm. But Saul was already spilling the beans, rendered senseless by Renatus's illusion of his deepest phobia.

Standing immediately behind the Dark Keeper, Aubrey's heart had thudded so loudly that he was surprised he'd not been caught. He'd dropped the ward for Saul and let him see him. He hadn't even needed to speak. Saul had played his part perfectly.

And he'd killed him for it.

And he'd nearly been killed himself when, in his guilty haste, he had run straight out the door and into Anouk. Thankfully she'd seemed too preoccupied with the gruesome excitement of the moment to stop and think about it, but Aubrey had slowed down after that, taking care to look out for obstructions and to clean up after himself, removing every last trace of himself as he went.

It was worthwhile, Lisandro had told him in the hours following. Saul had kidnapped and trafficked human beings across Europe and had never been brought to justice. He was the worst kind of person. Perfectly expendable; the only reason Lisandro didn't turn him away from the beginning. Having only met Lisandro properly for the first time the night before, Aubrey had remained unconvinced, but he could hardly take it back, could he? He'd followed this man blindly, accepting his offer when it was given through mutual acquaintances and betraying his new friends countless times. If it wasn't worthwhile, what was it?

It had to be worthwhile, which was why he'd stayed, even assisted Lisandro by pointing the blame at Renatus for a second time, while the stupid Dark Keeper was in the great Crafter's presence. Lisandro had suggested the twelve destinations in an earlier discussion, and then, a blessing – Renatus turning up unexpectedly. Leaving Shell with a mug that emanated his personal energy should Renatus reach out to check on him, he'd started off on his adventure, landing in a location and staying only long enough to trigger the security wards and falsify the energy that would come up if traced. And all of these people would waste no time tracing. It would have been quicker if Lisandro hadn't agreed to let Renatus see him, causing a huge hassle for Aubrey in trying to return unnoticed halfway through, but apparently it had been *worthwhile* for the conversation that had ensued and what Qasim would have scried.

Judging by the cohesiveness of the White Elm's attack tonight, Aubrey was failing to see how any of this Renatus-bashing had actually been *worthwhile*.

'What do you mean, you told her?'

Aubrey listened intently from the staircase as some students, a girl and a boy up way too late but without any councillors around to chastise them, chatted quietly in the hall on the second floor.

'I felt like I had to. You said yourself, it was *for* her.'

The girl was silent for a long moment, and then asked, 'How did she take it?'

'She seemed cool about it. Hopefully it helps her. Weird that none of them are back yet, don't you think?'

'Yeah, it's late.' The girl paused again. 'I should go to bed.'

'Alright. See you tomorrow?' The boy's voice was hopeful. The girl's response was dull, without promise.

'I suppose. I live here, don't I? Good night.'

'Night.'

The owners of the voices went into their respective rooms, and there was silence. Extending his senses all along that hall, Aubrey found that all of the students were in their rooms. Perfect. He stepped out of the stairwell and hurried along the hallway, reaching again for his key. It opened only one of these dormitories, but that was all he needed.

He slipped the key into the keyhole and turned it. His four students – Garrett, Joshua, Tyson and Enrico – were still awake, and turned to stare at him openly as he took back his key from the lock. He knew he looked terrible. It would help his case. His students had been quite partial to him before he'd left, but the shock of seeing him look like this would be a powerful influence on their compassion.

'Aubrey?' Tyson asked, hesitant. He was sitting on the floor between two beds, a dozen odd socks strewn across the carpet. Apparently he'd been trying to match them into pairs. Enrico was sitting on a desk, his feet on the seat of the chair. Joshua was lying across a bed, reading, and Garrett was sitting at his desk, folding paper.

'Guys, we've got to get out of here,' Aubrey told them. 'It's not safe here anymore.'

'What happened to you, man?' Enrico asked, hopping down from the desk. 'You look terrible.'

'We've got to go,' Aubrey said again, going to the nearest closet, which of course, belonging to a boy, was wide open with all sorts of things spilling out of it, and began searching for bags. 'Pack. Quick. The council will be back at any second and they could kill us all.'

'What are you talking about?' Josh asked, sitting up. 'The *council* is going to kill us? Who did this to you?'

Who ruined everything? Whose irritating apprentice had forced Aubrey into this situation?

'Renatus, and Lord Gawain,' Aubrey said. 'They didn't tell you? I've been on the run for weeks. I found out about their real motives. I've heard their plans; they want to be the only power. No more choice, no more options. Look what they're doing to Lisandro! They've turned half the world against him and they'll kill him if they get the chance, when all he did was say no to their ideas. I had to leave. I found some people who were sympathetic. We've got to go to them. Now, come on.'

'Are you saying Lisandro's just a victim?' asked Joshua, his tone implying doubt.

'I'm saying we need to leave, and then you can make your own mind up,' Aubrey said, thrusting Tyson's bag at him. He immediately began to pack. Josh dropped his book and jumped off his bed.

'What are you doing?' he demanded of Tyson, and of Enrico, who was piling his clothes up. 'We can't leave. What about our families? What are we meant to tell them?'

Enrico paused.

'My cousin is in dorm one,' he said tentatively. Aubrey shook his head. This was more difficult than he'd anticipated. He hadn't wanted to, but now manipulated the energy of the room to create a more obliging atmosphere.

'There isn't time. They won't hurt your cousin. He doesn't know anything about this. I'm just worried about you four because of your connection to me. You can contact your families when it's safe to do so. Now let's go, before Renatus comes back and destroys us.'

All four boys got to their feet and began packing their things.

'Just essentials,' Aubrey added, as Garrett carefully packed a hand-drawn picture between two pairs of jeans. Garrett nodded, quiet as ever.

These four boys didn't know it yet, but they were going to become the first students of Lisandro's, shaped and formed into what he most needed them to be. They would have the opportunity to become apprentices, just as Aristea had had here. It had come as a huge surprise to Aubrey to make the connection between Saul's "girl who sees through illusions" and Lisandro's mental commentary about Renatus's sudden power boost. It was, in fact, of course, Aristea. Why the White Elm had granted someone so young, so unstable and so suspicious the right to a young girl's life was beyond Aubrey's understanding, but he supposed that desperate times usually saw desperate actions.

'Come on, guys, let's go,' Aubrey hastened, unlocking the door and peering through. Still nobody, and he couldn't sense any of his former colleagues on the premises, either, although they couldn't be far away. Tyson was the first one ready, determinedly marching through the doorway and waiting in the hall for his roommates. Enrico and Josh followed, and Aubrey had to gesture hurriedly to Garrett. 'Garrett, come on.'

He was standing at his desk, writing something on his folded paper construction. Was it some sort of cube? A box?

'Garrett, what are you writing?' Aubrey demanded now, getting nervous. No clues, no traces...

'Garrett, hurry the hell up, man,' Enrico said. 'You can't leave notes – they'll be able to find us.'

'He's writing to his new *girlfriend*,' Josh snickered, and Garrett began to blush. 'That's right, we all saw you.'

'It's just a goodbye,' Garrett answered, putting down the pen and following them out. Aubrey could detect no betrayal in Garrett's aura or in his perpetually downcast eyes, so let it go. A silly little note wouldn't create any real problems, anyway. He pocketed his key, knowing it would be useless after tonight. He knew it was the last time he'd be in this house. There would be no coming back, dead or alive, or whatever he became after tonight.

'Quickly,' he murmured, leading the way.

THE END

Acknowledgements

At the close of this incredibly eventful year I find myself settling down to write the acknowledgements page of my second novel, which is an overwhelming thought considering that at this time last year, I had no published works at all. I feel so fortunate and almost bewildered to be where I am today, and it has all been made possible by the love, support and hard work of many people around me.

Firstly I need to thank the people who make this all worthwhile: the readers. Thank you to John Hudson for buying the very first copy of my first book, and thank you to every single person who took a chance on Chosen and gave it its opportunity to fly, whether you got a copy at the launch, bought one from me personally, grabbed it off your library shelf or ordered online. Your willingness to emotionally invest in a new, independent author is something I am immeasurably grateful for and your enthusiasm has been a massive source of inspiration for me. Sabrina, agent and editor, the only person who has looked at these works with an eye as critical as mine and still claimed to enjoy what you're reading: thank you. Your string-pulling and wand-waving and various other backstage tasks behind the scenes of my journey are much appreciated. I'm very grateful to the twist in destiny that had Matt meet you and put us in contact.

Thank you Jason Fenech, world's best boss, who let me print Chosen and Scarred from the office computer when I finally finished it the first time to save me having to pay for it at a printing shop. You can't possibly know how proud I was that day to take home the hundreds of loose pages that I called my 'book' but you made that day happen – thank you. The friends need their thanks, too, or there'll be riots. But in all seriousness, all of my friends deserve the deepest of thanks. I've been inundated with the most amazing support since publishing Chosen and it's been strongest in the circles immediately around me. Thanks to my wonderful, wonderful workmates, from my very patient and understanding angel of a teaching partner to the lovely ladies in the staffroom at first break who won't loan me Black Dagger Brotherhood because I "have a novel to finish for us first". Thanks to my test-dummies LJ, Ellen, Danielle, Mel, Mia, Tiffany, Matt, Mum and Dad for reading Scarred back when it was a gigantic bundle of printed pages, three times this length and a third the quality. Thanks to Katherine for flying for hours to be at my first book launch. Thanks to the incredible mummies and daddies who could have raised their eyebrows sceptically when their children came home claiming their teacher was publishing a book but instead came in excitedly, demanded to know all about it and threw themselves behind me and the series wholeheartedly. Thanks to the fabulous Kirsten, world's coolest and realest imaginary friend, for her completely selfless support of me and the books; thanks once again for the help with the French dialogue, for all the efforts you put behind The Elm Stone Saga and for the endless random chat. Thanks to Anna Malmi for being what has to be Chosen's most enamoured and devoted fan. I love how much you love it and I look forward to deconstructing Scarred with you, chapter by chapter, just as soon as you've read it. Thanks to my many incredible friends of the internet, whose realness cannot be entirely confirmed (though your knowledge of my book's plot and your enthusiastic support of my writing suggest you probably are real people, really reading, somewhere) but whose support is wholly appreciated.

Laura-Jane MacNamara, as always you have outdone yourself. In spite of life's demands and expectations, in spite of my demands and expectations (which I understand to be exasperating), you manage to produce something outside the scope of what I could possibly have anticipated. I guess this vision and talent is why you're the artist and I leave the pencils and the Photoshop alone. Your friendship remains precious to me and even if actual co-travelling looks impossible for us ("Hotel!"/"Hostel!"), I am so grateful to have you with me on all of my life's metaphorical journeys.

Again, as with my previous book, and probably as in all future publications, I would be amiss to not thank my teachers. Without these tireless, selfless and inspirational souls I would not have all these skills to play with. I would not know the joy of reading, the intrigue of learning, the exhaustion of researching or the peace of writing. Thank you to each of the women and men who had me in their class. Each of you played a part in making me the writer, and educator, I am; but perhaps none more so than Mrs Helen Barry of Year Five fame, who idly said to me one day, "You'll be an author one day." Before I heard those words it had never occurred to me that this was something I could do, and dreams were born that day.

My family is my rock, and in the wake of publishing Chosen this has not changed. Thanks to my cousins, aunts, uncles and grandparents who have supported me through this path and who have read my work. I'm so lucky to have family like you around me! Thank you to my brother Reegan for buying a copy of my book, even though I know you haven't read it yet (I saw it on your shelf, it's still in the bag... but that's okay), and for buying one of the t-shirts, though I can't recall ever seeing you in it. One day when all six books are out and I'm mega-famous you'll have six beautiful, unread, signed first editions and you can sell them for millions. Thank you infinitely to my amazing parents for their unwavering support and belief in me. I can't express enough how gracious I am for you and I hope you know I owe my every success to you and your sacrifices. In publishing Chosen, and now Scarred, my deepest dream of making you proud is realised and I hope to carry on doing so.

Matt, I love you. Thank you for trying to organise me when I'm in creative mode, for being an excellent soundboard for ideas, for your willingness to suspend belief and get right into it when I want to discuss something deep about the Elm Stone universe, for making sure I'm fed when I'd happily hole up in my study all day, for putting X-Files on for me when... well, pretty much all the time. Thank you for your love, your patience, your support, your friendship. Thank you for understanding that sometimes, I don't want to talk to you, and that it's not you – sometimes I just really need to write!